Dave Blackwell

Contact: dave.blackwell@live.co.uk

Printed Globally.

First Printing: March 2023

The Night Porter

ONE

Andy leaned back in the old office chair, reading a book. He is of average height and a stocky build with short spikey chestnut brown hair. He is wearing black trousers, polished black shoes, a white shirt and a black bowtie. He has hearing aids in both ears.

Behind him are two large filing cabinets, and down his right side a work counter, with files and papers. On his left side a wall planner, various photographs and a door leading to the reception corridor. Directly in front of him was a small desk with a fax machine, next to it a dated till and a computer. Bearing right in the L-shaped office is the reception counter where a computer sits under the counter. On the reception desk is a polished silver bell, a writing mat and a notepad and pen laid out.

The door opens and Dean walks in, holding two mugs of coffee. He is taller than Andy and a slim build, he has a shaved head and has a rough light blonde goatee, hardly noticeable. Also wearing black trousers, polished shoes and a white shirt with a black tie, swinging back and forth with each step.

"Black coffee," Dean said placing it on the counter next to Andy.

"Thanks," Andy said. "Took you ages!"

"Sorted a few things out," Dean said. "Less for us to do throughout the night."

"Oh cool," Andy said. "I did the Clockhouse earlier, not much needed doing."

"What time did you start today?" Dean said.

"Mark asked me to start at eight," Andy said. "So, I cleared the conference tables and hoovered the whole room."

"Bet that was fun!" Dean scoffed.

"It was fine," Andy said. "There were a couple of people still there, so I had a couple of drinks."

"Any new check-ins?" Dean said looking around the counter and then leaning against the table.

"No," Andy said. "Someone came in for directions."

"Weird," Dean said. "Long way to come for directions."

"I thought that too," Andy said shrugging his shoulders. "Saw the car pull up on the camera, attempted to do a three-point turn, gave up and drove down to the car park, hovered for five minutes and then drove up before walking in."

"Did he get out of the car in the car park?" Dean asked curiously.

"No," Andy said. "Just sat there, think he was on his mobile or his satnav."

"What was he looking for?" Dean said.

"Swanley station," Andy said. "Drew him a map."

"He was lost!" Dean exclaimed. "Anything happen while I was gone?"

"Nothing," Andy said. "Does the brasserie and bar need doing today?"

3

"Done it," Dean said. "You can do the room checks."

"Sure," Andy said putting the book down on the counter. "We have five rooms that need checking according to the handover."

"Yep," Dean nodded.

"Do you know why?" Andy asked. "Nothing on the handover."

"Deep carpet clean," Dean said. "Drinks stains in two rooms, two rooms had customers smoking in them and the last a fox took a dump in the middle of the room."

Andy scoffed and chuckled.

"It stank apparently," Dean said. "The delegates that smoked in the rooms have been billed."

"Good," Andy said. "You can smell smoke on the first-floor corridor."

"Yeah," Dean said. "Mark caught someone smoking the other night by the exit, the guy thought he would get away with it by opening the fire exit."

"Did he know it's alarmed?" Andy said shaking his head. "What an idiot!"

"I know," He smiled. "We saw it come up on the panel, so he went to investigate."

Andy picked up a clipboard and looked through the three sheets.

"Only three people in the hotel tonight," Andy said. "At least we can chill."

"We can when the third shows up," Dean said. "Have you met him?" Dean said. "Mr. Inkbroke?"

"Don't think so," Andy said.

"He comes here a fair bit," Dean said. "Has offices down in Crofton Business Park."

"What is he like?" Andy asked.

"Bit of a tosser," Dean said. "I don't like him."

"Oh great," Andy said. "But don't you say that about everyone?"

"Yeah," Dean nodded.

"What do you say about me when I am not around?" Andy asked curiously.

"Nothing," Dean shook his head. "I like to say it to your face," He said smiling and then laughing.

"True," Andy picked up his coffee. "Jesus! I am tired."

"Work today?" Dean said looking at his watch. "Yesterday rather."

"Yes," Andy looked at his watch. "Five past midnight," He mumbled. "I got two hours earlier so shouldn't complain!" He scoffed.

"Get some sleep once you have done the rooms?" Dean suggested.

"Might do," Andy said. "Might finish this book instead," He said, tapping the book.

"Want any food?" Dean said, putting his cup on the counter below the reception desk.

"No thanks," Andy said. "I had a bunch of cheese sandwiches in the Barn House Suite."

"Nice," Dean said. "I am going to go make some pasta, you okay waiting until I get back?"

"Yes," Andy said. "I'll head out to do the room checks and a security walk when you are back."

Dean gave a thumbs up as he opened the door, closing it heavily as he left and causing Andy to jump.

"You arse!" Andy snapped, hearing him laugh as he walked away.

Andy sat back in his chair, crossing his arms and closing his eyes.

A ring broke the silence and Andy opened his eyes, wondering if he had fallen asleep. He checked his watch and realised he had for half an hour.

"Anyone here?" A voice from the reception desk.

"Coming," Andy said, rubbing his eyes and yawning.

The entrance to the hotel is directly ahead of the reception desk, with large old oak doors with glass panels, next to it is a window that spans the length of the room.

On the left of the desk is a door leading to the brasserie and bar, in the middle, stairs leading up to the first floor, and next to the entrance, a door leading to the boardroom. On the right against the wall is a large fireplace with brass surroundings, and a hall leading to the reception, restaurant and staff access. A small lounge through a door by the windows. The carpet is thick green with diamond red patterns. The walls are a mixture of light pink and magnolia. A large brass ugly chandelier hung from the centre of the reception, and various vases were scattered around in the corners.

The man tall and slim with greying hair and glasses is wearing a three-piece black suit, a white shirt and a red tie.

Andy stepped around the corner and smiled.

"Hello there Sir," Andy said. "Welcome to The Range Hotel and how can I help you?"

"I have a reservation," The man said.

"Mr. Inkbroke?" Andy said.

"Inkbrook," He said. "It's Inkbrook."

"My apologies," Andy said, taking a registration card from a box under the counter.

"Not a problem," He said.

"Could you repeat that?" Andy said.

"Why?" Mr. Inkbrook asked.

"I am deaf," Andy said pointing to his ear. "I didn't catch what you said."

"I said it is not a problem," Mr. Inkbrook said. "Do you lipread?"

"Yes," Andy nodded.

"My nephew is deaf," Mr. Inkbrook said. "I think he plays on it."

"Don't tell anyone!" Andy joked. "We all do it!"

"Are you new?" He asked. "Not seen you here before."

"No," Andy said. "Been here a while, I don't usually cover the reception due to not being able to hear on the phone."

"Fair enough," He said. "Is Dean working?"

"Yes," Andy said. "Having his lunch break. You have the usual room you requested," Andy said. "Do you require a wake-up call in the morning or a newspaper?"

"No thank you," He replied. He said looking at his watch. "How far is the Crofton Business Park from here?"

"I'd say half an hour," Andy said. "Depending on what time you want to get there."

"Nine," He said.

"I would leave at quarter past eight at least," Andy said. "With the traffic from the bridge and so on, it gets busy."

"Thank you," He said.

"Could I get a signature and vehicle registration number please," Andy said pushing the card towards Mr. Inbrook.

"Would I be able to get some food?" He said. "I didn't get to eat."
Mr. Inkbrook filled in the card, checking it over and putting the pen down.

"Sure," Andy said. "We can do sandwiches, what would you like?"

"Can I just get cheese on brown bread?" He asked. "Maybe some nachos if you have them?"

"Yes that is fine," Andy said, writing it down. "Any drinks?"

"Coffee would be great," He smiled. "Been a long day!"

"I will get that up to you as soon as possible," Andy said. "Do you want me to show you to your room?"

"No, I know the way," Mr. Inkbrook said.
Andy handed him the room key, taking the registration card back.

"Thanks," Andy said. "Food will be ten minutes or so."

"Brilliant," Mr. Inkbrook said and walked away, making his way up the stairs for his usual room at the front of the hotel.
The door opened, and Dean walked in, a pint of water in one hand and banana in the other.

"Was that Mr. Inkbroke?" Dean asked, a smile on his face.

"Inkbrook!" Andy scoffed. "You bloody moron!"
Dean burst out laughing.

"I couldn't resist it!" Dean said. "What did he say?"

"Nothing," Andy said. He just corrected me. "Nice enough guy."

"Did he want anything?" Dean asked.

"Yes," Andy handed him a slip of paper. "You can sort that considering he asked after you."

"Sure, no probs, your sandwich-making sucks anyway!" Dean said placing the paper in his pocket.
"You may as well start on the room checks, get them out of the way."

Andy arrived on the second floor, looking down the long dark corridor for anything out of place, he looked at the notepad, checking which rooms needed checking. There are no rooms in use on this floor and the carpet had been cleaned during the day.

"Three on this floor," He said to himself as he flicked on the light switch, watching the hall illuminate slowly. He looked at the small table, with a telephone at the centre and a box of plastic overshoes next to it, a sign in block capitals 'TO BE WORN ON THIS FLOOR!!!'

He looked down at his shoes, noticing the water pooling around his feet.

Taking some overshoes, he leaned against the wall as he struggled to balance.

"Bloody things!" Andy moaned as he pulled them over his shoes.

Unlocking the first room on his right, he turned on the light and walked in, looking around.

On his right is the bathroom, the door closed. Straight ahead is the double bed at the centre of the room, with cabinets on either side. A three-panel window behind the bed, two of the side windows open, the drapes moving against the breeze. On the right of the bed is a wardrobe and a set of drawers with an old television mounted on the top. On the left side of the room is a desk and chair. The cream-coloured carpet is marked from being cleaned. The white walls are scuffed in places, there are various photographs are mounted of country scenes.

Andy sniffed deeply and then groaned.

"It stinks in here!" He said looking down at the outline by the bed, clearly where the wine had been spilt. "Well, that didn't come out did it!" Andy scoffed, pulling a notepad from the back of his pocket and writing down some notes, along with the room number.

Andy closed the windows and closed the drapes, checking over the room and bathroom before looking back and turning off the light.

Just as he is about the close the door, the telephone started ringing, causing him to jump in fright. Turning the light back on he walked over and looked at it, wondering who it could be. The red light flashed in between each loud buzzing ring.

"Who the hell is calling an empty room," Andy said to himself.

It continued to ring so Andy slowly answered it.

"Hello?" He said. "Who is this?"

No response.

"Hello?" Andy said again, listening and trying to focus.

No answer.

Andy put the phone back, walked to the door and turned off the light. Pausing for a moment, he then closed the door and locked it.

A noise from down the corridor and Andy looked around, expecting to see someone.

"Hello?" Andy said. "Anyone here?" He said louder.

No answer.

"There is no one up here you plank," Andy said. "Just get on with it!"

Three doors down on the right is the next room and Andy let himself in, muttering when the light was already on, so he made a note of it and recorded the room number.

"Bloody useless," Andy said. "They tell us to make sure lights are off in unused rooms and the idiots leave them on during the day!" He scoffed. "Lazy bastards!"

The room was the same layout as the previous one, only this room didn't have a desk and chair. He checked the bathroom and then closed the windows in the main room, looking around on the floor and sniffing loudly.

"Definitely a smoker," Andy said to himself in disgust.

Andy looked around the room again before walking to the door and turning off the light.

The telephone started to ring, and Andy turned the light back on to look at it.

"What is going on," He said curiously. "It's like a crappy horror film, only the killer doesn't realise I am deaf."

Andy walked over to the telephone and snatched it up.

"Who is this?" he asked.

Andy had a feeling it was Dean, pranking him.

A loud blowing noise came over the telephone and he listened, trying to work out what it was.

"Sod this," Andy said and put the telephone back, turning off the light and locking the room.

As Andy was about to enter the reception, he heard a loud noise coming from the kitchen.

"What is that?" He said, opening the door and looking down the white corridor, hearing the clangs coming from the kitchen. "Dean?"

Opening the swing door to the kitchen, Andy jumped in fright when a loud metallic clang echoed through the kitchen. The noise is frantic and loud, like a brick in a washing machine.

The kitchen is made up of two rows, one row with grills, ovens and hobs, and the other row of counters for food preparation. Straight ahead of the entrance is a pair of doors leading to the entrance, one for in and the other for out. Next to it is a glass cleaning and storage room. Just before the door, a worktop with a coffee machine and a large, automated toaster. At the far end of the kitchen is the dish-cleaning conveyor system. A door leads to the refrigeration and freezer storage room on the far end of the kitchen opposite the entrance.

Keith, the evening kitchen cleaner, is a tall and largely built man with a thick, messy beard and long scruffy hair. Looking like a villain from a horror movie, he avoided contact with people, keeping to himself and extremely quiet. In the year Andy had worked at the hotel, he had only spoken to him a couple of times, due to the point he couldn't understand him, and Keith hated everyone unless alcohol is involved.

Keith, holding a large frying pan is bashing it against the grill in the vegetable section, mainly used for vegetarian cooking.

"Keith!" Andy shouted. "Keith, what the hell are you doing mate?"

Keith stopped and looked up, breathing heavily.

"What?" Keith said bluntly.

"Why are you making so much noise?!" Andy asked. "Jesus we have people in rooms above the kitchen."

"Mouse," Keith said.

"What?" Andy said.

The door opened and Dean walked in, looking annoyed.

"What is going on?!" He snapped. "A guest just called down about the noise!"

"Mouse!" Keith pointed at the grill.

"Keith, can you leave the psycho vibes at home?" Dean said. "You saw a mouse?"

Keith nodded and grinned.

"So, you thought to beat it to death with a frying pan?" Andy scoffed. "Fruitcake."

Something caught Keith's eye and he dropped to his knees, proceeding to smash the frying pan against the floor.

"Keith stop!" Dean said, running round the kitchen and grabbing it from his hand. "For fucks sake Keith what is wrong it you?"

"Got it," Keith said laughing, picking up the small squashed and bloody mouse by the tail and dangling it. "Killed it."

"Was that really necessary?" Andy said.

Keith nodded.

"A lot of noise for something so small Keith!" Dean said. "If anyone complains, I am telling the restaurant manager it was you!" Dean turned and stormed out.

Keith turned on the grill, dropping the mouse on it.

"What are you doing?!" Andy snapped. "That is the vegetarian grill!"

"Don't care," Keith said. "Vegetarians are stupid."

"I am telling the head chef," Andy said. "You are disgusting!"

Andy shook his head, turned and left the kitchen.

Andy headed back to reception where Dean was, he stood at the reception and then tapped on the counter.

"Oi," Andy said. "Get off your arse for a change."

"What?" Dean moaned and got up, walking to the counter. "What do you want?"

"Did you call upstairs?" Andy asked.

"No," He said. "Waste of time considering you cannot hear. Why?"

"Well, I did the first room, and the phone rang, then the same with the second room," Andy said.

"Are you sure?" Dean asked. "Didn't imagine it?"

"No," Andy said. "Those phones are bloody loud."

"Odd," Dean said looking at Andy, shaking his head in confusion. "Wasn't me and nothing came up on the operator's desk."

"Anyone else on?" Andy asked. "Kitchen or restaurant?"

"They finished an hour ago," He said. "You know that."

"I answered them both," Andy said. "The first was quiet, the second sounded like wind."

"What do you mean someone farting?" He laughed.

"No!" Andy scoffed. "A blowing sound."

"Come on!" He laughed. "I bet you fell asleep and dreamed it!"

"No," Andy replied. "I am being serious."

"You are never serious!" Dean said. "You fell asleep in the brasserie last month and sleepwalked around like a retarded zombie!"

"Yes I know I did," Andy laughed. "But I was not asleep this time."

"Right!" He said. "Have you finished?"

"Three left," Andy said.

"Do those then we can have some food," He said looking at his watch.

"You already ate," Andy said.

"And?" Dean questioned.

"No reason," Andy said. "Didn't think you ate much anyhow."

"Go and finish the checks," Dean scoffed. "I'll start on the nachos in a minute."

"Fair enough," Andy said. "Was all okay with Inkbrook?"

"Yeah," Dean said. "He is a good tipper."

"I wouldn't know!" Andy said.

The telephone started to ring, and Dean picked it up.

"Reception, how can I help?" Dean said listening. "Hey Keith, what do you want?" Dean shook his head, leaning against the wall and holding up his index finger to get Andy's attention. "Keith said he is sorry and not to tell the head chef," Dean shook his head. "What did he do?" Dean asked Andy. "Other than kill a mouse and make noise?"

"He turned on the vegetarian grill and dropped it on there," Andy said.

"Did you really drop a mouse on the vegetarian grill and cook it?!" Dean said. "That is disgusting Keith!" Dean said trying not to laugh. "Well Keith I actually agree with Andy, but tell you what, I want you to clean that grill top to bottom," Dean said giving Andy a thumbs up. "We will check it later and if it is okay, we won't tell the head chef."

Dean hung up the call and put the telephone back, cringing.

"That man is nuts," Dean said.

"Tell me something I don't know," Andy said.

"Not as bad as his brother," Dean said. "Go on get lost," He said. "Finish the rooms and meet me in the brasserie in half an hour."

"Sure," Andy said and left, making his way back to the second floor.

Andy got to the third room, checked it and closed the window. As he is about to leave the room, he hesitated before sitting on the edge of the bed next to the telephone, watching it and waiting for it to ring.

"Come on," Andy said, tapping his fingers on the bedside cabinet. "Ring," He said. "I bloody dare you!"

Andy sat for a few minutes, waiting for the telephone to ring. He picked it up and listened to the dial tone.

"It works," He shrugged his shoulders. "Maybe they got bored?"

Andy put the phone down and stood up, straightening up the bed before walking back towards the door, cautiously watching the telephone.

At the end of the corridor, Andy unlocked the door to the fourth room and the smell hit him.

"Give me a break!" Andy exclaimed and groaned, his hand going to his nose.

The room layout is the same as the first, recently redecorated and modernized. The large flatscreen television is wall mounted. The two side windows are open and the drapes flap back and forth in the breeze. A desk lamp is on the floor, the thick plastic shade broken. In the middle of the carpet is a dark urine stain and closer to the wall, a pile of excrement.

"These foxes need to learn to use the toilet," Andy said. "Would make my job easier!"

Andy walked into the room, stepping over the mess and checking the room fully.

"What's up?" Dean appeared at the door.

"Shit!" Andy yelped. "Don't do that!"

"I was checking the fire exit," Dean said. "Got a warning light."

"Gave me a bloody heart attack!" Andy scoffed. "We had some visitors," Andy pointed to the mess on the floor.

"Oh great," Dean said. "Going to have to clean that up!"

"Tell me about it," Andy huffed. "Is the carpet cleaner on this level?"

"No idea," Dean said. "Want some help?"

"No, it's fine," Andy said. "I'll manage."

Andy looked at Dean's shoes.

"No overshoes?" He asked.

"Cannot be bothered," Dean said. "My feet are clean."

"Fair enough," Andy said.

"I'll check the door then head back to the reception," Dean said looking at his watch. "I'll do the newspaper order and stock the bar, should give you time to clean this shit up."

"Literally!" Andy said. "Looks like the sods had a party."

"This is why someone should have shut the windows at the end of the day shift," Dean moaned. "They don't have a bloody clue.

Dean shook his head as he walked to the fire exit, opening and closing the door, pushing it to confirm the latch had caught.

"See you later!" Dean said, waving as he walked past the room, fanning the air in front of his nose.

Andy put his keys and radio on the bedside cabinet, he headed back out to the corridor to the cleaners' cupboard which was only two doors away from the room and then the telephone started ringing again.

"Oh, come on!" Andy groaned. "What is going on?!"

Andy ignored it and walked to the small cleaning cupboard, grabbed a small bucket, detergent, spray cleaner, bags and a cleaning cloth.

He then walked back to the room, ignoring the telephone which was still ringing.

"Keep ringing," Andy said. "I don't give a toss."

Andy went into the bathroom, ran the hot tape and waited for it to slowly fill the bucket.

The telephone rang for a few minutes, and Andy got fed up, storming over and picking it up.

"Hello?" He said. "Who is this?"

All he could hear was static.

"Hello?" Andy said louder. "Who is there?"

No answer.

"Mental," Andy said and put the phone down, leaving it off the hook.

Andy cleaned up the mess, luckily the excrement was solid, and didn't leave a stain. The urine took more to clean, the strong smell making Andy cringe. Happy that he had cleaned up the urine, he put the cleaning items away. Picking up the lamp, he managed to pop the plastic shade back together, turning the lamp on and off to check it worked. He then closed the windows, leaning over the bed and his hand landed on a wet puddle of urine.

"Oh, you are kidding me," Andy groaned, sniffing his hand and then gagging. "If I find that fox, I am kicking it up the arse!" Andy said loudly out the window, then closing it and rolling up the bed sheets and quilt. He returned to the cupboard and got a large linen bag, shoving the sheets, quilt and the pillows into it. He put the bag into the bath, returning and checking the mattress to find it had seeped through slightly.

"Sod that," Andy said. "They can deal with that in the morning!"

The radio beeped.

"What does he want?" Andy said, picking up the radio and pressing a button on the side.

"Yes?" Andy said.

"Getting a warning that the telephone is off the hook," Dean said.

"What?" Andy said, not understanding what he was saying.

"I said, the phone is off the hook!" Dean said louder.

"I'll be down in a moment," Andy said. "Just leaving!"

Andy shook his head as he turned the radio off, clipping it onto the back of his belt. He then put the telephone back onto the hook and picked up his keys.

Walking up to the door, he turned off the light.

The telephone started to ring.

"Oh, nice try Dean," Andy said. "Gave yourself away there, you tosspot."

The telephone continued to ring.

"Too bad," Andy said and ignored it, locking the door and making his way to the staircase at the end of the corridor, the plastic overshoes crinkling and squeaking.

Just as Andy got to the door, he reached down to remove the plastic overshoes and the telephone on the table started to ring.

"What is with the phones in this place?" Andy said. "Like a crappy horror film."

Andy arrived at the reception counter, looking into the brasserie for Dean only to find it in darkness.

"You there?" Andy said tapping the counter.

"Yeah," He said and groaned before walking up, yawning.

"What did you say on the radio?" Andy asked.

"The phone in that room was off the hook," Dean said. "Operating unit kept beeping."

"I took it off the hook," Andy said. "It kept ringing!"

"Really?" Dean said in confusion.

"Sure, you ain't winding me up?" Andy asked.

"No," Dean said.

"You okay?" Andy asked. "Looking rough!"

"Thanks," Dean scoffed. "Feeling off," He said. "Fell asleep."

"Do you want to grab a few hours?" Andy said. "I can go off and leave you to it."

"Do you mind?" He asked. "I was supposed to clean the board room."

"I'll do it," Andy said. "And you can drop me home in the morning."

"That is fair," He said nodding. "Finished the rooms?"

"One to do," Andy said. "Bloody phones keep ringing it's freaky!"

"Did you answer them?" he said. "Or is that not possible?"

"I did," Andy replied. "Lots of static on the fourth room, so maybe on the blink. "Talking about that," Andy handed him a note. "That room has had a fox use it as a toilet," I said. "Needs to be taken out of action to be cleaned properly, did what I could for now, but the carpet needs power cleaning," He said. "don't want to wake up the customers."

"Thought you cleaned it?" Dean asked.

"So did I until I put my hand into fox piss on the bed," Andy said, smelling his hand. "I can still smell it!

"Good for your skin," Dean said. "Is the mattress wet?"

"Yes, I stripped the bed and put the stuff in a bag in the bath," Andy said.

"I will go up later with some spray bleach," Dean said. "Will let the cleaners know first thing in the morning."

"Well, I have the fifth room to check and then will do a security run," Andy looked at his watch. "And then I am getting some food and a pint!"

"Oh, might be worth checking the car park," He said. "We had two break-ins last night."

"You are kidding," Andy said. "Fine, I'll check it out."

Andy checked the fifth room and there were no surprises, the windows had already been closed and the telephone didn't ring. Picking up a torch from the security cupboard, he put on his jacket. He left the hotel at the staff entrance, making his way down the long dark road, dimly lit. He checked the back entrance to the Barn House Suite, looking through at the alarm panel, all showing green. He then checked the empty car park, looking around curiously.

"Where is your car, Dean?" He said. "Where have you parked it today?"
Walking around the front of the Barn House Suite, he shorn the torch in the building and the suites upstairs, he then realised one of the managers was staying there.

"Shit," Andy said aiming it at the floor, walking quickly towards the front of the hotel.
He checked the brasserie patio, winding down a couple of patio umbrellas that had been left up, collecting glasses and leaving them on the floor by the patio doors. The patio is quite small, with

granite floors and surrounded by plants, mini trees and thick ivy bushes. The thick cast iron chairs and tables made so much noise when Andy moved them, regardless of how careful he is.

"Useless!" Andy moaned.

He stopped, looking around in the corners, the shadows beginning to play tricks on his mind.

"Oh, piss off," Andy snapped. "Bloody wasting your time!"

He walked the length of the balcony across the front of the hotel, checking the back of the restaurant was locked and making his way down the steps towards the car park.

As he got nearer to the car park, he heard a loud thump in the distance and paused, looking across the green.

"Lights are off," Andy said to himself. "So, there will be no security lighting."

Security lights were always turned off on the lawn due to wildlife setting them off, various customers had complained, so at midnight, they were switched off.

"Let's see what that was," Andy said hesitantly.

He jumped down onto the green to cut across, gaining access to the car park from the back. It was the best way to surprise someone if they were there.

"Considering I cannot hear a thing," Andy said. "They are probably behind me with a metal baseball bat, getting ready to smash my skull into my brain," Andy scoffed. "Dean will find me at first light, foxes eating my eyeballs and humping my battered skull!"

Andy turned around and aimed the torch down the green, moving it around slowly.

"If my aunt was here," Andy said. "She would probably slap me for being morbid and then slap me again because," He paused. "Because."

Another loud thump, this time hitting concrete. Andy couldn't locate where it was coming from, and standing on the spot, he turned three hundred and sixty, looking around him with the torch.

Suddenly a football-sized concrete ball came rolling down the middle of the green and came to a stop, not far from him.

"What the hell?!" Andy said curiously, shining the touch at it.

The concrete balls were there for decoration on the old stone walls, there were about twelve of them starting from the Barn House Suite, all the way down to the car park.

"Hello?" Andy said. "Someone there?!" he called out, shining the torch.

No answer.

"Get a grip!" Andy said to himself.

Andy ignored the concrete ball and walked towards the small car park. It was oval-shaped, with trees and bushes at the centre. Dimly lit with security cameras at each end. There were only three cars parked up, close to each other. Two are delegates, the other is Deans. Checking around himself as he walked up the steps, he walked over to the vehicles, checking them over for any signs of breaking in.

Hearing something behind him, he turned around quickly to see a fox near the steps, looking dead at him.

"You better not be the little sod that messed up that room," Andy said.

The fox sat down.

"Was it?" Andy asked.

The fox yawned.

"Hope you haven't killed any of the swans," Andy stepped forward and the fox slowly stood up, getting ready to run. "Not going to hurt you mate," Andy said kneeling. "Come here."

The fox looked at Andy curiously.

"Shall I see if we have any bacon in the kitchen?" Andy asked.

The fox turned, ran down the steps and sprinted across the green.

"Fair enough!" Andy said, walking back to the hotel.

Andy attempted to open the doors at the entrance, only to find they were locked.

"Oh, come on!" Andy said looking towards the reception. "Dean?" He said, knocking on the window.

After a minute he made his way back in through the staff entrance, the security light came on and blinded him and he yelped in fright when Keith walked through the door nearly knocking him over. He wore a large black overcoat that touched the floor and a black beanie hat that made his head look odd with the amount of hair sticking out of the sides.

"Jesus Keith!" Andy said. "Thought death finally found me!"

"Cleaned the grill," Keith said. "Please don't tell the chef."

"I won't," Andy said.

Keith had learning difficulties and Andy knew that at times he did things that he didn't mean to do, even if it was bashing a mouse to death with a frying pan and dropping it on the grill.

"Thanks," Keith said.

"Just don't do it again," Andy said. "I don't eat meat and the thought of squashed bloody mouse in my food isn't good."

"Oh," Keith said.

"I prefer them live and wriggling," Andy said with a grin. "You okay getting home?"

"Walking," Keith said.

"Will you be okay?" Andy asked.

"Yeah," Keith nodded. "Clear night and I can see the moon."

"Good," Andy said. "Just don't go howling at the bloody thing."

Andy gently punched Keith in the arm who returned the favour, knocking Andy back a few steps.

"Damn," Andy said rubbing his arm. "See you tonight."

Andy opened the door, watching as Keith walked heavy-footed away, like a villain about to obliterate a hero.

"Wouldn't want to get into a fight with him!" Andy scoffed, closing and putting the latch on the door.

Andy quietly let himself into the reception, looking around for Dean only to find he wasn't in the reception.

"Where is he?" Andy asked.

He noticed a note stuck to the monitor under the counter.

"Gone to get some sleep," The note read. "Loads of love, Dean."

"Well, I hope no one calls down," Andy said and put the torch and radio away.

He checked the notebook for any messages and then looked at the security monitor, noticing two more concrete balls on the green,

"That can stay there until the morning," Andy scoffed. "Bloody things!"

Popping to the bar, Andy pulled himself a pint of lager and then went into the kitchen. Getting a large serving plate, he filled it with as many nachos as he could fit and covered them with grated cheese.

"This is going to be so good," He said, placing the plate into the microwave and starting it.

A loud buzz caused him to jump, and he looked around wondering what it was.

"What is that?" He said to himself, looking around the kitchen.

A prolonged buzz and Andy then remembered that there was an entry buzzer at the staff entrance.

"Who is that?" He moaned. "I bet that is Keith, probably can smell my pint!" Andy said, hiding the pint behind a chopping board.

He paused the microwave and walked through the kitchen to the staff entrance, unlocking the door and opening it to find no one around. The security light was also off, which was odd considering if someone had been there, it would have stayed on for at least two minutes.

"Weird," Andy said and returned to the kitchen, putting the microwave back on and watching as the cheese slowly melted.

A telephone started to ring, and Andy had no idea where it was. He noticed a red light flashing near the glass storage and hurried over. The telephone is wall mounted, the red LEDs flashing in between rings.

"Not answering," Andy said to himself and returned to the microwave when it beeped.

He took the steaming nachos out of the microwave, burning his fingers slightly as he dropped the plate onto the plastic worktop, blowing on them.

The telephone continued to ring.

"Oh, shut up!" I said to the ringing phone. "Give me a break!"

The telephone stopped ringing and Andy sighed in relief, drinking his pint and greedily eating the cheese-covered nachos.

As he finished them, he put the plate into the washer and put the pint glass into the glass washer. The telephone started to ring, causing him to jump.

"I am going to shove you in the washer!" Andy snapped at it. "Annoying!"

Returning to reception, Andy checked the security cameras.

"What?" He said, flicking through the camera channels. "What is going on?"

The concrete balls were nowhere to be seen, and the final camera revealed them back on the wall as if they had never fallen off.

"You are shitting me!" Andy scoffed.

Andy slowly flicked through each channel, double-checking each one in detail until he came across one of the car parks, a fox sitting in the middle looking up at the camera, its eyes reflecting.

"Bloody hell hound," Andy said. "I hope the swans kick your arse!"

Looking at the security rota hanging from the back of the door, Andy realised that Dean hadn't done a floor check, so he picked up a beep as well as a radio and headed to level one, signing off level two as complete.

Andy got to the first level, checking down to the fire exit and looking through the glass into the darkness. He pulled the release bar, checking it was solid.

The telephone at the end of the hall started ringing, causing him to exclaim and jump.

"Jesus!" Andy snapped. "Why is it so loud!"

Andy hurried down the corridor, picking up the phone.

"Yes?" Andy said.

"Hello?" A woman's voice.

"Who is this?" Andy asked, struggling to listen.

The woman continued to speak by Andy could not understand her.

"I'll be down in a few minutes," Andy said and put the phone down, making his way towards the reception, taking the quickest route that would bring him down the stairs in the middle of the reception. His beep then went off, and he checked it only to find the restaurant number come up.

"Odd," Andy said, knowing that no one was on shift. "Why is the restaurant beeping me?"

Andy arrived at reception to find the lights off, the only light coming off the computer monitor, he switched on the lights and went into the reception office, noticing flashing lights on the security monitor.

"What is going on?" Andy said. "Maybe I need to find Dean and call the police," Andy said.

The reception phone started ringing again and Andy jumped, looking at it.

"Bugger this," Andy said. "Ring all you want."

Andy ignored it.

Another phone started ringing, one from the hall by the restaurant. Andy opened the door, listening.

"Not answering any!" Andy said in frustration.

"Hello?" A woman's voice from the reception counter. "Anyone there?"

Andy returned to the reception counter to find a young woman standing there in a small t-shirt and boxer shorts. Andy recognised her from earlier, a German customer that was staying over with a friend. Her hair is messy, and she is drunk, steadying herself against the wall.

"I have locked myself out," She said. "Can you let me into my room?"

"Sure, not a problem," Andy said. "Do you want me to give you the spare?"

"Can you walk me up?" She said. "I am so drunk!"

"Sure," Andy replied. "Give me a moment."

Andy got a master key from the drawer and left the office, walking around to reception where the woman was leaning over the counter, resting her head.

"Ready?" Andy said.

"I cannot remember where it is!" She laughed loudly.

"What?" Andy asked.

"My room," She giggled, turning around and grabbing hold of his arm.

"I know where you are," Andy said.

Arriving at the room, Andy struggled to support the woman and unlock the door, after a couple of attempts, the door opened.

"Where have you been?" The woman said as she opened the door.

"He is letting me back in!" The drunk woman laughed.

"Why didn't you just knock?!" The woman said, tightening her white dressing gown around her waist. Taller than her friend, she has thick brown hair, tied up at the top in a bun and red-rimmed glasses.

"I forgot!" She laughed. "This porter brought me up!"

"I am so sorry," The woman said to Andy. "She cannot handle her drink!"

"It isn't a problem," Andy said as the woman took hold of her friend's arm.

"Where is the other guy?" The drunk woman said. "The good-looking one?"

"He is in his car I think," Andy said. "He isn't well."

"He was in the bar a few minutes ago," She smiled.

"Okay," I said curiously.

"Thank you," The friend said. "I'll tie her down!"

"Oh, you would like that wouldn't you!" The drunk woman said, slamming the door as Andy stepped back, inches away from getting hit.

"Charming," Andy said shaking his head. "I certainly get them."

Andy walked down the steps towards the brasserie when he heard laughing coming from the reception.

"Dean?" Andy said looking over the counter.

Dean is sitting in front of the monitor, pointing at me and laughing hysterically.

"It was you," Andy said. "Wasn't it?"

He nodded, not able to speak from laughing. After a minute, he calmed down.

"Oh my god, you made it so easy!" He said. "Watched you on the camera and called the phones when you were about."

"Funny," I said.

"I followed you outside and then diverted down the wall," He giggled. "Your face when the concrete balls rolled down."

"Laugh all you want," I said. "You can go and return them all!"

"Gonna need your help lifting them," Dean said.

"Too bad," Andy said. "You can deal with it.

"Ah come on mate," Dean said. "You are the powerlifter."

"Not at work I ain't," Andy said. "I am getting a pint!"

Andy left the keys on the counter and walked into the darkness of the brasserie, heading towards the bar.

TWO

Andy stood outside the entrance of the hotel, leaning against the wall with a mug of coffee. It is dark, the dim light coming from under the steps.

Andy leaned back with his eyes closed. Wearing black trousers, white socks and a white shirt opened at the collar.

He looked towards the road as a car made its way through the single lane, he shielded his eyes, trying to focus on it. The road curved at the front of the Barn House Suite, a U-shaped road that then connected to the lanes past the small lake, leading through the woods for half a mile to the entrance of the grounds.

"No more customers please," Andy groaned. "Please!" he begged.

As the car turned into the road towards the Barn House Suite and Andy sighed in relief when he recognised the police vehicle. It slowly stopped at the bottom of the steps and the driver's window wound down.

"Evening Andy," The officer said.

The ageing officer is bald with a rough greying beard, and visible tattoos on the back of his neck, fading. In uniform with a stab vest, he has a black and brown bruise under his eye.

"Hi," Andy said walking down the steps. "You after some food and drink?" Andy asked.

"No," The officer said. "Just doing a drive past, any problems?"

"All quiet tonight," Andy said. "Sure you don't want a coffee?"

"Thanks for the offer," He said. "But I cannot stay," He looked down at Andy's socks. "Someone stolen your socks?"

"Ha ha," Andy said in sarcasm. "New shoes, what happened to you?" Andy said pointing to his eye.

"Oh nothing exciting," The officer laughed. "I got called to a disturbance in town, someone threw a bottle and I happened to walk into the bar at the same time."

"Shit!" Andy scoffed. "Looks sore!"

"Not so bad," The officer said. "You take my advice?"

"Which advice?" Andy asked curiously.

"About slowing down?" The officer scoffed.

"Remind me," Andy smiled.

"Doing sixty in a thirty?" The officer said.

"My mistake," Andy said. "It won't happen again."

"Just count yourself lucky that we like your sandwiches and coffee," The officer laughed. "And expect them whenever we want."

"What happens when I leave?" Andy asked.

"Might pull you over for fun," The officer said. "Anyhow if all is okay, I am off."

"Thanks," Andy said. "Next time I'll sort out food and coffee."

"Good," The officer said, closing his window and driving down to the carpark and turning around, waving at Andy as he drove past.

Andy leaned back against the wall, yawning heavily and groaning.

"You okay Andy?" Mark said from the doorway.

Mark is Andy's line manager, tall and muscular. He is wearing a black suit, a white shirt and a black tie. His head is clean shaven and he is wearing black-framed glasses, holding a book in his hand.

"What?" Andy said turning around.

"Are you okay?" Mark asked.

"Not too bad," Andy said. "My head is booming."

"You can go home if you want," Mark said. "It's a quiet night, only seven people staying."

"I will be okay in a bit," Andy said. "Just needed some air."

"Where are your shoes?" Mark said looking down at his feet.

"By the door," Andy said. "New shoes, bloody killing me!"

"What did the police want?" Mark asked.

"Just a drive-by," Andy said. "Asking if everything was good."

"Did he tell you off for speeding again?" Mark exclaimed.

"Yes," Andy said. "Looks like sandwiches and coffee for life to buy his silence."

"It's your own fault," Mark scoffed. "I am going to stock the bar in a bit and then finish this book," Mark said holding up the book. "If you want to go, go," Mark said with a smile.

"I'll be good," Andy said. "I'll do the Barn house in a bit."

"Okay mate," Mark said, walking back into the hotel.

Andy walked down the steps, looking towards the Barn House when something caught his attention on the road.

"A frog," Andy said, walking over to it and expecting it to run away, but it didn't move.

As Andy got closer, he could see the frog had been run over, its internal organs hanging out of its mouth.

"Poor sod," Andy said. "Flattened by the local bobby."

Andy hurried up the steps, put his coffee on the wall and put his hand against the door as he put his shoes on. Opening the door, he yawned loudly.

"Mark?" Andy said. "You in there?"

Andy tapped on the counter.

"You there?" Andy said.

"You off?" Mark asked, walking round to the counter.

"No," Andy said. "There is a frog on the road, can you pass me a couple of plastic bags."

"Dead?" Mark asked.

"Guts hanging out of its mouth," Andy said cringing.

"Aww!" Mark moaned. "Poor Mr froggy!"

"Bags?" Andy asked.

Mark went round the corner and Andy heard a drawer being opened, followed by rustling. A few seconds later, he returned to the counter and handed the bags to Andy.

"I'll come and have a look," Mark said, leaving the office and catching up with Andy as he opened the door.

Walking down the steps followed by Mark, Andy bent down near the frog and wrapped the bag over his hand and reached forward.

The frog leapt forward and Andy fell back onto his backside, yelping in shock.

"You said it was dead!" Mark laughed. "Shit!"

"I thought it was," Andy said jumping up. "The poor sods guts are hanging out of its mouth!"

"Oh no!" Mark said. "You have to put it out of its misery!"

"Me?" Andy said curiously. "Why me?"

"Cause you don't have a heart," Mark said.

"Said who?" Andy asked.

"You told me," Mark said. "Idiot."

"Oh," Andy shrugged his shoulders.

"Just do the right thing!" Mark said pointing.

Andy groaned.

"Do it and I'll get the waitress's number for you," Mark said. "The one you keep banging on about."

"Really?" Andy said curiously.

"You are never going to ask her!" Mark said. "Bloody wimp!"

"She won't be interested," Andy said.

"How do you know?" Mark said. "Unless you ask, you will never know."

"Fine!" Andy snapped. "I'll ask her!"

Andy looked down at the frog.

"Sorry, buddy," Andy said and stepped on it, pushing down and hearing a crunch.

"Oh no!" Mark said. "That was horrible."

Andy lifted his foot and the frog jumped out from under it.

"What the fuck!" Andy exclaimed.

"Keep it down!" Mark warned him. "Maybe it's immortal?"

"Would you want to be mortal with your guts flapping on your chin?" Andy asked.

"Probably not," Mark said and stepped forward, pushing Andy out of the way. "I'll do it properly!"

Mark stepped on the frog, putting all his weight onto one foot. As he lifted his foot, the frog is still attempting to move.

"Thought you were going to do it properly?" Andy asked.

"Why won't it die?" Mark said. "Why?"

The door opened and Gary, Keith's brother stepped out, lighting a cigarette.

Garry is a middle-aged man, wearing blue jeans and a black t-shirt. Short black scruffy hair and his arms and neck were covered in badly designed tattoos. Most of his front teeth are missing and he has a crooked nose and one of his eye sockets is collapsed.

"What are you two cocks doing?" He asked.

"Nice," Mark said. "I am your manager you know."

"Don't care," Gary shrugged his shoulders. "What you gonna do, fire me?"

"Could you not smoke out here," Mark said. "I have just cleaned."

Gary held his hand under the cigarette.

"Happy?" He asked. "What are you two pissing about over?"

"Got an injured frog," Andy said.

"Kill it then!" Garry scoffed.

"Tried," Andy said.

"A car ran over it, he trod on it and then I did," Mark said. "Little bugger won't die."

"Wait there a moment," Gary said and went back inside.

"What is he doing?" Andy asked.

"I dread to think," Mark said.

A few minutes later, Gary came back outside holding a large meat cleaver.

"What are you doing with that Gary?" Andy asked.

"Bashing it over your fucking head if I don't get a drink!" Gary laughed.

"Gary?" Mark asked nervously. "Are you going to do what I think you are going to do?"

"Well, I ain't making you dinner!" Gary said a grin on his face.

"Does being a psycho run in the family? "Mark asked.

"What do you mean?" Gary said curiously.

"Well Keith has his moments," Andy said.

"He was dropped on his head as a baby," Gary said. "He wouldn't hurt a fly!"

"I know of a mouse that would have something to say about that," Andy said, shaking his head in sarcasm.

Mark looked at Andy curiously.

"What do you mean?" Mark asked.

"Will tell you another time," Andy said.

Gary held out the cleaver to Andy.

"What?" Andy said, looking at the old cleaver.

"Kill it," Gary demanded.

"I'll pass," Andy said.

"You vegans are all the same!" Gary snapped. "Bunch of bloody pussies!"

"I am not vegan," Andy said. "I am a vegetarian."

"Same shit," Gary snarled.

"No it isn't," Andy said. "Very different actually."

"One thing that vegans and vegetarians have in common is you should all be shot," Gary said.

"Move out of the way!" He moaned, shoving Andy to the side.

Mark indicated for him to not react, waving his hand, and shaking his head.

Gary got bent down and raised the cleaver.

"Let's do it properly!" Gary said, bringing the cleaver down as hard as he could.

He severed the frog in half, its legs still kicking.

"Did a good job of that," Mark said sarcastically.

"Thanks," Gary said smiling.

"That was sarcasm," Mark said. "It's still alive," He pointed.

Gary got down on his hands and knees, growling as hacked at the frog, bringing the cleaver down over and over.

"Stop Gary," Mark said. "Gary stop!" He reached in, tapping Garry on the shoulder.

"What?!" Gary snapped as he turned around.

"You are damaging the floor," Mark said. "Now clean it up."

"I ain't cleaning this up," Gary said standing up. "It's his problem," He pointed to Andy.

"No," Mark said. "You just went apeshit," Mark scoffed, trying not to laugh. "You clean it up."

"Fine," Gary said, looking at Andy. "I'll put it in the vegetarian quiche."

"I wouldn't," Andy said. "Your brother is already on warning for something similar."

Mark looked at Andy, nodding slightly.

"Dean told me," Mark said. "I'd be careful Gary," Mark said. "You know the vegetarian chef is dating the deputy manager, it won't go down well."

"Fuck you both," Gary said and stormed off, swinging the cleaver back and forth.

"How do they function in the real world?" Andy asked.

"Gary is getting worse!" Mark laughed softly. "Keith is usually fine, when his brother is not around."

"I'll clean it up," Andy said looking at the mangled bloody mess of what was once a frog.

"Hold on," Mark said looking down. "Did it just move?"

Andy looked at mark, shaking his head unimpressed.

"Go back to your book," Andy said. "You fruitcake!"

"I am making a coffee," Mark said. "Do you want one?"

"Normal or Irish?" Andy said.

"Irish obviously," Mark said. "You suck at making them, so I will do it, want one?"

"No I will grab a regular coffee later," Andy said. "Going to sort out the Barn House and hoover it."

"They fixed the leak," Mark said. "The sink in the apartment above sprung a leak, they only realised when it started dripping on the delegate meeting the other day."

Andy burst out laughing.

"Thought that would make you laugh," Mark said.

"They were bloody awkward," Andy said. "I nearly smacked one of them with his constant comments."

"I liked your comeback in the bar," Mark said.

"What comeback?" Andy asked curiously, trying to remember.

"When you pointed out that you were deaf because that guy thought you were being rude," Mark said. "But you couldn't hear him over the noise."

"Oh yes," Andy scoffed. "He said he wasn't being rude as he also had a disability."

"And you replied, being an arsehole isn't a disability!" Mark laughed. "I liked that."

"Did he complain?" Andy said.

"No," Mark said. "If he had, I would have reminded him that bullying isn't acceptable and cancelled his room."

"Mad," Andy said. "I bent over backwards for that group."

"I know," Mark said. "Don't worry about it."

"I am going to head over," Andy said pointing to the Barn House Suites.

"Got the key?" Mark asked.

Andy nodded and tapped his pocket.

"Could you take my mug in?" Andy pointed to the mug on the wall.

"Sure," Mark said, grabbing it as he passed it.

"Thanks," Andy said, walking towards the Barn House Suite entrance.

Andy yawned as he locked the door to the Barn House Suite, turning around and exclaiming in fright when Gary walked up the path.

"Have you seen Mark?" He asked.

"Jesus Gary," Andy said.

"Have you seen Mark?" Gary asked again.

"Is he not in reception?" Andy said. "That is where he said he would be."

"Where have you been?" Gary said. "Been bleeping you."

"Here," Andy said. "Mark told me not to bother with a bleep. What's up?"

"Got a customer in reception," Mark said. "Doesn't look too happy.|"

"You could have led with that," Andy said, shaking his head in annoyance and breaking into a run towards the hotel reception.

As Andy opened the door, he smiled at the man waiting by the counter. The man is wearing blue shorts and a white t-shirt. Slim with short blonde hair and silver-rimmed glasses.

"Apologies," Andy said. "Have you been waiting long?"

"Not long no," the man said. "The guy from the kitchen said he would find someone."

"How can I help? Andy asked.

"Would you have a spare room?" He asked.

"We do yes," Andy said. "Let me go round."

Andy let himself into the reception office, looking around the corner for Mark. His book is on the counter along with Andy's mug.

"Is there a problem with your room?" Andy asked.

"Not at all," he said. "My wife is not well and my snoring is annoying her. She forgot her earplugs."

"Sorry to hear that," Andy said. "Do you want a room nearby or?" Andy looked up.

"Is the room next door available?" He said.

"It is," Andy said. "Same cost."

"Could you link the charge to the details on record?" the man asked. "I don't have my wallet."

"Yes that would be fine," Andy said.

The man started to cry, his hand going to his mouth as he removed his glasses.

"Are you okay?" Andy asked.

The man sobbed, trying to stifle his cries. He turned around, hiding his face.

Gary walked in, stopping by the stairs.

"What is going on here?" He asked. "You upset him or something Andy?"

"No," Andy said. "I am not sure what happened."

27

"What did you say?" Gary said.

"We were discussing payment for his room," Andy said.

"Probably the prices set him off," Gary walked up to the guy. "I understand how you feel."

"No," The man said sobbing. "No, it's not that."

Mark descended the steps, pausing and looking at the crying man and Gary with his hand on his shoulder.

"What have I missed," Mark asked.

"Andy upset him," Gary said.

"No I didn't," Andy scoffed.

"Do you want to get back to the kitchen Gary," Mark said. "I will deal with this."

"Sure," Gary said. "Not into all this cry-baby rubbish," Gary said, storming off through the brasserie.

"Sorry about him," Mark said. "He is a moron."

"It's okay," The man said.

"Could I get you a drink or something," Mark said.

"No," The man said. "I will be fine, I am sorry!" He wiped his eyes, sniffing as he put his glasses on. "This man didn't do anything wrong."

"Is there anything we can help with?" Mark asked.

"I came down to book another room," The man said. "Andy here was ever so helpful."

"Another room?" Mark said curiously. "Is there something wrong with your room?"

"No," the man said. "The room is great."

"So what is the problem?" Mark asked.

"He snores," Andy said. "And doesn't want to disturb his wife as she is not well."

"Ah I get it now," Mark said.

"I couldn't sleep," The man said. "I had some news earlier."

"I am sorry to hear that," Mark said. "If there is anything we can do."

"It was good news," The man said. "I am going to be a father."

"I understand why you are crying now," Andy said. "I'd bloody cry if I were going to be a father."

"Shut up Andy," Mark said. "Could you give me the key to his room?"

Andy reached bent down and retrieved a key from under the counter, reaching out and handing it to Mark.

"Sure you don't want anything brought up?" Andy said. "Food or drink?"

"Actually," The man said. "Do you have anything sweet?"

"We have cheesecake," Mark said. "And some chocolate gateaux."

"What cheesecake do you have?" He asked.

"Lemon, strawberry, caramel and plain," Mark said. "What was the other?" He said looking at Andy.

"Coffee," Andy said. "But it's not good."

"He is right," Mark said. "It's not good."

"Could I get caramel?" The man said. "With some cream."

"Yes," Andy said. "Will bring that up shortly."

"And some water," The man smiled.

"Water in the room, but if you want any more, just call down," Mark said. "I will take you up."

"Thanks," The man said to Andy. "Sorry for being a nuisance."

"Not at all," Andy said. "And congratulations."

Andy watched as Mark led the man upstairs, he turned and gave Andy a thumbs up.

Andy opened the door to the kitchen from the restaurant entrance, looking around for Gary.

"Gary?" He said. "You here?"

No answer.

"Hey Gary, do you want a pint?" Andy said louder.

No answer.

"Thank god for that," Andy said. "Annoying pleb!"

Walking round to the desert station opposite the refrigerator, he took a plate from the shelf, checking it was clean and then opened the small stainless-steel door to the small refrigerator under the counter, taking out a metal jug and smelling the contents.

"Smells great," Andy said. "Fresh cream!" Placing the jug on the counter next to the plate.

He made his way over to the walk-in refrigerator, opened it and walked in. Three rows of metal shelving racks, one against the wall, one in the middle and the third against the side wall. Another row is against the back, where the deserts are stored.

On the first rack are various cooked types of meat, on the second are vegetables and on the third dairy products.

Andy walked to the end of the refrigerator, looking at the various covered cheesecakes, individually sliced.

"Two slices," Andy said picking up the place with half a dozen slices of caramel cheesecake. "One for the crying man and one for me."

There is a clunk as the door closes, followed by a click.

"What?" Andy said turning around. "What is going on?"

Walking to the door and putting the cheesecake on the vegetable shelving, he attempted to open the door but it is locked.

"Oh come on!" Andy said, knocking on the door. "Hello?" He said looking through the small, stained window. "Gary?!" He called out.

The lights went off in the kitchen and only the small emergency light in the refrigerator barely lit up the area.

"Gary!?" Andy yelled out.

Andy pulled at the latch, pushing at the door.

"You arsehole!" Andy snapped.

Andy bent down, looking at the latch, trying to work out why he couldn't open it in the dim light.

"Must be locked from the other side," Andy said to himself. "Should it do that?" He said curiously.

Andy banged on the door three times as hard as he could.

"Gary!" He called out. "Mark?"

Andy remembered when the breakfast chef had shown him around the kitchen on his first day, explaining that the refrigerator was practically soundproof. Andy had asked him if people get locked in, only for the chef to say if the latch is locked, then yes, people could be locked inside.

"Give me a break," Andy said, rubbing his hands together as the cold started to get to them.

He looked around the room, hoping there was another door or latch, but there is only one way in and out.

"At least I won't starve," Andy joked. "Or die of thirst!" He noticed the bottles of water stacked in the corner.

Andy leaned against the wall next to the door, sliding down as he sat down and crossed his legs.

Half an hour passed when the lights came on and Andy looked up.

"Hello?!" Andy called out. "Can someone let me out!"

Mark appeared at the small window and then unlocked the door.

"Been looking for you everywhere," He said. "What happened?"

Andy got up from the floor, groaning.

"I came in to get the cheesecake and someone locked the door," Andy said. "And then turned the lights off."

"Why didn't you just pull the emergency latch?" Mark said.

"Because it doesn't work," Andy said.

"That isn't good," Mark said. "I'll speak to maintenance in the morning."

"If I had been on my own," Andy laughed. "I'd have been there until breakfast!"

"Gary," Mark scoffed, shaking his head. "it could only have been him."

"Arsehole," Andy said, picking up the plate of cheesecake. "I'll get him back."

"You okay?" Mark asked. "Cold?"

"Headache has gone," Andy chuckled. "Arse has gone to sleep!"

"Don't want to know," Mark said. "The customer doesn't want the cheesecake anymore," Mark said looking at it. "I fancy a slice though."

Andy handed the plate to Mark.

"You having some?" Mark asked.

"Sure," Andy nodded. "Right after I use the loo!"

Andy hurried away, diverting into the changing rooms.

Andy sat down in the reception, taking off his shoes and groaning as he stretched his feet. He picked up his book and leaned back, opening it.

Mark opened the door, popping his head in the door.

"Hey," Mark said. "I just need to pop home, is that okay?"

"Sure," Andy said.

"I'll only be gone for an hour," Mark looked at his watch. "Maybe less."

"It's fine," Andy said. "I am going to read, everything is done."

"Thanks," Mark said. "We will do the brasserie floor tomorrow."

"Varnish?" Andy asked.

"Yes," Mark nodded.

"I hate that," Andy said.

"You sweep and mop," Mark said. "I'll do the varnish."

"Deal," Andy said. "How is Dean?"

"Bored," Mark said. "He called earlier."

"I bet," Andy said.

"I'll see you in a bit," Mark said. "Stay in reception in case the police do a drive-by."

"Will do," Andy said as Mark closed the door.

Andy watched the monitor as Mark walked towards the door and stopped, walking back to the reception counter.

"Hey Andy," Mark said tapping the counter.

Andy hot up and walked round to the counter.

"Could you lock the door," Mark said.

"Sure," Andy said, leaving the office and following Mark to the door, letting him out and then locking it. Mark waved as he hurried down the steps, walking fast towards the car park.

Andy returned to the reception office, sipping coffee, and reading his book.

Several minutes passed when a car caught his attention on the monitor and he looked closer, not recognising it. It wasn't a police car and was Mark.

31

"Oh great," Andy said, watching as the car went past the hotel towards the carpark.

Switching the channels, the car slowly turned around and slowly pulled up outside the hotel. Andy put on his shoes and walked to the window, looking at the taxi.

"Wonder who this is?" Andy muttered to himself. "Everyone is in tonight."

A woman got out of the taxi, making her way up the steps and pushing the door, crashing into it lightly.

"Hold on," Andy said and laughed, walking to the door and unlocking it.

"Good evening," Andy said with a smile. "How can I help?"

The woman is tall and slim, wearing a black mini skirt, a silver t-shirt and a leather jacket. She has long frizzy blonde hair.

"This is a hotel right?" She asked.

"Yes," Andy said.

"We need a room or two," She said. "Have you got any available?"

"We do," Andy said.

"Great," She sighed in relief. "I'll get my friends!"

Andy watched as she ran towards the taxi, nearly tripping on the steps in her heels. He let the door close and returned to the reception, standing by the counter, watching on the monitor as two of them struggled with getting one out, extremely drunk. They are wearing the same outfits as the first woman. One of them is shorter and athletically built with short black hair, and the drunk one is average height and build, with heavy make-up on. Her long bleached blonde hair is immaculate.

They paid the taxi driver and then all took turns to hug him, one of them slapping his backside as he walked away.

Andy looked up when they walked into the reception, the two supporting their drunk friend, each holding an arm.

"Hi," the one that Andy had met at the door said.

"Good evening ladies," Andy said looking at his watch, it had just turned one in the morning. "Well good morning rather! My name is Andy."

"Hi, Andy," The woman from the door said. "I am Marina," She pointed to her drunk friend. "This is Charly, the blushing bride that is drunk!" She scoffed and laughed, pointing to the woman with short black hair. "That is Ellen."

"Good to meet you all," Andy said. "How was your day?"

"Eventful!" Marina said. "We have just been out to a hen night but cannot find any rooms at the hotel we wanted, so we were recommended here," She said.

"Could you repeat that," Andy said, struggling to lipread her when she looked away.

"What?" Marina said giggling.

"Could you repeat that?" Andy asked.

"Why?" She asked.

Ellen pointed to Andy's hearing aid, whispering to her friend.

"Oh I am sorry," Marina shouted, attempting to do sign language. "Is this better?"

"No just talk normally," Andy said chuckling. "I don't sign."

"Let's try and not upset the guy that is looking after us tonight," Ellen said.

"It is okay really," Andy said. "Everyone reacts differently. I rely on sound and lipreading ton communicate so just be normal."

"Okay," Marina nodded.

"She is far from normal!" Ellen scoffed.

"I haven't met a disabled before," Charly slurred.

"Charly!" Ellen exclaimed. "Stop it, that is rude!"

"First time for everything," Andy said. "Not sure if any of us are left in the wild."

Charly giggled.

"Ignore her," Marina said. "Stupid mare is drunk!" She looked at her, shaking her head and indicating to her to be quiet. "Do you have any rooms?"

"We do," Andy said. "Three rooms or?"

"Could we two," Marina said, looking at Ellen who nodded in agreement. "One of us needs to keep an eye on this one!" She indicated towards Charly, who nodded drunkenly.

"Sure," Andy said and pulled out a booklet from out under the counter that showed all the prices. "These are the current prices."

"That is fine," Marina said. "Pricey but fine."

"Tell me about it," Andy said. "I can promise you will get looked after."

"Oh is that right!" Charly giggled.

"Behave!" Ellen pulled at her arm. "You already disturbed the cab driver with your advances."

"Did I?" Charly said in confusion. "I don't remember!"

"He will," Marina said. "Poor bastard."

Andy handed her a form, pointing to the sections to fill out.

"Please fill this out and if I could take payment," Andy asked with a smile. "I will then take you to your rooms."

Marina handed Andy a credit card and he ran it though a reader, also recording the details and handed the printed invoice for her to sign.

"Just tell us where the rooms are and we will manage," Ellen said. "Is the hotel busy?"

"No not today," Andy said. "Fairly quiet," He handed two keys over. "Your rooms are next to each other and on the next floor in the middle. If you head up those stairs," Andy pointed toe staircase. "Rose rooms six and seven."

"Would it be possible to get some food brought up?" Marina asked. "What about wine?"

"I can do sandwich platters and crisps," Andy got out a notebook. "What would you like?"

"A selection is fine," She said. "You decide."

"Six bottles of white wine," Charly said with a mischievous grin.

Andy chuckled.

"No," Marina said sternly. "Two is fine for now."

"Bloody party pooper!" Charly moaned.

"I have a good feeling that as soon as you lay down," Ellen said. "You will pass out."

"I will have the food and drink up to you in the next twenty minutes," Andy said. "If you need anything further please let me know."

Marina took the keys and got hold of Charly's arm, turning and leading her towards the staircase with Ellen's help.

"I feel sick!" Charly said and both her friends stopped.

"Really?" Ellen asked.

"No!" Charly burst out laughing.

"You are a bitch!" Marina said.

"I know," Charly said. "I want more wine!"

"Maybe," Ellen said. "A big maybe!"

Andy shook his head as he watched the three woman make their way up the stairs, giggling and talking over each other.

Covering the large sandwich platter in clingfilm, he looked up when the door to the kitchen opened and Dean looked in.

"There you are," Dean said. "Where is Mark?"

"He had to pop home," Andy said. "What are you doing here?"

"Bored," Dean said. "Thought I'd come in and see Mark."

"Miss me too?" Andy laughed.

"Fuck no," Dean shook his head.

"Charming," Andy scoffed. "Three women on a hen night just showed up," Andy said raising an eyebrow. "That is what you are missing today."

"What are they like?" He said.

"They are okay" Andy replied. "One is off her face but they are harmless."

34

"Just three of them?" He asked.

Andy nodded.

"I am just going to take these up and then sorting out some wine," Andy said. "I'll sort you a coffee when I am back."

"What wine do they want?" Dean asked.

"Just the house white," Andy said. "Two bottles and three glasses."

"I'll get it ready and leave it by reception for you," Dean said. "I am going to grab myself a pint."

"Thanks," Andy said, picking up the platter and bowl of crisps.

"Was Mark okay?" Dean asked.

"Not sure," Andy said. "He seemed a little distracted."

"Oh right," Dean said. "Hopefully he is okay."

"He will be okay," Andy said. "Ask him about the frog when you see him," Andy said and laughed. "And also me getting locked in the fridge."

"You got locked in the fridge?!" Dean exclaimed.

"No," Andy said. "I was locked in the fridge!"

"Keith or Gary?" Dean said. "Neither of them like you."

"Tell me about it," Andy said. "It was Gary."

"Nice of him wasn't it," Dean said. "Making a complaint?"

"No," Andy smiled. "I have a plan in motion."

"Oh yeah?" Dean said curiously.

"Going to give him a c-section," Andy said with a grin on his face.

"A what?" Dean asked. "Why?"

"C-section," Andy said.

"I know what a c-section is, but don't understand what you mean," Dean said.

Andy put the platter and the bowl down, he put his finger under his ear and drew it all the way down across his nick to his other ear, in the shape of a C.

"Oh I get it," Dean sniggered. "Sounds good," Dean said.

"You can be my alibi," Andy said.

"Fuck that," Dean said. "I'll get some rope and bricks and we can drop him in the lake."

"I knew I liked you," Andy smiled, picking up the platter and bowl. "I need to get these delivered," He said, hurrying as he made his way through the restaurant.

Andy knocked at the door with his foot, with a platter in one hand and a bowl of chips in the other.

No answer.

Andy knocked again, harder.

The door suddenly opened and Marina stood there, wearing black knickers and bra.

"Sorry," Andy said trying not to look.

"I did say come in!" Marina said slightly annoyed.

"I cannot hear, so it's safer to wait," Andy said holding up the platter.

"Oh I am sorry," She covered her mouth. "I forgot!"

"No problems," Andy said. "Where do you want these?"

"On the table," Marina smiled and pointed.

Andy walked into the room where Ellen sat in a chair against the wall, still dressed. Charly laid in the bed in her underwear and Andy turned away when he saw her, she had her hand down her knickers, playing with herself and a pillow over her face, oblivious.

"That is new," Andy said.

"What?" Marina asked curiously.

"Of all the things I have seen at this hotel, that one is new," Andy smiled.

Marina looked at Andy in confusion, and then at the bed.

"Oh for god's sake Charly!" She yelped and ran over to the bed, throwing the bed clothes over her. "I am sorry you saw that!"

Ellen groaned and then covered her mouth, stifling laughter.

"It's her hen night," Andy laughed. "She is entitled to a bit of fun."

"Embarrassing!" Marina said. "I will be using that against her forever!"

"I second that," Ellen said. "Maybe a counter best man's speech?"

Andy laughed, placing the sandwiches and crisps on the table.

"I will bring up the wine next," Andy said walking to the door.

"Let yourself in," Marina said. "It's open."

"Thanks Andy," Ellen smiled.

"Maybe Ellen will give you a show when you come back!" Marina said.

Andy paused at the door.

"Shut up you bitch!" Ellen scoffed. "Ignore her Andy!"

Andy smiled at Ellen and then left the room, gently closing it behind him.

Andy arrived at the reception desk, picking up the tray with two bottles of wine in an ice bucket and three glasses next to it.

Mark came round the corner.

"Everything okay?" He asked.

"All good," Andy said. "Three new admissions, just finishing off the room service."

"Three?" Mark said. "Odd number."

"Three women," Andy said. "They were on a hen night."

"Nice?" He asked.

"They are okay," Andy said. "One of them is really cute."

Mark gave Andy a thumbs up.

"Strangely enough," Andy said. "When I just went up there, one in her underwear, one sitting down dressed and the third, drunk as anything, was lying in bed with a pillow on her face," Andy paused and chuckled softly. "Masturbating."

Mark looked at Andy wide eyed.

"You serious?" He asked.

"Yes," Andy said.

"Of all the nights I have to go home," Mark scoffed.

"You would have left me to do it anyhow," Andy said.

"Depends on how hot they were," Mark said with a grin on his face.

"Behave!" Andy laughed. "I am taking this up and then grabbing a coffee break, is that okay?"

"Sure," Mark said. "I am reading."

"Everything okay?" Andy asked.

"Yes," Mark nodded.

Andy knocked on the door and then opened it, walking into the room.

"Oh thank god!" Marina said. "I need a cold glass of wine, I am so hot!"

Andy walked to the table, avoiding looking at the bed. He put the tray on the table, taking off the glasses and the bucket.

"She is out of it," Marina said. "Absolutely zonked."

"Looks like she had a fun day," Andy said looking at Charly in bed, snoring softly.

"Are you married?" Marina asked.

"No," Andy said.

"Girlfriend?" Marina asked. "Or boyfriend?"

"I am straight," Andy said. "And single."

"Why?" Marina said. "Shy?"

"A little," Andy said. "Would you like anything else?"

"No thanks," Ellen said. "All good," She yawned loudly.

"If you do," Andy said. "Just give reception a call, otherwise have a great night."

Andy left the room, stopping in the corridor and taking a deep breath.

"Damn," He said.

Leaning back in the chair, Andy had his eyes closed and his arms crossed.

"Tired?" Mark asked as he stepped from the reception.

"What?" Andy said, opening his eyes and sitting forward.

"Tired?" Mark said again.

"A little," Andy said. "Been a long day."

"Do you want to go?" Mark said. "Only have a four hours left."

"No it's okay," Andy said. "I'll go grab a coffee."

"I'll get you one," Mark said. "I am just going up to the offices first to get some paperwork, and then will be down. Give me twenty minutes."

"Sure," Andy said and stood up. "Thanks."

Mark left the reception, walking to the staff corridor to take the lift up to the third-floor offices.

Andy sat back down, yawning heavily and closing his eyes.

The operator telephone started to ring and Andy stood up, walking over and looking at the panel.

"No number displayed," Andy said. "Crap!"

Ignoring it, Andy hoped that Mark would be able to connect it from the offices.

After a minute, it stopped ringing and Andy closed his eyes again.

A few minutes later, Andy opens his eyes when he hears someone knocking on the counter.

"Just a moment," Andy said and stood up, rubbing his eyes and trying to focus.

Andy walked around to the counter and found Ellen standing there in her underwear.

"Hello there," Andy said. "There are dressing gowns in the room."

"I have gone and locked myself out," She laughed. "I also cannot remember which room I am in!" She burst into fits of giggles.

"I went to call my friends, and then realised I don't know the number," she shook her head. "Crazy. I then called reception, and completely forgot!"

"Forgot what?" Andy asked.

"That you were deaf," She covered her mouth. "Sorry."

"No I am sorry," Andy said. "My colleague is usually here but he has popped out for a bit." She laughed, attempting to cover herself.

"Hold on?" Andy said.

Picking up a bunch of keys and his overcoat hanging on the back of the door, Andy met Ellen at the desk, putting the jacket over her shoulders.

"Am I embarrassing you?" She asked.

"No I am just being polite," Andy said. "I will take you up to your room and let you in."

"Thank you," Ellen said smiling.

The front door opened and a police officer walked in, the one that Andy had seen earlier.

Ellen turned around, the front of the overcoat open.

"What is going on here?" He asked. "Everything okay miss?" He said, looking at the Ellen and then at Andy.

"I locked myself out of my room," She said. "I was going to call down but remembered that this man is deaf, so it was easier to come down."

"Fair enough," The officer said.

"I am taking her back to the room," Andy said. "Go take a seat and I will get you some coffee shortly."

Andy walked Ellen up to her room, unlocking the door and opening it for her.

"There you go," Andy said,

"Thank you," She replied. "Do you want to come in?" she smiled.

"I don't think that will be appropriate," Andy said. "Plus I have some things to do and a police officer to look after!" He laughed. "Do you need anything?"

"There is something yes," She said and without warning stepped forward, kissing Andy on the lips. He felt her tongue push inside, the taste of wine, cigarettes and vomit taking him by surprise. She backed away and Andy froze.

"You taste good," She said smiling. "Maybe we can go on a date one day?" She said.

Andy nodded, unable to talk.

"Here," She said, taking off the overcoat and handing it to him. "I'll leave you a note in the morning, with my number."

She went into the room and closed the door.

Andy stood staring at the door for several seconds, trying to work out what had just happened.

Andy walked into the brasserie to find Mark sitting with the police officer, both had grins on their faces.

"Give me a minute," Andy said.

Andy walked into the bar, opened a bottle of water and drank some, swishing it around in his mouth and spitting it into the sink.

"Great kiss," He said to himself. "Wrong time."

Andy walked back into the brasserie with a bowl of peanuts.

"Everything okay?" Mark asked.

"Fine," Andy said sitting down. "Mine?" He pointed to the coffee.

"Yes," Mark said. "Steve was telling me you had a woman down her in her underwear."

"Locked herself out of her room," Andy said. "So I took her up."

"Why did she have your overcoat?" Mark asked.

"Because I wanted to do the right thing," Andy said.

"Hell of a view," Steve said. "And I mean wow!"

"You are married," Mark said.

"No harm in looking," Steve smiled.

"She invited me into her room," Andy said.

"Bloody hell that was a quick one," Steve said.

"Nothing happened," Andy said. "She was drunk so it wouldn't have been a good move."

"Good," Mark said.

"She grabbed hold of me, kissed me and shoved her tongue in my mouth," Andy scoffed. Steve exclaimed and then looked at Mark, shaking his head.

"Wow," Mark said. "Good?"

"It was," Andy said. "But the taste of cigarettes and vomit ruined it."

"Oh no!" Steve groaned. "That is wrong!"

Andy nodded and then smiled.

"Is that your first kiss?" Mark asked.

"No," Andy said. "First in a long time though!"

"She likes you!" Steve said. "You should ask her out."

"She wants to date," Andy said.

Andy leaned forward, picking up his coffee and then leaned back in the chair.

"Eventful night," Andy said. "Women in their underwear."

"Not forgetting the drunk one masturbating," Mark said. Steve choked on his coffee and then looked at Mark in shock.

"What?" Steve asked, then looked at Andy.

"When I delivered some food," Andy said. "One was lying in bed with a pillow over her face," He paused. "And her hand down her knickers, going to town."

"I am in the wrong bloody job!" Steve said. "I help out tonight?"

"I think not," Andy laughed. "They may steal your handcuffs!"

Andy groaned, looking at his watch.

"If it is okay with you Mark," Andy said trying not to yawn. "I am going to head off, is that okay?"

"Yes," Mark said. "Thanks for tonight."

"No problems," Andy said.

"I forgot to ask," Mark said. "Are you able to help out on Friday?"

"Sure," Andy nodded. "How come? Thought you were both on?"

"It's Valentine's night event," Mark said.

"Oh you, are kidding me," Andy moaned. "All those loved-up annoying people everywhere."

"Please," Mark said. "It would help us both out a lot."

"I am not doing the bar," Andy said. "Anything but the bar."

"Deal," Mark gave him a thumbs up.

"Or dealing with any more immortal frogs!" Andy said.

"Immortal frogs?" Steve said curiously. "What is that about?"

"That is a long story," Mark said.

"Probably an idea to leave the meat cleaver out," Andy said laughing.

"Should I be worried?" Steve asked.

"No," Mark said. "You ran over a frog earlier and the bloody thing wouldn't die."

"Until the kitchen psycho came along," Andy said.

"Go home Andy," Mark pointed to the door. "Get some sleep!"

"Thanks," Andy said and got up. "Good night to both of you."

Andy left the brasserie, collecting his jacket before he left.

THREE

Tracy stood at the counter, smiling at the couple that are filling out a form. Tracy is a redhead, her hair long and curly, tied up into a ponytail. She is average height and slim, wearing a black skirt, a white blouse, and a black jacket.

"Would you like someone to show you to your room?" She asked the couple.

"No thanks," The man said. "We have stayed here before," He said looking at the woman who smiled. The woman is wearing a long black dress and a leather jacket, large on her and most likely belonging to the man. The man, wearing black trousers and a white shirt. His right hand is heavily bandaged.

"The champagne is in the room as requested," Tracy said. "I will have the desert brought up as soon as possible."

"No rush," The woman said. "Thank you."

Tracy took the form and handed a key to the couple, watching as they walked away, holding hands awkwardly.

"So sweet," She whispered.

A knock at the door and she looked at it, realising the latch was on.

"Coming," She said, hurrying over and unlatching it.

Andy opened the door and walked in.

"Hi Tracy," He said. "You are here late. Thought you finished at six?"

"Helping out," Tracy said. "What on earth happened to you!"

Andy has a thick graze down the side of his eye and cheek, his eye is also bruised and his lip split. He is wearing black trousers, a white shirt, and a black tie.

"Long story," Andy said.

"Fighting?" Tracy asked.

"No!" Andy scoffed. "Got jumped by two morons the other night," Andy said. "I am okay."

"That looks so sore!" Tracy exclaimed. "Did you go to the hospital?"

"No," Andy shook his head. "Not worth the hassle."

"What happened?" She asked.

"I went out for a walk late at night," Andy said. "Going down an alleyway, two guys came the other way, drunk out their heads."

"Oh dear," She said.

"Long story short, they grabbed me and I fell, bashing my face on the wall and kissing the council standard paving stone!"

"How did you get away?"

"Poor you," She said. "It's a busy one tonight!"

"I saw," Andy said. "Restaurant and brasserie are full and I gather all rooms are sold?"

"All but two," Tracy said. "Strangely enough."

"Oh they will go," Andy said. "Are Dean and Mark in yet?"

"No not yet," She said. "Thought you didn't start until ten?" She said looking at her watch.

"Mark asked me this morning if I could come in early," Andy said. "Saying they were short staffed?"

"We had no porters today," She said.

"You are kidding," Andy said. "How have they managed?"

"They asked some of the bar staff to help out," Tracy moved to reception, checking no one was there. "Would you be able to do a room drop off for me?"

"Sure," Andy said. "What is it?"

"Desert," Tracy said, handing Andy a piece of paper. "They just arrived."

"I'll do it now," Andy said, opening the door and checking it was clear.

Andy knocked on the door, holding a silver tray with a bowl of strawberries and another small bowl of whipped cream. He leaned towards the door, listening in case he was asked to come in.
The door opened and a man stood there in boxers and a t-shirt.

"Hi," He said.

"Good evening," Andy said. "I have this for you."

"Bloody hell!" He said. "What happened?"

"Nothing, why?" Andy asked.

"Your face," He pointed. "Looks sore."

"Love bite gone wrong," Andy said.
The man laughed, shaking his head.

"Could you put it on the table please," The man pointed. "My hand is useless."

"What happened to you?" Andy asked.

"Put my hand through my mother's greenhouse," The man chuckled. "Sliced it right across the middle!"

"That sounds sore," Andy hissed as he placed the tray on the table.
As he turned around, a woman walked from the bathroom completely naked before noticing Andy and quickly running back in, closing the door.

"Oh dear," The man said. "That's me in trouble!"

"I doubt that," Andy said raising his eyebrows. "Enjoy!" He said and left the room, closing the door behind him.

"Wow," Andy said. "Lucky sod!"

Andy stepped into the office and Tracy smiled at him.

"All good?" She asked.

"Yes," Andy said. "Just done a couple of deliveries."

"Did mine didn't you?" She asked.

"I did yes," Andy said. "Guy with the bad hand?"

"That's the one," Tracy said.

"His partner walked out of the bathroom completely naked," Andy said grinning.

"No," She exclaimed.

"Yes," Andy nodded. "Little tattoo on her tummy."

"What of?" Tracy asked curiously.

"No idea," Andy said. "She ran away pretty quickly."

"Poor girl!" She said.

"He is a lucky guy!" Andy scoffed.

"How many valentines cards did you get?" Tracy asked.

"None," Andy said. "Who is going to send me any?"

"I thought maybe the girl from last week?" Tracy said smiling. "The one that forced her tongue down your throat?"

"I never heard from her," Andy said. "Not surprised, to be honest, she was drunk."

"Did you send any?" She said.

"One yes," Andy said.

"Someone here," She asked.

"You know the answer to that," Andy said. "I sent a card and had a rose delivered."

"I know," She laughed. "It came in earlier today."

"Has she said anything?" Andy asked nervously.

"No idea," Tracy said sighing loudly. "Been stuck in here all day."

"What time did you start?" Andy said looking at his watch.

"Eight this morning," She said. "The new girl never showed up."

"That isn't good," Andy said.

An elderly lady walked up to the counter, smiling when Tracy moved into view. The lady is wearing a blue dress and a red jacket.

"Hello there dear," She said. "I just wanted to inform you that there is a young couple arguing on the terrace."

"Thank you for letting me know," Tracy said. "We will keep an eye on things."

"Could you advise where the nearest lavatory is please?" She said.

"Through the brasserie, past the bar and on your left," Tracy said. "Do you want me to show you?"

"No thank you, dear," She said smiling. "I will manage."

The lady walked away, clutching a black walking stick.

"What was that?" Andy asked.

"Someone arguing outside," She replied. "On the terrace."

Andy flicked the channels on the security monitor until he found the camera on the front of the hotel, the image is in black and white and not clear.

"Bless her," Tracy said.

"Who?" Andy said looking up.

"Fiftieth anniversary," She said. "Her and her husband come here every year."

"That is nice," Andy said. "I am going to go for a walk around the terrace."

Stepping out of the entrance, Andy looked down the end of the terrace near the restaurant. There is a young couple, arguing. The tall and thin man is wearing black jeans, a white shirt with a goatee and a shaved head. The woman, short and petite wearing a long cream dress and a small grey jacket, her long curly blonde hair down to her buttocks.

The man was irate, red in the face as he got close to the woman's face, pointing at her.

"Everything okay here?" Andy asked.

"Fine," The man said. "Just mind your own business."

"I would," Andy said. "But there have been complaints."

"I don't give a fuck mate," The man said calmly.

"Stop," The woman said slapping his arm.

"Well could you take it somewhere else that isn't next to the restaurant," Andy said. "Your room maybe?"

"Don't you have a job to do?" The man asked.

"I am doing it," Andy said. "Can I get either of you anything?" Andy asked. "Coffee? Tea?"

"No," The woman said. "Thank you."

The man sighed.

"Sorry," He said. "It's been a long day."

The man walked away, heading towards the green, the woman looked at Andy and shook her head, following him.

Andy leaned against the wall, watching as the woman caught up with the man.

"What's going on?" A voice said behind Andy.

"What?" Andy said, turning around.

Spencer is tall and muscular built, wearing black trousers, a white shirt, and a black tie. Andy struggled to understand him at times due to his strong Nigerian accent. He has a shaved head and a thick, well-groomed goatee.

"Is he giving you problems?" Spencer asked.

"No," Andy said. "Gave me some lip, but nothing major."

"Lip?" Spencer asked curiously.

"Attitude," Andy said.

"What happened to you?!" Spencer said pointing to Andy's face. "You been in a bust-up?"

"Not really a bust-up," Andy said. "More a couple of drunken idiots trying their luck."

"You okay though?" Spencer asked.

"Yeah I am good thanks," Andy said. "Just a little sore."

"Looks it," Spencer hissed.

"I woke up today and forgot," Andy chuckled. "Rubbed my face!"

"Damn!" Spencer said shaking his head. "Need me to hang around," Spencer laughed.

"I'll be okay," Andy said. "Will keep an eye on them for a little while," Andy yawned, covering his mouth. "How are you doing? How's the shoulder?"

"I am good thanks," Spencer nodded in appreciation. "My shoulder is much better, but no training for some time."

"What happened?" Andy asked.

"I was benching alone," Spencer rolled his eyes. "My right arm is not so good, so when I put more push into it, it went."

"Popped it?" Andy asked.

"Yes," Spencer said.

"Oh bloody hell," Andy cringed. "Lucky you didn't drop the bar on your head."

"My girlfriend lifted it," Spencer said. "And drove me to the hospital."

"How about we train together," Andy said. "When you recover?"

"I cannot lift what you lift!" Spencer exclaimed.

"It's just training," Andy said. "Not a competition."

"It is a deal," Spencer smiled. "Oh is it true?"

"Is what true?" Andy asked curiously.

"Come on man!" Spencer laughed.

Spender reached over, punching Andy in the arm.

"Did you send Marie a card and rose?" He asked.

"I did," Andy said nervously. "Why?"

"I knew it," Spencer exclaimed.

"Well I was told she liked me," Andy said. "By one of the waiters."

"Oh," Spencer said. "She was surprised," Spencer took a mobile phone from his pocket.

"I'll see if she is around," Andy said. "Is she still at work?"

"She is covering with the restaurant tonight," Spend said. "I need to take a call."

Spencer hurried off round the corner of the building towards the garden entrance to the restaurant. Andy noticed the couple are no longer on the green, he walked down the steps, waiting as a couple of cars drove past slowly and then descended the second set of steps down to the green, the harsh lights flooding the length of green in bright light.

"Hopefully they sorted it," Andy said.

Andy had completed a security check of the hotel floors and grounds, working his way up to the staff entrance where there are two waitresses on a break. One of them, tall and slim, wearing black tights, a short black skirt, and a white blouse. She has short brown hair and glasses. The second girl, Marie is shorter, slim with long dark brown hair, wearing the same clothes.

"Good evening," Andy said.

"Hey Andy," The first girl said. "How are you?"

"Not too bad," Andy said smiling. "You okay Marie?" He said, slightly nervous.

"Yeah fine," Marie said, avoiding eye contact.

"What happened to your face," The first girl said, prompting Marie to look at Andy.

"Got jumped the other night," Andy said. "Looks worse than it is."

"That is terrible," The first girl said. "Sure you are okay?"

"I am good," Andy said. "Got five minutes to chat?" He asked Marie.

"Andy," Marie said, sighing heavily. "The flower and card were nice, but I am not interested."

"I'll wait in the staff room," The first girl said, walking around Marie and opening the door, smiling at Andy as she closed it.

"Not interested?" Andy said.

"No," She said bluntly. "I go for taller guys," She said, looking him up and down. "And it wouldn't work, with the hearing thing."

"Oh," Andy said, lost for words. "Wasn't expecting a knockdown that brutal."

"Brutal?" Marie said.

"Yeah," Andy replied. "Being blown out for two things I cannot control."

47

"I've got to go to work," She said. "Just give me some space, yeah?" She said, walking back into the hotel.

"Wow," Andy said, shocked.

After a couple of minutes, he walked into the staff room.

The small staffroom is lit with a single fluorescent lamp, flickering every few seconds. A round table in the middle of the room with six chairs around it, on the right next to a small window, is a large urn, sink, and refrigerator. Next to the refrigerator, is a large pedal bin.

"Hi Charlotte," Andy said. "You okay?"

"Shit Andy," Charlotte said. "That was bitchy of her."

"You heard that?" Andy asked.

"Yes," She said. "The windows don't work for shit."

"Was a bit of a shock," Andy said. "Especially when I was told she liked me."

"Who was it?" Charlotte asked.

"Simon," Andy said. "Works in the bar."

"What an arsehole," Charlotte said. "I am sorry."

"It's fine," Andy said, walking over to the cupboard and taking out a cup, placing it under the urn. "Do you want a drink?" He said pointing to the cup.

"No," She smiled. "Just had one."

"Did your boyfriend spoil you?" Andy asked.

"No," She said. "Not yet, but he is picking me up after work so who knows?"

"When do you finish?" Andy said looking at his watch.

"Eleven," She said yawning and groaning. "Maybe twelve depending, it's a manic night."

Making himself a black tea, he strained the teabag and carried it to the bin, flipping the lid up and looking into it.

"What?" Charlotte said curiously.

Andy reached into the bin, pulling out a single red rose and a torn-up card.

"Well wow," Andy said.

"No way!" Charlotte scoffed. "That is totally uncalled for!"

Charlotte got up and walked over to Andy, taking the flower and card off him.

"It's not a problem," Andy said.

Charlotte grabbed him and hugged him.

"Thank you," Andy said.

When Charlotte broke away, he took the card from her and dropped it into the bin.

"Can I have this?" She said, holding the rose.

"Won't your boyfriend get the hump?" Andy asked.

"No," She smiled. "I'll give it to my mum if that is okay?"

"Sure," Andy chuckled.

He picked up his tea and walked to the door.

"So what happened the other night?" She asked.

"With what?" Andy said pausing.

"The attack," Charlotte said.

"I couldn't sleep," Andy said. "So decided to go for a long walk around town, just after midnight."

"As you would," She shrugged her shoulders and smiled.

"I was walking down an alleyway, next to a graveyard," Andy said chuckling. "It was quite dark, barely any lighting down there."

"Next to the school?" Charlotte asked. "I know the one."

"Two guys came towards me and I could tell they were drunk, part of me said to go back the other way but I couldn't be bothered," Andy rolled his eyes. "As they approached me, one of the spoke but because it was dark I couldn't lipread them, so I moved so I could and that is when it went wrong."

"How?" Charlotte asked.

"One of them grabbed me and I lost my balance, falling into the wall and causing this," He pointed to his face. "And then hitting the floor hard. I was dazed a few seconds but as I tried to get up, they kept pushing me down, laughing and so on."

"Oh shit," She said shaking her head, her hand on her mouth.

"I could spell pee and poo, and I snapped," Andy took a deep breath. "I forced my way up, grabbing the leg of the main guy and just flipped him into the bushes," He laughed. "The second guy came at me, throwing punches like a moron, so I just body slammed him into the wall and then threw him into the bushes, funnily enough, he ended up in the graveyard."

"Oh, Andy!" Charlotte gasped.

"I then walked away, met by police officers at the end of the alley, which was pretty strange!" Andy said.

"What happened," She said. "Did they get arrested?"

"They asked if I wanted to press charges, but there is no point," Andy said. "Nothing will come of it. Besides, both of them had their karma."

"Are you sure you are okay though," Charlotte asked. "Did you go to accident and emergency?"

"No," Andy said. "They would clean it and send me on my way, so I cleaned it myself with spray bleach."

"You idiot!" She groaned.

"I tell you though," Andy said. "None of that hurt more than what Marie just did!" He burst out laughing, pausing and then shaking his head, biting down on his lip.

"Surely you need a tetanus update?" She said. "God knows what was on the wall or floor."

"Pee and poo," Andy chuckled. "I had a jab last year, so all good."

"I better head back to the office," Andy said. "Catch up with you later?" He said.

"Yeah," She said. "Look after yourself and see you later."

Andy sat down in the reception, putting the tea on the workshop, watching as Tracy was dealing with a customer. He watched as the middle-aged man shook her hand before walking away, and she stepped round the corner.

"Bloody creep!" She said.

"What?" Andy asked curiously.

"He asked me out!" She scoffed.

"Lucky you!" Andy said laughing.

"He is here with his wife!" She said. "Bloody cheek of it!"

Andy stood up, looking at the security feed on the monitor.

"Tell your other half!" Andy said. "I am sure he will go mad."

"I think not," Tracy said. "I was hoping he would pop the question."

"Nothing?" Andy said.

"Not yet," She sighed in frustration. "Have you heard our news?"

"What?" Andy said picking up his mug.

"Have you heard our news?" She said again.

"No," Andy said. "What news?"

"We are getting a new addition," She smiled, placing a hand on her stomach.

"Getting a dog?" Andy asked.

"No," Tracy shook her head.

"A cat?" Andy tried again.

"Come on!" Tracy said, both of her hands on her stomach.

"A tarantula?" Andy smiled.

"You are the weirdo that would get a tarantula as a pet!" She scoffed. "Try again!" She pointed to her stomach."

"Pregnant with twins?" Andy said, bursting into laughter.

"God I hope not!" She said. "I want one to start and see how that goes.

The elderly woman from before came to the reception counter again, smoking.

"Hello there," Tracy said. "Sorry but you cannot smoke here."

"Oh, I am sorry dear," The elderly lady held up a hand, walked into the brasserie and threw the cigarette onto the log fire, and then returned to the counter.

"I just wanted to let you know," She said. "There is a young lady outside, crying."

"Oh no," Tracy said. "Whereabouts?"

Tracy waved at Andy, indicating for him to check the security camera, but because he couldn't hear the conversation, he had no idea what she wanted from him.

"Just outside near the bar," She said indicating.

"Thank you," Tracy said. "We will check up on her and make sure she is okay."

Tracy watched as the elderly lady walked away and then turned the security camera to the front of the hospital, pointing to a woman.

"What?" Andy asked.

"Apparently," Tracy smiled. "She is crying."

"Okay," Andy said shrugging his shoulders. "So?"

"Go and check on her you sod," She scoffed. "Not a good night for someone to be upset."

"Tell me about it," Andy said.

"Why?" Tracy asked.

"Marie found out the card and rose were from me," Andy said. "Ripped up the card and threw the rose in the bin!"

Tracy is lost for words, her mouth opened in shock.

"I know," Andy said shaking his head.

"You are kidding mate!" She said in anger. "Okay, not being interested is one thing, but that!"

"I spoke to her," Andy said. "Before I found the stuff in the bin, apparently I'm too short and she cannot handle the deaf thing."

"Oh, Andy!" Tracy said, holding out her arms to hug him.

"No it's okay," Andy said. "It's getting to me!" He wiped his eyes, exclaiming in embarrassment.

"Oh no," Tracy said, pulling a sad face.

"I am going to check on this girl," He said. "And when everyone buggers off to bed, I am having a drink or ten."

Andy quickly left the office, wiping his eyes as he walked to the entrance, and stepped out.

The woman sat on a cast iron chair, her legs resting against the table. Her head pressed against her knees as she sobbed. It is the woman from earlier that Andy had seen arguing with her boyfriend.

"Excuse me?" Andy said softly. "Are you okay?"

"No!" She cried.

"Can I help you with anything?" Andy said, moving closer.

She looked up, her makeup running from tears.

"He dumped me," She said and sobbed.

"I am sorry to hear that," Andy said. "And if I am honest, it's his loss."

"I don't know what to do!" She cried.

"Well," Andy said. "If I were you, I would try and enjoy the night," He sighed. "Do you have a room?"

"Yes," She nodded. "I don't want to do this on my own!"

"How about calling a friend," Andy said shrugging his shoulders. "A girls' night or something, anything to be honest."

"I don't know!" She cried.

"Can I get you a drink?" Andy said. "On the house of course."

"Can I have vodka?" She said. "And soda?"

"Sure," Andy smiled and nodded. "It's cold out here, do you want to come inside?"

"No," She said. "I want to stay here."

"Okay," Andy said. "I'll bring you a drink shortly."

"What happened to your face?" She asked.

"Cut myself shaving," Andy said.

The girl laughed.

"You laughed!" Andy said and walked through the patio towards the bar.

Andy walked through the brasserie and up to the bar where several people stood, a couple sat at the bar and Charlotte was on her own.

"You okay?" Andy asked.

"Fine," Charlotte said. "It's a quiet moment."

"Now you have said that," He grinned. "It's going to turn manic!"

"What is with the girl?" She said pointing through the brasserie entrance where he had come.

"She got dumped," Andy said shaking his head.

"No way!" Charlotte gasped. "On Valentine's day? That really sucks!"

"I know," Andy said.

"Trying your luck?" Charlotte smiled.

"What?" Andy said, not hearing her correctly.

"Are you going to try and get in there?" She said with a grin.

"No," Andy exclaimed. "She is nice, but not the right time for it! Could you do me a vodka and soda," Andy said. "For her, not me."

"Sure will do," Charlotte said and got a clean glass, pouring two shots of vodka and then adding the soda. "Fancy a chat before I go later?" Charlotte said. "My other half cannot collect me until after twelve."

"Sure," Andy said. "Give me a shout when you are ready," Andy said.

The elderly lady from the reception walked over to Andy, stopping to get her balance, Andy reached out to offer his arm.

"Are you okay?" He asked.

"Yes thanks, dear," She said. "I am looking for the toilets."

"There," Andy said pointing.

"Thank you," She said. "I am here with my husband," She said and pointed to an elderly man sitting in the bar lounge, he raised his hand at Andy.

"Very nice," Andy said. "I hear you are celebrating fifty years!"

"Fifty years!" Charlotte said. "That is so sweet!"

"Congratulations," Andy said. "What is your secret?"

"Wine," The elderly lady laughed. "Lots of it, the main reason I am constantly going to the lavatory!"

"I get what you mean," Charlotte said.

"Could you sort out that small bottle of champagne for me?" The elderly lady said to Charlotte.

"Of course," She smiled. "I'll get Andy to bring it over to you in a moment, is that okay?"

"That would be wonderful," The woman said patting Andy's hand and looking at his face. "What happened to you?" She asked.

"Charlotte over there punched me for not doing as I was told," Andy said. "She packs a mean punch."

"Did you deserve it?" The lady asked, staring at Andy.

"Yes he did," Charlotte said. "Won't do it again will he."

The old lady burst into laughter, walking towards the toilets.

"That is going to give you a bad name," Andy said, picking up the drink from the bar. "Give me a shout if you need anything."

"I would," Charlotte said. "But you won't hear me!" She exclaimed.

"You are so funny!" Andy said. "Not!" he shook his head in mock disgust as he walked away, heading through the brasserie.

Andy got to the table on the terrace to find the woman had gone, he looked up and down to see if she had moved.

"Oh bloody hell," Andy said.

"Andrew?" A man called down from the entrance. "Andrew?!" He said louder.

Andy looked at the entrance to see a tall, well-groomed man in a three-piece suit in black with a light grey waistcoat. His black hair immaculately styled, short on the back and sides, long on top. His trimmed goatee looks like it had been sprayed on. He has a thick French accent and Andy always struggled.

"Andrew come here!" He called out.

"It's Andy," Andy said. "Not Andrew."

"Same thing," He said.

"How can I help you Allen?" Andy asked.

"My name is Allain, "He said.

"Same thing," Andy said smiling.

"No it is not," He said. "What are you doing?"

"Looking after customers," Andy said.

"Are you drinking?" He snapped.

"No," Andy said. "I was bringing a drink for a lady who was sat at a table here," Andy pointed.

"Are you working on the bar?" Allain asked.

"No I am floating," Andy said. "Based in reception until ten."

"Where is Dean?" He asked.

"Starts at ten," Andy said.

Allain looked at his watch.

"Did you need me for something?" Andy asked.

"I received a call from the restaurant," Allain said.

Andy looked at him, confused, waiting for him to say something further.

"Okay?" Andy said.

"Do you understand me?" Allain asked.

"Yes," Andy nodded. "You had a call from the restaurant," He said. "And?"

"There was an argument between a couple," Allain said. "I came to investigate."

"I already sorted that one," Andy said. "Was a while ago, the girl was the one I was getting a drink for, she was upset."

"Why?" Allain demanded. "Did you do something wrong?"

"No idea why you would assume I did anything," Andy sighed. "But no, her partner ended the relationship."

"That is not good," Allain said. "Could you keep her away from the customers, she will only ruin the mood."

"She is a customer," Andy said.

"I don't want depressed people around tonight," He laughed. "We have a reputation to keep.

"Okay," Andy said. "Anything else?"

"What happened?" Allain said, pointing to Andy's face.

"Insect bite," Andy said.

"Really?" Allain said in disbelief. "It looks bad, can you not cover it up?"

"I forgot my mask," Andy said.

"Mask?" Allain said, confused.

"Yes," Andy said. "I don't I'd make a good phantom though, my singing voice isn't great."

"I don't understand," Allain said. "Can you put make up on it?"

"No," Andy said.

"Why not?" Allain said, unhappy with the response.

"I am allergic," Andy said. "If I put anything on, I'll get sick."

"Don't do that," Allain said. "Try and turn your head to the side when people talk to you, so they cannot see it," Allain said in disgust. "When is Mark in?" He asked.

"Ten," Andy said, turning his face to the side, almost looking away from Allain.

"And Dean?" He said, checking his watch.

"You asked that," Andy said. "Also ten."

"Tracy leaves soon," Allain said. "You need to look after reception."

"I cannot do that," Andy said. "The phones need to be manned."

"Then you do that," Allain said bluntly.

"I can't," Andy said.

"Why not?" Allain said.

"Because he is deaf," Tracy said at the doorway. "I am working until ten, so it's fine."

"Well I am glad I have put these things into place," Allain said. "Please keep the terrace clean Andy!"

"You are needed," Tracy said. "Customer complaint."

"Could you ask the on-call manager to deal with them?" Allain said nervously.

"We don't have one," Tracy said. "You are covering."

"I forgot," Allain said, walking back into the hotel.

Tracy stepped outside, walking over to Andy.

"He is such a tosser," Tracy said. "A lazy tosser too!"

"Tell me about it," Andy said. "Keeps calling me Andrew."

"Idiot!" Tracy moaned. "You okay?"

"I am good," Andy said. "The girl has gone."

"I saw her walk through," Tracy said. "Went upstairs."

"I am going to get rid of this," Andy said. "And then do a floor check."

"See you later," Tracy smiled.

Andy went let himself into the small bar, watching as Charlotte restocked the refrigerators.

Behind the bar are three different house beer pumps, a second counter with glasses, fruits, and juice. An ice machine and dishwasher side by side. Behind the bar are refrigerators, four individual ones with a selection of various bottled drinks. Above them are countless spirits hanging from holders, the mirrored wall giving the impression there are more. At the end, a door leading to the storage and pump room.

"Hey," Andy said.

"What do you need?" Charlotte said looking up, balancing awkwardly.

"Nothing," Andy said tipping the drink into the stainless-steel sink and putting the glass into the dishwasher next to it. "She disappeared."

"Waste of vodka," Charlotte shook her head.

"Need any help?" Andy said, looking at the two people sitting at the bar.

"No," Charlotte stood up. "It's quiet, just did some drinks for the restaurant."

"Bad news," Andy said. "The French moron is on."

"I know," She rolled her eyes. "Took him three attempts to pull a pint earlier."

"He is useless," Andy said.

"What time do you finish?" Charlotte said, wiping down the bar.

"Six in the morning," Andy said. "All depends on how busy it is."

"Guess you will get lumbered into doing the Barn House tonight?"

"I don't mind," Andy said. "It is quite relaxing doing the hovering."

"Never thought I would hear a guy say that!" Charlotte scoffed.

"The Barn house always reminds me of you," Andy said.

"I know," Charlotte said. "All because Dean told you I was mean with a nasty temper."

"You can imagine my fear when I walked into you that day," Andy laughed. "Expecting you to beat me to death with a bottle!"

"Still scared of me?" She asked innocently.

"Petrified!" Andy exclaimed.

The telephone behind the bar started to ring and Charlotte answered it.

"Where?" She said trying to listen over the noise. "Okay I will send Andy round."

"What is it?" Andy asked as she put the telephone down.

"Drunk guy in the staff room," Charlotte said. "Freaked out Lindsay so I said you would pop round and see how it is."

"Lindsay is in?" Andy said. "I thought she left?"

"Helping out," Charlotte said. "We need it!"

As Andy was about to open the door of the staff entrance leading to the staffroom, the kitchen door opened.

"Hey Andy!" One of the chefs called out. "Andy come here!"

Andy stopped and turned around.

Scott is the lead vegetarian chef, a tall and heavily build man with a large beard and a shaved head. He is wearing white trousers and a white top, stained.

"Evening Scott," Andy said. "You okay?"

"Yeah," He said indicating for Andy to go over to him. "Come here."

"What's up," Andy said nervously. "Is this about the vegetarian quiche from last week?"

"No that is history," Scott said. It's cool."

"So what's up?" Andy said. "You need something?"

"A favour," Scott said. "Could you send Tracy down to the lake?"

"Could I what?" Andy scoffed. "You planning to kill her or something?!"

"No!" Scott exclaimed and laughed. "I am not that brave!" He got closer to Andy. "I am going to propose."

"About time!" Andy said. "Where abouts near the lake?"

"The bench," Scott said. "The new one, not the duck shit covered one."

"They are both covered in duck shit as far as I know," Andy said. "Sure, when?"

"Ten minutes," Scott said looking at his watch. "Make something up about me being there."

"Like what?" Andy asked.

"You did acting at college didn't you?" Scott asked. "I am confident you will think something up. Ten minutes!" He said, giving Andy a thumbs up before returning to the kitchen.

Andy stepped out of the staff entrance and saw Lindsay standing by the staffroom with a cigarette hanging from her lips. She is taller than Andy, muscular and wearing black trousers, a white shirt, and a black tie. Her short black hair is combed over her ears.

"Hey!" Andy said. "Thought you left!"

"I did," Lindsay said.

"You never said goodbye!" Andy said. "Thought you loved me."

"Love is a strong word," Lindsay laughed.

"Okay, liked," Andy corrected himself.

"That is a strong word too," She scoffed.

"Okay," Andy said. "You win."

"What happened to you?" She asked. "You drop your barbell on your face again?"

"I did that once," Andy said. "And I was drunk!"

"Who benches when they are drunk!?" Lindsay scoffed.

"Me," Andy said. "So no copying otherwise I will sue for copyright."

"Spoilsport," Lindsay whined.

"What's going on with the guy in the staffroom," Andy asked.

"It's not so bad," Lindsay said. "His girlfriend walked out."

"Another one?" Andy said.

"What do you mean?" Lindsay asked.

"Just had to deal with a poor girl that got dumped," Andy said.

"What are you doing to these people," Lindsay said. "You are bad luck!"

Andy nodded slowly.

"I heard about Marie," Lindsay said. "That is rough."

"Never mind," Andy said. "She showed her true colours."

"You can do better," Lindsay smiled and hugged him. "If you tell anyone I hugged you, I'll kick you to death."

"Naturally," Andy said. "Let me check on this guy."

Andy knocked on the door and then let himself into the room.

The man is sitting on one of the chairs, holding a bottle of beer in one hand, and a cigarette in the other. He is wearing black jeans, a white shirt untucked and brown leather shoes. He is clean-shaven, with short brown heavily gelled hair.

"Hi there," Andy said. "Sorry but you cannot smoke in here," Andy said pointing to a fire sensor. "If that goes off, there will be a shitstorm."

The man dropped the cigarette onto the concrete floor, treading on it.

"Are you okay?" Andy asked.

"Not really," The man said. "My bird dumped me."

"Sorry to hear that," Andy said.

"She wanted me to propose," The man said sighing heavily. "But I am not ready."

"Sorry," Andy said. "And sorry to do this, but I need you to move to a customer area."

The man ignored Andy, looking down at his feet.

"Do you think I am wrong?" He said.

"Do I think what?" Andy asked. "Didn't catch that."

The man looked up at Andy.

"You don't look foreign," He said.

"I am deaf," Andy said. "I need to lipread."

"Oh," The man said. "Not meet a deaf person before," He nodded. "What's going on with your face?"

"Got attacked," Andy said. "Nothing to worry about."

"You have that Seven of Nine vibe going on," He said, laughing lightly.

"What?" Andy said in confusion.

"Seven of nine?" The man said, expecting Andy to know what he meant.

"What is that?" Andy asked.

"Star Trek?" the man said. "Borg in Voyager."

"Not seen it," Andy said. "Is it good?"

"Yeah," The man said, finishing the contents of his beer.

"What is your name?" Andy asked.

"Nick," He said.

"Nick," Andy said. "Could I show you back to the bar and I will get you a drink on the house?" Andy said.

"Two?" Nick smiled.

"Possibly," Andy said.

Nick got up, handing the bottle to Andy as he opened the door and walked out, heading towards the carpark and lake.

"Tonight isn't going to be a quiet one," Andy said to himself. "I know it."

"Andy?" Allain said. "What are you doing here?"

Andy turned around, and Allain stood in the walkway, not wearing a jacket. His shirt sleeves rolled up.

"Is there a problem?" Allain asked.

"No," Andy said. "Just one of our customers was in the staffroom."

"Why?" Allain asked.

"No idea," Andy said.

"Are you drinking?" Allain asked, looking down at the bottle in Andy's hand.

"No," Andy said. "It was the customers."

"That is the second time I have seen you with a drink in your hand today," Allain said.

"You will get to see it more when I clear the bar later," Andy smiled. "Clearing away bottles and glasses is part of my job."

"I know that," Allain said.

"So why do you think I am drinking?" Andy moaned.

"Sometimes you look drunk," Allain said. "Uneven on your feet."

"Balance," Andy said. "It's due to my hearing loss, would be happy to have a test."

Allain shook his head.

"It's not a problem," Andy said. "I can ask the police when they visit."

"Now you are being silly," Allain scoffed. "What are you doing now?"

"Helping at the bar," Andy said. "And then back to reception."

"Is Mark in?" Allain asked. "Or Dean?"

"No," Andy said looking at his watch. "Half hour or so."

"Why are you in earlier today?" Allain asked. "You start at ten, do you not?"

"I was asked to come in early," Andy said. "Due to the Day porter shortage."

"I see," Allain said. "Could you have not come in earlier?"

"No," Andy said. "I had a hospital appointment."

"Are you sick?" Allain asked.

"No," Andy said. "Just a hearing test."

"But you are deaf?" Allain said. "Why would you need hearing tests?"

"Don't worry about it," Andy said. "I need to get on."

Walking through the bar back to the reception, Andy tapped on the counter.

"Hi," Tracy said. "What do you need?"

"Scott said could you meet him down by the lake?" Andy said.

"Why?" She asked.

"He has a headache," Andy said. "He asked if you could take some headache pills."

"I cannot leave reception," She said.

"Ask Lindsay to cover for ten minutes," Andy said. "She has done reception before and knows her way around."

Andy saw Lindsay leaving the lounge with a tray of glasses.

"Lindsay," Andy called her over. "Here give me that."

"Why?" Lindsay said curiously, walking up to Andy, smiling at Tracy.

"Could you cover the reception for ten minutes?" Andy asked. "I can't in case phone rings and Tracy needs to pop out for ten."

"Lazy bastard!" Lindsay said under her breath. "What is it worth?"

"What do you want?" Andy said smiling deviously.

"Hover the restaurant?" She said.

"Bloody hell," Andy moaned. "Fine," He said as Lindsay handed him the tray of glasses.

Tracy left the office with her handbag, leaving via the entrance and Andy rolled his eyes.

"He bloody owes me!" Andy said softly.

"What was that about?" Lindsay appeared behind the reception.

"Scott wanted Tracy to meet him at the lake," Andy said. "I think I know why."

"No!" She exclaimed. "Took him long enough!"

"I said the same!" Andy said as he walked away.

Andy returned to the bar, smiling at Charlotte as he caught her eye, walking through the double doors.

"Another broken heart," Andy said, pausing when he saw Marie near the bar with Charlotte.

"What?" Charlotte said curiously.

"The guy in the staff room," Andy said. "His girlfriend walked out on him because he hasn't proposed to her this year."

"Bloody hell," Charlotte said. "Lots of shit hitting the fan today."

"He said he was coming to the bar, but I haven't seen him," Andy said, squeezing past Marie and looking across the bar. There are over a dozen people sitting around, standing and drinking.

"Maybe he went to his room to sleep it off?" Charlotte said.

"I knew it was going to be one of those days," Andy said. "Let's hope that no fights break out."

"Where you here last year?" Charlotte asked. "I cannot remember."

"No," Andy said. "I was off and had a date."

"Oh a date on Valentines," Charlotte exclaimed. "How was it?"

"She blew me out," Any chuckled. "Stood outside the restaurant for a good hour before I left, had an email from her saying she had a change of heart."

"Oh no," Charlotte said. "Did you find out why?"

"She had an issue with my deafness," Andy said. "Must be a common thing."

"Andy?" Marie said stepping closer to him.

Andy didn't respond.

"Andy can I have a word?" She said again.

"Is it work related?" Andy asked.

"No," Marie said.

"Then I don't want to know," Andy said.

"Come on Andy," Marie said. "You cannot ignore me."

"I can," Andy said. "You made it clear what you think of me, so I'd rather not waste my time."

Andy turned around and Marie looked at him for a few seconds, hesitating before leaving the bar.

"Well that was awkward," Charlotte said.

"She say anything to you?" Andy asked.

"No," Charlotte said. "But I said I thought what she did was unfair."

"Never mind," Andy said looking at his watch. "You need any help?"

"No thanks," Charlotte said. "Darrell is in at ten."

"I am going to go back to reception," Andy said. "If you need anything, let me know."

"Too nice for your own good," Charlotte joked.

"I know," Andy said and left the bar, making his way through to the reception.

As Andy opened the door, Dean appeared behind it.

"Password?" Dean asked.

"Let me in or I'll go home and leave you to the loved-up zombies," Andy said smiling.

"You bloody would," Dean said. "You okay?"

"Great thanks," Andy said walking in and closing the door, looking at the reception. "Where is Tracy?"

"Taking a break," Dean said. "Poor cow has been on all day."

"I know," Andy said. "I got in at eight."

"Why?" Dean asked.

"Mark asked," Andy said. "Issues with the day porters."

"Mark isn't going to be in," Dean said. "Did he tell you?"

"No," Andy said. "How come? It's going to be manic tonight."

"I know," Dean said. "We have Gary staying late and a couple of the waiters to help with the Bar and food."

"Cool," Andy said. "I finish at six."

"Fair enough," Dean said. "I am working until eight."

"We had a couple of relationships end," Andy said. "One girl crying on the balcony and a guy drunk in the staff room."

"In the staff room?" Dean scoffed. "Give him his marching orders?"

"Yes," Andy said. "Also Allain is annoying today, keeps asking when you and Mark are in."

"I do not like that guy," Dean said.

"Me neither," Andy said, putting his finger to his lips when he saw Allain walk up to reception.

"Tracy?" Allain said. "You should be at the desk."

"Tracy is on a break," Dean said walking to the counter. "She needed it."

"Please maintain a presence at the desk," Allain said. "We must maintain a professional standard."

"Did you want me?" Dean asked. "Apparently you have been asking after me?"

"No," Allain said. "Is Mark in?"

"Mark is sick," Dean said. "So it's just myself and Andy working tonight."

Allain went to walk away and then stopped, turning around.

"Does Andy have a drinking problem?" Allain asked.

"No," Dean shook his head. "Why?"

Allain sighed heavily.

"I saw him with a drink earlier," Allain said. "And then in the staff room with a bottle of beer."

Andy walked around the corner and Allain looked up in surprise.

"The first drink was for a lady that was sitting on the terrace, when I came back she had gone, so the drink was thrown away," Andy said. "The second bottle, empty I may add, was from the man that was drinking and smoking in the staff room."

"I understand," Allain said. "I was just asking."

"I don't drink when I am working," Andy said.

"I have to go," Allain said. "I need to help out in the restaurant."

"See you later," Dean said as Allain walked away, disappearing around the corner towards the restaurant. "You prick!"

"He is hard work," Andy said. "Does he actually do anything?"

"General managers huh" Dean said. "Fucking useless."

"There is a couple in tonight," Andy said. "Celebrating fifty years."

"Jesus!" Dean exclaimed. "That is a long time."

A woman hurried over to the reception desk, dressed in black trousers, a red blouse, and black high heels. She is tall and slim with long blonde hair and dark lipstick.

"Hi," She said. "Just to let you know that something is happening on the stairs."

"What do you mean?" Dean asked.

Andy tried to look at the stairs from the corner, but a fake tree was blocking his view.

"There is a couple," She said softly. "On the stairs."

"Okay," Dean said, confused. "Is there a problem?"

"They are doing the deed," She smiled. "On the stairs, leaving noting to the imagination."

"I will check it out," Andy said.

Andy walked round to reception and looked up at the old-style staircase with brass handles, split into two, one leading up curved to the right to a single room at the front of the hotel, the left leading to the first-floor rooms.

The woman is laying on her back against the stairs near the single room, holding onto the banister with one hand and the around the guy who was thrusting away, his trousers around his ankles. His hands on the step where the woman rested her head, his knuckles white from gripping the carpet. Andy could see everything from where he stood, as well as smell it.

"Like being in a porn movie," Andy said softly. "Excuse me!" Andy said.

The couple ignored him, the woman moaning loudly as the man grunted with each thrust, getting faster and faster.

"You are going to get some serious carpet burns," Andy said, walking up the steps. "Hey!" He clapped his hands together loudly and they stopped, breathing heavily.

"What?" The woman said.

Andy recognised her from the front of the hotel, the man from the staff room.

"Looks like our recently made singles have found their matches," Andy scoffed.

The man stood up, pulling up his trousers and Andy turned away as the guy turned and unintentionally flashed his genitals at him. The woman pulled her dress down, smiling at Andy.

"What is the problem?" The woman said.

"Apart from shagging the living daylights out of each other in the middle of reception," Andy said. "We have other guests in the hotel and we cannot have this kind of thing going on, there could be children here."

"Oh," The man said. "Didn't think it was a problem."

"You both have rooms," Andy said. "Consider using those, less chance of carpet burns."

The woman giggled.

"What happened to my drink?" She said.

"You disappeared," Andy said. "Looked everywhere for you."

"Sorry man," The man said. "Got carried away in the moment."

"No harm done," Andy said looking at the woman by the reception in hysterics, Dean shaking his head with a grin on his face. "In future," Andy said. "Use your rooms, I would hate to have to throw you out if we get any complaints."

"No problem," The man said, holding his hand out for the woman who took it, leading her towards the bar.

"Excuse me sir," Andy said.

"Yeah? "The man said, stopping at the bottom of the stairs.

"Your fly," Andy said. "Don't want that thing to catch a cold do you?"

The man looked down, exclaimed, and laughed as he pulled up the fly. The woman looked at Andy, giving him a little wave as they left.

Returning to reception, Andy sat down and picked up a clipboard, looking through the list.

"Full house," Andy groaned. "I know those last two rooms would go."

"She looked good," Dean said.

"Who?" Andy said.

"That girl," Dean indicated towards the bar. "From the stairs."

"She is nice," Andy said. "Has a little tattoo on her tummy."

"What of?" Dean asked curiously.

"No idea," Andy said. "His arse was in the way."

"Both pissed," Dean said. "Let's hope they don't give us any problems, I am not in the mood."

"Strangely enough," Andy said. "They are the man and women that split with their partners."

"No shit!" Dean laughed. "Well, looks like it worked out okay for them.

The door opened and Tracy walked in, not saying anything as she walked to the reception desk, looking around, covering her hand.

"You okay?" Dean asked her.

She nodded.

"We have it under control here if you wanted to go home," Dean said. "Been a long day for you."

She shook her head, not saying anything.

"What is going on? Dean asked. "You are never quiet."

Tracy held up her hand, a smile breaking out.

"He proposed?" Dean said, noticing the ring on her finger. "Took the sod long enough!"

"Congratulations," Andy said.

"You played that one well," Tracy said. "You had me convinced."

"The acting came in use there," Andy said.

"You can act?" Dean asked. "Really."

"Well everyone thinks I like them," Andy said. "That is how good I am."

"Apart from Marie," Tracy said, rolling her eyes and shaking her head.

"What is going on with Marie?" Dean asked curiously. "What did I miss?"

"I will tell you later," Andy said. "Hey Tracy, you just missed all the fun."

"Why?" Tracy asked, checking the counter.

"A couple banging on the stairs," Dean said. "Right at the top by the single room."

Tracy looked confused, stifling a yawn.

"Banging what?" She asked.

"Each other," Andy said laughing. "It was like a three-dimensional porn!"

Dean burst out laughing.

"Nothing to the imagination," Andy said. "Smelt pretty strong too."

"Of what?" Tracy asked.

"Of sex," Dean said. "They were really going for it, and I mean, really!"

"Lots of carpet burns!" Andy sniggered.

Tracy groaned, shaking her head.

"Does Allain know?" She asked.

"No," Andy said. "Guess who they were?"

"Who?" Tracy asked curiously with excitement in her voice.

"The recent singles," Andy said. "The girl from the front and the man from the staff room."

"At least they met each other," Tracy said nodding. "it's a start."

The phone started to ring and Tracy cleared her throat before answering it.

"Hello this is reception," She said. "How can I help you?"

Tracy got Dean's attention by tapping him on the shoulder.

"Okay," She said, trying not to laugh. "I will get someone on that."

"Now what?" Andy said in frustration.

"Check the camera for the green," Tracy said giggling.

Dean flicked through the channels until the green showed up, and in a spot where the green banks up, is the couple again.

"Are they?" Tracy asked Andy.

"Looks like the same couple," Andy said.

"They must be on speed or something," Dean said. "At least they aren't in the middle of reception."

"No," Tracy said. "But the whole hotel will get a show."

"I will go and speak to them," Andy moaned. "Again."

"Go for it," Dean said. "I am not getting involved in that one!" He sniggered.

Walking down the steps by the carpark, Andy saw the couple on the embankment. The man on his back, holding the woman by the waist who is sitting on top of him, rocking back and forth, moaning loudly. The man has a cigarette in his mouth and for every thrust, is a puff of smoke.

"What am I going to do with you two?" Andy said as he walked down the green towards them. The woman stopped, breathing heavily.

"Hi," She smiled. "Are we doing something wrong?"

"Apart from banging in public," Andy smiled. "You really need to use your room for this."

"We are not mothering anyone," The man said. "Are we?"

"You are on camera," Andy said. "Two of them pretty much, and one of the front rooms rang down because they caught your show."

"We won't charge," She moaned and started to rock back and forth, the main gripping her hips and groaning.

"Come on!" Andy said. "Count yourself lucky I cannot call the police, and trust me, I wouldn't but someone may."

"Okay," The woman said, standing up. The man let out a grunt, laying there and breathing heavily. Andy turned away, shaking his head.

"I don't want to see that again," Andy exclaimed. "Will have to charge it for a room if I see it again."

"Put your cock away," She said giggling. "It might catch a cold."

The man let out a laugh as he put himself away, pulling up his trousers and zipping them up.

"Shall we go to your room?" He asked. "Or mine?"

"Let's get a drink first," The woman said, holding out her hand as the man stood up.

Andy watched as they started to walk down the middle of the green.

"This way please," Andy said pointing to the stairs leading to the path. "Don't want you slipping."

"She is already slippery!" The man laughed, slapping the woman's backside.

"Too much information," Andy said. "Go on, off to the bar with you, don't give me any more grief, please!"

"Aw, we are not that bad surely?" The girl said, turning around and walking backwards.

"Well," Andy said. "Neither of you are shy, I give you that!"

"I bet this happens all the time?" She said.

"No," Andy said. "Not at all."

"Really?!" The girl said in surprise.

"Most people probably use their rooms," Andy said.

The girl giggled and ran up the steps, making her way towards the hotel, followed by the man who was struggling to tuck his shirt in.

"Fruit cakes," Andy said quietly as he walked up the steps, heading to the car park to do a security check.

Standing by the reception counter, Andy looked into the bar where half a dozen people sat quietly, including the old couple.

The elderly woman noticed him and called him over. Andy put his hand up to acknowledge her, putting a bunch of keys behind the counter before walking over to her.

"Hello there," Andy said. "How are you?"

"Very well thank you," She said.

He husband sat next to her, fast asleep, leaning against the armrest.

"Is he okay?" Andy asked curiously.

"I don't think he is dead," The woman laughed softly.

"You don't think he is what?" Andy said, not hearing what she had said.

"Dead," She said. "He looks dead sometimes when he sleeps."

"Not at all," Andy said shaking his head. "I want to sleep, to be honest!"

"Any update on our taxi?" She asked.

"We have just chased it for you, and they are on the way," Andy said. "I am sorry we couldn't sort out a room for you."

"That is okay dear," She said. "It is my fault for leaving it so late."

"Have you had a nice day?" Andy said kneeling down.

"Oh yes," She smiled. "An amazing day. How about you, did you do anything for your special lady?"

"No special lady I am afraid," Andy said.

"Special man?" She grinned.

"No," Andy said. "I definitely like the ladies."

"What about that lovely girl behind the bar," She said. "I cannot remember her name!" She groaned.

"Charlotte," Andy said looking towards the bar, catching a glimpse of her as she handed a drink to a man at the bar. "She has a partner."

"Oh that is no good," She said. "I could run him over for you if you like?"

"Thank you," Andy laughed. "That is nice of you, but I think she is happy with him."

"There is someone out there for you," She said. "You seem like a lovely young man."

"Thank you," Andy said.

"I have put up with this sod for a long time," She said pointing at him.

"That is because you love me," The old man mumbled.

"Go back to sleep," She scoffed.

The door leading to staff access opened and Allain stepped out, pulling on his coat.

"Are you busy Andy?" He asked.

"Just helping this customer," Andy said. "Did you need something?"

"Could you empty the bins?" Allain asked.

"Bins?" Andy said. "Where?"

"Kitchen," Allain said.

"Gary does that," Andy said looking at his watch. "He should be in soon."

"Okay," Allain said. "Could you look busy please?"

"This young man was assisting us," the woman said. "And he has been very helpful."

"Good," Allain nodded.

"We have been coming here for a very long time," The woman said.

"That is good," Allain said uninterestedly and walked away.

"What a rude man!" The woman said. "Who is he?"

"General manager," Andy said.

"General nuisance!" The woman scoffed.

Dean appeared at the entrance by the reception, pointing to the couple.

"I think Dean has your taxi sorted," Andy said standing up.

"Oh wonderful," The woman said. "I need a proper cup of tea!"

"Did they not offer you one?" Andy said.

"It is disgusting!" She said, nudging the old man.

"Should have asked me," Andy said. "I am an expert!"

"Did your grandmother teach you?" The woman said standing up, holding on to her husband's arm as he groaned.

"My great aunt," Andy said. "Extremely fussy with her tea and I mean extremely!"

"Aw that is good to hear," She said as the old man stood up. "A good cup of tea is hard to find."

"Fifty years and I am still looking for a decent cup of tea!" The old man said laughing.

The woman turned around, glaring at him.

"I think she wants a divorce!" The man said.

"No chance," The woman said. "Til death do us part!"

"Now I am worried," The man said, leading her to the door. Andy followed, stopping by the reception counter. He watched as Dean led them to the door and helped them down the steps to the waiting taxi.

Dean walked in, yawning as he walked back into the reception and around to the counter.

"Nice couple," Dean said.

"You okay?" Andy said. "Looking tired."

"Yeah," Dean said. "Didn't sleep well."

"Well once we get rid of this lot you may as well grab a couple of hours," Andy said.

"Restaurant has a couple of people left," Dean said. "Two groups in the lounge and the Barn House has just closed up, staff are clearing it up for us."

"Oh cool," Andy said.

Gary came storming through the bar, out of breath when he got to the reception counter, red in the face.

"What's up?" Dean asked.

"I am in the kitchen," Gary said. "Cleaning, all the chefs have gone home!"

"Okay," Dean nodded. "And?"

"Is Mark in?" Gary snapped. "I need a manager!"

"Allain is still in," Andy said. "I think."

"Fuck him!" Gary moaned. "He is bloody useless!"

"What is the problem Gary?" Dean asked. "Andy will sort it," He said in frustration.

"There is a couple shagging in the kitchen!" Gary said in anger.

"Okay keep it down!" Dean hushed him. "Don't want people knowing."

"I thought the glass machine was broken," Gary said quietly. "So went to fix it, only to find a couple fucking over the glass washer!"

"Stop swearing Gary," Dean said. "Go have a cigarette and Andy will sort it out and then get you a pint," Dean said nodding to Andy. "Is that okay?"

"Sure," Andy said. "I have a pretty good idea who it is."

Andy slowly opened the door to the kitchen, looking down into the small room housing the glass washer.

"Knew it," Andy scoffed.

The same couple from earlier are up to their antics again, the girl bent over the washer with her dress over her head. The guy behind her is thrusting so hard that the glasses on the shelving were clinking and rattling. Andy is surprised the washer hadn't fallen off the counter.

"Okay guys," Andy said. "Going to send you to your rooms now."

They didn't respond.

"Excuse me!" Andy said.

The man let out a loud groan, falling forward and laying against the woman's back, stroking her hair.

"Finished?" Andy said bluntly.

The man stood up in fright, stepping away from the woman and causing her to groan. Andy turned around, trying to avoid the view. The man realised and pulled her dress down and then put himself away, struggling to do his trousers up.

"How long you been there?" the man asked.

"Long enough to know there may be a surprise in nine months," He scoffed, trying not to laugh.

"Is the bar open?" The woman said as she stood up, straightening her dress.

"No," Andy said. "But if you go to your room," He said. "Or rooms, I will bring some up."

"Why is the bar closed?" She moaned.

"It's just gone one," Andy said. "And if it was someone else here, you would have been thrown out."

"Sorry," The man said. "We both really like each other."

"I know," Andy said.

"What gave it away," The woman scoffed, a smile on her face.

"Have you found any knickers?" The man asked.

"I don't get into the habit of looking for knickers," Andy said. "Why?"

"She lost hers," He said giving her a playful shove.

"Did you check the stairs?" Andy said. "And the green?"

"Yeah," The man said. "We also checked the lake."

70

"I got duck shit on my dress because of that bench!" The woman complained.

Andy laughed, shaking his head.

"Got a good tour of the hotel then," Andy said. "You are going to be mind blown when you see the rooms," Andy said in sarcasm. "Beds, chairs and baths!"

"Oh my!" The girl said in fits of giggles.

"I think I need coffee," The man said.

"Come on," Andy said, leading them to the door. "I recommend you both go to bed, no more, please. Not in public."

"I am spent mate," The man said.

"I don't care," Andy said. "Shift it."

Allain walked in via the restaurant access doors, looking at Andy leading the couple away.

"Andy?" He said. "What is this?"

"They got lost," Andy said. "Someone gave them the wrong directions to the toilets."

Andy turned around.

"Don't say a thing," Andy whispered.

"Lovely hotel," The man said. "This boy has really looked after us."

"Boy?" Andy scoffed.

"He is lovely!" The girl said loudly. "I need a wee!"

"On that note," Andy said. "I need to show them out," Andy said to Allain who nodded, brushing him away.

Andy led them through the doors and then the single door into the brasserie, walking them to the toilets and stopping by the bar, watching them as they both headed towards the ladies' toilets.

"Hey!" Andy said.

The man stopped and turned around.

"Other side for you," Andy said. "You are not going in there together!"

The man moaned and turned around, waving to the girl childishly.

"What is going on?" Charlotte said through the gate of the closed bar.

"I'll come in," Andy said, walking to the swing doors and pushing them open.

Charlotte is leaning against the bar, drinking a coffee.

"There you go," She said pointing to a mug of black coffee on the counter. "Don't say I don't do anything for you," She smiled.

"You okay?" Andy asked.

"Yeah," She nodded. "What was with that couple? They were at the bar earlier, drinking a ton."

"Caught them three times doing the deed in public," Andy said smiling. "Stairs, the green and then the glass cleaner in the kitchen."

Charlotte started to laugh, putting her mug down as she struggled to control herself.

"I saw quite a bit," Andy said.

"Oh no!" She said. "Poor you."

"Crazy," Andy said, sipping at the coffee. "You okay?"

"Tired," Charlotte said. "My other half texted and said he cannot pick me up."

"You are kidding," Andy said. "Why?"

"No idea," Charlotte said. "But I think he doesn't feel the same about me anymore."

"No," Andy said. "Why?"

She shrugged her shoulders.

"I don't know," Her voice broke and her hand went to her mouth as she fought back tears.

Andy walked over to her, putting down his mug and putting his arms around her, hugging her softly.

"I am sorry," Andy said. "How are you getting home?" Andy asked.

"I will walk," She said. "It's not far."

"It's late and dark," Andy said. "Do you want me to drop you home?"

"You are working," She said.

"You live in town don't you?" Andy asked.

She nodded, wiping her eyes.

"I will drop you," Andy said. "Dean won't mind."

"Thought your car was out of action," She said.

"Got it back yesterday," Andy said. "Even if it was, I would walk you home."

"Are you sure?" Charlotte said. "I don't want you to get into trouble."

"I get a half-hour break," Andy said. "And I am taking you home."

"Thank you," She said forcing a smile. "I really appreciate it."

"Have you finished?" Andy asked.

Charlotte nodded, wiping her eyes.

"let me get my keys," Andy said. "And then we can walk down."

"Thanks," she smiled.

Andy got to the reception counter and knocked on it.

"You there Dean?" He said.

"Yeah," Dean said. "What's up?"

"I am dropping Charlotte home," Andy said. "Going to take my break if that is okay."

"Yeah sure," Dean said. "You know she has a boyfriend right?"

"He cancelled on her," Andy said. "Poor girl is upset and I am not letting her walk home in the dark."

"Shit," Dean said. "Yeah take her home mate."

"Could you grab my keys?" Andy said. "Inside pocket."

"Want your coat?" He asked.

"No," Andy said. "It isn't so cold."

Andy walked round to the door and then back with the keys, handing them to Andy.

"Where are you going," Allain said walking up behind Andy.

"Taking my break," Andy said.

"Could you clear the corridor first," He asked. "There are some trays."

"I will do it," Dean said.

"I asked Andy to do it," Allain said.

"Andy is busy," Dean said. "I need to go to one of the rooms, so I will do it."

"Andy should be doing more because he is deaf," Allain said. "He cannot fully do his role."

"What does that mean?" Andy said.

"You cannot hear on the telephone," He said. "And you struggle to understand me!"

"No offence Allain," Dean said. "But most people here struggle to understand you."

"That is not true," Allain said. "I have an accent."

"That is my point," Dean said.

"We will discuss your role properly soon," Allain said.

"Okay," Andy said. "I want an official meeting with a witness, and a copy of my signed contract and I will bring my Job centre representative."

"Why?" Allain asked. "Why do you have to be so difficult."

"Because after nearly six months of working here," Andy said. "You want to discuss my role because you have an issue with my hearing disability."

"Not me," Allain said. "I have had complaints."

"Good," Dean said. "You will need to sit down with a witness and another manager, list those complaints and discuss them."

"What complaints?" Andy asked.

"I cannot remember," Allain said. "But I didn't imagine it."

"Name one complaint?" Andy asked.

"I cannot remember," Allain said.

"Fine," Andy said. "I will pop to the job centre later and get some advice."

"No no no," Allain said. "Let's forget about it."

"Convenient," Dean said.

"Maybe I got my wires cross," Allain said and walked away in a hurry."

"Going to get some wire around your throat one day," Andy said. "Prick!"

As Andy was about to walk away, a tall and athletic man in blue jeans and a black leather coat walked in and Andy recognised him, it is Charlotte's boyfriend.

"Evening," Andy said. "Can I help?"

"I may have pissed off Charlotte," He said. "Is she still here?"

"She is in the bar," Andy said.

"Can I?" He asked nervously.

"Yes," Andy said pointing to the bar.

Charlotte looked at Andy when she saw her boyfriend walking towards the bar and mouthed the words 'I am sorry'. Andy watched as he walked into the bar, throwing his arms around her, and hugging her, kissing her passionately.

"Shit," Dean said.

"Seems the ladies like the arseholes," Andy said. "Never mind," Andy handed the keys back to Dean. "I am going to do a corridor walk for our wonderful general manager."

Andy looked at the bar to see Charlotte still hugging her boyfriend, he turned and walked to the stairs, looking when the couple from earlier stepped out from the lounge.

"Behaving?" Andy said.

"Yes," The girl smiled. "The other guy made us coffee."

"Glad to hear it," Andy said. "Going to your rooms now?"

"Heading back to hers," The man said. "Going to have a bath and then she wants more."

"Stop it!" She snapped at him.

"Enjoy the rest of your stay," Andy said. "Nice to meet you."

And ran up the stairs, turning at the corner and gripping the brass banister as he lost his balance, slipping on a step and falling forward.

"The perils of being deaf," He said in embarrassment. "You didn't see anything!"

The couple followed Andy up the stairs, cuddling and kissing on the way.

FOUR

Andy walked through the door to the storeroom behind the bar, wiping the front of his shirt. Charlotte looked around and started to laugh, noticing the front of his shirt wet.

"No one told me there was going to be a wet shirt competition!" She laughed.

"Very funny," Andy said. "The valve was stuck," He said, picking up a hand towel from the counter. "Whoever put it in didn't do it properly and it erupted!"

"Oh no!" Charlotte giggled. "Are you okay?"

"I am fine," Andy said. "I have changed the barrel and cleaned up the mess."

"It's not so bad," She said, covering her mouth.

"Going to look like pee when it dries!" Andy scoffed.

"It will be fine," She said. "Just don't drive home!"

"I have no plans to!" Andy said. "I walked in today, it is a nice evening."

A man wearing a suit walked up to the bar, placing two empty pint glasses in front of Charlotte.

"Hi Love," He said. "Same again please."

"Sure," Charlotte said, putting the glasses under the bar and getting clean ones and began to pull a pint.

"What is that?" He said looking at Andy. "Is it a secret service thing?"

"What?" Andy said, not sure if he was speaking to him.

"It's a hearing aid," Andy replied.

"Why do you have a hearing aid?" the man asked.

"Why do you think?" Andy said.

Charlotte smiled, shaking her head.

"Why do you think he would need a hearing aid?" Charlotte asked.

The man scoffed and shrugged his shoulders.

"I am deaf," Andy said.

"Deaf?" he said. "Really?"

"Yeah," Andy nodded.

"You can't be," he said.

"Why?" Andy asked.

"Well you can hear fine," He said. "And you don't seem the kind," He said.

"What do you mean?" Andy glared at him. "What is the kind?"

"I have seen deaf and dumb people on the telly," He said. "You are not like them."

"Don't say that!" Charlotte exclaimed. "It's offensive."

"What?" The man said in confusion.

"Dumb," She said. "It's rude."

"Well?" The man said. "Isn't that what it is?"

"No," Charlotte said. "I forget the right word."

"It's mute," Andy sighed. "Don't say dumb, it's offensive and ignorant. Deaf people are different from one another, so ignore the crap you see on television."

"Oh," he shrugged his shoulder. "So you are really deaf?"

"Severely," Andy replied. "But it is getting worse."

"Wow," The man scoffed.

"Yeah," Andy nodded.

"So do you do the hand stuff?" He asked, attempting to sign. "I see it on the telly a lot, really bloody annoying."

"What sign language?" Andy asked. "No I don't sign."

"And those subtitles too," He groaned. "All they do is get in the way!"

"Yeah that is a simple case of hearing people not giving a shit if deaf people can understand what is going on," Andy said bluntly.

"Well can't they read a newspaper instead?" He laughed.

"Why a newspaper?" Andy said, looking away.

"So tell me," He said and thought about it. "What do I sound like?"

Andy looked at him and shook his head. "Sure you want to know?" Charlotte asked. "Andy is blunt as anything!"

He nodded.

"Pretty annoying!" Andy said bluntly. "You have one of those voices I just want to switch off, almost wishing I could mute out."

"Fair enough!" The man laughed. "My girlfriend says the same!"

Andy looked at Charlotte who is trying not to laugh as she placed the pint in front of him and started to pull the second one.

"You got a bird?" He asked. "A deaf one?"

"No," Andy replied.

"What about a normal one?" He said.

"Define normal?" Andy said, walking closer to the bar.

"Yeah," He said. "One that isn't disabled.

"No," Andy asked. "What about you? Does your girlfriend have a normal boyfriend or did she lose a bet and get stuck with you?"

"You are funny," He laughed. "I like you."

"Feeling isn't mutual," Andy replied.

"Be nice Andy," Charlotte said, looking at him and rolling her eyes.

"Can you date normal girls?" He asked.

"What kind of question is that?" Andy said looking at him. "What do you mean?"

"Non-disabled," He said.

"Do you class yourself as normal?" Andy asked him.

"Yeah," He nodded. "I don't have any disabilities."

"Oh, I think you may have a couple," Andy muttered. "In fact I can think of one beginning with A."

Charlotte let out a giggle.

"Can I ask a question?" He said.

"Do I have a choice?" Andy said.

"If you had kids," He paused. "Would you keep them if they were disabled like you?"

"Oh that is not on!" Charlotte exclaimed.

"Keep them?" Andy said. "Of course, what else would I do?"

"Well," he said. "Some women have abortions if the kid is disabled," The words came out of his mouth so normal and blunt.

"A what?" Andy asked, not sure if he had heard him right.

"Termination," He said. "like when women find out that the kid is heavily disabled and don't want to go through with it."

"What is this?" Andy scoffed. "The nineteen twenties?!"

Charlotte looked at the man, shaking her head in disbelief.

"Well it's true," He said.

"It's backward," Ryan said. "And no, I wouldn't abort a child if it was going to be deaf!"

"I am different," He said smugly. "Why bring a kid into the world that will struggle?"

"It's about support," Andy said. "My parents didn't support me, but I turned out okay."

Charlotte placed the second pint on the bar.

"Paying here or charge to your room?" She asked.

"Can you charge to the room please," The man said, showing her his room key number.

"No problems," She said smiling.

The man picked up the pints.

"Hope they find a cure for you," He said to Andy. "You seem like a nice enough bloke."

Andy watched as he walked away.

"What an arsehole!" She said under her breath.

"I have heard worse," Andy said. "If being an arsehole was a disability, he would have it rough!"

Allain caught Andy's eye as he approached the bar from the toilets, holding up a finger to get Andy's attention.

"Good evening Allen," Andy said.

Andy is wearing a black suit, white shirt, a grey waistcoat and a bright red tie.

"It is Allain," Allain corrected him.

"Ah my mistake," Andy said. "Did you need me?"

"Yes," Allain said. "Did you get my message?"

"No," Andy said. "Which message?"

"About the room checks?" Allain said. "You forgot to do them last night."

"I wasn't on last night," Andy said.

"Yes you was," Allain said. "We spoke!"

"No," Andy said. "I wasn't in last night, Mark wanted me to come in tonight instead."

"Are you sure?" Allain said.

"I didn't see him yesterday," Charlotte said. "He would have been helping me otherwise," She looked at Andy and smiled.

"Do you need me to do anything tonight?" Andy asked.

"Yes," Allain said. "The rooms still need checking."

"Sure I will do that," Andy said.

"Also Andy," He sighed. "Please shave!"

Andy had some minor stubble as he had not shaven in a couple of days, but he is still tidy.

"Why?" Andy said.

"You need to be clean shaven and presentable in this role," Allain said. "I have said that before!"

"But you have a goatee," Andy said. "What is the difference."

"I am a manager!" Allain said. "And I can grow one."

"Okay," Andy said. "Can I get that in writing?" Andy asked.

"Why?" Allain said.

"Well if it is in my contract, I must have missed it," Andy said. "Also do the rules apply to everyone or just the resident deaf person?"

Allain laughed awkwardly and waved his hand, trying to brush it off.

"Have you been drinking?" He asked.

"No," Andy said. "We have had this discussion before, I do not drink at work."

"What is that?" He said pointing at Andy's shirt.

"A shirt," Andy replied.

Charlotte laughed.

"No," Allain said. "What did you spill?"

"Nothing," Andy said. "Someone didn't install a barrel correctly and it blew."

"Did we lose anything?" Allain asked.

"I am fine thanks," Andy said. "Just thought I would put that in there in case the wellness of your staff isn't important."

"You look fine," Allain said.

"The barrel was nearly empty," Andy said. "No, nothing was lost."

"Do you have spare shirt?" Allain asked.

"No," Andy said. "I usually keep a spare, but someone stole it."

"Maybe you need to go home," Allain said. "I don't want people to think you are a drunk."

"I can go home," Andy said. "Not a problem for me."

"Is Dean in?" Allain asked. "Or Mark?"

"No," Andy said.

"Oh you better not go home," Allain said.

"He doesn't smell of beer or anything," Charlotte said. "So he will be fine."

"Can you check the rooms before I leave?" Allain asked.

"Yes," Andy said.

"And you will let me know?" Allain asked. "If the rooms are okay?"

"Yes," Andy said.

Allain nodded, straightening his tie.

"Must go," Allain said. "Very busy!"

Andy and Charlotte watched as Allain hurried away, making his way past the small group in the bar and out the staff access door.

"What an absolute prick," Charlotte said. "How do you stay so calm through that?"

"My parents were just as bad," Andy said. "My mother was a psychological bully."

"Is?" Charlotte said. "Did she die?"

"No," Andy said. "Unfortunately, she is dead to me though."

"I am sorry to hear that," Charlotte said.

"It's fine," Andy said. "I am close to my Great Aunt, practically my mum!"

"That is sweet," Charlotte said, leaning against the bar. "Andy I am sorry about the other night."

"Other night?" Andy said. "What happened?"

"Valentines," She said.

"Oh that," Andy said. "Seriously it's fine, I am glad you sorted things out."

"We are splitting up," Charlotte said. "And I am fine with it."

"I am sorry," Andy said.

"No," Charlotte said. "I am fine with it, we have drifted apart and I am glad it is happening now rather than years down the line."

"Want a hug?" Andy asked.

Charlotte walked over to him and gently hugged him, rubbing his back.

"Did you do this to make me wet?" She said.

"Excuse me?" Andy said grinning.

Charlotte slapped him and rolled her eyes.

"You know what I mean," She said.

The bar doors opened and Dean walked in.

"Hey Dean," Charlotte said.

Andy looked at his watch.

"Thought you were in later?" Andy asked.

"I was bored," Dean said. "Thought I'd come in, you okay Charlotte?"

Charlotte smiled and nodded.

"What the fuck happened to you?" Dean pointed to Andy's shirt.

"Someone didn't connect a barrel correctly," Andy said. "Soon as I released it, bang!"

"Shit," Dean said. "Same thing happened to me a couple of weeks ago!"

"It's probably Charlotte," Andy said pointing to her.

"No it isn't!" She scoffed. "I am not that stupid."

Allain walked up to the bar, paused and is about to say something before turning around and hurrying away.

"What's with him?" Dean asked.

"I swear he has probably had a couple of strokes," Andy said.

Charlotte let out a suppressed giggle, her hand covering her mouth.

"He was in a strop about me not checking rooms last night," Andy said.

"You were not here," Dean said. "He left me a note and I checked them."

Allain appeared at the bar, leaning over.

"It was me that you left the note for last night," Dean said. "I have checked the rooms."

"What rooms?" Allain said in confusion.

"The rooms you asked me to check," Andy said.

"I have no idea what you are talking about," Allain said. "Dean, are you free to have a catch up now?"

"No," Dean said. "I don't start for an hour."

"Oh," Allain said. "I finish in a minute."

"What's it about?" Dean asked.

"Keith," Allain said.

"What about him?" Dean asked.

"I need to talk about his role," Allain said. "Is he doing it correctly?"

"I am not his manager," Dean said. "So you shouldn't be talking to me about him."

"Are you not?" Allain said.

"Head chef," Dean said. "You need to talk to the head chef."

"Oh I understand," He said and walked away.

Dean stepped forward and looked over the bar, watching as Allain walked through the staff access.

"Fucking hell," He scoffed. "What is going on with him?"

"What is right with him?" Andy said.

"You two crack me up!" Charlotte laughed and rolled her eyes. "Can you mind the bar while I pop to the loo?" Charlotte asked Andy.

"Of course," Andy said.

"I am getting coffee," Dean said. "Is it busy?"

"No," Charlotte said. "Just a group in the bar and a group of girls in the lounge, but they aren't drinking much."

"I nearly got trapped in there earlier," Andy smiled. "They thought I was a discounted stripper!" Charlotte giggled.

"And then had a million and one questions about being deaf," Andy scoffed. "I was close to jumping through the window!"

"Are they cute?" Dean asked with a smile on his face.

"Pervert," Charlotte said, punching him as she walked past and left the bar.

"You good?" Dean said.

"Not too bad," Andy said. "You?"

"Knackered," Dean said. "What happened?" Dean pointed to Andy's shirt.

"Someone put a tap on wrong," Andy said. "It was stuck, so when I managed to get it off, it exploded on me."

"Shit!" Dean laughed.

"Had to wipe the floors, ceiling, bottles and myself," Andy scoffed. "Worried because I may have got some in my mouth and Allain would have got the evidence he wanted!"

"Fuck him," Dean said. "He is a moron."

"Go get your coffee," Andy said. "Will catch up with you soon."

Dean left the bar and Andy stood by the counter, leaning over to check the bar seating area. The fire had been on for a few hours and there is a strong smell of burning wood, Andy loved the smell.

"Wonder who will be clearing out the fireplace later," he said to himself.

One of the girls from the lounge, tall, slim with long blonde hair walked up to the bar, slightly drunk and struggling in heels. She is wearing a black jacket, red blouse and a black, glittery mini skirt.

"Hi," Andy said. "How is your evening going?" He asked.

"Hey," She smiled. "It is brilliant!" She placed her small black handbag on the counter, groaning.

"Are you okay?" Andy asked.

"These heels are killing me!" She moaned. "God knows why I thought they would be a good idea!"

"Self-inflicted!" Andy laughed. "How can I help?"

"Could we get some beers?" She asked. "Just one round before we head off?"

"You can," Andy said. "Same as before?"

"Please," She nodded.

"Do you want me to put it on the main bill?" Andy asked.

"Yes," She said. "We are paying at the reception, is that okay?"

Andy smiled and nodded, removing half a dozen beers from the refrigerator and lining them up.

"I'll bring them into you," Andy said. "Unless you want to try your luck at balancing them on a tray?"

The woman burst out laughing, shaking her head slowly as she looked down at the heels.

"Me and my mates are curious," She said. "After chatting with you about your disability."

"Why are you curious?" Andy asked.

"Well," She laughed nervously. "How do deaf people," She hesitated. "You know?"

"What?" Andy asked.

"Sex," She said. "How do deaf people have sex?"

Andy looked at her.

"How do deaf people have sex?" Andy said, not sure he had heard her correctly.

"Yeah," She giggled.

"Really?" Andy said sarcastically. "Why?"

"Well we have not met a deaf person before," She said. "So we were just wondering."

"The same way you lot do," Andy replied. "But in silence."

She burst into hysterics.

"You mean you don't make any noise?" She said.

"No," Andy said, removing the caps from the beers. "We make noise."

"Oh," She said thinking. "Weird."

"Deaf people are still human," Andy said. "Do you want me to draw a picture?"

"They told me to ask you," She laughed. "Like I said, we haven't met a deaf person before."

"Well lucky you," Andy said. "Don't tell everyone, it's a special opportunity."

"Can you hear anything?" She said. "During you know what?"

"I'll let you know when I try it out," Andy said. "Unless you want to give me a trial run?" He smiled at her.

"No," she giggled. "I am not that drunk yet."

"Charming," Andy replied.

"And you are too short for me," She said. "I like them tall."

"Right," Andy said. "I'll bring these out to you soon."

"Thanks," She said smiling. "I'll take one now," She said taking a beer from the middle, nearly knocking them over.

Andy watched as she walked away, struggling to keep her balance, Charlotte came through the staff access, moving out of the way when the woman nearly walked into her.

"What was that about?" Charlotte said as she walked into the bar. "That mini skirt is practically a belt!"

"You wouldn't believe me if I told you," Andy put the beers onto a black plastic tray.

"Try me," She said grinning.

"Let me get rid of these beers," Andy said.

"Tell me when you are back," She said. "I need a laugh."

"Good," Andy said, grinning madly as he left the bar, walking backwards through the swing doors.

Andy sat behind reception, watching the security monitor as he sipped at a mug of back coffee. Dean stood behind the reception, looking at the mirror mounted on the wall that gave a reflection of the bar.

"Looks like the group in the bar have gone," Dean said. "All we need now is for the last two woman in the lounge to go."

"I thought they went?" Andy said. "We stopped serving drinks an hour ago."

"Looks like they are making the ones they had last," Dean looked around. "Isn't that cold?" He pulled a face in disgust.

"What?" Andy asked curiously.

"That coffee," Dean said. "I made that over an hour ago."

"It's okay," Andy shrugged his shoulders. "Once they go, I'll do a floor check."

"We only give four people in the hotel," Dean said. "It's going to be a quiet night."

"I am tempted to make a pizza," Andy said. "Scott had the ingredients left over from today and said to help ourselves."

"I hate pizza," Dean groaned in disgust.

"More for me," Andy said. "What are you going to have?"

"Might do some pasta," Dean said. "That pesto Scott made is quite nice."

"Don't tell Gary," Andy whispered. "It's vegetarian!"

"I am telling him," Dean said. "I saw him eating it earlier! Saying that, he did have a ton of bacon on it."

"Keith in?" Andy asked.

"I think so," Dean said. "It has been a long day with two events."

Dean put his finger to his lips when he heard a door open and then pointed towards the lounge. A woman dressed in red leather trousers, red heels, a white blouse and black leather jacket walked up to the reception, her short blonde hair is messy.

"Hey," She said bluntly. "We need more drinks in here."

"Apologies," Dean said politely. "We are not allowed to serve drinks to non-hotel customers."

"Said who?" She asked.

"It's the law," Dean said.

"Piss off!" She snapped. "You are having me on!"

"No I am not," Dean said. "I did explain to you an hour ago that we could not serve any drinks after a certain time."

"Come on," She said. "Who is going to know?"

"It isn't worth losing my job over," Dean said.

Andy put his mug down and stood up, turning the security screen to show the reception desk, watching the woman.

"Come on," She said. "I'll pay you."

"Your account has already been closed and we are unable to make any more charges," Dean said. "This has been explained."

"Well how do I get a drink then?" She demanded.

"You can purchase a room for the night," Dean said.

"I don't want to stay in this piece of shit hotel," She snapped. "I want a drink and you have to serve me!"

"No," Dean said. "I really don't."

"Get a manager!" She demanded.

At this point the woman that Andy had served at the bar left the lounge and joined her friend at the reception counter.

"What is going on?" She asked.

"He won't serve us drinks," She said.

"I told you they won't," her friend said. "Come on Emma lets go," She looked at Dean, embarrassed. "Could you call us a cab?"

"Yes," Dean said. "Where to?"

"Into Dartford," She said. "My name is Claire."

"Sure," He nodded. "Take a seat and I will have that here as soon as possible."

"No," Emma said. "I want a drink."

"You can't," Clair said.

"We can offer tea, coffee or water," Dean said. "Nothing alcoholic I am afraid."

Emma grunted in annoyance, looking at Dean in disgust.

"I am going to report you," She said.

"Emma stop it," Claire said. "We have had a good day, don't ruin it."

"One beer," Emma said. "And I will leave."

"I am sorry," Dean shook his head. "No alcohol."

"I am going to report you for sexual harassment," Emma pointed at him.

"Emma!" Claire gasped. "That isn't true."

"I would like to warn you that you are on camera," Dean said pointing to the camera above the reception. "And if you continue, I will call the police and press charges, I will let you have coffee, on the house."

"Those cameras aren't real," She said.

Andy stepped round and made himself seen.

"They are recording," Andy said. "And I am a witness."

Emma picked up the bell on the counter and threw it at Andy, missing him completely. She stormed off and walked out of the entrance, sitting down on the steps.

"Oh my god," Claire said. "I am so sorry, I have no idea what is going on with her."

"Anymore and we will call the police," Dean said. "We are being quite relaxed about threats and attempted assault."

"Attempted assault?" She said curiously.

"She just threw a bell at me," Andy said trying not to laugh as he bent down and picked it up, placing it on the counter.

Dean reached over and tapped it, the bell rang out loudly.

"Bloody hell," He said. "Works better than before."

"I am sorry," Claire said. "As soon as the cab shows up, we will be gone."

"No problems," Dean said. "She is dangerous and I hope that she gets help, when she sobers up."

Dean picked up the telephone and dialled a number, smiling at Claire as she left reception and joined her friend on the steps.

"Fucking hell," Andy said. "What a nut job!"

"I agree with you there," Dean said. "I will still be letting the police know, in case she decides to try anything."

"I'll switch the tape," Andy said. "Just so we have it."

"Hi there," Dean said on the telephone. "Could I have a taxi to The Range Hotel please to collect a couple of rabid morons?" Dean laughed. "Yes you may need a cage," he said trying not to laugh. "One of them bites!"

Andy shook his head as he listened, a grin on his face.

"Ten minutes?" Dean said. "No problems, thanks," Dean put the telephone down. "What a bunch of morons," He said. "She was as nice as anything earlier," Dean leaned against the cabinet at the back of reception. "Turned nasty pretty quickly."

"You okay," Andy asked.

"Fine," Dean said. "As if I would sexually harass that piece of shit."

Andy scoffed and laughed, sitting back down and picking up the mug.

"Why don't you go and get a fresh one," Dean moaned. "That must be disgusting!"

"It's fine," Andy said. "And I want to stay here in case she kicks off again," He smiled.

"Fine," Dean said. "I am getting a cold drink," he looked at his watch. "Want anything?"

"No," Andy said. "When they go I am going to do some food."

Keith suddenly appeared at the reception desk, causing Dean to jump in fright. Keith is wearing blue jeans, heavily stained on the thighs, a black t-shirt and a thick plastic apron. His beard and hair are messy and greasy, he also has rice in the front of his beard.

"Jesus Christ Keith!" Dean gasped, his hand on his chest. "Was the rice nice?" Dean asked when he noticed.

"How do you know?" Keith mumbled.

"Half of it is in your beard," Dean pointed in disgust.

"Oh," Keith said and ignored it. "Pint?" He said pointing towards the bar.

"You want a drink?" Dean asked.

"Yeah," Keith nodded. "Pint!"

"Give me a few minutes and I will bring one in," Dean said. "Lager yeah?"

Keith nodded.

"Gary want anything?" Dean asked.

Keith shrugged his shoulders.

"I'll bring him a whiskey," Dean said shaking his head. "Go on," He said. "You know you are not supposed to be here."

Keith walked away, giggling like a child.

"He is going to kill me one day." Dean said.

"Is Gary in?" Andy said. "I haven't seen him."

"Yeah he is in," Dean said nodding. "He and Scott had one hell of an argument earlier."

"Why?" Andy asked.

"Gary put a bowl of sliced bacon in the vegetable section refrigeration," Dean said. "Said it was an accident but Gary kept laughing about it so Scott threw him out."

"Shit," Andy said. "Why didn't you tell me?"

"Well you wanted to look after the women didn't you," Dean scoffed. "All because you fancied the bride to be."

"I didn't know she was the bride to be," Andy said. "Simple mistake."

"Plonker!" Dean snapped. "Is that why you gave them free champagne?"

"No," Andy said. "Allain told me to."

"Bloody hell he is getting soft," Dean said. "Anyway," He walked to the door. "Won't be long, any issues bleep me."

"Sure," Andy said, watching the security display as Dean left the office.

Someone knocked on the door and Andy looked up.

"Come in?" Andy said. "It's not locked."

The door opened and Charlotte walked in, holding her thick winter jacket and a rucksack.

"Can I have a quick chat?" She asked, dropping the bag onto the floor along with the jacket.

"Sure," Andy said. "You okay?" And stood up, stretching.

"Yeah," She smiled. "Tired. You?"

"Tired too," Andy said. "Rather be in bed."

"What time do you finish?" She asked.

"Six," Andy said. "It's going to be a quite night anyhow."

"Didn't sound it," Charlotte scoffed. "Did the bell hit anyone?"

"You saw that?" Andy laughed. "That was funny."

"She was a bitch to me earlier," Charlotte said. "Wonder what her problem was?"

"Are you walking home?" Andy asked. "Want me to walk with you?"

"It's okay," She said. "My dad is getting me."

"Okay," Andy said.

Charlotte stepped closer to Andy.

"What's up?" Andy said nervously.

Charlotte leaned in and kissed Andy on the lips. Andy froze, taken by surprise.

"I am sorry," She said.

"No," Andy stuttered. "Don't be sorry, I am just shocked."

"Why?" Charlotte said.

"Been a while," Andy said. "Since I had a kiss."

"Really?" Charlotte said, leaning in again and kissing Andy, gently pushing her tongue into his mouth. Andy kissed her back, passionately and tightened his grip around her, pulling him closer.

"You taste good," She said. "I have been wanted to do that for most of today."

"Wow," Andy said nervously. "I mean, well wow."

"You liked that?" She said smiling. "Maybe we can go out," She said. "Grab a coffee at some time?"

"I would like that very much," Andy said.

"When you two have finished sucking face," Dean said from the counter. "Could I have the keys?"

"Sure," Andy said grinning. "Hold on."

Andy picked up the keys and handed them to Charlotte who walked around the front of the counter, handing them to Dean.

"What do you see in him?" Dean said. "He likes pineapple on pizza!"

"So do I," Charlotte smiled. "You don't know what you are missing."

"Gross," Dean said and walked away. "Just wrong!" He called out.

"Want to wait outside with me?" Charlotte said picking up her jacket. "Don't let my dad see anything," She said. "Too soon for him."

"Sure," Andy said reaching down and picking up her bag. "After you."

Andy had fallen asleep in an armchair in the bar when Dean shook him awake, he woke up in fright, disorientated.

"What?" He said. "What is happening."

"Apart from your snoring shaking the place apart," Dean laughed. "I could hear you from the reception!"

"What do you want?" Andy asked.

"We may have trouble," Dean said.

"What has Gary done now?" Andy moaned. "Has he set the alarms off again?"

"No nothing like that," Dean said. "Something much worse."

Andy stood up, stretching and groaning.

"What time is it?" He said looking at his watch.

"Two," Dean said. "Keith and Gary have gone, but there is a car circling."

"Where?" Andy asked.

"It went to the staff carpark first," Dean said. "And then the main carpark, it then left but is back again."

"Called the police?" Andy asked.

"Not yet," Dean said. "I want to check it out first."

"Okay," Andy nodded. "What's the plan?"

"I will head towards the main carpark through the restaurant," Dean said. "If you can go via the staff entrance, check the staff carpark in case," Dean handed Andy a large torch. "Here, be careful."

"This isn't another one of your pranks is it?" Andy asked. "I am too tired to care."

"No," Dean said. "I am serious."

"Bloody hell," Andy groaned. "Was having a good dream too."

Andy got to the staff carpark only to find it empty, he had made his way there, listening out only for the silence to be broken by wildlife.

"Why are the lights off?" he said looking around, noticing that the lamps had been smashed, glass at the bottom of the poles. "If you are winding me up Dean," Andy said to himself. "I am letting down all your tyres!"

Andy froze when he heard an engine, turning off his torch, he looked around in the darkness, briefly catching the rear lights of a car heading from the side road towards the entrance.

"Should have brought a radio," Andy said.

Andy walked through a path between the hotel and the Barn House, seeing the car as it turned into the main car park. He then saw Dean walk out from the terrace and into the road, looking down at him. Andy waved, trying to indicate what he had seen but Dean was aware, making his way towards the carpark.

"Bloody idiot," Andy moaned. "Not even had coffee yet!"

Walking towards the carpark, Andy watched as Dean disappeared and a minute later, he started to run back towards the hotel.

The small car squealed as the tyres tried to grip the stone covered road, with no lights on the old red metro roared down the road towards Dean and Andy flinched as he expected Dean to get run down. Dean turned and dived into a bush, the car just missing him as it attempted to swerve, clipping a wall and knocking one of the concrete balls off. Andy watched as it fell to the green and started to roll down the middle, his attention then turned to the car heading for him.

"Fuck this," Andy said and stepped backwards until he felt the gate against his back. "Not paid enough for this crap!"

The car sped up as it approached the bend, the back end spinning out and knocking down the wooden fencing. Andy looked into the car, seeing the strain on the young boys face as he fought to control the car, the passenger attempting to conceal his identity.

"Morons!" Andy yelled out.

The car attempted to straighten as it passed the lake, only to hit the side of the kerb and flip over onto the roof with an echoing bang as the passenger and rear passenger windows exploded. The roar and

89

whine of the engine dying down when it cut out, the wheels freely spinning. The car slid down the embankment, stopping a couple of meters away from the lake.

Andy stood looking for a few seconds, before bursting into hysterics. Looking towards where Dean had dived into the bushes, he caught a glimpse of Dean crawling out from the bushes and jump to his feet, breaking into a sprint.

"Andy!" Dean called out. "You okay?"

"Fine!" Andy called out. "You?"

"Go and help," Dean said. "I'll call the emergency services."

Dean ran into the hotel and Andy saw two young boys in tracksuits climb out from the car and run into the woods, disappearing in seconds.

"Bloody chavs!" Andy said, running towards the car.

Placing the torch on the floor and illuminating the inside of the car, Andy could hear someone crying hysterically.

"My mum is going to kill me!" He cried out. "Oh shit my mum is going to kill me!"

"Hello," Andy said looking inside. "Are you hurt."

"Don't hurt me!" He cried. "I am stuck!" He tried to unlock the belt.

Andy looked up at the boy in his mid-teens, trapped upside down in the driver's seat. Wearing grey jogging bottoms and a matching jacket. He has short blonde hair and a red bandanna around his neck.

"Hi," Andy said. "Wonderful driving skills!" Andy laughed.

"I am sorry!" He cried. "My mum is going to kill me!"

"Well what do you expect," Andy said. "Messing around on private property and driving like a twat!" Andy scoffed. "Are you hurt?"

"No," He cried. "I cannot get out!"

"I'll do you a deal," Andy said. "I'll get you out, but promise you won't run, you need to do the right thing."

"I don't want to go to prison!" He cried.

"Stop crying and listen," Andy said. "It's bad enough trying to lipread you when you are blubbering upside down."

"I didn't do anything wrong," He said sniffing. "I was just out driving with my mates."

"How old are you?" Andy asked.

"Twenty!" He said.

"Yeah," Andy scoffed. "Of course you are!"

Dan came running down the road, his white shirt bloodied and torn.

"Shit," Andy said standing up. "Are you hurt?"

"Fucking thorn bush," Dean said. "I had to dive into a thorn bush."

The boy is still crying.

"Are you hurt?" Dean asked.

"No!" The boy sobbed.

"Then shut up before I give you something to cry about," Dean snapped. "Little shit!"

The boy continued to cry.

"Got your penknife?" Andy asked.

"Yeah," Dean said. "We cutting his fingers off?"

The boy gasped and cried.

"No Dean," Andy said, covering his mouth as he laughed. "Need to get him out."

Dean bent down, looking into the car as liquid trickled down the boy's face onto the roof of the car.

"Shit," He said. "Fuel leak?"

Andy bent down, sniffing and then looking at the wet patch around the boys crouch.

"No," Andy said. "He has wet himself," Andy stood up, noticing the steam coming from the engine. "Might be an idea to get him out though, just in case this thing decides to go up in smoke."

"We are going to let you out," Dean said. "But if you run I am going to break your legs!"

"He won't run." Andy said then tapped the car. "Will you?"

"No," The boy cried. "I promise."

"Go grab a blanket or something," Andy said. "It's chilly and he could go into shock."

"Will with my foot up his arse," Dean said.

"Go on," Andy said. "I'll get him out.

Andy handed a small penknife to Andy, shaking his head as he walked towards the hotel.

"Right," Andy said getting down on his knees, yelping when he put his knees into glass, he reached into the car when he noticed a magazine, spreading it out over the glass. "Let's get you out of the car you plonker."

"I won't run," He sniffed. "I promise."

"I know," Andy said. "Hold onto the wheel," Andy reached up. "When I cut the belt you will need to lower yourself down, don't want you falling and breaking your neck."

"Okay," Andy reached up with the penknife, pulling at the belt and cutting it. Dean was always sharpening the knife, and it cut through effortlessly.

The boy let out a yelp as he fell down headfirst, panicking as he tried to sit up and kicked out, catching Andy in the face.

"Jesus!" Andy said, falling back into the grass, his hearing aid falling out.

"Sorry!" The boy yelled out. "I didn't mean to!"

Dean turned up holding a blanket, looking down at Andy laying on the grass, blood trickling from his nose. Dean is wearing a black bomber jacket, unzipped.

"What happened?" Dean asked, picking up the whistling hearing aid and handing it to Andy.

"An accident," Andy said sniffing. "He accidentally kicked me."

"Going to accidently kick him in a minute," Dean said kneeling down, looking at the boy sitting there, almost as if he were thinking of running. "You better not be thinking of running!"

"No," The boy shook his head.

"Get yourself out," Dean said. "And sit on the wall over there," Dean said pointing to the low wall." The boy crawled out, attempting to cover his jogging bottoms that he had messed.

"Here," Dean said, wrapping the blanket around him. "Warm yourself up."

Andy stood up, moaning when blood ran from his nose, down his face and the front of his shirt.

"Hides the beer stain," Dean said laughing.

"You can talk," Andy said pointing to the spots of blood all over Deans shirt.

"The back is worse," Dean said. "Hope you are good with tweezers!"

"Did you have to dive into a thorn bush?" Andy said trying not to laugh, pinching is nose.

"Funny," Dean said.

"You okay though?" Andy said.

"I am fine," Dean said. "I blame you!"

"Why?" Andy asked.

"You said it was going to be a quiet night," Dean scoffed.

Andy looked up at the front of the hotel when a light came on and someone opened the window, looking out.

"What is going on?" The male customer called out. "I am trying to sleep!"

"I can only apologise," Dean said. "Kids today," He pointed to the car. "No driving skills."

"Okay," The customer said. "Fair enough."

The man closed the window and after a few seconds, the light went off.

"My mum is going to kill me," The boy said.

"Yes," Andy said. "You keep saying."

"Is that her car?" Dean asked.

The boy nodded.

"He is right," Dean exclaimed. "She is going to kill him!"

Andy stood by the reception, looking down at the ambulance parked by the Barn House and the two police cars behind it. A car slowly drove up the road, stopping outside the hotel and Allain got out, wearing a blue suit and a white shirt.

"What has happened?" He said walking up the steps. "Where is Mark and Dean, why do you have a dirty shirt ,do you have a spare?"

"I get the feeling you don't like me very much?" Andy scoffed. "I got kicked in the face, hence the blood, Dean is being treated in the ambulance and Mark is off."

"What happened to Dean?" Allain said in a panic. "Is he okay?"

"Dived into a thorn bush," Andy said.

"Why did he do that?!" Allain gasped.

"I thought the same," Andy said. "But when a car is coming at you full blast, you tend to get lost in the moment."

Allain looked at Andy in confusion.

"They were up to no good," Andy said. "When they were disturbed they tried to escape and flipped the car," Andy reached up, checking his nose for blood. "Two boys ran away, left one trapped."

"Any property damage?" Allain asked.

"Wall, fences and grass," Andy said. "Mark said to contact you."

"Thank you for calling me," Allain said. "I wonder if the boy is okay?"

"We are fine by the way," Andy said. "I am glad that staff wellbeing is considered."

"You look fine," Allain scoffed.

Another car drove up the road, slowing down near the upside-down car before a police officer asked them to park near the hotel.

"I need get a coffee," Allain said. "Please deal with this."

Allain walked into the hotel and Andy watched as the car came to a stop at the bottom of the steps.

A short woman wearing blue jeans, slippers and a red jacket got out of the car, she looked up at Andy before climbing the steps.

"Hello," She said. "Where is he?"

"Inside," Andy said. "With the police."

"Is he hurt?" She asked.

A man got out of the car, tall and heavily built. He is wearing a white t-shirt, black shorts and white trainers. Balding with a beard, he looks tired.

"No," Andy said. "Shocked."

"Do you work here?" She asked Andy.

"Yes," Andy nodded. "I am one of the night porters here."

"Did he do that to you?" The man asked, pointing to Andy's nose.

"Not intentionally," Andy said. "Was an accident when I helped him out."

The man turned and looked at the car.

"Was he driving it?" He asked Andy.

"Yes," Andy nodded. "Two others in the car ran away."

"Did you see who they were?" He asked.

"No," Andy said. "Too dark and there was a bit going on."

"Can we see him?" She said, tears in her eyes.

"Sure," Andy said. "Follow me."

Andy walked into the bar where the boy sat on a couch, a female officer next to him and a male on a chair opposite.

"Hi," Andy said. "His parents have arrived."

The boy started to cry.

"Okay send them in," The male officer said as the female officer.

The mother walked in and went straight up to boy, grabbing hold of him as he stood up and hugged him.

"I am sorry mum," He cried.

"Are you okay?" She said. "Are you hurt?"

"He has been assessed by a paramedic," The female officer said. "He has no injuries."

The woman stepped back and took a deep breath, before slapping the boy across the arm, causing him to fall back into the couch, crying.

"Woah," Andy said, trying not to laugh.

"Don't do that please," The male officer said. "I think he has learnt his lesson!"

"Why do you think your father isn't in here?" The woman said. "You have broken his heart hanging out with those lowlifes, did they talk you into it?"

"No mum!" He cried.

"Look at my car!" She snapped.

"I will pay for it," He cried. "I am sorry!"

"How are you going to pay for it in prison!?" She yelled at him.

"I cannot go to prison," He cried. "Please don't take me to prison!"

"Let's all sit down and discuss this," The female officer said. "I would like to remind you that no one has pressed charges yet."

"I am going to wait outside," Andy said. "Give me a shout if you need anything."

Andy walked into the reception, looking down at his bloodied shirt and then noticing Allain sitting in the corner with a cup of coffee.

"Should be you in there," Andy said. "As the general manager."

"We are going to press charges," He said defiantly.

"A scuffed wall, broken fence and damaged grass," Andy said. "Hardly worth the hassle if you ask me, and he made a mistake."

"He deserves prison!" Allain said. "You must press charges."

"For what?" Andy asked.

"Criminal damage of course," Allain said.

"As the general manager," Andy said. "That is for you to do."

"Me?" Allain said. "Why me?"

"Because you are the general manager," Andy repeated himself. "I am just a badly paid porter."

The male officer came to the reception counter, tapping on it.

"Anyone here?" He said.

Andy pointed to the counter and Allain shook his head.

"Coming," Andy said shaking his head in annoyance as he walked around the corner.

"Is a manager in?" The officer asked.

"He is," Andy said,

"Can I speak to him regarding charges?" The officer asked, opening a notepad.

"Sure," Andy walked round the corner. "Police would like to speak to you Allain."

Allain sighed as he reluctantly got up and walked to the counter.

"Hello there," The officer said. "And you are?"

"Allain Jean Paul," Allain said. "I am the General Manager here at The Range."

"Do you wish to take things further?" He asked.

Allain looked at Andy who looked away, ignoring him.

"No," Allain said nervously. "No charges, we will speak to the parents about any damage."

"Okay," The officer said. "Thank you," The officer walked back into the bar.

"We need that car gone before the morning," Allain said. "It is very unsightly."

"Nothing can be done until the morning," Andy said.

"Why not?" Allain demanded.

"It's in the middle of the night," Andy said. "The police are dealing with it."

"Can you and Dean do something?" Allain asked.

"Do we look like we can flip a car and move it?" Andy asked.

"I don't know," Allain said. "But what if the owners turn up, it will make me look bad."

"Well as a General Manager," Andy said. "It is your job to fix these things."

"I am delegating," Allain said, annoyance in his voice.

"I am a night porter," Andy said. "Not a superhuman car mover."

The door opened and Dean walked in, looking at Allain and then at Andy.

"You finally showed up," Dean said to Allain. "Took you long enough."

"I was asleep," Allain said. "And I am not on duty."

"Your name is on the duty roster," Dean said pointing to the wall. "Did you forget?"

"All good?" Andy asked.

"Yeah," Dean nodded. "Just some cuts and scratches, the paramedic pulled out some thorns."

"Do you need to go to hospital?" Allain asked.

"No," Dean said.

"Allain was asking if we can move the car," Andy said. "In case the owners show up."

"We are night porters," Dean said. "Lifting cars isn't in my contact."

"Allain will not be pressing charges," Andy said.

"The boy made a mistake," Allain said. "He needs a second chance."

"Not what you said on the phone," Dean scoffed. "But that is fair enough."

"I will go and speak to them," Allain said. "Offer them a room for the night."

"Why?!" Dean said.

"They must be tired," Allain said and left the reception, walking round into the bar.

"God forbit he thinks of the staff," Andy said.

"The twat is stuck in the past," Dean said. "Treating the staff like crap is normal to him."

"Should have seen the mother slap the shit out of the kid," Andy laughed. "She walked in, hugged him, asked him if he was okay and then wallop!"

The boy's father walked through the entrance, making his way to the counter and dean walked round.

"I just wanted to apologise on behalf of my boy," He said. "He isn't a bad kid, just mixed with the wrong crowd."

Dean walked into view, removing his jacket.

"I spent time in prison for the same reason," Dean said. "Mixed with the wrong crowd, stole some cars and got caught, did some time in my teens, wasn't fun."

"We will be compensating you both," The man said. "For your troubles."

"It's cool," Dean said.

The man walked into the bar and both Dean and Andy started to laugh when they heard the boy crying.

"So much for a quiet night," Dean said. "I was looking forward to a kip."

"Me too," Andy said. "This shirt is ruined."

"Mine too," Dean scoffed and laughed. "When you in next?"

"Next Friday," Andy said. "And Saturday for the wedding."

"I am off on the Saturday," Dean said. "It's me and you on Friday, guess who is in?"

"Who?" Andy asked curiously.

"The car salesman," Dean laughed.

"Oh no," Andy groaned. "Not him again!"

"We are going to get Gary to stay again," Dean said. "Hopefully the loser will take a hint and go to bed."

"That would be good," Andy said.

"Oh yeah," Dean said pointing a finger at Andy. "When are you seeing her then?"

"Who?" Andy said curiously.

"You know who you deaf twat," Dean scoffed. "Your new face sucking friend."

"We are meeting tonight," Andy said. "Coffee date."

"Isn't it a bit soon?" Dean said. "She just split with her guy?"

"That is what is worrying me," Andy said. "But I will chat to her about that."

"Don't get me wrong," Dean said. "She is an amazing girl!"

"I know," Andy smiled. "Do you want a coffee?" Andy said. "I certainly need one."

"Yeah," Dean said. "I need sugar in mine."

"Two?" Andy asked.

"Don't be silly," Dean exclaimed. "Three."

Andy shook his head, laughing sarcastically as he left the reception, heading for the kitchen.

FIVE

Andy sat watching the security monitor, the camera over the reception, standing up when he saw the woman walk up to it, leaning over the counter.

"You in there?" She said.

"Oh hey Charlotte," Andy smiled. "Thought you weren't working today."

Charlotte is wearing grey jogging bottoms and a black sports jacket.

"I am not," She said. "I had my dad's car and thought I would pop by."

She leaned over, smiling.

"You going to give me a kiss or not?" She said.

Andy leaned over, kissing her on the lips. She pulled him closer, kissing him passionately, her tongue against his.

"You taste nice," Andy said. "What is that?"

"Raspberry lip balm," She laughed. "Is it busy?"

"No," Andy said. "Dean is in the kitchen making sandwiches for a customer and I am just keeping an eye out for one of our guests."

"Okay," She said. "I was going to ask if you wanted to grab breakfast in the morning?"

"That would be great," Andy said.

"They do vegetarian stuff," She said. "My mum doesn't eat meat."

"Nice," Andy said. "I cannot wait."

"Good," She smiled.

Andy saw the headlights of a car coming up the road, reached over and switched the monitor over.

"Want to come in here," Andy said. "I have heard this guy is a bit of a pervert."

"Oh not the car salesman?" She groaned. "I cannot stand him."

"I have heard nothing good," Andy said.

Charlotte walked around, letting herself into the office and sitting on the worktop.

"He is really good with tips though," She said. "When he isn't trying to screw everything."

"I have never met him," Andy said. "Dean told me everything."

"He creeps out the girls," Charlotte said. "He even tried on me once."

"No way!" Andy exclaimed.

"Yeah," She shivered. "On my eighteenth."

The car stopped outside the front of the hotel, pulling up close the wall. Andy watched as the man in a black suite, white shirt and red tie pulled a case and bag from the passenger seat. He is bald and clean shaven.

"Is that him?" Andy pointed to the monitor.

Charlotte leaned in.

"Yeah," She said. "Looks fatter than before."

The man walked up to the front of the hotel and pushed the door open with his foot. Charlotte moved round the side so she couldn't be seen and Andy smiled when he approached the counter.

"I have a booking," He said. "Brian Smith."

"Good evening sir," Andy said, removing the registration card from under the counter and placing it in front of Brian who dropped his bags on the floor, groaning and stretching. He took a credit card from his pocket, placing it in front of Andy.

"It's my wife's," He said. "It's registered."

"That is fine," Andy said, confirming the details matched. "Could you just fill in the card and sign it please."

"Of course," He smiled. "Do I have my usual room?"

"Yes," Andy nodded.

"I have a friend joining me later," He said. "She said she may arrive at midnight."

Charlotte laughed silently, shaking her head as if she knew something.

"That is fine," Andy replied. "Dean is expecting you."

"Where is he?" Brian said looking at his watch.

"Security run," Andy said.

Brian signed the card and pushed it towards Andy.

"Could you drop my bags to my room?" He asked. "Save me going up?

"Sure," Andy said.

He bent down, lifting up his black leather case and handed it to Andy, followed by a smaller leather case.

"Just stick them in the cupboard for me," He said.

Andy nodded, placing them on the floor next to the counter.

"Could I grab a drink?" Brian asked.

Andy saw Dean walking through the bar in the mirror.

"Dean is just coming," Andy said. "He will be able to sort that for you."

"Fancy joining us for a pint?" He asked. "Not met you before, will be good to know more."

"Will do after I have done my jobs," Andy said.

"One last thing," Brian removed a bunch of keys from his pocket. "Can you drive?"

"Yes," Andy said.

"Manual?" He asked.

"Of course," Andy smiled.

"Could you park it for me," He said. "Closest to the front as possible," He handed the keys to Andy.

"I will do that in a moment," Andy said. "And bring the keys back."

"Thanks mate," Brian said giving him a thumbs up before walking into the bar, met by Dean who grabbed his hand and shook it, leading him to the bar.

"So?" Charlotte said.

"What?" Andy asked.

"Freak huh?" She cringed.

"Seemed friendly enough," Andy shrugged his shoulders. "But I know what you mean."

"Want to grab a coffee before I go?" Charlotte said. "I fancy a chat," She smiled.

"Sure," Andy said. "Staff room?"

Charlotte nodded.

"Meet me there in five," Andy said.

"Black coffee?" Charlotte asked.

"Yeah," Andy said and kissed her on the cheek as he opened the door.

Charlotte slapped his back side as he walked through and he hissed in pain.

"Wimp!" She said, turning the corner towards the staff access and running when Andy went to grab her.

Andy sat in the bar, looking at the fireplace, watching the flames dance amongst the wood, cracking and spitting. Four of them sat around a coffee table, Andy, Dean, Gary and Brian.

"How about you?" Brian said to Andy.

Andy didn't respond.

"Is he ignoring me again?" He asked Dean.

"No," Dean said. "Daydreaming probably."

"Oi!" Gary snapped, throwing a beer mat at Andy and caught him on the forehead.

"What!" Andy moaned, rubbing his head. "What do you want you tosser?"

Brian started laughing.

"Brian asked where you see yourself in ten years," Dean said.

"No Idea," Andy said. "Not thought that far ahead."

"Come on, come on!" Brian said. "You must have an idea?"

Andy sighed, crossing his legs.

"Programming," he said. "I would like to become a self-employed computer programmer."

"Oh, very nice!" Brian. "You can fix my photocopier!" He said.

"Not quite the same thing!" Dean responded.

"What is so funny?" Brian said.

"He is deaf," Gary said. "How is he going to be a programmer?" He said.

"Surely that isn't a problem?" Brian said and then looked at Andy. "I didn't know you were deaf!" He said in surprise. "You hide it well."

"You did," Dean said. "You asked him all about it the last time you were here."

"Did I?" He looked confused. "Don't remember."

"The same day you were chatting up the eighteen-year-old bar girl," Andy scoffed. "You traumatised the poor girl!"

"No!" Brian said. " She wasn't that young!"

Dean looked at him and nodded.

"Shit," Brian said. "Never mind, no harm done." He turned to Andy. "So how deaf are you?"

"Completely without my hearing aids," Andy responded.

"Wow!" Brian said and put down his drink and sat forward.

"Bloody deaf people!" Gary moaned. "They should be drowned at birth!"

"I wasn't born deaf you inbred moron," Andy snapped back.

Gary glared at him as he finished his drink.

"Have you seen that film?" Brian said to Gary.

"What film?" Gary replied. "There are millions out there."

"The Night Porter?" Brian said.

"They made a film about the two sad bastards?" Gary laughed pointing at Dean and Andy.

"Not quite," Brian said. "You should check it out."

"About time you did the fridge check," Dean said.

"One more drink," Gary said. "Brian promised me one!"

"He is right there," Brian said. "Sambuca?"

"I am not going to have any," Dean said and looked at Andy. "You want one?"

"No," Andy said. "My ears are bad enough without amplifying them anymore."

"Okay," Dean said and got up. "I'll grab them for you," Dean walked to the bar, looking at Andy and shaking his head in frustration as he walked backwards into the bar, the swing doors squeaking.

"What time is your guest due?" Andy asked.

"She said about midnight or so," Brian said looking at his watch. "She is working."

"Fair enough," Andy said, covering his mouth as he yawned heavily.

"Which room do I have?" Brian asked.

"The usual as requested," Andy replied. "You stay with us so much you practically have your own room."

"I do like that room," Brian nodded.

"Is your guest your fancy bird?" Gary asked bluntly.

"No," Brian said. "No, just a friend."

"Cool friend," Gary said. "I wouldn't mind a young lady friend turning up at my house in the middle of the night."

"I bet," Andy said.

"The ladies like me!" Gary said confidently.

"Really," Andy said grinning.

"Yes," Gary said. "I know how to deal with them in the bedroom!" He growled.

"Don't want to know," Andy said screwing his face up in disgust.

"You banged Charlotte yet?" Gary asked.

"Who is Charlotte?" Brian asked.

"Not saying a word," Andy said.

"Go on," Gary said. "Tell me!"

"No," Andy said.

Gary grunted in annoyance.

"I'll find out!" Gary said.

"How was your date at the weekend?" Andy said. "From the bar?"

The smile disappeared off Gary's face, replaced with annoyance.

"Thought that would shut you up," Andy said.

"Fine," Gary snapped.

"What is that about?" Brian asked.

"Nothing," Gary said, looking up as Dean turned up with two shots of Sambuca.

"There you go," He said as he put them on the table in front of Gary and Brian.

Gary picked his shot up.

"Wait," Brian said. "Got to light it first!"

"What?" Gary said. "What do you mean?"

"You light it first," Dean said. "Then blow it out before you drink it."

"Why?" Gary said.

"Just do it," Brian said, tapping the table for him to put the shot down.

Gary grunted and put the shot on the table next to Brian who picked up a lighter and set both shots alight.

"Now you can have it," Dean said.

Gary picked up the shot and didn't blow it out, he choked when he greedily downed the shot, spilling it down the front of his chin. The thick stubble caught alight and he attempted to put it out, smearing the flaming sambuca over his face.

Dean stood up and picked up a glass of water, throwing it into Gary's face and then stood there, looking at him rubbing his face and spluttering.

"You were supposed to blow the flame out!" Dean said. "You idiot!"

Andy was in hysterics, trying to speak.

"You can shut up!" Gary snapped at him.

"So when are you going to tell me about your date?" Andy asked.

"You need to fuck off!" Gary growled at him.

"Go finish off in the kitchen Gary," Dean said.

Brian is quiet, watching what was happening.

"Now piss off or no more drinks," Dean pointed to the door leading to the kitchen. "Go on."

Gary stuck up two fingers and then a middle finger at Andy before walking off to the kitchen, slamming the door behind him.

"What is his problem?" Brian said. "Why is he always angry?"

"Because he failed in life," Dean said. "And now wants to drag everyone down."

"Does his brother still work here?" Brian asked. "Not seen him in a while."

"Oh yes he still works here," Dean said. "He took the staff door off the hinges last week!"

"That was him?" Andy said. "How?"

"One of the waiters locked him in as a joke," Dean said. "So he kicked it."

Andy laughed.

"Took out half the frame as well," Dean said shaking his head.

"I didn't notice," Andy said.

"Was repaired," Dean said. "Turns out he doesn't like tight spaces."

"The size of the guy," Andy scoffed. "Everywhere must be tight for him."

"Did you ever hear the story about the waiter that got on his bad side?" Dean asked.

"No," Andy said. "Who?"

"This was a couple of years ago," Dean said. "A waiter was bothering one of the young waitresses, Keith overheard her talking about it so he stormed into the bar and lifted him up by the throat!"

"Shit!" Andy said. "All he needs is a mask and a chainsaw and we have a villain no one can stop."

"Is he a bit retarded?" Brian asked.

"Don't say that," Dean said.

"Well, I can't say mental can I?" Brian said bluntly.

"He has learning difficulties," Andy said. "Don't say anything like that in front of Gary."

"He is very protective of Keith," Dean said.

Brian shrugged his shoulders.

"So," Brian. "Can I ask you a personal question?"

"Sure," Andy said.

"How do you know you are deaf?" He asked.

Dean looked at Brian in confusion and then at Andy, a grin on his face.

"Well," Andy started. "I lost all hearing in my left ear overnight." He pointed to his left ear. "The other ear went slowly over a couple of months." He pointed to his right.

"Yes," Brian said holding up his hand. "But HOW do you know you are deaf?"

"What are you banging on about?" Dean asked him.

"Who said you are deaf?" Brian said and sat forward.

"A specialist and an audiologist," Andy responded. "Had all the relevant tests."

Brian shook his head and laughed.

"What?" Andy said, looking at Dean in confusion.

"That doesn't mean anything," Brian responded, a smug look on his face.

"I have hearing tests every now and then," Andy said.

"Humour me," He said. "I'll buy you a drink!"

"Bottle of Vodka?" Andy asked with a grin on his face.

"Fine," Brian said shrugging his shoulders, indicating he didn't care.

Dean sat back in the chair, crossed his legs, and watched.

"Come here a moment," Brian said. "I want to try something."

"What?" Andy asked.

"It's something I picked up from a specialist friend of mine," He said.

"Does he fix cars?" Dean asked.

"No!" Brian huffed. "He is a medical expert."

Andy shook his head and sighed.

"Okay," Andy said. "You better tip well tonight."

He got up and walked over to Brian.

"Okay," He said and stood up. "Just need to feel behind your ears."

Brian pressed under Andy's ears and moved his fingers down the side of his neck, chucking and nodding like he had done a good deed.

"Just what I thought," He said. "You are not deaf, your tubes are blocked."

Dean started to laugh.

"Get out of it," Andy said. "I have had all the tests going."

"If you blow your nose it will solve all your problems!" Brian said. "Trust me!"

Andy sarcastically hit the palm of his hand against his forehead.

"I think I have blown my nose more than a few times since I went deaf!" He said.

Gary walked into the lounge, holding a large plastic bowl of pasta.

"What is going on?" He said. "What's all the fuss about?

"He isn't deaf," Dean said. "Turns out his tubes are blocked!"

Gary let out a loud gasp and dropped the bowl of pasta, he then fell to his knees, shouting in sarcasm.

"It's a miracle!" He cried. "Praise the lord!"

"Jesus Gary keep it down!" Dean said trying not to laugh.

"Maybe you can cure my brother!" Gary said.

"Gary!" Dean said laughing.

Gary got to his feet and shook his head.

"Stick to selling cars you daft bastard," He walked to the door, just about to open it.

"Gary," Dean said. "You gonna clean this up?" He pointed to the plain pasta on the floor, the red plastic bowl had rolled under a table.

"Are you not right in the head?" Brian said.

"What is that supposed to mean?" Gary said defensively!"

"Gary!" Dean warned him.

"I am shitting you," Gary smiled. "I'm just as fucked in the head as my brother!"

Gary got down on his knees, grabbed the bowl and scooped the pasta into it, putting a piece into his mouth and chewing it.

"I hate pasta!" He moaned. "Tastes so bland, I need meat!"

"Speaking of needing meat," Andy said. "How was your date?"

Gary paused, glaring at Andy before shaking his head and forcing a smile.

"Not saying a word," He said. "I am going!"

Gary stormed out, slamming the door against the wall, muttering all the way to the kitchen.

"What was that about?" Brian asked.

"Have you heard?" Dean said to Andy.

"I heard something," Andy said. "From one of the waiters."

"Tell your version," Dean said.

"From what I heard is that Gary went out with a group on Saturday," he said. "And he got talking to a woman at the bar."

"Right?" Brian said.

"Bearing in mind Gary hates everyone and everything unless they are white and perfect," Dean sighed. "If you are coloured, gay or disabled, Gary automatically hates you."

"Everyone warned him about this woman that he was getting overly friendly with," Andy said. "But he just thought they were jealous and eventually went home with her."

"I don't get it?" Brian said.

"Turns out she had a bigger dick than he does," Dean said.

"Oh," Brian scoffed, trying not to laugh. "A chick with a dick?"

"Transexual yes," Dean said. "I know her, she is a really nice person."

"He," Brian said.

"No, she," Dean said.

"Whatever," Brian said curiously. "So, who shagged who?"

"Nothing happened," Dean said. "Gary passed out."

Andy chuckled.

"Why?" Brian asked.

"He drinks like a fish every day!" Andy said.

"But some people are winding him up," Dean said. "Saying he took it like a champ!"

"Oh no that is wrong," Brian said. "I know some people like that kind of stuff, but still it is wrong."

A woman arrived at the reception counter. Tall and slim with a short black skirt, white blouse, and a black leather jacket. She has long blonde hair and long nails, painted red.

"Hey Chloe," Brian said standing up.

"Hi Brian," Chloe said, walking into the bar. "Hi, guys."

"Want a drink?" Brian asked.

"Can we go up?" She said. "I am so tired."

"Sure," Brian smiled. "Did you drop my bags in the room?" Brian asked Andy.

"Yes," Andy said. "Placed them inside the cupboard as you requested."

"Thanks," Brian said. "We may order some food?" He said looking at Chloe who smiled and nodded.

Andy stood up as they left, watching them turn the corner and he turned to Dean, shaking his head in amazement.

Dean held up his hand, listening as they walked up the stairs, their voices trailing off into the distance.

"Nice arse," Dean said nodding in agreement.

"Girlfriend?" Andy asked.

"Call girl," Dean said. "She has to be, I mean look at the state of him!"

"I know," Andy said. "Crazy. I thought he was married."

"He is," Dean said. "He is using his wife's credit card!"

"You are joking!" Andy laughed.

"Can you clean the bar?" Dean asked. "I'll sort the reception."

"Sure," Andy said and made his way towards the bar, stopping when Gary opened the door.

"Hi," Gary said. "Any chance of a pint?"

"Sure," Andy said. "Come on."

The telephone started to ring in reception and Andy paused, waiting for Dean to answer it.

"Help yourself," Andy said to Gary. "Just don't go nuts."

Andy caught Dean's reflection in the mirror, trying to get his attention. Andy walked into reception, leaning up against the counter.

"Andy is popping up," Dean said. "Stop yelling in my ear please," Dan squinted and flinched.

"Andy is coming up!" Dean put the telephone down, shaking his head.

"What is it?" Andy asked.

"Problem with his room," Dean said picking up a key. "He has asked for another room but want's someone to go up."

"What is wrong with the room?" Andy asked.

"He wouldn't say," Dean said. "But demanded someone go up," Dean handed a key to Andy. "Room opposite, practically the same."

"Bloody pain in the arse," Andy said.

Brian and Chloe stood outside the hotel room, watching as Andy approached them.

"What appears to be the problem?" Andy asked.

"Have a look," Brian snapped. "It isn't acceptable!"

"All was well when I dropped off the bags," Andy said, trying to think in case he had done something.

"Just look," Brian said.

Andy opened the door, he first noticed the smell of excrement followed by growling and screeching. Two foxes are on the bed, one laying on its stomach and the other mounting it, thrusting violently.

"Could I see your receipt please?" Andy stepped forward.

The male fox jumped up and out of the window, looking back before bolting. The female lay there for a few seconds, before looking up and not responding.

"Come on," Andy pointed at the window. "Get out of it!"

Andy stepped forward and she let out a surprised yelp before also jumping out of the window, avoiding the pile of excrement and urine, Andy leaned over the bed and closed the window.

"I am not happy about this," Brian snapped. "This is not acceptable."

"I can only apologise," Andy said.

"What are you going to do about it?" Brian demanded.

"We have another room for you," Andy said holding up the key. "Practically the same."

"I want a full refund," Brian said. "Otherwise I will take this further."

Dean appeared at the doorway, looking in.

"Foxes?" He asked.

"Yes," Andy said.

"I want to know what you are doing about this," Brian said.

"I have sorted the opposite room out for you," Dean said. "It's much better than this one."

"I want a full refund," Brian demanded.

"Come on," Chloe said. "Let's go inside."

"No," Brian said. "I know how these things work and I am a regular customer."

"Please Brian," Chloe begged him.

Brian took the key off Andy, handing it to Chloe.

"Give me a few minutes," Brian said. "Go run yourself a bath."

Chloe nodded and let herself into the room opposite, smiling at Brian as she closed the door.

"So?" Brian asked.

"Unfortunately this cannot be helped," Dean said.

"The room should have been checked before," Brian said.

"We offered to show you to the room," Dean said. "You refused."

"Well I want a refund," Brian snapped.

"Will you be leaving tonight?" Dean said.

"No," Brian said. "I am staying."

"So," Dean said. "The room is chargeable."

"I can make your life very uncomfortable," Brian said. "Could even get you sacked."

"Maybe we should do a refund," Andy said.

"What do you mean?" Dean said.

"Well," Andy said. "We would have to call the owner of the credit card, explaining that a room has been refunded for two persons."

"What are you banging on about?" Brian said.

"He is right," Dean said. "Refunds are confirmed with the credit card owner," Dean sighed. "Does your wife know you are meeting up with young ladies on your business trips?"

Brian glared at Andy, red in the face.

"Is that a no?" Dean said. "Because threatening me is like a dare, and I wouldn't hesitate to tell your wife everything."

"You better watch it," Brian pointed a finger. "You are on thin ice."

"So are you," Dean said. "Your wife runs the business, not you."

"You cannot treat me like this," Brian said. "I will have your job."

"Okay," Dean said walking away. "I am up for a challenge."

Andy walked into the room, removed a case and a small bag for the cabinet, placed them in front of the opposite room door and then closed the door to the soiled room, locking it.

"I will be in reception if you need anything," Andy said. "Have a lovely stay," He said sarcastically, walking away and grinning.

Andy walked into the kitchen, Gary and Dean standing by the restaurant doors.

"What an absolute tosser!" Dean snapped. "He has no clue!"

"What happened?" Gary asked, downing half of a pint and letting out a prolonged belch.

"Brian," Dean said. "Threatened our jobs because he won't get a refund."

"Why?" Gary scoffed. "What's he want a refund for? I thought he was okay."

"There were foxes shagging in his room," Andy said. "They have shit everywhere too."

"So give him another room," Gary said.

"We did," Dean replied. "He wants more."

"Tell him to fuck off elsewhere then!" Gary growled. "Want me to get Keith in?"

Dean laughed.

"Andy suggested calling his wife as part of the refund process," Dean grinned.

"I don't get it," Gary shrugged his shoulders.

"He is here with his hooker," Dean said. "Do you think someone young and sexy is going to date a random guy in his late fifties?"

"I did okay," Gary said.

Andy was about to speak when Gary pointed his finger at him, warning him.

"Don't fucking say anything you deaf twat!" He snapped.

"Gary," Dean said. "Everyone knows she has a dick, and you know what, no one cares!"

"What?" Gary stuttered.

"Nothing happened between you both," Dean said. "You passed out on the bed and she slept on the couch."

"Really?" Gary said.

"No one wanted to say anything," Andy laughed. "It was more fun watching you squirm."

"Fuck me!" Gary exclaimed. "You really had me worried."

"You give it just as much," Dean said.

"I bet she wanted to give it just as much too," Andy scoffed, trying not to laugh.

"You are a funny fucker," Gary said. "Good for you I am in a good mood."

"Are you?" Andy said. "Want a pint?"

"Sure," Gary said.

"Can you go and grab him one," Dean said. "The brasserie floor needs doing."

Andy let out a long groan.

"Did you forget?" Dean smiled.

"I was hoping I didn't have to do it," Andy said.

"Remember when you did it for the first time?" Dean said.

"You keep reminding me," Andy said.]

"What happened?" Gary asked.

"The lacquer," Dean said. "You forgotten?"

Gary shook his head in confusion.

"Mark asked Andy to clear all the furniture, sweep and mop the brasserie floor," Dean said. "Once it dried, to lacquer it."

"No," Gary said. "Don't remember."

"Well Andy didn't let it dry out properly and most of the chairs got stuck," Dean laughed. "Apparently it was bedlam the next day."

"I sorted it out after," Andy nodded in sarcasm. "I blame Mark."

"Probably had his nose in a book," Gary said. "He goes through so many books!"

"Oh that reminds me," Dean said. "Head chef wanted me to talk to you Gary."

"About what?" Gary asked.

"There have been some complaints," Dean said.

"I don't give a fuck," Gary replied, shrugging his shoulders. "What about?" He asked.

"Your hygiene," Dean said.

"My what?" Gary scoffed.

"Hygiene," Dean replied. "Body odour."

"I don't understand," Gary said.

Dean groaned.

"You stink," Andy said bluntly.

"Oh," Gary laughed. "It's cos I work hard."

"Well some of the kitchen staff have moaned, so could you either use deodorant or have a shower," Dan grinned. "Preferably both."

"I'll check my payslip and see if it is worth it," Gary said. "I fancy that pint now."

"Better get to reception," Dean said looking at his watch.

Andy walked into the bar, the swing doors squeaking loudly, he looked into the brasserie, free of furniture and sparkling.

"Half an hour then I can varnish," Andy said.

Gary suddenly appeared at the shutter over the bar, growling and rattling it like a crazed chimpanzee in a zoo.

"Blimey," Andy said. "Like being in a zoo."

"Pint!" Gary pointed to the tap.

"Magic word?" Andy asked.

"Now, you deaf twat!" Gary snapped.

"That isn't nice," Andy said.

"Why," Gary said. "You are deaf and you are a twat."

"Fair enough," Andy nodded. "What do you want."

"Anything," Gary said.

Gary started walking towards the brasserie floor and Andy yelped.

"You dare," Andy said.

"You cleaned it?" Gary said leaning down and looking at the glistening floor. "Did you use dirty water or something?"

"Yes," Andy said. "Just stay off it!"

"Grumpy bastard," Gary said and pushed the swing doors, breathing in deeply and sighing.

"What?" Andy said.

"I love that smell," Gary smiled. "The smell of a bar and dishwasher soap!" He burst out laughing.

"How's your brother?" Andy asked.

"Same old," Gary said. "Broke a bone in his hand."

"Oh," Andy said. "How did he manage that?"

"Pinched his telly," Gary scoffed and laughed.

"Why?" Andy asked.

"Well our old mum used to tap the side of the telly if it played up," Gary shrugged his shoulders. "He must have picked it up."

"What happened?" Andy asked.

"It flew off the table and hit the wall," Gary exclaimed. "Blew the main fuse box as well."

"Did he go to the hospital?" Andy said, reaching for a pint glass and pulling a pint.

"No," Gary shook his head. "He doesn't do hospitals."

"How do you know he broke a bone?" Andy said curiously.

"It makes a cracking noise," Gary said holding up his hand, opening and closing it.

Andy moaned, shaking his head, and finishing the pint, handing it to Gary.

"Thanks Andy," He said. "You know I like you really."

"Where there is alcohol concerned," Andy said. "I know."

Gary laughed, downing the pint in several gulps.

"Excuse me?" Brian said from the bar, causing both Andy and Gary to jump in fright.

"Jesus!" Gary yelped. "I nearly shit myself!"

"Gary!" Andy groaned. "Stop it. How can I help you?" He said to Brian.

111

"I wanted to apologise," Brian said. "For what happened earlier."

"No skin off my nose Brian," Andy said. "Do you want a drink?"

"No," Brian smiled. "Too late for me."

"How's your bird?" Gary asked bluntly.

Brian nodded with a cheeky grin.

"Lucky bastard!" Gary scoffed.

"Could I get some Sandwiches?" Brian asked. "Chloe is hungry."

"After all that sausage?!" Gary exclaimed. "Greedy cow!"

Brian laughed awkwardly.

"Okay Gary," Andy said trying not to laugh. "On that note, you need to go and Brian, could you give your order to Dean at the reception," Andy said, noticing Dean arrive from a security walk. "I will get started on them."

Andy leaned against the bar, holding a pint of water and yawning. His shirt is wet with perspiration, reaching for a towel, he wiped his face.

"All done?" Dean said from the bar.

"Bloody knackered!" Andy said, had to mop it over a couple of times after Gary decided to write words over the tiles."

"He is a tosser," Dean said shaking his head. "Looks good though."

"Shit," Andy said.

"No it looks good," Dean said.

"Look," Andy said pointing to near the open door. "We have a bloody visitor!"

Dean looked through the shutter.

"Where?" He asked.

"Look at the size of the croaking sod!" Andy said. "That is going to ruin the floor!"

A large frog sat looking towards the bar just inside the open door.

"It's going to stick," Gary laughed. "Shall I get my cleaver?"

"No," Andy warned him. "You will not."

"Why?" Gary asked in disappointment.

"One, you will make a mess and two, how will I explain the damaged tiles?" Andy said.

"Fair enough," Gary said.

"I supposed I could go outside," Andy said. "Grab it before it gets any further."

"All yours," Gary said. "I have my pint and don't care anymore."

"Thanks Gary," Andy said shaking his head as Gary walked away, stopping to turn and laugh as he walked through the door.

The frog jumped forward, making a squelching slap against the tiles as it landed.

"Stop!" Andy moaned. "Or ill feed you to the foxes!"

The frog jumped forward again.

"Screw it," Andy said and walked directly at it, bending down, and grabbing it. As he turned, he slipped and fell backwards, landing flat on his back and cracking his head on the floor. His vision became a mass of stars, the metallic taste building at the back of his mouth and noise as he lay there with his eyes closed, moaning softly.

"Oh shit," Andy groaned and dropped the frog.

The frog landed on his chest, facing him.

"That hurt," Andy said, putting his arm over his eyes, after a couple of minutes, he began to snore.

"Andy?" Dean said. "Andy, wake up," He kicked Andy's foot.

"What?" Andy said opening his eyes.

"Why are you sleeping on the floor?" He asked.

Gary stood next to Dean, a pint in his hand.

"Did that frog put you on your arse?" Gary laughed.

"What frog?" Dean said looking at Gary.

"There was a frog in the middle of the brasserie floor," Gary pointed.

"Oh bloody hell," Andy said. "I'm stuck."

Gary burst out laughing, followed by Dean.

"How long have you been there?" Dean said, reaching down and grabbing hold of Andy's arm as he sat up, his shirt sticking to the floor.

"No idea," Andy said. "When did you go into the kitchen?" He asked Gary.

"Half an hour ago," Gary said.

"Must have passed out," Andy said.

"Did you crack your head?" Dean said, worry in his voice.

"A little," Andy said, feeling the back of his head and noticing the blood on his hand.

Andy stood up pulling himself away from the varnish that gripped at his trousers and then looked down at the outline where he had been laying.

"Oh for fucks sake!" Andy moaned.

"I'll sort it," Dean said. "Go sit down, get some rest."

Andy looked around the brasserie floor.

"What you looking for?" Gary asked.

"Wondering where that frog got to," Andy said.

"Probably imagined it," Dean laughed.

"I saw it," Gary said.

"You are always drunk Gary!" Dean scoffed. "You see all kinds of weird crap."

"I need to sit down," Andy groaned, walking over to an armchair, and sitting down.

"Feel sick or anything?" Dean asked.

"No," Andy said. "Thirsty."

"Could you get Andy some water," Dean said to Gary who nodded and hurried into the bar and began to pull a pint. "What are you doing?"

"Getting myself one too," Gary said.

"Could you get Andy some water first?" Dean scoffed.

Gary mumbled, picking up a small glass.

"You want ice Andy?" Gary said.

"Gary asked if you wanted ice?" Dean said.

Andy nodded.

After some noise and banging around, Gary came out and handed the glass to Andy who gulped at it, sighing in relief.

"Thanks Gary," Andy said, laying back in the chair and closing his eyes. In less than a minute, he is snoring.

"Bloody hell," Dean said. "I wish I could get to sleep that quickly."

Dean started to mop over the floor where Andy had been laying.

"Is he still working days?" Gary said staring at Andy.

"Don't think so," Dean said.

Gary walked into the bar.

"What are you doing?" Dean looked back.

"Clearing up," Gary said. "That okay?"

"Sure," Dean said curiously and returned to moping the floor, scrubbing at the outline.

Gary crept out of the bar, holding a fire extinguisher, a grin on his face as he approached Andy who was gently snoring.

"This is going to be fun," Gary said under his breath, giggling as he aimed the nozzle at Andy's thigh. "This will teach you!"

Gary discharged the fire extinguisher and within a few seconds, Andy woke up in fright yelping, jumping from the chair.

"What the fuck!" Andy cried out.

"Gary!" Dean snapped. "What are you doing!?"

Dropping the fire extinguisher on the floor, Gary ran out of the bar, closing the door to the staff access, leaning up against the glass and pointing at Andy, laughing.

"Tosser!" Andy growled and ran at the door, only to find Gary had blocked it with his foot to stop Andy getting in. Pushing and shoving at the door, Andy tried to get it open.

"That is for winding me up," Gary said through the glass, laughing hysterically.

Andy looked down at his thigh, the vapor rising from a white patch of frost.

"Oh shit," Dean said noticing. "You okay?"

"I am going to beat him to death!" Andy growled.

Gary laughed loudly behind the reinforced wired glass window.

"Grow up Gary," Dean said. "That was dangerous."

"Don't care," Gary said shrugging his shoulders.

"It is also a sackable offence to tamper with fire extinguishers," Dean said. "I will have to report that it has been discharged."

"Don't care," Gary sniggered.

"Come here," Andy indicated to Gary.

Gary put his face up against the glass, sticking his tongue out and taunting Andy.

"Prick," Andy said under his breath and without warning, he punched the glass.

Gary fell backwards, clutching his face.

"Oh bloody hell Andy," Dean exclaimed. "This is going to be hard to explain!"

Andy watched as Gary walked into the kitchen.

"I think you hurt him," Dean said.

"And?" Gary said. "He had it coming."

"I know," Dean moaned. "But look," He pointed to the door.

"I'll sort it," Andy said. "Watch," Andy opened the door and took the cover off the door slowing mechanism. "Grab me a knife," Andy asked.

"Why?" Dean said.

"Or a flathead," Andy said. "I don't care which."

Dean walked over to the brasserie, bending down by a trolley and picking up a knife before walking back to Andy.

"You aren't going to stab him are you?" Dean asked.

"Not yet," Andy said. "Plenty of decent knives in the kitchen."

Gary walked out from the kitchen and Andy glared at him.

"Truce," Gary held up his hand in defence, his other hand holding a wet towel against his eye.

"You two need to stop," Dean said. "Otherwise there won't be a hotel left."

"That would make a good book for you to write!" Gary laughed.

"Trust me," Andy said. "You don't fare well in my stories."

"I am sorry," Gary said. "I went too far."

Dean looked at Andy, waiting for him to say something.

"What?" Andy said.

"You going to say sorry too?" Dean asked. "Or you going to be the arsehole?"

"I will be an arsehole until my leg defrosts," Andy said.

Gary started laughing.

"Promise you won't stab him," Dean said handing the knife to Andy.

"Yes, for now," Andy said. "Hold the door for me," Andy asked.

Dean held the door as Andy reached up and turned a screw a couple of turns and then stepped back.

"Let it go," Andy said.

Dean let the door go and it slammed closed, echoing through the bar and brasserie.

"Shit," Dean said. "Nice one!"

"I'd never have thought of that," Gary scoffed. "You done that before?"

"Yes," Andy said. "Accidently broke a door at college."

"How about the fire extinguisher?" Dean asked.

"Easy," Andy said. "I'll say it fell off the wall and went off because the pin was missing."

"There wasn't a pin in it," Gary said.

"Problem solved," Andy said.

A croak from the brasserie got Deans attention and he turned, looking in the direction.

"What?" Andy said.

"Did you hear that?" Dean asked.

"No," Andy said. "But then again, I am deaf."

"Sounds like the frog," Gary said.

The frog jumped into view, stopping in the middle of the bar and brasserie.

"Little shit," Andy groaned. "I swear that thing is trying to kill me."

Gary burst out in laughter, removing the towel from his face to reveal a little cut on his brow.

"Bloody hell," Andy said. "Was that me?"

"Yeah," Gary said. "It's fine."

Andy felt the back of his trousers.

"I think I need new trousers," Andy said. "And a shirt."

"Like glue isn't it?" Dean said. "I have been there, although I slipped."

"Yeah," Gary added. "Didn't go and sleep in it like you did you bloody idiot."

Andy walked over to the frog, carefully bending down, and picking it up, holding it between his cupped hands.

"Gonna kill it?" Gary asked.

"No," Andy said. "Going to take it down to the lake."

A loud ring came from the reception counter and Dean looked at the mirror, seeing Chloe standing at the counter.

"Are you okay there?" Dean asked.

"Could you call me a cab?" She asked tearfully.

"Where are you going?" Dean asked.

"Dartford," She said sniffling.

"Are you okay?" Dean asked her.

"He is an arsehole," She said, fighting back tears.

"Do you want a cup of tea or coffee?" Gary asked.

"No," She said. "I just want to go home."

"I am happy to take you home," Dean said. "Due a break anyhow."

"Are you sure?" She said.

Andy walked up to the reception, smiling at Chloe who looked at his hands.

"That isn't a spider is it?" She said worryingly.

"No," Andy said. "A frog."

"Dinner," Gary scoffed.

"Aw no!" She said. "I love frogs."

"This one is a psychopath!" Andy said, laughing as he walked past Chloe. "I'll let this sod go and then head back," Andy said. "Give me five minutes."

Andy yawned, sitting in reception with his feet up on the counter and reading a book.

"Good morning," Brian tapped the counter. "You there Dean?"

Andy got up, put the book down and walked round to the reception.

"Hi there sir," Andy said. "How can I help?"

"Do you know where Chloe went?" He asked.

"She left a couple of hours ago," Andy said.

"Why?" Brian asked abruptly.

"Because she wanted to," Andy said. "She got a cab home."

"Why was I not informed of this?" Brian snapped.

"Because she is an adult," Andy said. "We don't have to inform others if someone chooses to leave the premises.

"Where is Dean?" Brian said. "I want to speak to him."

"Dean is on a break," Andy said.

"Get him," Brian demanded.

"He isn't on site," Andy said.

117

"And left you on your own?" Brian scoffed. "That was silly."

"Why is that?" Andy asked curiously.

"You are deaf," He said. "You shouldn't be allowed on your own."

"I suggest you stop there," Andy said. "That kind of attitude is discrimination."

"No," Brian shook his head. "It's an opinion."

"So everyone is allowed an opinion?" Andy said.

"Of course," Brian said.

"Well you are an arsehole," Andy said. "Treating people like shit just because you think you are important."

"You cannot talk to me like that," Brian growled. "I could have your job!"

"You couldn't do my job," Andy laughed. "You are literally a salesman for your wife, meeting call girls in hotels and hoping she doesn't find out."

"Is that a threat?" Brian said pointing.

"No," Andy said. "A threat would be, if you give me any more crap, then I will be informing your wife."

"You wouldn't be able to," Brian scoffed. "You have no idea where she lives!"

"Your home address is on the registration," Andy said. "Plus, I am pretty sure I could track down one of your sales offices."

"You are on thin ice," Brian warned him.

"I don't care," Andy said. "I don't take kindly to discrimination and threats."

"Who do you think they will believe?" He laughed and shook his head in defiance. "Me, a regular customer that happens to be a millionaire, or you, a minimum wage disabled porter that will never amount to anything?" He said through clenched teeth.

"Firstly," Andy said holding up a finger. "This is my first job, and there will be other opportunities," He held up another finger. "Secondly, you are on camera," Andy pointed to the camera behind him. "I am pretty sure that is all I need to shut you down," And smiled. "And thirdly, if your wife cuts you off, I am pretty sure you will no longer have access to her millions and will have to enjoy a minimum wage."

Brian is red in the face, his eyes darting to the camera and then to Andy as he struggled to respond.

"Now unless there is anything realistic I can help you with," Andy said. "Go back to your room and have a think about the way you treat people," Andy said.

The door opened and Dean walked in, stopping when he saw Brian at the counter.

"Everything okay?" He said looking at his watch.

"Yeah," Andy nodded. "Everything okay sir?" He said to Brian.

"Yes," Brian said forcing a smile. "I was just asking Andy if I could get a paper but left it too late."

"If we have any spare," Dean said. "I will let you know,"

Brian nodded and then looked at Andy.

"Thank you," Brian said before walking up the stairs, returning to his room.

Dean approached the counter, listening until he heard a door close.

"What was that about?" Dean said. "It was not about papers!"

"He got into a temper," Andy said. "Threatening me and everything."

"Why?" Dean asked.

"He demanded to know why we let Chloe go," Andy said. "I explained we cannot detain people."

"He is a tosser," Dean said.

"Why was Chloe upset?" Andy said. "Did he hurt her?"

"He was horrible to her," Dean said. "Promised her money to spend the night and changed his mind when she got there, so she said she was leaving."

"Bloody hell," Andy said.

"Yeah," Dean said. "He then threatened to send her nude photos to her family and colleagues if she said anything."

"What an arse," Andy said.

"Well," Dean said. "His loss and my gain."

"What?" Andy said curiously.

"Looks like we are dating," Dean said. "Just spent the last couple of hours talking to her."

"Thanks for that," Andy nodded. "Leaving me on my own with Gary."

"Was it okay?" Dean said, feeling bad.

"It was fine," Andy said. "He finished the brasserie floor and we chilled with a pint and food." Andy yawned. "Police showed up as well, did some checks on the carpark and guess what?"

"What?" Dean said, also yawning.

"Brian's car," Andy laughed. "No tax or MOT."

"You are kidding!" Dean exclaimed. "A car salesman, with a millionaire wife, has no tax or MOT on a company car!"

"No," Andy said. "So I gave them his information."

"Brutal," Dean shook his head. "Deserved, but brutal."

"They also said a car has been abandoned in the staff carpark," Andy said.

"It's not abandoned," Dean said. "Broken down."

"Oh," Andy said. "I didn't recognise it."

"What are they doing about it?" Dean asked.

"Nothing," Andy said. "I said I would check with you first," Andy looked at his watch. "Half hour and I am done."

"Go now if you want," Dean said. "I'll finish up."

"I am meeting Charlotte," Andy said. "So I will hang around."

"Oh yeah," Dean smiled. "You both hit it off quick."

"I like her," Andy said. "She is amazing."

"Well take it slow," Dean said. "She was with her guy for a few years."

The door opened and Charlotte walked in, wearing the same clothes from the previous day.

"Bloody hell don't you sleep?" Andy said.

"I am a student," Charlotte smiled. "You know the answer to that one!"

"Morning," Dean said. "Go on Andy," Dean said. "You can finish now."

"Sure?" Andy asked.

"Yes," Dean laughed. "Been a long night for you."

Andy grabbed his jacket and left the reception, walking up to Charlotte and kissing her on the cheek. She grabbed him and hugged him.

"You are warm," She said and then exclaimed, looking at her hands. "Why are you sticky?"

"He slipped while varnishing the brasserie floor," Dean scoffed. "Silly twat passed out."

"Oh my god!" She said. "You should have gone to hospital!"

"Cut his head too," Dean said.

"Behave!" Andy said. "I am fine."

"I think a change of clothes would be good before we go out," Charlotte said. "I'll drop you home first."

"I agree," Andy said.

"Just bugger off," Dean said. "I am sure I have a car salesman temper fallout to deal with."

"What happened?" She asked.

"I will tell you in the car," Andy said. "You are going to love this!" He took her arm gently, leading her towards the entrance.

SIX

Andy stood next to the bar, watching the various people standing and seated, talking and drinking.

"Long day," Lindsay said. "You okay?"

"Yeah," Andy said. "Rather be in bed."

"Me too," She said grinning. "Not sure who with though."

"What?" Andy said, not hearing what she said.

"Not sure who with," She smiled and laughed. "Sorry about Charlotte," She said. "No idea what is going through her head."

The storeroom opened and a tall and slim girl walked out, wearing black trousers, white blouse and has short brown hair, she is struggling with a case of bottled beers.

"Want any help?" Andy asked.

"No thanks," She said.

"This is Andy by the way," Lindsay aid. "He is one of our night porters."

"Hi," She smiled. "I am Gemma."

"Nice to meet you Gemma," Andy said. "First day?"

"Yeah," Gemma said.

"It's all downhill from here," He laughed. "No seriously it's okay, the people are really friendly."

"Some of them!" Lindsay scoffed.

"True," Andy said looking around. "Charlotte not on tonight?"

"She is helping in the restaurant tonight," Lindsay said. "Joining the bar in an hour."

A couple of women came to the bar, both wearing identical bridesmaid dresses in light blue, their long blonde hair styled and platted. Both are the same height.

"Are you twins?" Andy asked.

"Everyone thinks that!" One of the women said. "We are not even related!"

"Switched at birth?" Lindsay said.

"Who knows!" The second woman said. "We are from the Barn house wedding," She said. "There should be a large bottle of champagne behind the bar for the bridesmaid group?"

"Yes there is," Lindsay said. "Could you get the bottle I told you about," She said to Gemma. "Andy will help if you need it?"

"I will be fine," She said and left the bar, walking into the store.

"How is the evening going?" Andy asked.

"It's beautiful," One of the women said.

"Shame the groom is pissed out of his head," The second said. "He is always an arsehole when he is pissed."

"Any problems?" Andy asked.

"Nothing we cannot handle," The second woman said.

Gemma opened the door, awkwardly carrying the large bottle of champagne.

"Let me help!" Andy said and walked into the bar, gently taking the bottle from her.

From the ground, the bottle was up to his hips.

"Can you bring it into the lounge?" The first woman said. "With eight glasses?"

"Sure," Andy said. "Do you want to bring the glasses and I will take this round for you?"

"That would be great Andy," Lindsay said. "Gemma, the glasses are on the bottom shelf," She pointed to the cupboard. "Check them over before you take them."

The two women made their way through the bar to the reception.

"This thing is ridiculous," Andy said. "How is anyone supposed to lift this!"

"Will keep them quiet for a while," Lindsay said.

"More like half hour," Andy scoffed. "They have been going through the booze like there is no tomorrow!

"Thanks for helping," Gemma said. "That weighs a ton!"

"Gonna have to get you down the gym," Andy said. "Start you on a light bench."

"What do you call light Andy?" Lindsay asked.

"Let's say about a hundred?" Andy said thinking. "Maybe eighty, seeing as I am generous."

"He lifts," Lindsay said. "Useful when it comes to heavy stuff."

Gemma giggled.

"Go on," Lindsay said. "Take it round."

Andy opened the door for Gemma as she walked into the lounge, smiling at him and thanking him as he closed it, walking over to the reception.

"Hey Tracy," Andy said. "You okay?"

"Yes," Tracy said covering her mouth as she yawned. "Marina is taking over shortly."

"You had enough?" Andy asked.

"Not sleeping," She said. "Didn't want to come in today but Allain said they were short staff and guilt tripped me."

"Arse," Andy said under his breath.

"So they bought the bottle in the end," She indicated towards the lounge.

"Yes," Andy said. "They are waiting on the rest of the bridesmaids to show up for a speech or something."

"I am so looking forward for tonight to be over," Andy said. "Bloody hate days like this."

"Any tips?" She asked.

"Couple," Andy said. "Nothing major. One customer thought fifty-two pence was a good tip."

"Oh no," Tracy started to laugh.

"Tell me about it," Andy said. "I will put it towards a house."

"That might take a while," Tracy said.

"True," Andy said. "A very long time."

"Where are you now?" She asked.

"Got a flat in Swanley," Andy said. "Neighbours are a pain in the arse but it's okay once I remove my hearing aids."

"Sounds painful," She shook her head.

"Only last year the old girl upstairs had a faulty washing machine," Andy said. "I woke up to find water pissing down from the light, went round to talk to her and she demanded I help her and her son clean up the mess."

"Bloody hell," Tracy said. "Did you?"

"No," Andy said. " After she had reported me to the housing association several times for noise, even though I was working, so I left her to it."

"She still giving you issues?" Tracy asked.

"She left early this year," Andy said. "Council threw her out for shit stirring, turns out that was her eight eviction!"

"Eighth!?" Tracy exclaimed.

"Girl living there now is no better," Andy said. "She keeps coming round and telling me she is lonely and needs a man."

"Aww," Tracy said. "And?"

"Not my type," Andy said. "I gave her a yellow pages."

"Mean!" Tracy snapped.

"Her brother was responsible for vandalising my car!" Andy scoffed. "Told them I had it on camera, so he started being all nice."

"Bloody hell!" Tracy snapped. "I will be avoiding Swanley!"

A loud crash followed by a high-pitched pained scream came from the Lounge.

"Oh shit what was that?" Tracy said. "It came from the lounge, go and check!"

Andy run over to the lounge, pulling open the door and looking inside. The two bridesmaids are leaning over Gemma who is kneeling over, crying hysterically. The bottle of champagne is on its side, the puddle around it growing.

"What happened?" Andy asked, looking down at the blood dripping from Gemma's hand.

"The cork hit her in the face," the bridesmaid said. "It was an accident."

"Let me have a look Gemma," Andy said kneeling down next to her.

Tracy opened the door and looked in.

"What's happened?" She asked.

"Hit in the face with a cork," Andy said. "Could you get the first aid kit please, under the counter."

Tracy nodded and walked away.

Gemma became quiet and still, falling forward.

"Gemma?" Andy said. "Gemma are you okay?"

"I think she has passed out," one of the woman said.

The door opened and Lindsay walked in, looking around.

"Shit," She said. "What happened."

"Looks like the cork hit her in the face," Andy said. "Help me lay her down, she has passed out."

"Could you both leave," Lindsay said to the two bridesmaids.

They nodded and hurried out as Tracy came in holding a small green first aid box.

"Marina is calling an ambulance," She said. "She is coming down in a while."

"Thanks," Andy said as he and Lindsay laid Gemma on her side.

"Gemma?" Andy said. "Gemma can you wake up?"

Gemma mumbled and groaned.

Lindsay gentle moved her hair to the side, gasping in shock when she saw Gemma's eye. The top of the eyelid had been torn and there is heavy swelling, blood trickled down the side of her face, the colour draining from her.

"Any gauze or eye pads?" Andy asked.

Tracy opened the box, finding a couple of packs of eye pads and opened them, placing them back-to-back and handing them to Andy who placed them over Gemma's eye.

"Sorry!" Andy said as Gemma hissed in pain.

"I want my mum," She sobbed. "Please call my mum."

"I will do that for you," Lindsay said holding Gemma's hand.

"Do you know what happened?" Andy asked as he applied tape to the edges of the eye pads, taking care not to press down too much.

"She undone the top," Gemma sobbed. "And knocked the bottle over!"

"Can you stand up?" Andy asked.

"I feel sick," Gemma said.

"Let's stand you up," Andy said. "Make you more comfortable."

Andy and Lindsay carefully pulled her up and sat her on the couch, Tracy sat down next to her, holding her against her.

"I am going to keep an eye on reception," Andy said. "Are you both okay to stay with her?"

"Yes," Tracy said.

"I will get cover for the bar," Lindsay said. "And get your phone for you, then we can call your mum yeah?"

Gemma nodded, mumbling as her hand went to her face.

"Don't touch it," Tracy said. "Do you want some water?"

Gemma nodded.

"I will get it," Andy said. "And clean up," he said, looking at his bloodied hands. "Will also get rid of this," He bent down, picking up the champagne bottle and leaving the lounge, closing the door behind him.

The man walked into reception, average height, stocky with black heavily gelled hair. He is wearing a dark grey suit, electric blue waistcoat and matching tie. He has a small brown and white duck under his arm and a bottle of beer in the other hand.

"Service!" He yelled as he approached the reception.

"Can I help you?" Andy said appearing at the reception counter and then noticing the duck. "Why have you got a duck?"

"I found it!" He laughed.

"Let it go," Andy said.

The man lifted his arm and the duck dropped, running around reception flapping its wings and quacking hysterically as it tried to find its way out of the reception.

"Why?" Andy groaned.

"I am the best man!" He said loudly. "I want a beer!"

"Bar to your left," Andy said.

"Can you grab me one?" He asked. "Save me walking in there."

"Sorry I am busy," Andy said.

"Busy doing what?" He challenged.

"Busy catching a duck because a moron brought it into the hotel," Andy scoffed. "If it decides to shit anywhere, we will charge you."

"Oh," He said.

"And if anything happens to the ducklings," Andy said. "You are getting a visit from the police!"

Andy left the office and saw the duck heading towards the restaurant. Lindsay stood by the door, turning and looking at the duck and then at Andy.

"Close the door!" Andy said.

Lindsay closed the door and the duck stopped, quacking softly.

"It's okay," Andy said. "I am going to take you back to your kids," He said. "Unless you would like a room to escape them for a day or two?"

The duck turned and faced Andy.

"Shit," Andy said. "Did you just understand me?!"

A elderly woman walked out from the toilets and stopped, looking at the duck and then at Andy. She is wearing a black skirt, white blouse and a black jacket. Her short grey hair is curly and recently permed.

"Did you order the duck?" Andy said.

The woman smiled and chuckled.

"I just need to grab it," Andy said.

"Are you going to hurt it?" She asked.

"No," Andy said. "This one is a mother, a moron from the wedding thought it would be funny to grab it."

"What a childish person!" She said. "Let me help."

The woman reached for a table by the door, where there is a bowl of bread. She picked up a slice and carefully bent down, offering it to the duck.

"That might work," Andy said. "The customers hate it, but the wildlife don't care."

The duck moved closer to the woman, taking the bread from her hand. Andy walked up behind it slowly and suddenly reached down, grabbing the duck.

The duck let out a prolonged screaming quack, attempting to get away from Andy.

"Chill out Donald!" Andy said. "I am trying to help!"

Andy bent down and picked up the small piece of bread.

"Even got you dinner!" he scoffed.

Andy turned around and Bradley, the restaurant manager stood by the reception office.

"What are you doing?" He said. "I forget your name."

Bradley is a tall and slim ban with long black hair tied up at the back, wearing a black suit and a multi-coloured waistcoat and tie. He never displayed emotion and hardly moved his lips when he spoke, making it hard for Andy to understand him.

"The best man from the wedding decided to be an idiot and bring this into reception," Andy said.

"Why didn't you stop him?" Bradley asked.

"Didn't really get a chance," Andy said. "Getting rid of it now."

"You are lucky that didn't get into the restaurant," Bradley said. "Otherwise it would not have looked good for you," He shook his head and sighed. "Why is the door closed?"

"I asked Lindsay to close it to stop the duck getting into the restaurant," Andy said.

"Well I am glad she had the sense to do the right thing," Bradley said. "You have much to learn."

Bradley kept his distance as he walked past Andy, waving his hand to indicate Andy to go away.

"Let's get you back to your children before this horrible man eats them for dinner," Andy said to the duck.

"Do behave," Bradley said. "We have an image to maintain here."

"I know," Andy said. "But the duck isn't impressed."

Andy walked away, making his way to the entrance.

"Bloody robot," Andy muttered under his breath as he opened the door by leaning against it.

He walked down the steps and looked around before walking round to the Barn house towards the lake.

Mark stepped out from the bar entrance, walking over to Andy with the duck tucked under his arm.

"I don't want to know do I?" Mark asked.

"Bloody best man!" Andy said. "Brought it into reception and let it go!"

"Idiot!" Mark moaned. "This night has been the worst!"

"Things bad?" Andy said, letting the duck go and watching as it half flew and ran towards the lake, quacking like a lunatic.

"The groom is drunk," Mark said. "Probably on something too but keeps picking arguments."

"I sorted out the lounge," Andy said. "Might take a while for the carpet to dry but got the blood out."

"Anyone heard from her?" Mark said. "The new girl?"

"Gemma," Andy said. "No."

"I saw the paramedic pull up," Mark said. "Was worried for a moment, I thought you had finally killed someone."

"What do you mean finally?" Andy scoffed.

"You telling me you already have?" Mark asked curiously.

"Not telling you," Andy smiled. "I need to go and wash my hands."

"Who is in reception while you are playing with ducks?" Mark asked.

"Marina," Andy said. "She popped to get a coffee."

Marina stood at the reception, using the computer. She is short and stocky, wearing a navy-blue suit, her shoulder length black hair brushed back over her ears.

"That is our last room gone," She said to Andy. "I don't envy you guys working tonight!"

"Tell me about it," Andy said. "Bloody hate weddings."

"Not getting married then?" She asked.

"Not a chance," Andy said. "The ladies only like me when they want something or are on the rebound."

"Oh dear," She shook her head.

The telephone began to ring and Andy jumped, groaning.

"Hello," Marina said picking up the telephone. "Reception here."

Andy looked at Marina, hoping that he didn't have to do any room deliveries.

"Yes he is here, hold on," Marina said, handing the telephone to Andy.

"I cannot hear on the phone," Andy said. "Could you relay the message?"

"Oh Sorry," She laughed. "I forgot," She put the phone to her ear. "Hi Mark," She said. "What is the message?"

Andy looked at Marina as she nodded and smiled through the conversation, finishing with a gasp and putting the telephone back on the hook.

"Well that isn't good," She said.

"What?" Andy asked. "What did Mark have to say?"

"The wedding has finished at the Barn House," Marina said, looking at her watch. "There was a fight."

"You are kidding!" Andy scoffed.

"The bride and the bride's mother are heading over," Marina said. "Mark said could you look after them."

"When are they coming over?" Andy asked.

"Now," Marina said.

"Did he say what happened?" Andy asked.

"No," Marina said. "Just that there was a fight."

"Bloody hell," Andy exclaimed. "Not something you want on your wedding day."

Andy turned the monitor channel to display the front of the hotel, looking at the two figures walking towards the entrance, one in a wedding dress.

"Here they come," Andy said.

"Will you be okay looking after them?" She asked.

"Yes," Andy said. "Will be fine."

"I knew it was going to be one of those evenings," Andy said. "I had the best man kidnap a duck!"

"I heard about that," She said. "Bradley told me about it, he was annoyed with you."

"I didn't do anything other than catch it," Andy said. "I don't think he likes me much."

"Don't take it personally," she said. "He doesn't like anyone."

"Wonder how Gemma is?" Andy said.

"Poor kid," Marina said. "The bridesmaids were ever so upset."

"Those bottles are lethal," Andy said. "Few months ago someone got me in the nuts with a champagne cork."

"Oh no!" Marina groaned.

"I walked funny for a few hours," Andy said laughing.

The bride and the mother of the bride walked into reception. The bride in a figure-hugging white wedding dress, simple and short. He long blonde hair, platted and styled, her face is red and her eyes wet. The mother, short and thin is wearing a dark blue dress, a man's jacket over her shoulders. Her lip is cut and she has a red mark on the side of her face.

They both walked up to the reception counter.

"Good evening," Marina said. "How can I help you."

"Could we sit somewhere quiet?" The bride's mother said. "Things have gone a little wrong tonight."

The bride started to cry.

"Oh I am very sorry," Marina said. "Andy could you help?"

"Hi," Andy said. "Our lounge is free if you want to use that?" He said pointing to the front of reception. "The floor is still wet after the accident earlier."

"That is not a problem," The bride's mother said. "We heard about the poor girl, how is she?"

"Still waiting to hear," Andy said.

"Please keep us informed," The bride said. "We feel responsible."

"It was an accident," Andy said. "Would you like some drinks?"

"Could we get some tea?" The bride asked. "Please?"

"Of course," Andy said.

"I don't want John over here," She said.

"John?" Marina said in confusion.

"Her husband," The mother said.

"Ex-husband," She snapped. "It's over!" She sniffled.

"Now don't be rash," The mother said. "This can be sorted out."

"He attacked you mum!" She said. "That isn't the kind of man I want to be with!"

Andy looked into the bar, noticing people were watching.

"If you would like to go into the lounge," Andy said. "I will make sure John stays away from the hotel," He said smiling. "I will also update my colleague."

"Thank you," The bride said, putting her arm around her mother and leading her into the lounge, closing the door behind them.

"Well shit!" Marina said. "Getting married and breaking up on the same day cannot be good!"

"Could you call Mark," Andy said. "And warn him about John and the Brides request?"

"Yes," Marina said. "Do you want me to let the bar know about the drinks?"

"No," Andy said. "I will do it."

Andy stood by the bar waiting to be served. Charlotte is behind the bar along with Lindsay.

"Hey Andy," Lindsay said.

Charlotte avoided eye contact with Andy, pretending she hadn't noticed him.

"Hi," Andy said. "Could I get tea for two please," He said.

"Sure," She smiled. "Want me to charge it?"

"No," Andy said. "It's on the house for the bride and mother."

"They are drinking tea?" Lindsay scoffed. "It's a wedding!"

"Long story," Andy said. "I will tell you about it later."

"Okay," Lindsay said. "I called Gemma earlier, her mum answered."

"How is she?" Andy asked.

"Not good," Lindsay shook her head. "Her eye is a mess apparently so they are waiting for a specialist."

"Poor girl," Andy said. "Hopefully they can sort her out, she was in so much pain."

"Hi Andy," Charlotte said.

"Hey," Andy nodded in acknowledgement.

"Got time to talk?" She asked.

"Not at the moment sorry," Andy said. "Too busy."

"What about after?" She said.

"I don't really want to talk," Andy said.

"What is going on with you two?" Lindsay said in concern.

"Nothing," Andy said. "I just made a mistake."

Lindsay looked at Charlotte and then at Andy, groaning and shaking her head.

"This is the reason I don't date," She scoffed. "More hassle than it's worth!" She placed a metal tray on the bar, loaded with a pot of tea, sugar, milk and two cups and saucers.

"I'll catch you later Andy," Charlotte said.

"You made your choice Charlotte," Andy said. "You picked him over me, which is fine, but you didn't have to play with my feelings," Andy said, turning and walking way, balancing the try in his right hand.

"What happened?" Lindsay asked. "I thought you two were getting on?"

"My dad," Charlotte said. "He wasn't happy with me seeing Andy."

"Why?" Lindsay said. "Seems like a solid guy."

"Because he is deaf," Charlotte said. "My dad said if I carried on seeing Andy, I wouldn't have a home."

"Why did you go back with the loser?" Lindsay exclaimed.

"I don't know," Charlotte said. "I didn't want to be alone."

"You are an idiot," Lindsay scoffed.

"I just cannot please anyone," Charlotte said. "No matter what I do I am wrong."

Andy knocked on the door to the lounge, opened it and popped his head in.

"Just me with your tea," Andy said. "Okay to come in?"

"Yes," The mother of the bride said. "Come in."

The lounge is fairly small, with a fireplace in the centre of the room with large vases on each end, the fire is lit. In front of it a large antique style coffee table, in front of that a large cream four-seater couch. On either end a single armchair in dark green, with a floral design. Under the full-length window is a smaller coffee table, with a single wooden chair at either end. On the opposite side of the room is a large wood and glass cabinet with various bottles, glasses and plates on display. A large mirror with a gold frame above the fireplace, reflecting the painting on the opposite side of the room of the hotel. On the mantlepiece are various small vases, fake antiques.

"Do we pay now or charge to the room?" The bride asked.

"No charge," Andy said.

"Don't be silly," The mother said.

"On the house," Andy said. "No arguments."

Andy placed the Tray on the table, laying the cups and saucers in front of the ladies.

"Would you like any cakes or biscuits?" Andy asked.

"No thank you," The mother said, moaning and bringing her hand to her lip.

"That looks sore," Andy said. "Would you like some ice?"

"No thank you," The mother said.

"What happened?" Andy asked.

The bride started to cry.

"Oh I am sorry," Andy said.

"It's not you," The mother said.

"John hit my mother," The bride sobbed.

"You are kidding!" Andy exclaimed. "Do you want us to call the police?"

"No," The mother said. "It is over and done with."

"He needs to be held responsible for what he did mum!" The bride cried. "I had no idea he was like that, in ten years he has never shown that side."

"Why did he hit you?" Andy asked. "If you don't mind me asking."

"I asked him to slow down on the drinking," The mother said. "He was getting out of control."

"Is this the guy that kept chasing the ducks earlier?" Andy asked. "Average height, stocky with lots of hair gel?"

The bride nodded.

"I know him," Andy said. "Told me where to go when I caught him peeing up a tree."

"Oh my god!" The mother said trying not to laugh.

"I am so sorry," The bride said.

"Stop crying," The mother said.

"I don't want to see him," She sniffed. "Can you stay with me tonight?"

"Can I stay with my daughter in the Bridal suite?" She said. "Of course!"

"I wish dad was here," She said, wiping her eyes.

"Are you sure about that?" The mother scoffed. "It would have been a bloodbath."

"Is your father no longer with us?" Andy asked.

"Oh it's not like that!" The mother laughed. "He has taken my sister home, she isn't well."

Andy laughed, nodding in understanding.

"Is there anything else I can help with?" Andy asked.

"If I pack his things," The mother said. "Would you be able to leave them behind reception?"

"Yes that would be fine," Andy said.

"I am sorry for this," The bride said. "It is so embarrassing."

"Stop it," The mother said. "It is not your fault, drink your tea and we can go to the room."

"I will be in reception if you need anything," Andy said.

The mother nodded and Andy left the room, gently closing the door behind him.

Mark walked up to him when he left the lounge, tapping him on the shoulder.

"Who is in there?" He asked.

"Bride and mother," Andy said. "Just sorted them out tea."

"It's a mess," Mark said. "The groom kicked off after they left and his mates had to restrain him, he is off his head."

"Drunk," Andy said bluntly. "He was a tosser earlier."

"I think he is on more than drink," Mark said. "One of his mates thinks he is on the white stuff!"

"Moron," Andy shook his head. "Did you see what happened?"

"No," Mark said. "I was helping out at the bar when it went quiet. The band stopped and the mother of the bride walked in holding her face. Few seconds later the bride was yelling at the groom and threatening to kick his head in, so I stepped in."

"He hit the mother," Andy said.

"I know," Mark shook his head in disappointment. "I found out after."

"They don't want him coming over," Andy said.

"I have told his friends," Mark said. "None of them are staying here, so they are taking him with them."

"I asked if they wanted the police, but they said no," Andy said.

"I have already called and asked for a presence," Mark said. "We also had a suspicious car in the carpark, so I want that looked into."

"Marina has the number plate," Andy said.

"How did she get that?" Mark asked curiously.

"She took it when the car drove past earlier," Andy said. "Lightning reflexes!" Andy said.

"Good hearing too," Marina called out from the counter. "Just had a call from the team saying that everyone is leaving," Marina said. "The groom apparently got into a fight with his friends and they have left."

"Oh great," Mark moaned. "So we are stuck with him?"

"Not we," Marina smiled. "Just you two."

"Is Dean not in tonight?" Andy asked. "Thought he was helping out."

"He didn't show up," Mark said. "Called him but he isn't picking up."

"Odd," Andy said.

"Very," Mark said. "I just hope he is okay."

"What do you want me to do?" Andy asked.

"Stay in reception," Mark said. "Marina is going to be here for a bit longer to help out with the phones."

"The things I do for you," Marina rolled her eyes.

"It's your own fault for being the duty manager," Mark laughed.

"Well you could have had Allain helping out," Marina smiled in sarcasm.

"Pass," Andy said. "He hates me."

"He doesn't hate you," Mark said. "He is just set in his ways."

"Discriminative and stuck up his own arse?" Andy said bluntly.

Maria burst out laughing, nodding at Andy in agreement.

"He does more harm than good," Marina said. "God knows how he got the job."

"Friends in the right places," Mark said. "Doubt he will be here much longer."

"You going back over?" Andy asked.

"Yes," Mark replied. "Going to maintain a presence in case he decides to try his luck."

Andy nodded in agreement.

"Call if you need anything," Mark said and left the reception, Andy stood by the window watching as he walked over to the barn house, looking round for signs of the groom.

"What is going on?" Lindsay said.

"The groom smacked the mother of the bride," Andy said. "They are in the lounge so keep it down."

"Oh no," She said, a smile breaking on her face.

"Stop it," Andy said.

"Do they need anything?" Lindsay asked.

"No," Andy said.

"Charlotte told me," Lindsay said. "About what happened."

"That her father didn't want her dating a deaf guy so she ran back to her ex," Andy scoffed. "She took me for a ride."

"She likes you Andy," Lindsay said. "A lot."

"As I said," Andy looked at her. "She didn't hesitate to run back to the guy she claims she didn't love anymore, so I give up caring."

"Talk to her," Lindsay said.

"If he father controls her life enough to stop her dating people," Andy said. "Nothing I say will make a difference."

"I am sorry," She said.

"Welcome to my world where I am reminded daily I am deaf," Andy said. "Doesn't bother me, but everyone seems to make a big deal of it."

"Is it that bad?" Lindsay asked.

"Well hearing girls seem to have an issue with me being deaf, and deaf girls seem to have an issue with me being too hearing," Andy scoffed. "I am buggered."

"Stop it," Lindsay said. "Just talk to Charlotte."

"Can we not talk about this anymore?" Andy said. "Please?"

Lindsay nodded, putting her hand on Andy's shoulder before walking back to the bar. Andy looked out the window for a couple more minutes before returning to the reception.

Mark opened the door to reception, sighing in relief.

"You okay?" Andy asked.

"Yeah," Mark said. "Barn house is empty and there are only a couple of people in the bar."

"The bride and the mother have gone to their room," Andy said.

"Has the father turned up yet?" Mark asked.

"No, I haven't seen him," Andy shook his head. "Most of the guests have gone to their rooms. It's strangely quiet."

"Calm before the storm mate," Mark scoffed. "Calm before the storm."

"It will be fine," Andy said. "Gary and Keith are in the kitchen," Andy shook his head. "They had a full-blown argument and one of chefs had to spray them with water!"

Mark burst out laughing, his hand going to his mouth when he realised there were still people in the bar.

"Police didn't show up," Andy said.

"That is annoying," Mark scoffed. "Never here when you need them."

"Where is the groom?" Andy asked.

"If he isn't here then he must have gone home," Mark said. "Have you seen him come in?"

"No," Andy said. "One of his friends came over and asked for coffee so we sorted that, otherwise no more from any of them."

"Good," Mark said.

"Can I grab a coffee?" Andy asked.

"Sure," Mark said. "Grab me one too. Anyone in the bar?"

"No the girls have gone home," Andy said.

"Did you talk to Charlotte?" Mark asked. "You really need to talk."

"So everyone keeps telling me," Andy said. "But what will come of it?" He grunted. "Her dad doesn't want her dating a disabled guy."

"I get what you mean," Mark said. "But you are going to be working with her, so you may as well sort things out."

"Maybe," Andy said. "Coffee."

Andy left the Reception, closing the door heavily behind him.

Balancing two mugs of coffee, Andy walked through the bar, pausing when he heard yelling and banging.

"Oh bloody hell," Andy said, putting the mugs down and hurrying into reception.

Mark stood by the entrance with his hand against the door, a frustrated look on his face. The groom was outside, trying to get in, punching, kicking and running at the door. He doesn't have his jacket on, his white shirt arms rolled up, blood on his knuckles.

"Could you get me the phone," Mark said, reaching up and bolting the door.

Andy leaned over the reception, grabbing hold of the cordless telephone and then returning to the entrance to hand it to Mark.

"I thought he left," Andy said.

135

"So did I," Mark shook his head and looked at the groom. "I suggest you calm down," He warned him.

"Let me in!" He demanded. "I'll fucking have you when I get my hands on you!"

"You sure about that?" Mark said.

The groom growled and ran at the door, kicking and punching it.

"You will never get in," Mark said.

"I'll smash the windows in!" The groom shouted.

A young woman came down the stairs, average height and athletic, wearing a white t-shirt, blue tracksuit bottoms and barefoot. Her short brown hair is damp.

"What is going on?" She asked. "What's with all the noise?"

"Sorry about that," Andy said. "We have a rather agitated groom."

"Groom?" She said and walked over to the reception. "That is my cousins husband."

"Oh," Mark said. "I guess you haven't heard."

"Heard what?" She asked.

"I think it's better coming from family," Mark said.

"What happened?" She said to Andy. "Tell me."

The groom continued to kick and punch the door.

"Paul stop it," She snapped. "Why are you acting like an animal?!"

Paul stopped, breathing heavily.

"He punched the Bride's mother," Andy said softly. "So the bride ended it."

"You punched my aunt?" She raised her voice. "Why would you do that?!"

"She was winding me up!" Paul said. "She made me do it."

"You are winding me up!" The woman said. "Maybe I should give you a kicking!"

"I only give her a slap," Paul said. "Wasn't even that hard."

"She has cancer you tosser!" The woman yelled. "She is having chemo you waste of space!"

Mark dialled a number on the phone, putting it to his ear.

"Who you calling?" Andy asked.

"Police," Mark said.

"Good," The woman said. "He better not get in here, or ill kick him to death."

"What is going on?" The bride came down the stairs.

She is wearing a dressing gown over white shorts and a pink t-shirt.

"Lisa," The woman said. "I am so sorry!"

"It's okay," Lisa said. "What is happen Sandi?"

"Look," Sandi pointed at Paul. "Reckon he is rabid?"

"Stop it Paul," Lisa said. "Just go home and sleep it off before you make things worse."

"I need you to listen to me," Paul said. "Your mum has never liked me!"

"She told me to marry you!" Lisa said. "You bloody idiot!"

Paul paused, looking down at the floor.

"Why did you hit her?" Lisa exclaimed. "You know my mum is sick and you had to go and hit her!"

"It was an accident!" Paul said. "I didn't mean it."

"I saw you," Lisa said. "It was not an accident."

"Please," He begged. "Please take me back."

"No," Lisa shook her head. "I don't want to see you again, so go away!"

Paul howled in anger, kicking the door and running at it. Mark dropped the phone and groaned, kicking it over to Andy who picked it up.

"I am going to deal with this," Mark said. "Could you both stand back."

Mark unlocked the door and stood back, watching as Paul ran at it, the door swung open and came back, hitting him in the face.

Paul fell to the floor, moaning and mumbling.

"Right you," Mark said, picking him up like around the waist like a rag doll and carrying him over to a large armchair by the window. "Sit down and shut up!"

Paul stood up and walked towards Lisa, only for Mark to push him back into the chair.

"Get away from me," Paul growled at him. "I have a good lawyer!"

"Good," Mark said. "Maybe he will keep you out of prison for assault and criminal damage."

"Bullshit," Paul snapped.

The entrance door opened and two police officers turned up.

"Hi there," Mark said.

"We had a call from a member of the public," The male officer said. "Is there an issue?"

"Yes," Mark said. "This gentleman is having a hard time listening to anyone."

"Paul," Lisa said. "Just walk away."

The male officer, the same height and build as Mark walked over, bending down and looking at Paul who is close to crying.

"Are you going to be a problem?" He asked him.

"No," Paul shook his head.

The female officer, short and stocky stood by the door, writing down notes. She reached up, locking the door.

"Could someone explain what is happening please?" The male officer asked.

"Do you want me to explain?" Mark looked at Lisa who is being comforted by Sandi.

"I will," Lisa said. "We got married today, but he got drunk," She looked at him. "And is clearly on something, he attacked my mother."

"I didn't attack her!" Paul said. "I just slapped her."

"Well you have just confirmed to me you assaulted someone," The male officer said.

"It was her fault!" Paul said. "She wound me up!"

"She has been nothing but nice to you!" Lisa snapped.

Sandi started to laugh softly.

"What are you laughing at bitch?!" Paul snapped.

"If you keep up the attitude, I will be inclined to cuff you," The officer warned him.

"God help you when Bill finds out," Sandi shook her head, a grin on her face.

"That is what I am worried about," Lisa said.

"Who is Bill," The officer asked.

"My dad," Lisa said. "Paul has only ever seen his nice side."

"Lisa," Paul said. "Lisa please listen to me!"

"Go home Paul," Lisa said. "I do not want to see or speak to you today, you ruined what was supposed to be the happiest day of my life!"

Someone knocked on the reception door and Andy walked over, smiling at the female officer as she moved out of the way. Andy unlocked the door and opened it.

"Good evening," He said. "Can I help you?"

The man is in his late sixties, wearing a dark grey suit and a blood red waistcoat, his white shirt is opened at the collar. He has a thick grey beard and thinning grey Immaculately styled hair.

"I am with the wedding venue," He said. "Do you know where everyone has gone?" He looked at his watch. "I thought it would still be going on?"

"Dad?" Lisa said walking over to the entrance. "Oh dad!" She cried.

The man let himself in, grabbing hold of her as she sobbed.

"What has happened?" He said. "Is it your mother?"

"No mum is fine," Lisa said, wiping her eyes. "It's over between me and Paul."

"Don't say that!" Paul yelled. "Bill please tell her to listen to me!"

"Keep it down," The officer said. "There are guests here."

"I don't care!" Paul snapped.

"I gathered that," The officer said.

"Why is It over?" Bill asked.

Paul stood up and the officer stepped back, silently warning him.

"What happened?" Bill asked Lisa.

"He hit mum," Lisa said nervously.

"He what?" Bill said calmly.

"It was an accident," Paul said. "Please!" He pleaded.

"Paul," Lisa shook her head and sighed. "Accidently became an arse and slapped mum."

"You are a bitch," Paul scoffed. "Just like your mother!"

"Watch your mouth kid!" Bill snapped, pointing at Paul. "You do not speak to daughter and wife that way."

Bill walked over to Paul, calmly and focused.

"I suggest you go home," He said. "And think about this in the morning, and I am sure Lisa will listen to you when you are free of drugs and booze!" Bill said. "You are a mess Paul."

Bill turned around.

"Cancer is too good for her!" Paul said, grinning and stumbling.

"Sorry I didn't quite catch that," Bill said turning around.

"I said!" Paul leaned in.

Bill lashed out, punching Paul dead in the nose and sending him falling back into the armchair, yelping in shock and pain, his hands going to his nose. He then stepped back, putting his hands up in defence when the male officer stepped in, the female officer pulling pepper spray from her belt.

"Sorry," Bill said. "We came at me and I reacted."

"One thing you don't know about my dad Paul," Lisa said. "Is that he was boxing men twice his weight before your parents even dreamed you up!"

"I am prepared to drop you home," The officer said. "But if this continues, I will arrest you for disturbance and being a general nuisance!"

Bill walked over to Lisa, shaking his hand.

"That hurt," He said looking at his bloodied knuckle. "He is all mouth!"

"I am sorry dad," Lisa said.

"Behave," Bill said. "Where is your mum?"

"Asleep," Lisa said.

"I am proud of you Sandi," Bill smiled.

"Why," Sandi said.

"How you didn't kick his head in," Bill scoffed. "I will never know."

"Can I offer you drinks?" Andy said. "On the house obviously," Andy looked at Mark who nodded.

"I'll leave you to it," Sandi said. "I am up early and really need to sleep," She looked at Paul. "Now he has stopped screaming like a toddler, maybe I can."

"Bitch," Paul mumbled.

"One more word from you and I will arrest you," The officer said. "Go on, give me a reason to handcuff you and drag you to my car!" He pointed at Paul. "I will even let my colleague here pepper spray you, she is itching to try it out, you going to behave?"

Paul nodded.

Lisa and Bill followed Andy into the bar, and Mark closed the bar doors.

"Where can we drop you?" The officer asked.

"I will sleep in my car," Paul said.

"No you will not," The female officer said. "You are under the influence and will not be staying in your vehicle."

"Why?" Paul asked.

"It's illegal!" The male officer said. "You can pick your car up tomorrow once you have sobered up."

"I did everything for her!" Paul said, holding back tears.

"And threw it away by hitting a woman," The female officer said. "You have some issues to sort out and I suggest you do before you bump into someone who hits harder than that old man."

Andy stood at the bar, looking across at Bill and Lisa, he had his arm around her. He noticed Andy and gave him a smile and thumbs up.

Mark came in from the storeroom, locking it behind him.

"Had a call from the hospital," Mark said. "It's not good for Gemma."

"What?" Andy asked.

"She is having surgery," Mark said. "They cannot do anything for her eye, it's too badly damaged."

"Oh shit!" Andy exclaimed.

"Poor kid," Mark said. "Can you write up a statement before you go?"

"All I did was carried it into the room," Andy said. "The two bridesmaids piss arsing about is what caused the accident."

"We know," Mark said. "They have admitted everything and accepted full responsibility."

"Who would have thought a cork could do so much damage," Andy said. "Her face looked as if someone had shot her!"

He looked at the swing doors when they squeaked and Charlotte walked in, looking at him.

"I will let you update Charlotte," Mark said. "I need to get back to reception."

"Update me on what?" She looked at Andy.

Mark left the bar, controlling the door as it swung shut.

"Gemma has lost her eye," Andy said. "They cannot do anything for it, so she is having surgery."

"Oh my god!" Charlotte exclaimed. "Poor girl!"

"Very sad," Andy said. "Shouldn't have happened."

"I hear you helped her," Charlotte said. "That was good of you."

"I didn't do much," Andy said. "Just common sense."

"Proof we need a first aider," Charlotte said.

"And a first aid box that is actually in date," Andy scoffed. "The pasters went out of date when I was at college!"

Charlotte forced a smile and nodded.

"Can we I talk to you?" She asked.

"Okay," Andy said leaning against the refrigerators.

"I fucked up okay," She said. "My dad loves me to bits, but he is old fashioned."

"Judgmental and stuck in the dark ages is the correct saying," Andy said. "But there you go."

"I want us to still be friends," She said.

"No," Andy said.

"What do you mean no?" Charlotte said. "Why not?"

"I thought you were better than Marie," Andy said. "But what you did was no different."

"It's not me," She said. "It's my father!"

"So you are going to let him control your life forever?" Andy said. "Treat you like an object?"

"I do like you Andy!" Charlotte said.

"No," Andy shook his head. "You don't. One minute we are having breakfast, holding hands and kissing. The next minute daddy tells you to avoid the disabled guy because he is a discriminative bigot, and then you run back to your ex-boyfriend who will probably drop you once he feels like it."

"I know how it looks," Charlotte said, sighing heavily.

"You played with my feelings," Andy said. "Girls like you, are the reason I hate myself so much!" Andy said. "Girls like you are the reason that negativity tortures me!"

"I can help you," Charlotte said. "I know someone that would like you."

"Charlotte," Andy said. "Please go away."

Charlotte looked at Andy, trying to speak but nothing would come out. She started to cry and left the bar, storming off.

"That wasn't good," Bill said approaching the bar, placing two empty mugs on it.

"Sorry you had to hear that," Andy said.

"Sorry you had to go through that," Bill scoffed. "Don't give up though," He smiled. "Life seems to have more downs than ups."

"Tell me about it," Andy scoffed.

"Thank you for looking after my wife and daughter," Bill said. "I will be making up to you."

"You don't have to," Andy said. "It's what I do."

"Goodnight," Bill said, reaching over and taking Andy's hand and shaking it. "I hope you get less grief from our crowd tonight!" He chuckled.

Andy watched as Bill walked over to Lisa, pulling her up from the couch. She waved at him and smiled as she followed her father out of the bar.

Andy walked into the store, locked the door behind him. His hand went to his face as he stifled sobs, crying softly.

SEVEN

Walking around the front of the Barn House, Andy shone the torch through the windows, checking what he could see. He then checked the door was locked, rattling it several times.

"Locked like it was earlier," He said to himself. "I swear Mark just wants me out of the way." As he walked back towards the hotel, he turned around and looked up at the apartment when something caught his eye.

"What was that?" Andy said.

He looked at the double balcony windows, noticing an outline of someone walking back and forth, lights flickering.

"The apartment is empty," Andy said. "Who is that?"

He walked around the side of the Barn house and walked up the metal fire exit staircase, looking through the window into the apartment kitchen and noticing a light was on in the hall.

Suddenly Marina walked into the kitchen, wearing only white underwear. She is muscular and toned, her hair wet from having showered. She looked towards the window and screamed in fright, attempting to cover herself before running away, closing the kitchen door behind her.

"Shit!" Andy yelped and stumbled, falling backwards and losing his footing. He slipped down several stairs on his backside, shouting out in pain and surprise. Laying at the bottom of the steps for several seconds, his hand on his lower back as he hissed in pain and groaned.

After a minute he got up, picked up the torch and hurried over to the hotel entrance, looking back at the Barn House apartment as the main room lights came on.

"Bollocks," He muttered and let himself into reception and walked up to the counter where Mark stood, looking at him curiously.

"What's with you?" He asked.

"Who is staying in the apartment?" Andy asked.

"No one," Mark said. "Been empty all week."

"Well I saw movement," Andy said. "And decided to investigate."

"And?" Mark said.

"Saw a near nude Marina," Andy said. "So I will probably be looking for a new job!"

"Marina?" Mark said picking up a clipboard with a printout. "She is on leave."

The telephone started to ring.

"Wait there," Mark shook his head and answered the telephone. "Reception, Mark speaking."

Mark listened and started to laugh.

"Yes it was Andy, and it isn't his fault," Mark said. "The handover states the apartment is empty all week," Mark said, nodding and laughing."

"Tell her I am sorry," Andy said shaking his head in embarrassment.

"Andy said sorry," Mark said. "I can assure you he is not a pervert on this occasion."

"Funny!" Andy scoffed.

"She said not to worry," Mark said. "And to keep it to yourself."

"I will do," Andy said. "Could I ask a question?"

"She said yes," Mark nodded.

"What is the tattoo of?" Andy asked.

Mark started to laugh.

"She said she will tell you another time," Mark said. "How come you are there Marina?" Mark asked. "I will update the paperwork in case Andy uses it as an excuse."

"You are not helping," Andy said.

"Sorry to hear that," Mark said. "Let me know if you need anything," Mark nodded and smiled. "Take care."

"Damn," Andy said. "I have to say, she has an amazing body!"

"It's a butterfly," Mark said grinning.

"How do you know?" Andy asked.

"She just told me," Mark said. "She has a couple."

"Where is the other?" Andy asked curiously.

"Don't know," Mark shrugged his shoulders.

"How come she is staying there?" Andy asked.

"Her flat flooded," Mark said. "Washing machine in the flat above leaked."

"Bad luck," Andy said.

"I bet you were behind it so you could perve on her!" Mark scoffed. "She said you fell down the stairs?"

"Yeah," Andy exclaimed. "Hurt my arse!"

"You okay?" Mark asked.

"Fine," Andy said. "I've some trays upstairs to collect so will do that before I get some food."

"Turn around a minute," Mark said.

"I am not falling for that," Andy scoffed. "I know you like looking at my arse!"

"Not this time," Mark grinned. "You have something on your back."

"Really? Andy said. "Do I look that stupid?"

"Yes," Mark said. "Just turn around!"

Andy turned around and Mark laughed softly.

"You have a black mark on the bottom of your shirt," Mark said.

"Probably from the last step," Andy said. "I felt that!

"Got a spare?" Mark asked.

"Should have," Andy said. "Unless someone has stolen that one too."

"Go get changed and then do the floor check," Mark shook his head, chuckling softly.

Andy opened walked into the staff changing rooms, groaning at the mess. Directly ahead are four toilet cubicles, the second taped up with a note stating it is out of action. On the left are six sets of double lockers, a six-person bench and hanging rack in front of it. On the right are four washbasins, one with a chunk missing out of the side and an attempt to repair it with silicon. The floor is covered in rubbish and various clothes, mainly the kitchen staff. The white walls are marked and damaged from years of use, the double strip florescent lighting barely illuminating the room.

"What a shithole!" Andy scoffed. "People are disgusting."

"Hello?" Keith called out. "Who is that?"

"What?" Andy said, noticing the feet at the bottom of the third toilet and recognising the large boots. "That you Keith?"

"Yeah!" Keith shouted.

"You don't have to shout remember Keith," Andy said. "Doesn't help me at all."

The door opened and Gary walked in, bumping into Andy.

"Sorry!" Gary said. "What the fuck you doing standing around."

"Changing my shirt," Andy said. "Look at the state of this room."

"I know," Gary said. "I refuse to clean it."

"Don't blame you mate," Andy shook his head in disgust. "Keiths in here."

"Keith," Gary said. "You having a poo or are you looking at nude photos again?" Gary said loudly. Andy started laughing.

"Where did you get that one?" Andy asked.

"Found it," Keith said. "It's mine, keeping it."

"You can keep it Keith," Gary said. "But you need to finish your chores before you bang one out."

"Oh no!" Andy groaned. "I am going elsewhere!"

Gary burst out laughing, followed by Keith who then opened the door, his belt undone.

"Put it away!" Gary said, pointing to the belt.

Keith put the magazine in his mouth and put his belt on properly, pulling it tightly around him.

"Don't put that in your mouth!" Gary exclaimed. "You don't know where it's been!"

"Did Mark speak to you about the Barnhouse Kitchen?" Andy said. "Just remembered.

"All done," Gary said. "God knows what they dropped in there but it took some bloody hard scrubbing and a ton of detergent!"

"I know," Andy said. "Took them a day to let us know about it."

Gary laughed.

"Word of advice," Gary said. "Never mix bleach with that detergent, I went to a whole different place!"

"You plonker!" Andy rolled his eyes.

"Was it you that walked it through onto the carpet?" Gary sniggered.

"No," Andy said. "One of the waiters walked into the kitchen and slipped on it, cracked his head. He then stumbled through the hall to use the phone."

"Shit!" Gary exclaimed. "Who was it?"

"No idea," Andy said. "He is new, not sure of his name, tall and skinny."

"Oh you mean the paki?" Gary said.

Keith started laughing.

"Pakistani," Andy said nodding. "You cannot say that."

"I say it how it is," Gary shrugged his shoulders.

"Besides," Andy said. "He is Indian, not Pakistani."

"What's the fucking difference?" Gary scoffed. "They both eat curry and dress weird!"

"Behave," Andy shook his head. "I am off!"

Andy squeezed past Gary.

"Will catch you later," Gary said to Andy and then looked at Keith. "Come on big guy," Gary said. "Wash your hands and finish your chores then you can read your magazine."

Andy put the tray on the small table, looking down the corridor at the fire exit, noticing the door is open.

"Bloody people!" He moaned, walking down towards it.

The man was resting against the wooden walkway that bridged the fire exit to the embankment, wearing jeans and a red shirt. Average height and slim, he has short brown hair and glasses. He is smoking, holding a mug of coffee in the other hand.

"Excuse me," Andy said. "You shouldn't be smoking out here."

"Not doing anyone any harm," He said.

"This door is alarmed," Andy said. "It set off our panels downstairs."

"Oh," The man said. "I didn't know that."

"That's okay," He said. "You must have missed the big sign that states the door is alarmed."

146

"No need to be rude," He said.

"Not being rude," Andy said. "Just trying to avoid our customers having to go outside the front of the hotel on a cold night because someone opened an alarmed fire door."

"I am going to complain," He said. "Making a big deal out of nothing."

"That is fine sir," Andy said. "Check the registration paperwork before you do," Andy said smiling and opening the door.

"I'll close it," He said.

"I need you to either come in or go the long way round," Andy said. "Legally I need to close this and check the alarm stops, so are you in or out?"

"Bloody jobsworth!" The man snapped at Andy.

"I agree," Andy said. "Bloody jobsworth keeping the customers safe!" He scoffed. "How dare I do that huh?"

"Feel free to speak to my line manager," Andy said. "I can promise you I am tamer compared to him."

The man grunted as he pushed past Andy, stopping by his room door.

"What is your name?" He demanded. "I am going to complain."

"Ivor," Andy said and walked past the man, heading back to his tray on the table.

"Well Ivor," The man said. "You may not have a job tomorrow!"

"Is that supposed to scare me?" Andy said.

"I am pretty sure a piece of a shit porter like you couldn't get a decent job!" The man said in a nasty tone. "Loser in life huh?"

"I don't care," Andy said. "At least I won't have to worry about nicotine-induced cancer."

Andy walked away, ignoring the man speaking to him, the man raising his voice as Andy got further away.

Andy looked back when he heard a door slam.

"Idiot," Andy scoffed. "Better give Mark a heads up."

Pressing the call lift button, Andy stood by the lift door listening to it.

"Come on!" He said, balancing a tray with several plates on his arm. "Not attempting the stairs with this!"

A grinding clunk followed by the lift door juddering, and then slowly opening.

The lift was small, designed for a wheelchair or a maximum of two people. Andy rarely used it unless he had a lot to carry, and with his balance being bad, he didn't want to risk slipping on the stairs.

"About time!" Andy moaned, stepping into the lift and pressing the button for the ground floor.

The door didn't close.

"Weird," Andy leaned forward and pressed the button again.

The door failed to close.

"Bloody thing!" Andy exclaimed, and as he stepped forward, the doors closed causing him to suddenly stop and jolt, nearly dropping the tray. "Jesus!" Andy growled.

The lift vibrated and rocked as it lowered to the ground floor, clanking as it stopped.

"Better get this reported," Andy said. "Sounds like it is going to collapse!"

The lift door didn't open so Andy awkwardly leaned in, pressing the button and waiting for the door to open.

"Bloody thing," Andy scoffed and pressed the alarm button, getting close to the speaker as he could. After a few seconds, it crackled and hissed, and he could barely make out someone talking.

"Hi," Andy looked up at the panel, where a label said 'Lift Ref: RCHH'. "I am stuck in lift number RCHH. Nothing seems to be working and the doors won't open."

The voice at the end started to speak, very quietly and there was so much background noise.

"Sorry I cannot understand," Andy said. "I am deaf, so I am struggling to hear anything."

No response.

"Hello?" Andy pressed the button. "Anyone?!"

No answer.

Andy put the tray down on the floor and thumped the lift door several times.

"Hello!?" Andy yelled. "Someone must be able to hear me I am sure of it!"

Andy hit each side of the lift, pausing when the display flickered.

"I'll text Mark," And said to himself. "He will be able to help."

Andy pulled out his mobile phone but had no signal.

"Wonderful!" He said in sarcasm. "I really need the loo!" Andy said.

He looked down at the water bottle next to the plates on the tray.

"No," Andy said to himself. "It hasn't got to that point yet!" Andy pressed the emergency button, holding it down for ten seconds. "Is anyone there?"

No answer.

"This is gonna be fun!" Andy looked around, realising it was a sealed lift and it was warm. There was no access panel above. He tried to prise the doors open, but they were stuck solid.

Leaning against the wall, Andy looked at his watch.

"Hopefully Mark will investigate," Andy said. "He is bound to wonder why it took me so long to collect several trays," He sighed. "I hope!"

An hour had passed and Andy still had not heard anything or anyone.

"Hello!" Andy said loudly. "I am stuck in the bloody lift!"

The lift rattled and grinded, moving slightly.

"Hello?!" Andy pressed the emergency button again and the lift started to move downwards with a squeal. "What is going on with this bloody thing!"

He looked at the panel, realising the lift had gone down to a floor that wasn't listed.

"Am I going to a secret basement?" Andy said to himself. "Oh great," he said. "Like a dodgy horror movie."

The lift door opened and Mark stood there with a large bald man wearing blue overalls.

"He don't look dead," He said to Mark.

"Dead?" Andy said. "What are you talking about?"

"Someone said they were stuck in a lift and dead," he laughed.

"Deaf!" Mark corrected him. "He is deaf!"

"Oh that actually explains why you didn't pick up the phone," The man laughed.

"What phone?" Andy said and looked at the panel.

"There hasn't been a phone on this for some time," Mark said.

The man reached in, opening a to a compartment below the control panel, revealing a telephone.

"Oh," Mark said. "He wouldn't have been able to hear anyhow."

"Why not?" The man asked. "All he needed to do was talk."

"Because he is deaf," Mark said.

"I tried texting," Andy said. "But no signal."

"Sorry," Mark said. "Been looking for you everywhere."

"I showed up and gave it away," The man laughed.

"If you don't mind grabbing the tray," Andy said to Mark. "I need a pee before I wet myself!"

Andy stepped into the room, looking around.

"The basement?" He said. "Why haven't I seen this before?"

"The wine cellar is through that door," Mark said pointing. "This room is hidden."

"Cool," Andy said. "Excuse me."

"You okay?" Mark asked.

"Close to pissing myself," Andy said. "Changed my shirt but don't have any spare trousers!"

"Go!" Mark exclaimed. "I am not changing your nappy."

The man looked at Mark, confused.

"I am kidding," Mark said. "It gets boring around here so we wind each other up."

Andy opened the door to reception, sighing in relief and smiling at Mark.

"Better?" Mark asked him.

"Much," Andy said. "Lift sorted?"

"Out of action until they come back with parts," Mark said. "Not good considering that is the only one we have!"

"Just means the porters will be doing more lifting," Andy said.

"Let's hope we don't get any customers with mobility issues," Mark said. "Otherwise it will be embarrassing."

"Do we get any?" Andy asked. "Not seen a single wheelchair user since I have been here."

"Take a wild guess," Mark said. "The whole hotel is anti-disabilities. Steps leading into the hotel, no ramps."

"Crazy," Andy said.

"Someone requested a hearing loop system once," Mark said. "But upper management refused it."

"Why?" Andy said. "I don't like them to be honest and every deaf person is different."

"Because upper management are arseholes," Mark shrugged his shoulders.

"I thought all managers were," Andy said grinning. "Did you get a complaint about me earlier?" Andy asked.

"In fact I did," Mark said. "You are a bad boy, punish, punish, punish," He said sarcastically pointing a finger.

"He was a tosser," Andy said. "Didn't seem bothered about setting off the door alarm just so he could have a fag."

"I know," Mark said. "He has your full name now," Mark laughed. "Ivor Gotten!"

"Ah I couldn't resist," Andy said.

"He has my name too," Mark said. "Said he will complain for not backing him up."

"Prick," Andy scoffed.

"I pointed out the hotel fire regulations and stated I could have him removed from the hotel," Mark said. "So, he is now going to get us both fired."

"Let me know when that happens," Andy said. "Shall we give him hourly wake up calls?"

Mark laughed, shaking his head.

"Dean popped in earlier," Mark said. "While you were bunking off in the lift."

"That thing is dodgy," Andy said. "How is he?" Andy asked.

"You know that girl?" Mark said. "Chloe I think her name was?"

"Yeah," Andy said. "They are dating."

"Oh you know?" Mark said in surprise.

"Yeah," Andy nodded. "I was there that day."

"You were," Mark slapped his forehead. "I am getting old."

Andy stood in front of the counter, looking at the mirror into the bar.

"It's dead," Andy said. "Hopefully it will stay this way."

"Did you see if Gary was in?" Mark asked. "He was starting late."

"He is," Andy said. "Saw him in the changing rooms, Keith was hiding in one of the stools with a porn magazine!"

"Sounds like Keith," Mark scoffed. "He cannot read, only likes the ones with pictures!"

Andy laughed.

"That changing room is disgusting!" Andy exclaimed. "I ended up using the toilets by the bar."

"Don't blame you," Mark said. "I never go in there. Will probably need a tetanus daily if you do!"

Tyler walked down the stairs, looking out the window and then at the reception.

"Is this reception?" He asked.

"Yes," Andy said.

"How can we help you sir?" Mark asked.

"Is there a cigarette dispenser?" He asked, looking around.

"No," Mark said. "We don't sell cigarettes."

"We have cigars at the bar," Andy said. "Do you want to see the selection?"

He shook his head.

"No, not my thing," he said. "Where is the nearest shop?"

"There is a twenty-four-hour corner shop in town," Mark said.

"Can someone run there and get some?" He asked.

"I am afraid not," Mark said. "We have to remain on site."

"Shit," He moaned. "Don't think I can wait until the morning."

"Sorry," Mark said.

Bobson came down the stairs, heavy-footed and jumped down the last few. He is of average height and African American. Andy had struggled to understand him when he first met him due to his accent, however, after some practice, he started to get it. He is wearing a light grey suit and is clean-shaven and bald. Tyler is Korean, short and skinny, with long black hair and a beard, also wearing a light grey suit.

"Where is the dispenser?" He asked Tyler.

"They don't have one," Tyler said. "But there is a shop in town."

"No dispenser?" he scoffed angrily. "What kind of a hotel doesn't sell cigarettes?" He walked up to the counter.

"This one," Mark said. "We have cigars in the bar if that interests you."

"Oh that sounds interesting," He said turning to Tyler. "What do you think?"

Tyler shook his head.

"Got a price list?" Bob asked.

151

"Sure," Mark said and picked up a folder tucked away in the side of the desk, flipping over the pages and showing Bob. Tyler then walked up, standing next to him.

"They are expensive," Tyler said.

"Money is no object," Bob said, flicking Tyler on the chest. "Live a little, what do you want?"

Tyler shook his head.

"Could I get two packs of those," He pointed to the photographs on the page. "And two of those."

"Of course sir," Mark said. "Would you like to pay now or charge to your room?"

"Stick it on the room," Bob said. "Could I also get a bottle of champagne?"

Mark turned the pages in the folder, showing him a list of champagne.

"What's with those prices?" Bob exclaimed. "Could get a couple of cases back home for that!"

"They are the prices I am afraid," Mark said.

"If you want to wait here," Andy said. "I will go and get your goods."

"Nah," Bob said. "You are a bellboy," He scoffed. "You can bring them up for me."

"Bellboy?" Andy said. "What is a bellboy?"

"Isn't that what they call the porters in America?" Mark said.

"Sure," Andy said. "I will bring them up."

"Thanks!" Bob said, turning away and making his way up the stairs.

Tyler watched as Bob turned the corner, walking up to the counter.

"I will collect them at the bar," Tyler said. "He is being an arse."

"Sure," Mark said. "Do you want to meet Andy at the bar?"

Andy walked into the bar, only to find Gary pulling himself a pint.

"What are you doing?" Andy said.

"Pulling a pint!" Gary scoffed. "What does it look like you twat!?"

"You aren't supposed to be in here," Andy said. "You know that."

"Fine," Gary said putting the half-pulled pint down.

"What do you want?" Andy asked. "I'll bring it to you."

"Anything," Gary said.

"Anything?" Andy said. "You sure?"

"Yes," Gary nodded and left the bar.

Tyler stood by the bar, looking at the section of drinks while Andy removed the cigars from the cabinet, handing them to Tyler.

"Anything else?" Andy asked.

"All good thanks," Tyler said and walked away, reading the back of the cigar back.

Picking up a pint glass, Andy took a shot from several of the spirits behind the bar until the glass was three-quarters full and then topped it off with lager.

Gary returned to the bar, pushing his head through the doors.

"I smell a pint," Gary said.

"Keep it down," Andy said handing Gary the pint as he walked in.

"Who was the Chinese guy?" Gary asked.

"Korean," Andy said.

"Same shit," Gary said. "They all look the same to me!" He took a sip at the pint and exclaimed in surprise. "What is in this?"

"Bit of everything," Andy said. "Should keep you happy for a while."

"It's good!" He scoffed.

Andy noticed Marina walk up to the reception.

"Shit," Andy said. "Marina is here."

Gary leaned over the bar, looking towards the reception and Andy pulled him back.

"Dickhead!" He snapped. "Go on, out the back!" He pushed him towards the door.

Gary muttered as he opened the door, walking into the darkness.

"Keep quiet," Andy said. "Don't want to lose my job because you have a drinking issue!"

As Andy turned around, Marina walked through the double doors.

"Who were you talking to?" She asked Andy.

"Myself," Andy said. "I am nuts like that."

Andy returned to the bar, collecting the dirty glasses.

"Everything okay?" Marina asked.

"Yes," Andy said. "Sorry about earlier."

"It's okay," She laughed. "Mark explained everything, it's partially my fault."

"It's cool," Andy smiled. "Got to say, nice physique."

"Behave!" Marina exclaimed. "I currently have an addiction to working out."

"Me too!" Andy laughed. "Benching mainly!"

"My bench sucks," She said.

"How come you are here?" Andy asked.

"Just checking up on things," She said. "We had some difficult customers earlier."

"Oh," Andy said. "Not heard anything, do you want a drink?"

"No thanks," She said. "I am going to do some work upstairs. Will grab a coffee from the kitchen first."

"Sure," Andy said. "Let me know if you need anything."

"Thank you," She said. "Is Gary on by the way?"

"Yes," Andy said. "Last in the kitchen when I saw him."

"He creeps me out," She shivered.

"He creeps everyone out," Andy said smiling.

"Have you heard the story?" She whispered. "About the woman that took him home?"

"The one with the third leg?" Andy said and laughed.

"Yes!" She laughed loudly, covering her mouth. "Did they?"

"What?" Andy asked.

"You know?" She said. "The deed?"

"Oh!" Andy said. "I don't want that image in my head!"

"Neither do I," Marina walked to the bar doors. "I'll be upstairs if needed."

Marina walked out of the bar, letting the doors swing and squeal aggressively.

"Need to find some oil for that," He said, looking at the door. "You can come out now," Andy said.

The door opened and Gary looked in, hesitating.

"She has gone," Andy said.

"What did she want?" Gary asked. "What was she talking about? Cannot hear shit in there!"

"Just work," Andy said. "She was checking everything was okay with the problem customers."

"Chuck them out!" Gary said.

"I wish," Andy said. "I need to eat."

"Chef left out some ploughman sandwiches for you," Gary said with a smile, drinking his pint.

"Oh that is good of him," Andy said. "I am looking forward to those."

"I ate them," Gary burst into hysterics.

"Choke on your drink," Andy said. "it will be your last!"

The telephone started to ring and Mark picked it up.

"Reception," He said. "How can I help you?"

Andy sat down, picking up a mug of cold coffee.

"I apologise for that," Mark said.

Andy looked up, trying to listen.

"I will ask them to keep it down," Mark said. "Apologies again," Mark put the phone down.

"Problem?" Andy said.

"Yeah," Mark sighed. "Noise from one of the rooms again, the room above is complaining."

"Want me to go and have a word?" Andy said. "I need fresh coffee and food after."

"Nachos?" Mark said licking his lips. "I am hungry!"

"Thought you were on a diet?" Andy said.

"Do you want to fall out?" Mark asked. "I could have you do the brasserie floor again."

"Surely you need the exercise," Andy said.

"I'll put you with Gary and Keith for a week," Mark said.

"God no!" Andy shook his head. "They will try and get me into the National Front!"

"They aren't that bad!" Mark said quietly.

"They are," Andy said. "So bad that even the National Front would ban them."

"Go do some work!" Mark said, pointing to the stairs.

Andy laughed, sticking up his middle finger when he left the reception.

Knocking on the door, Andy took a deep breath.

No one answered the door.

"I can hear the television," Andy said quietly. "I know you are in there."

He knocked again, slightly harder and stepped back.

The door opened and Andy recognised the man from earlier in the reception. Two men, one black and one Asian visiting from the states had met up with a couple of young women at the hotel and then invited them up to their room for food and drinks. Andy had asked the girls for identification due to not being sure of their ages, but they assured him they were not drinking alcohol and were not staying at the hotel.

The two girls are sitting on a bed, both in blue jeans and t-shirts, one is blonde and slim, the other athletic with black hair.

"Yeah," Bob said. "What you need?"

"Hi," Andy smiled. "We have had a complaint about the noise," Andy explained. "Unfortunately the walls are thin, but could you keep it down please, it is getting late."

"Yeah sure," He said. "Sorry man."

"Do you need anything?" Andy asked.

"No man," He said. "All good, what's your name?"

"Andy," He said.

"I am Bobson, but prefer bob," Bob said. "That is Tyler," He pointed to the Korean man. "What are your names again?" He pointed to the girls.

"I am Jo," Jo said and waved. "This is Lesley," She said as Lesley smiled.

"Nice to meet you all," Andy said.

Bob nodded and closed the door, Andy stepped back when it nearly hit him.

"Arsehole!" He muttered and walked away.

Andy looked into the kitchen, noticing Mark speaking to Keith.

"All done?" Mark asked.

"Yeah," Andy said. "Hopefully they won't cause any issues."

"The girls still up there?" Mark asked.

"Yeah," Andy said. "Bit odd."

"Why?" Mark asked.

"Not sure," Andy said. "It feels off."

"We will have to keep an eye on it," Mark said. "I am going to give Keith a lift home," Mark said. "He has hurt his back."

"Sure," Andy said. "When you going?"

"In a minute," Mark said. "Will let you eat first and then shoot off."

"Thanks," Andy said.

"Nachos ready in the microwave for you," Mark said.

"Brilliant!" Andy said and walked over to the microwave, starting it as Mark and Keith left to go to the bar.

Andy sat against the worktop, watching the cheese melt over the nachos. The microwave humming along with the loud wiring of the extractor fans and the dishwasher.

"I am really looking forward to this," Andy said.

"Hey man!" Bob said at the top of his voice and slapped Andy on the shoulder, causing him to yelp in fright and suddenly turn around.

"Jesus Christ!" Andy snapped. "What are you doing in here?"

"Looking for someone," Bob said. "No one in reception."

"Mark is in the bar," Andy said breathing heavily. "And I am here having a heart attack!"

"Did you not hear me?" Bob asked.

"No," Andy said.

"Why?" Bob said. "I was loud."

"I am deaf," Andy said.

"No you are not," Bob scoffed. "You don't seem the type."

"What do you mean by type?" Andy asked.

"You don't talk funny," Bob said. "Or do that sign language stuff."

"I lipread," Andy said. "What can I help you with?"

"We need more drinks," Bob said. "Can you come up?"

"If you go to the Bar," Andy pointed to the door. "Mark will be able to help you."

Bob nodded, gave Andy a thumbs up and walked away. Andy watched as walked to the door, looking both ways.

"Straight ahead," Andy said loudly.

"You what?" Bob called out.

156

Andy sighed and talked to the door, opening the second door to the bar.

"There you go," Andy said pointing to Mark at the bar. "Found him in the kitchen," Andy said. "He wants drinks."

Mark gave Andy a thumbs up.

"Cheers mate," Bob smiled. "See you around."

Andy rushed back into the kitchen, groaning when he noticed the smoke coming out of the microwave.

"No!" Andy moaned. "Not my day!"

Andy opened the microwave, looking at the smoking crisp cheese.

"Doesn't look too bad," Andy said. "It will do."

Andy was sat in reception, his feet up on the worktop as he read a book, struggling to keep his eyes open.

"Come on Mark," he said to himself. "Where are you dropping him off, Brighton?!"

Andy looked at his watch.

"An hour?!" He scoffed. "Bet the git has fallen asleep in his car again!"

Andy jumped in fright when a man suddenly appeared at the reception desk, tapping the counter impatiently. Tall and slim wearing black shorts, grey t-shirt. He has short blonde hair and a well-trimmed goatee.

"Hello?" He said. "Is anyone here."

"Coming," Andy said, putting down the book and getting to his feet, hurrying around. "How can I help sir?"

"I called down earlier about noise coming from the room below me," He said. "It's still loud."

"I am sorry to hear that," Andy said. "I did speak to them but must have gone in one ear and out the other. I will speak to them again," Andy said. "Could I get your room number?"

"Of course," The man said holding up a key. "I have to be up early and it's driving me nuts!"

"I understand," Andy said. "I will sort it out."

"Thank you," He said. "I would be happy to move to another room, but why should I?"

"I fully agree," Andy said. "I will go straight up and speak to them, and again, I apologise."

"Not your fault," The man said smiling. "Thank you."

Andy watched as he walked away and then sighed in frustration, picking up the master keys he then locked the reception and made his way back to the room in respect.

Andy got to the door and breathed in heavily, shaking his head as knocked on the door, stepping back and waiting.

No answer.

He knocked again, louder.

The door is pulled open aggressively and Bob stood there, anger in his face.

"What do you want?" He snapped.

"You really need to keep the noise down," Andy said. "I could hear it down the corridor."

"Not deaf then are you?" He scoffed. "Knew you were lying man."

"We have other customers to think about," Andy said. "If you don't keep the noise down, I will have to ask you to leave."

"You can try," Bob scoffed and laughed. "I wouldn't if I were you though."

"Well you aren't me," Andy said. "So keep it down yes?"

"No," Bob shook his head. "You are beginning to piss me off man."

"Sorry you feel that way," Andy said. "But like I said, we have other customers."

"Don't come here anymore," Bob said. "I don't want to see you anymore."

"Then keep the noise down," Andy said. "It's a hotel, not a theme park."

Bob pulled up his shirt to reveal a handgun tucked into his belt.

"Don't piss me off," Bob said. "I ain't afraid to use this!" He said leaning forward. "No go away little man and get on with whatever it is you do, bitch."

"No need to be rude," Andy said, biting down on his tongue.

"Look," Bob said while doing mock sign language. "Walk away boy," He said slowly. "Go back down to your little office and stay out of my face, or else," He emphasized and waved his hands around patronisingly.

He slammed the door in Andy's face and he stood there for a minute, thinking.

"Okay," Andy nodded.

Mark was in reception when Andy came down the stairs.

"You got the keys?" He asked Andy.

"Yes," Andy said and threw the keys to Mark who caught them, walking round and letting himself into reception.

Andy followed, let the door closed and stood there.

"Sorry I was late," Mark said. "I took him to hospital, poor sod was crying in pain!" Mark said and looked up. "You okay?"

"We have a problem," Andy said.

"What?" Mark said.

"A customer came down to complain about the noise," Andy said. "Same one that called down."

"Again!?" Mark exclaimed.

"Yes," Andy nodded. "So I went up and spoke to them again."

"Asian and black guy?" Mark asked. "Same guy from the bar earlier?"

"That is the one," Andy said. "He threatened me with a gun."

"He what?" Mark said looking at Andy, concern in his face."

"Showed me a gun in his belt and said he isn't afraid to use it," Andy scoffed, chuckling softly.

"Was it real?" Mark asked.

"Cannot tell," Andy said. "But as far as I am concerned, he threatened me with it," He paused. "So."

"You okay?" Mark asked him.

"I am fine," Andy said. "I grew up with arseholes so that was a walk in the park!" Andy laughed.

"I am calling the police," Mark said.

"Good," Andy said. "Hopefully they will shoot his kneecaps out."

Andy stood by the door when the three police officers walked into the reception, two male officers in tactical gear, armed. A plain-clothed female officer led them in, making a beeline towards Andy leaning against the radiator. Taller than Andy and slim, with long black hair, tied up at the back, so tight that it looked uncomfortable.

"Andy?" She asked. "Mark has explained everything to us."

"Okay," Andy said.

"Do you know what prompted the treats?" She asked him.

"I guess he didn't like being told to keep the noise down," Andy said. "I went to the rooms a couple of times."

"Did you see the full weapon?" She asked, writing down notes.

"I saw the grip and slide," Andy said. "But it was tucked into his belt, however," He paused. "I am pretty sure it's a fake."

"Thank you," She said. "It probably is a fake, but we don't want to take chances, my colleague will explain to you what happens next, and if you are comfortable assisting him that would be great."

"Sure," Andy said and walked over to the officer who explained what the next move was.

Andy stood outside the hotel room, looking at the armed officers on either side of the door. One of them nodded, giving Andy a thumbs up.

Andy could hear the music pounding, the laughter from the girls and the Asian man's voice.

"Noisy as always," Andy whispered.

Andy knocked on the door and stood back.

No answer.

"Hello?" Andy knocked on the door again.

The door opened slightly and bob looked out.

"Got the drinks?" He asked.

"No," Andy said. "I need to point out the noise issues again.

The door is aggressively yanked open and before Bob had a chance to speak, Andy stepped back and the two officers burst into the room.

"On the floor," One of them yelled. "Hands behind your head!"

The girls threw themselves on the floor, screaming and Tyler, drunk, slowly sunk to the floor, his hands behind his head.

"It isn't real!" Bob yelped. "Don't shoot it isn't real, it's a fake!" He panicked. "I was only playing!"

"Hands on your head!" The officer yelled at Bob.

"It's a replica!" He cried out. "I was only playing!"

"Hands on your head!" The officer said. "Do not move or I will shoot!"

The second officer slowly moved forward, pulling the gun from Bob's belt and examining it, confirming to his colleague it was a replica.

"Are there any more weapons in this room?" He asked, his weapon still trained on Bob.

"No," Bob said shaking his head.

"Are you certain," The officer demanded.

Bob nodded.

The girls are shaking and crying.

"I was only playing with you man," Bob said looking at Andy. "You didn't have to call the police on me man!" He said nearly in tears.

"Shouldn't have threatened me then should you?" Andy said and bit his lip, trying not to laugh at Bob's reaction, considering he went from gangster mode to a scared primary school child.

A couple of doors started to open and heads pop out, looking down the corridor at the commotion.

"It's okay," Andy said. "If you call reception, you will be given an update. Please return to your rooms."

A female officer at the end of the corridor called Andy over.

"Are you okay?" She asked.

"I am fine," Andy said. "Had a feeling it was a fake."

"Regardless," She said. "We still have to treat it as a real weapon. Is there somewhere we can take the girls?" She asked. "I have a feeling they made some bad choices."

"The lounge," Andy said. "Also we couldn't confirm their ages for alcohol," Andy said. "Not sure how old they actually are."

"We will find out," The officer said. "Would you join your colleague, if we need anything, we will contact you, thank you for your time."

Andy nodded and walked away, laughing quietly as he descended the stairs, looking at Mark behind the counter on the telephone.

"Yes," Mark said. "I apologise for that and can confirm there is no danger," Mark nodded. "Thank you."

He put the telephone down and shook his head.

"Wow," Mark said. "Those that heard the police are in a panic."

"You should have heard him," Andy sniggered. "Screamed like a girl!"

"I heard," Mark said. "You okay?"

"I am fine," Andy said. "Just going to go grab a drink."

Mark nodded.

"Come back here after in case the police want to speak to you," Mark said.

Andy walked up to the coffee machine in the kitchen, groaning when he realised it was turned off.

"I bet that was Gary," He scoffed.

"Gary what?" Marina said walking up behind Andy who jumped in fright. "You okay?"

"Yeah," Andy said. "All good."

"Mark updated me," She said. "I have just been speaking to the officer."

"Crazy night," Andy shook his head. "Would be nice to have a quiet night for a change so I can get a couple of hours' sleep."

Marina burst out laughing, putting her hand on his shoulder.

"You handled it well from what I hear," She said. "What has been your highlight of the evening so far?"

Andy thought about it for a few seconds.

"Seeing the hot gal in the apartment with a solid bod!" Andy exclaimed. "That is the highlight!"

"Stop it!" She laughed.

"It wasn't getting threatened with a fake gun," Andy scoffed. "It was your abs!"

"God!" Marina said. "I was so embarrassed."

"I am sorry though," Andy said. "I am not a pervert or anything, I promise!"

"It's fine," She said. "I usually walk around naked."

Andy looked at Marina, shocked.

"That shut you up didn't it," She shook her head.

"Coffee?" Andy asked.

"No," She shook her head. "I am on the early shift and coffee keeps me awake."

"How's your place coming along?" Andy asked. "Hear there was a leak."

"Leak has been fixed," She said. "My father is now sorting out the damage to the ceiling and replacing the carpet for me."

"Fair enough," Andy said. "What's the apartment like?" He asked curiously.

"Never seen it?" She said in surprise. "Thought you would have by now?"

"No," Andy said.

"I'll show you one day," She said.

The door to the restaurant opened and Mark stuck his head in.

"Could you come through mate?" He asked. "They have the girls in the lounge and one of the fathers is on the way."

"Did they get their ages?" Marina asked.

"Both fifteen!" Mark said. "Not looking good for them."

"Shit!" Marina said. "This is going to be a fun report to write up!"

"I have done most of it," Mark said. "Will need one from Andy though."

"I'll start on that once everything is done," Andy said.

"Could you find out if they want drinks," Marina said. "Ring it though and Andy and myself will sort them out."

"I think they wanted tea," Mark said. "But I will confirm and let you know."

Marina and Andy entered the reception from the bar and Marina stopped awkwardly, looking at the armed officers, their weapons clipped to the front of their vests.

"It's okay," Mark said from the reception. "You can go through."

"Don't worry," The officer said. "Not loaded."

"Thank god for that," Marina said. "Not a fan of guns."

The other officer nodded at Marina as she walked past, followed by Andy who looked at Bob and Tyler, seated and handcuffed by the window.

"Oh," Bob said. "You have tea for us?"

"No," The officer said. "Just sit down and be quiet."

"Yes shut up Bobson," Tyler snapped. "You have turned today into a shit show!"

"Both of you be quiet!" The officer raised his voice.

"Could I get some water please?" Tyler asked. "Feeling ill."

"I could get some bottled water in a moment," Andy said and looked at the officer. "If that is okay with you?"

"That is fine," He said.

"No tea?" Bob asked, laughing.

"You are an idiot," Tyler groaned. "First time I visit England and you ruin it!"

"Do I need to gag you both?" The officer said sternly. "Because I will if you keep it up."

"Sorry," Tyler said, his lip quivering as he turned, hiding his face.

Marina opened the door to the lounge as Andy walked in holding a tray of four mugs of tea and a plate of various biscuits. The girls sat on the couch, a female officer sitting on either side of them.

Jo was crying softly, her head buried in her hands. Lesley sat back looking bored, her arms crossed.

"Hi there," Marina said. "I have some tea for you."

"Thank you," One of the officers said. "Could I ask who you are?"

"I am Marina," She said. "I am one of the duty managers and this is Andy, our night porter."

"Good to meet you both," The officer said and stood up. "You are the one that was threatened."

"With a toy gun yes," Andy scoffed, placing the tray on the table."

"I didn't know he had a gun!" Jo blurted out. "I didn't know!"

"Stop it Jo!" Lesley scoffed. "It's no big deal!"

"This is quite serious," The female officer said. "Two grown men in a room with two underage girls, and a handgun replica used to threaten a member of staff."

Jo started crying heavily.

"What were you thinking?" The officer asked. "Did

"Your father is on his way," The officer said and then looked at Lesley. "We have been unable to contact your father."

"Probably working," Lesley shrugged her shoulders.

"Jo will be free to go once her father arrives," She said. "However you will have to remain until we can get hold of someone."

"Can I call my uncle?" Lesley asked.

"Yes," The officer said. "Maybe we borrow a telephone?" She asked Marina.

"Of course," Marina said. "We have one in our boardroom opposite."

"Come on then," The officer said.

"I will meet you back at reception," Marina said to Andy who nodded.

The officer left with Lesley, flanking her as they followed Marina out of the room.

"Here you go," Andy placed the mug in front of Jo, along with a jug of cream and a bowl of various sugar cubes.

"Thank you," Jo said, hiding her face.

"Biscuits too," Andy said. "Count yourself lucky, they won't let us have them!"

Jo looked up, forcing a smile.

"Anything Else?" Andy asked the officer.

"No thank you," She said.

"I am sorry," Jo sniffed.

"What was that?" Andy asked.

"She said she is sorry," The officer said.

"It's okay," Andy said. "You didn't do anything wrong, and no one got hurt."

"Still," She said. "I am sorry, I should have said something."

"It's okay," Andy nodded. "The police are dealing with dumb and dumber."

Andy left the lounge, pausing by the door when a man in his late fifties walked up to the door, knocking on the glass. Short and stocky wearing blue jeans, a white shirt and a brown leather jacket. His hair is buzzcut and dark brown, and he is clean-shaven with thin-rimmed glasses.

"I'll get it," Andy said to one of the officers who nodded.

Andy walked over to the door and unlocked it.

"Can I help you sir?" Andy said. "Are you a resident?"

"No," He said. "The police contacted me, and said my kid was here?"

"Yes," Andy said. "Please take a seat."

"I am good thanks," the man said.

The man stood by the window, leaning against the radiator.

The boardroom opened and the female officer walked out with Lesley.

"Look," Bobson said. "It's the one you like."

"What was that?" The man said.

"My mate likes that one," Bobson said with a grin. "I like her mate."

The man looked at Lesley as she noticed him and then looked away.

"You like the other one?" The man said.

"Yeah," Bobson nodded. "Would have had my way with her if that porter hadn't kept bothering us!" he looked at Andy.

The man walked over to Bobson and the officer put his hand up in warning.

"That girl is my fifteen-year-old daughter," The man said. "And only just."

"Oh," Bobson said. "She clearly is an early starter!" He scoffed and laughed.

The man growled and kicked out, kicking Bobson full-on in the face and causing him to fall back in the chair, landing heavily against the fireplace.

The officer stepped forward, placing his hand on the man's chest.

"I fully understand why you reacted that way," He said. "But I need you to calm down and let us deal with this, he will be charged."

"What the fuck man!" Bobson yelled out.

Tyler remained quiet in his chair, looking down at the floor. The female officer stood with Lesley, holding onto her arm.

"We weren't going to do anything with them," Lesley said to the man. "He said he had some money for us, and all we had to do was chill out with them."

"Did they touch you or Jo?" The man asked.

"No," Lesley shook her head. "Bobson was a pervy freak, but Tyler was nice to us."

"Shut up!" Bobson snapped.

"No, you shut up!" Tyler yelled. "Nothing would have happened," Tyler said to the man. "It was just food, drinks and talking."

"Did you know they were underage?" The man asked.

"We didn't tell them," Lesley said.

"You are a dangerous young woman," The man said walking up to her and pointing at her. "I don't want you anywhere near my daughter again, this isn't who she is, this is you!"

"It's no big deal," Lesley said. "Nothing happened!"

"But what if it did?" The man said. "What if it did?"

The man moved away, looking down at Bobson in disgust.

"Let's go back into the boardroom," The female officer said, leading Lesley into the room. "Could you show this gentleman into the Lounge?" She asked Andy.

"Sure," Andy said. "Follow me," He said, showing him towards the lounge.

"Thank you," he nodded.

Andy opened the door and Jo looked up and started to cry, the officer stood up and let the man sit down next to her, and she lay against him, sobbing heavily.

"Let me know if you need anything," Andy said and closed the door, watching as the officer helped Bobson up.

"These cuffs hurt," He moaned.

"Aww what a shame," Andy said in sarcasm and walked round to reception. "Can I wait in the kitchen?" He asked Mark who nodded.

Marina was making a sandwich on the cold food counter when Andy walked through the kitchen.

"Hi," She said.

"Need any help?" Andy asked.

"I think I can manage a sandwich," She laughed.

"No, I meant," Andy stuttered. "Are they for a customer?"

"No," She shook her head. "For me," She smiled. "Want some?"

"No," Andy said. "I'll eat later after my rounds."

"How's it going out there," She said.

"You missed the fun," Andy scoffed.

"What?" Marina said, picking up half a ploughman's sandwich, and taking a large bite. And leaned against the worktop, reaching across for the metal rectangular bowl full of cheese, taking a handful of slices.

"The father of one of the girls came in," Andy said grinning and eating. "Just as one of the guys dropped a comment about sleeping with one of the girls."

"Oh my god!" Marina said. "they are only fifteen!"

"Yeah," Andy nodded. "The father kicked him right out of his chair!"

"Which one?" Marina said.

"Which one what?" Andy asked, folding a slice and shoving it into his mouth.

"Which of the men got kicked?" She said laughing. "Watch your fingers!"

"Bobson," Andy said. "Black guy."

"I bet he wasn't smiling after that?" Marina said. "What a night!"

"I just want everyone to get lost," Andy said.

"I will be going once the police go," Marina said. "I need to assist the police, they are auditing the room and collecting the belongings."

"Need my help?" Andy asked.

"No," Marina said.

The door opened and Mark looked in.

"Sorry Andy," Mark said. "Could you open the bar?"

"Oh you are kidding me," Andy said. "Who?"

"Residents," Mark said. "Awake due to all the noise and called down asking if they could have drinks at the bar."

"Sure," Andy said. "On my way."

EIGHT

Andy stood at the reception counter. Watching the monitor as the Silver Audi pulled up outside. The heavily built man with thinning blonde hair, wearing a grey suit and a white shirt pulled a small leather case from the boot of his vehicle. He looked around before locking the vehicle and walking up the steps, his nose in his mobile phone.

"Come on," Andy said. "Hurry up so I can get some food!"

The man walked into reception, pushing the door against the wall aggressively and not looking up from his phone as he approached the counter.

"Hello there," Andy said.

"Key," He said bluntly.

"Name please," Andy asked with a smile.

The man looked up.

"Are you new?" He said. "The staff here know who I am."

"Apologies but I have not met you before," Andy said. "So I will need your name."

"I don't accept your apology," The man said. "My surname is Jones and I will be speaking to the manager about this."

"Could you repeat that?" Andy asked.

"Why?" Jones said.

"I am deaf," Andy said.

"I don't care what your name is," Jones scoffed.

"No," Andy rolled his eyes. "I am deaf, as in hearing impaired."

"Good for you," Jones said. "I said, my name is Jones and I will be speaking to a manager," He said slowly and patronising. "I don't get why they would have someone with a learning difficulty dealing with high-profile customers."

"It's not a learning difficultly," Andy said. "I just have trouble hearing."

"Is there a difference?" Jones asked.

"Yes," Andy said. "I am sorry you had to repeat yourself."

"I am still going to complain," Jones said, annoyance on his face.

"That is fine," Andy said and reached below the counter for the room key. "Is there anything else I can help you with?"

Jones took a key from his pocket, slamming it down on the counter.

"Get that parked by someone who isn't disabled," He pointed to the key.

"Sure," Andy said.

"Repeat that back to me," He demanded.

"You said, get that parked by someone who isn't disabled because I am ignorant," Andy said.

"Did you just call me ignorant?" He said, putting his mobile phone into his pocket.

"Yes," Andy said smiling.

"Why?" He snapped. "What gives you the right to speak to me like that?"

"What gives you the right to speak to me like that?" Andy asked.

"Like what?" Jones said. "I just think that disabled people shouldn't be in roles that they cannot do."

Mark walked in from the bar, stopping at the door.

"Everything okay here sir?" He asked.

"No," Jones said. "This disabled boy was extremely rude to me."

"Probably best not to call him a disabled boy then," Mark said. "I heard the whole conversation, there was no need to bring up his hearing disability."

"And who are you?" Jones said. "Do you know who I am?"

"I am Mark," Mark said. "The night porter manager and yes, we have met."

"I want to speak to someone higher!" Jones demanded.

"Just to confirm," Mark said. "You want me to wake up a duty manager because we won't let you treat staff like it's the Victorian era?"

"I will not be made out to be the one at fault," He said.

"As you will be aware," Mark stepped forward. "Our reception has a camera installed."

"And?" Jones said, looking up at the camera.

"If you continue to attack my staff member, I will have you removed from the hotel," Mark said. "So if there is there anything else I can do for you?"

"I know people high up in this hotel, that includes the owners," Jones said. "You may not have a job tomorrow."

"I know the owners as well," Mark said. "I have known them for several years, so by all means, do speak to them," Mark smiled.

"I am not dropping this," Jones said.

"That is fine," Mark said.

Dean walked in from the bar, his shirt arms rolled up.

"Hello," Dean said.

"Dean," Jones said. "I am glad to see you, could you park my car?"

Dean looked at Mark who nodded.

"Sure not a problem," Dean said reaching for the key on the counter. "Anything else?"

"You could give these two lessons on how to treat customers," Jones said.

Mark shook his head at Dean.

"I am going to my room and will call down for a food order," He looked at Andy. "I would rather he did not take my order, I am not in the mood for any more mistakes tonight."

"What mistakes have I made?" Andy asked.

"Don't argue with me," Jones said pointing a finger in warning.

"What mistakes?" Mark said. "As his line manager, I would like to know."

"He didn't hear me when I spoke," Jones said. "Not acceptable."

"Hardly his fault," Dean said. "He is deaf in both ears."

"Then he shouldn't be working with customers," Jones said. "Especially high-profile customers." Andy scoffed.

"I am a high-profile customer," He said to Andy. "And the customer is always right!"

"If you would like to go to your room," Dean said. "I will look after you," Dean smiled. Picking up his bag, Jones glared at Andy as he walked away, making his way up the stairs. Mark listened for a minute and then turned to Andy, shaking his head.

"Don't take it seriously," Mark said. "He is like it with everyone."

"Well I am not taking that shit from him," Andy said. "Anymore and I will make his stay uncomfortable."

"I will deal with him," Dean said. "His bark is worse than his bite."

"He won't have any teeth to bite with once I smack him!" Andy growled.

"Ignore him Andy," Mark said. "I have your back."

"Better make sure we drop his bread," Dean said with a smile. "And cough over his mayo." Andy laughed.

"Maybe get some foxes to eat some coffee beans and crap it out," Andy said. "Probably take too long though."

"Just ignore him," Dean said.

"Good job I am not parking his car for him," Andy shook his head. "Otherwise I'd park it into a fudging wall!"

"I'm tempted to take it for a joy ride!" Dean said grinning.

"Please don't!" Mark begged. "I don't want to have to deal with him anymore!"

"Is he always like that?" Andy asked.

"No," Dean said. "I bet he has had a bad day." Mark nodded in agreement.

"He is nicer after a few drinks," Dean said. "Last time he was here, he was tipping generously and buying drinks for people."

"Probably just hates the disabled ones then," Andy laughed.

"No," Mark said. "Don't think so."

Dean looked at Mark, rolling his eyes.

"I am going to grab a coffee before I do a security walk," Andy said. "Will be in the staff room."

"Sure," Mark nodded. "I'll be in reception."

"I will be finishing at two," Andy said. "Taking time back, just reminding you."

"That is fine," Mark said looking at his watch. "Could you do the brasserie floor tonight?"

Andy nodded.

"Try not to fuck it up this time!" Dean exclaimed.

"Alright! Alright!" Andy scoffed. "Glad me cracking my head didn't ruin your night!"

"Go," Mark waved him away. "Go get your coffee."

Andy sat in the staff room, scrolling through messages on his mobile phone. The door opened and Keith walked in, sporting a shaved head. Wearing black combat trousers, black shirt and a long black overcoat.

"Hey Keith," Andy said.

Keith nodded.

"You okay?" Andy asked him, putting his mobile into his pocket.

"Yeah," Keith said. "Where is Gary?"

"Not seen him for a while," Andy said. "Probably in the kitchen, he was going to clean the floor before he knocked off."

"Going out tonight," Keith said in excitement. "Clubbing."

"Oh right," Andy nodded.

"You want to come?" He asked.

"No I don't do clubbing," Andy said. "Not my thing."

"We are going on the pull for bitches!" Keith grunted.

"Oh," Andy said. "Okay."

The door opened and Charlotte walked in, pausing when she saw Andy before walking to the counter to make a drink. She is wearing a black blouse and black trousers, a beer label is stuck to the side of her leg.

"Hey Char!" Keith said. "We are going clubbing."

"That is nice Keith," Charlotte replied.

"You want to come?" He said. "Bring your man?"

"I am not seeing him anymore," Charlotte said.

"Sorry to hear that," Andy said. "You have a label on your leg," He pointed.

Charlotte smiled and bent down, pulling it off and throwing it into the open bin.

"It's okay," Charlotte said. "It was doomed to fail. I was stupid enough to believe he really wanted to save what we had, and make it work," She sighed. "Seems his brain wasn't doing the thinking."

"Never mind," Andy said. "Plenty more fish in the sea."

"Did you want to grab breakfast in the morning?" Charlotte asked him.

"I am at my aunts in the morning," Andy said. "Only here for half a shift."

"Okay," Charlotte nodded. "Maybe another time?"

Andy nodded.

"Want a drink?" She asked him.

"Already have one thanks," Andy said.

"Keith?" Charlotte asked. "Do you want one."

"I want beer," Keith said and laughed.

"It's tea or nothing," Charlotte said. "No beer in here."

"Aww!" Keith moaned.

The door opened and Dean walked in, hurried over to the counter, and playfully pushed Charlotte out the way.

"Hey!" She snapped. "Stop it."

"What!?" Dean said, turning around and looking at Dean. "Parked the car for your mate," Dean scoffed.

"What?" Andy said looking up.

"Your favourite customer," Dean said. "Parked the car for him."

"Sounds like he is best buddies with you!" Andy said. "He is a tosser."

"Who is that?" Charlotte asked.

"Jones," Dean said. "He is staying for a few days."

"He is the one that thinks the sun shines out of his arse," Charlotte said. "I cannot stand him."

"He is okay," Dean said.

"He wanted me to stay out of the public eye because I am deaf!" Andy scoffed. "Not much of that is okay."

"Want me to kill him?" Keith said.

"No," Andy said. "I do my own killing."

"I am going," Charlotte said. "Got to cash up the tills."

Andy nodded, looking down at his mobile phone as Charlotte left, closing the door behind her.

"Not going to give her a chance are you?" Dean said.

"What do you mean?" Andy asked.

"She made a mistake," Dean said. "She likes you a lot."

"She didn't when her ex came running back," Andy said. "Who's to know she won't go running back again?"

"What if she doesn't?" Dean said.

"It hurt what she did," Andy said. "I get messed around all the time and I am not in the mood."

"Fair enough," Dean said. "But I think you should give her a chance."

"Will see how I feel tomorrow," Andy said. "Maybe give it a while to see if she is interested or runs to someone else."

The door flew open causing the three men to jump, looking to see Gary standing in the doorway, laughing.

"You should see the look on your faces!" Gary laughed loudly.

"Keep it down!" Dean said. "Rooms above us."

"Fuck the lot of them!" Gary snapped. "You ready?" He gently punched Keith.

Keith stood up, nodding.

"Mark wants you both by the way," Gary said. "Something to do with security didn't hear what he said, wasn't really listening."

"Thanks, Gary," Dean said sarcastically. "So helpful."

Dean and Andy walked into the front of reception via the bar, stopping by the counter and waiting for Mark who is on the telephone.

"Wonder what is going on?" Dean asked Andy who shrugged his shoulders.

Mark put down the telephone and looked at Dean and Andy curiously.

"What?" He asked.

"Gary said you wanted to see us," Andy said. "Something about security?"

"No," Mark said. "He is winding you up."

"I hate that idiot!" Dean stormed off through the bar.

Mark looked towards the stairs when he heard them creak and Jones stepped down.

"Hello there," Mark said. "How can I help you?"

"Is the bar open?" He asked.

"Yes," Mark nodded. "Dean is in there now."

"Good," Jones said and walked up to the counter, causing Andy to step back. "Could someone go to my car and collect my mobile and laptop?"

"Sure," Mark said. "Whereabouts are they?"

"In the car," Jones said. "Wherever Dean parked it."

"No, I mean the laptop and phone," Mark asked.

"Back seat," Jones said, putting his keys on the counter and walking into the bar.

Mark nodded and picked up the telephone, pressing a button.

"Hi Dean," He said. "Customer on the way to you for drinks."

Mark put the phone down and handed Andy the key.

"Could you get the laptop and phone?" He asked.

"And stick it on eBay?" Andy asked.

"What's that?" Mark asked.

"It's an online auction thing," Andy said.

"I don't go online," Mark said. "Not into all that rubbish."

Andy laughed, making his way to the entrance.

Andy walked down the steps, looking down the road towards the carpark and noticing the man towards him. The man, taller than Andy and slim with a shaved head and a thick beard is wearing a black jacket, black jeans, and brown boots.

"Everything okay there?" He called out.

"Fine," The man said with an American accent. "I am a customer here."

"Yeah," Andy said. "I recognise you from earlier. Did you find the store?"

"I did," The man said. "Cannot miss it, takes up most of the town huh?"

"It does," Andy said. "Also the biggest employer in the area."

"Some strange people there too," The man laughed.

"Last night today?" Andy said. "What time are you flying tomorrow?"

"Yes," The man said. "I wish I could explore London more. My flight is at eleven."

"It was good to meet you," Andy said. "Planning to head back?"

"Yes," The man said. "But I will not be staying here, didn't like it much at all," He shook his head. "Sorry."

"Oh I don't care," Andy said. "I only work here, and trust me, I wouldn't stay here!"

"Extremely expensive!" The man scoffed. "And some of the staff are a little stuck up."

"You met Allain earlier didn't you?" Andy asked.

"I did," He shook his head. "The guy is a fucking idiot!"

"We all agree," Andy said. "I dislike him with a passion!"

"Sorry you have to work with the likes of him," The man said looking around. "You finishing for the night?"

"No," Andy said. "We have an arsehole staying and he is upset that a disabled person works here."

"A disabled person?" The man said. "I have not seen any disabled people."

"Me," Andy responded, pointing to himself.

"You?" The man exclaimed. "You are not disabled."

173

"Well in the eyes of most ignorant people," Andy said. "I have a hearing disability."

"Doesn't mean you are disabled," She scoffed. "So what if your ears don't work properly, it means you are better with other things!"

"Like killing and disposing of residents!" Andy growled.

"You are studying programming," The man said. "Computer programming right?"

"Yes," Andy said. "Doing evening classes, a change in my path."

"Stick to it," The man said. "Paths change in life, I set out to be a doctor, and now I am a lawyer!" The man laughed. "Bloody boring too!"

"You can always retrain!" Andy said.

"I can," He shivered. "I am getting a drink at the bar, join me if you are allowed?"

"Sure," Andy said. "Once I have checked the arseholes car!"

The man laughed and hurried away, waving with his back turned to Andy.

"Why can't all our customers be friendly!" Andy said. "Would make my life so much better!"

As he approached the start of the car park, Dean parked the car at the far end and reversed into the space. He aimed the key fob at the vehicle, pressing the button. There is a beep and a click as the locks popped up.

"Right," Andy said. "Let's get the laptop and phone for this arsehole."

As Andy approached the vehicle, he noticed the rear passenger window open.

"That isn't good," Andy said.

It wasn't open, it had been smashed.

"Shit," Andy ran over, looking into the vehicle.

The black leather seats are covered in glass, with no phone or laptop on the back.

"Bollocks!" Andy snapped and checked the front, but the vehicle is empty. He then checked the boot, only to find that was also empty.

He ran back to the hotel.

Andy walked up to the reception where Mark stood, looking at him with worry.

"Laptop?" He said. "Mobile?"

"Car has been broken into," Andy said. "Passenger rear window smashed."

"Oh shit," Mark said. "Hold on."

Mark picked up the telephone and pressed a button, listening on the end.

"Want me to check the others?" Andy asked.

Mark shook his head.

"Dean," Mark said. "Could you pop to the reception? Thanks." Mark put down the phone.

"Did you see anyone?" Mark asked.

"No," Andy said. "Only a customer walking back."

"Did he have anything?" Mark said. "Look suspicious?"

"No," Andy said.

Dean walked into reception, looking at Andy and then Mark.

"What?" Dean asked. "What's up?"

"The car had been broken into," Mark said. "Laptop and mobile are gone."

Dean laughed and then paused, looking at Mark.

"You aren't kidding?" Dean said. "Oh great!"

"Do you want me to speak to him?" Mark asked.

"No I will," Dean said.

Dean walked into the bar and Andy watched as he approached the bar counter where Jones sat, holding a pint.

"This is going to be interesting," Andy said.

"It really isn't," Mark shook his head. "He has a temper."

Jones jumped up from his stool and made a beeline towards reception, his face red.

"Here he comes," Andy said.

Jones stopped at the reception, looking Andy up and down and then at Mark.

"Are you having me on?" Jones said. "My car has been broken into?"

"Unfortunately yes," Andy said.

"No," He pointed a finger at Andy. "I am talking to this man here, not you!"

"Fine by me," Andy said, backing away.

"Andy checked the car only to find the back window had been smashed," Mark explained calmly. "He has checked and cannot find your laptop or mobile phone."

"Can someone else check," Jones said. "He probably didn't look properly."

"Ears are the issue," Andy said. "Not my eyes."

"You are getting on my nerves," Jones said. "Can you go away?"

"Sure I can do that," Andy said. "Rather not be in the company of someone so discriminative and backward."

Andy walked away, making his way towards the door of the reception. He opened it quietly and let himself in, gently closing the door behind him.

"Why does he work here?" Jones said. "Is it some kind of job centre thing to get more disabled people in to bridge a gap or something?"

"I don't know what your concern with Andy is," Mark said calmly. "But Andy is good at his job and I will not hear any more, would you like me to call the police?"

"No," Jones said. "I want you to find my laptop and Mobile."

"Do they have trackers installed?" Dean asked.

"No," Jones said bluntly.

"Then how can we find them?" Dean asked.

"Has someone checked that deaf person's belongings?" Jones said. "I bet he has stolen them?"

"I watched him walk down the carpark, and walk back with nothing," Mark sighed. "He is not a thief."

"Maybe check his car?" Jones said.

"He walks into work," Dean said. "I can promise you it wasn't Andy," Dean said.

"Cameras?" Jones said.

"Not in that location," Dean said. "I have mentioned before that we have no cameras there and you have been insistent on having your car in that spot," Dean explained.

"I will call the police," Mark said.

"No," Jones said. "No police."

"Do you want me to clean up the glass and cover up the window with plastic, in case it rains?" Dean said.

"Do you mind?" Jones said.

"No," Dean said.

"Just keep that kid away from me," Jones said. "I don't want to see him, he has been nothing but bad luck."

Jones walked back into the bar.

"What, an absolute tosser!" Andy said. "What is his problem?"

"Don't take any notice," Mark said. "It isn't personal."

"Feels bloody personal!" Andy said, sitting down angrily. "This job is more stress than it's worth."

"At least you get paid," Mark said.

"Paid?" Andy scoffed. "Hardly call three pounds fifty an hour pay!"

"Well hopefully you will get a response about your pay rise request," Mark said. "Allain is the person to speak to."

"He is in today isn't he?" Dean said. "Worth talking to him."

"Think I might do that," Andy said. "Is he upstairs?"

Mark nodded.

"Okay to pop up?" Andy asked Mark.

"Go for it," Mark said. "Chill out for a bit."

Andy knocked on the door, putting his ear to it and listening.

The door opened and Allain stood there, wearing a grey suit and a black shirt.

"Yes?" Allain said.

"Could I have a quick word?" Andy said.

"It will have to be quick," Allain said. "Very busy man I am."

Allain opened the door and Andy stepped in.

The office is quite small, set in the corner of a converted roof. Dead ahead is a small window with a view of the green. On either side of the room is a desk with a computer mounted on it and a chair behind it. Marina sat behind one of them, smiling and nodding at Andy as he walked in. The room is dimly lit, most of the light coming from desk lamps on the desk. Against the wall under the window are several filing cabinets, boxes in front of them full of paperwork. The floorboards are varnished wood, chipped and worn from years of use.

There are various maps, charts and photographs stuck to the wall around the room. At the centre of the room is a small fan heater.

"Not been up here before," Andy said.

"You are not missing anything," Marina scoffed. "It's depressing."

Allain pushed out a chair and put it in front of his desk, sitting down.

"So what is the problem?" Allain asked.

"Did you get my letter?" Andy asked.

"Which one?" Allain said, looking at the paperwork scattered on his desk.

"I only sent one," Andy said. "About a pay rise request."

"Did you?" Allain said. "Why do you want a pay rise?"

"My hourly rate is quite low," Andy said. "When I started I was told it would go up after three months."

"Has it been three months?" Allain asked curiously.

"It's been a year," Andy scoffed.

"What is your hourly rate?" Allain said.

"Three fifty an hour," Andy said.

Marina scoffed.

"Bloody hell," She said. "I thought porters were on more than that."

"That is a good wage," Allain said.

"Would you work for that?" Marina asked.

"No," Allain said. "But I am not a porter."

"Still," Marina said. "That is shocking."

"Andrew," Allain said.

"It's Andy," Andy said. "Not Andrew."

"We did a good thing when we took you on," Allain said. "From what I heard, it was very hard for a disabled person like yourself to get a job and the hotel changed that for you."

"Okay," Andy said. "What are you getting at?"

"You have the owners of this hotel to thank," Allain said. "For giving you a chance when no one else did."

"So they can pay me peanuts?" Andy scoffed.

"You cannot do your job properly due to your disability," Allain said.

"In what way?" Andy asked.

"You cannot speak to customers or answer the telephone," Allain smirked.

"I can speak to customers," Andy said. "And the hotel was aware of the telephone issue when they offered me the role."

"But I have seen you with customers," Allain said. "You struggle to understand simple things."

"Not true," Andy said.

"It is Andy," Allain said. "That is why your wage is very low."

"That is a little unfair," Marina said.

"So my request has been refused?" Andy asked.

"Yes," Allain said. "So the letter I have stating my wage will increase after three months is a lie?" Allain looked at Andy and then at Marina.

"I do not remember a letter," Allain said.

"You didn't interview me," Andy said. "It was the reception manager at the time."

"Well I am sorry," Allain said. "I will speak to my manager and get back to you, but the answer will be the same."

"Okay," Andy nodded.

"Andy does a lot more to help out here," Marina said. "He has solved quite a few of our computer problems, which has saved a fair bit of money."

"Really?" Allain said curiously. "Maybe that is the path you should be taking."

"I am," Andy said. "Currently studying."

"Does that impact your work here?" Allain asked.

"No," Andy said. "It doesn't."

"Let me speak to my manager," Allain said. "And I will get back to you."

"Fine," Andy said. "Marina, just so you are aware, we have a customer that has taken a dislike to me."

"Never mind," Marina said.

"His car was broken into," He said. "His mobile and laptop were stolen."

"Why did this happen?" Allain snapped. "Who is responsible."

"He left the items on the back seat," Andy said. "Dean parked the car in his usual spot for him and a while later, he requested someone collect his things."

"Who found it?" Marina asked.

"I did," Andy said. "So he now believes I am responsible."

"Sounds like an idiot!" Marina scoffed. "Police been contacted?"

"No," Andy said. "He refused the police."

"Please look after him," Allain said. "Give him drinks and food on the house."

"Dean is looking after him," Andy said. "He doesn't want me near him."

"Did you do something to upset him?" Allain asked.

"No," Andy said.

"Then why does he have a problem with you?" Allain asked.

"I will look into it Allain," Marina said. "I need to check a few things, so you can go if you want to."

"Are you sure?" Allain said.

"Yes," Marina said.

"Well I am getting back to work," Andy said. "Seeing as my pay rise was refused."

"That is life," Allain said.

"Can I have the refusal in writing please?" Andy asked.

"No I am not sure I can do that," Allain said.

"Allain he will need it in writing," Marina said.

Allain groaned.

"Fine, fine I will do it tomorrow for you," Allain said. "Please get back to work and keep our customers happy."

Andy closed the door to reception and sat down, picking up a book and opening it.

"Did you speak to him?" Mark asked.

"Yes," Andy nodded.

"And?" Mark said. "Getting a raise?"

"Refused," Andy said. "Apparently they are doing a good thing offering a disabled person a job, so they can continue to pay me peanuts."

"You are joking," Mark scoffed. "Did you mention your contract?"

"Yes," Andy said. "He is going to speak to his boss."

"I hope they agree to it," Mark said. "You are good at your job and I don't want to lose you."

"Well you know I am looking elsewhere," Andy said. "And I am working part-time in a store that would love for me to go full-time."

"That Is what I am worried about," Mark said.

"Seventy-five pence extra for day work," Andy said.

"Not as much free food and drink though," Mark smiled. "Or a cool boss?"

"Dream on," Andy scoffed. "You aren't cool!"

"I really am," Mark said.

"Nope," Andy shook his head.

Jones appeared at the reception, holding half a pint of beer.

"How can I help you?" Mark asked.

Andy hit round the corner, out of sight.

"I want to see someone higher up," Jones said. "Above you."

"Sure," Mark said. "If you would like to wait in the bar I will give them a call."

"I will wait here thank you very much," Jones said, sipping at his pint.

"Of course," Mark picked up the telephone and pressed a button, listening to the phone ring until it was answered. "Hi Marina," Mark said. "Are you able to come down and deal with a complaint?"

"Is there not a male manager?" Jones asked.

"Hold on a moment," Mark said covering the speaker. "Excuse me?" Mark asked, not sure he had heard properly.

"I would prefer a male manager," Jones said.

"Marina is the site manager," Mark said.

"What about the hotel manager?" Jones said. "I forget his name, the French guy."

"He isn't working today," Mark said looking at his watch.

"Fine," Jones said. "I'll speak to the woman, maybe she is hot enough for me to put up with."

Andy shook his head, watching Jones on the security monitor.

"Could you pop down to reception please?" Mark asked. "The customer is Jones."

Mark put the telephone down and smiled.

"On her way," Mark said. "Shouldn't be a couple of minutes."

"I will wait," Jones said.

Andy quietly left the reception, knowing which way Marina would come, he wanted to pre warn her before she met Jones.

Andy stood by the stairs, looking up when he heard Marina descend the stairs, stopping when she saw him.

"What are you doing?" She asked.

"Giving you a heads up," Andy said.

"I looked up his file quickly," Marina said. "Appears he is a serial complainer!"

"First time I have met him," Andy said. "And he hates me."

"What does he want to talk about?" She asked.

"No idea," Andy said. "But he wanted someone senior and wasn't too happy the manager is a woman."

"Oh really!" She exclaimed. "Well he is going to love me!"

The lift opened and Dean stepped out, looking at Marina and then at Andy.

"What are you two up to?" Dean asked curiously.

"Nothing," Marina said. "Jones wants to see a senior manager."

"Oh you are fucking kidding!" Dean groaned. "I thought he gave up that idea."

"Why?" Marina asked.

"He was moaning at the bar," Dean said. "Wants Andy to be held responsible for the car break in."

"But it wasn't Andy," Marina said. "Was it?" She looked at Andy who shook his head.

"He has the arse," Dean said. "Not sure how it will go as he doesn't like woman managers," Dean said holding up a hand. "No offence."

"I have dealt with all kinds of idiots like that," Marina said. "I am no stranger to this. What has gone missing?"

"A mobile and laptop," Dean said. "Left the on the back seat."

"What a bloody idiot!" Marina scoffed. "What did he think was going to happen?"

"That is what I said," Dean said. "I didn't notice them when I parked the car, so not convinced."

"So why is he blaming Andy?" Marina asked.

"No idea," Dean said. "He has taken a dislike to him since he came here."

"Odd," Marina shook her head. "I will go and sort this out. Has he said what he wants?"

"Wants the hotel to reimburse him," Dean scoffed and laughed.

"He has a fright coming his way," Marina shook her head. "Self-entitled prick."

Andy let Marina walk into the reception and after a minute he followed, diverting into the reception quietly. Dean returned to the bar, watching.

"So how can I help you, Mr Jones?" Marina said as Mark moved out of the way, letting her have the reception counter.

"My car was broken into," Jones said. "Due to the incompetence of your staff."

"Could you expand on that please," Marina said. "Why my staff?"

"That deaf guy," Jones said. "I am pretty sure he broke into my car and stole my stuff."

"Why?" Marina said. "Why would he have done that?"

"Doubt he gets access to that kind of stuff," Jones shrugged his shoulders. "Being disabled."

"Okay Mr Jones," She sighed. "I need you to stop attacking Andy over his disability and attempt to be civil, otherwise I will not be taking you seriously."

"This is why I didn't want a woman manager," Jones said. "Too soft."

"I can deal with your complaint," Marina said. "Or I can have you removed for abusing staff."

"I haven't abused anyone!" Jones snapped, slamming the pint glass down on the counter.

"Since your arrival, you have taken a disliking to a disabled staff member," Marina said. "And now a female one."

"Prove it?" Jones demanded.

"There is a camera above me," She said.

Jones looked up at the camera and then at Marina, sighing deeply as he picked up the pint glass.

"So," Marina said. "How do you want to go about this?"

"I believe the hotel should reimburse me," He said. "For my missing items."

"Unfortunately," Marina said. "We are not held responsible for possessions left in cars, the signs are clear."

"But my car was broken into!" Jones said. "Surely you have security that should be checking?"

"We do regular security checks," Marina said. "We also recommended you parked in the central carpark where there are security lights and cameras."

"So it's my fault?" Jones said.

"I didn't say that," Marina smiled. "I simply stated that we advised you."

"How on earth did you become a manager here?" Jones scoffed. "Did you use your looks?"

"I would be very careful about what you say next," Marina said.

"I don't like empty threats," Jones laughed.

"Not a threat," Marina said. "But if you drop another comment like that, I will have the police remove you from the hotel."

"How about we get back to my problem?" Jones said.

Marina took a deep breath.

"Where did you leave these items?" Marina asked.

"On the back seat," Jones said.

"Not a good choice was it?" Marina said.

"I forgot them," Jones said. "I am only human."

"I understand that," Marina said.

"You don't," Jones said. "I want the hotel to replace my goods."

"The hotel will not be replacing your laptop or mobile," Marina said. "We would be happy to call the police for you to make a statement?"

"I don't want the police," Jones said.

"Could I ask why?" Marina asked curiously.

"No," Jones said. "In fact, I am going to take this up with the hotel manager tomorrow!"

"That is not a problem," Marina said. "I stand by my decisions."

"Good luck," Jones said. "You will be looking for a new job tomorrow!" He walked away, muttering to himself.

Marina turned around the corner, squeezing past Mark who returned to the counter and looked in the mirror, watching as Jones sat down at the bar, clearly upset.

"What an arsehole!" Marina said under her breath. "Oh my god!"

"I had that as soon as he arrived," Andy said. "Staying away from him before I belt him."

"He is quite difficult," Mark said. "Much worse this year for some reason."

"Why doesn't he want the police?" Marina asked.

"Probably hiding something," Andy said. "Certainly acts like he is on something!"

"I am sorry," Marina said to Mark. "Not sure what more I can do."

"The last time we had issues with him, Allain panicked and gave him his stay free of charge," Mark explained. "So I would imagine he is aiming for the same thing again."

"Is there anything you want me to do?" Marina asked.

"Don't worry," Mark said. "We will deal with him."

"You get the rope and bricks," Andy said to Mark. "I'll kill the fucker."

"Rope and bricks?" Marina said curiously.

"So we can dispose of him in the lake," Andy said emotionlessly.

"You crack me up!" She laughed. "I am going back upstairs, anyone want a coffee before I go?"

"No thanks," Mark said.

Andy shook his head.

"Know where I am if you need me," She said and left the office.

"Just ignore him," Mark said. "I know it's annoying, but don't give him any reasons."

"I know," Andy said. "I'll just play dumb all night."

"You do that anyway," Mark laughed, reaching across, and punching Andy playfully in the arm. "I am going to the loo," He said. "Keep an eye on the desk."

"Oh thanks a bunch," Andy said. "You will come back and find his severed bloody head on the counter!"

"That is fine," Mark opened the door. "But you are cleaning it up!"

"Fine," Andy said and sat down, picking up his book as Mark left, the door softly closing behind him.

Andy glanced up at the monitor in front of him when someone caught his eye.

"Oh for fucks sake!" Andy said under his breath.

"Hello?" Jones said tapping the counter. "Someone there?"

Andy put the book down and stood up, stretching before walking to the counter.

"Hello," He said. "How can I help?"

"Is there an adult around?" Jones said, looking at Andy in frustration.

"Not at the moment," Andy said. "Only this kid," He pointed to himself. "What can I help you with."

"Dean said to come here to order food," Jones held up a menu. "Can you manage that?"

"Yes," Andy nodded and picked up a notepad and pen. "What would you like?"

"Could I have two rounds of cheese ploughman's, no pickle," He looked through the menu.

"Sure," Andy wrote it down. "Anything else?"

"Do you have plain nachos?" Jones said.

"Yes," Andy replied.

"Those as well," Jones said and dropped the menu on the counter. "Now repeat that back to me so I know you got it right."

"Two rounds of cheese ploughman's, no pickles and plain nachos," Andy said.

"Good," Jones said nodding. "Fast as you can please," Jones said, snapping his fingers as he walked away.

"With a side of spit," Andy said clearing his throat. "Will have a mint first so the cheese has a hint of minty, you twat."

The door opened and Mark walked in, looking at Andy by the counter holding the notebook.

"What did he want?" Mark asked.

"Food," Andy said.

"You okay to do that?" Mark asked.

"Definitely," Andy smiled. "Two rounds of cheese ploughman's, plain nachos and a side of spit."

"Don't," Mark shook his head, trying not to laugh.

"Fine," Andy said in disappointment. "Can I rub the bread on the floor?"

"No," Mark shook his head, mock crying. "Please don't!"

Andy left the reception, laughing.

Opening the door to the bar area with a plate of sandwiches and a bowl of crisps, Andy made his way to the bar where Jones sat. Dean was behind the bar, cleaning and sorting glasses.

"Here we go," Andy said, placing the plate and bowl on the bar.

"Took your time," Jones said looking at his watch.

"Anything else?" Andy asked, ignoring the comment.

"No," Jones waved him away.

Andy looked at Dean and rolled his eyes before turning and walking away.

"Hold on," Jones said.

And stopped and turned.

"Where is the pickle?" Jones asked.

"You said no pickle," Andy said. "And asked me to repeat it and it was no pickle."

"You misheard," Jones said.

"So I misspoke it as well?" Andy said. "When you asked me to confirm?"

"No idea what you are talking about," Jones said. "I asked for pickle and you cannot even get that right!" Jones groaned. "Why is it so hard for you?"

"It isn't hard," Andy said. "You are just messing around with me."

"Maybe customer service isn't for you," Jones laughed.

"I am not even going to bother answering that," Andy said.

"Well, what are you going to do to correct this?" He asked. "It has been one thing after another with you."

"Name one?" Andy asked.

"Because of you my car was broken into," Jones scoffed.

"Are you accusing me of theft?" Andy asked.

Jones shrugged his shoulders.

"I will make some fresh sandwiches if you wish?" Andy asked. "Or I can bring a jar of pickles out for you to look at to feel better about yourself?"

"I am the customer," Jones said. "The customer is always right."

"In all fairness," Dean said. "You have always asked me for no pickles."

"Well I changed my mind today," Jones said.

"If you want to call it that," Andy said.

"What do you mean by that?" Jones demanded.

"You are a bully," Andy said bluntly. "Going out of your way to bully me because it makes you feel important."

"I don't need to feel it," Jones said. "I am."

"Well," Andy said. "I refuse to serve you anymore."

Andy turned and walked away.

"Don't turn your back on me kid," Jones said. "I can destroy your life."

"Try," Andy said. "I have given up caring."

Andy calmly walked away stopping at reception.

"What is going on?" Mark asked.

"He is an abusive arsehole," Andy said. "Going for a walk to cool off before I smack him in the face."

"Okay," Mark nodded. "Go over to the Barn house," Mark handed him a key. "Get a drink."

Andy took the key and left the reception, looking back when Jones walked up to the counter.

Just as Andy approached the Barn house, a police car slowed down and Steve got out.

"Hey Andy," Steve said. "All good."

"Could be better," Andy said.

"Problems?" Steve asked.

"Customers," Andy said shaking his head. "You know the kind."

"Could I grab a cold drink?" Steve asked. "Forgot my water."

"Sure," Andy said unlocking the door and turning on the lights to the bar.

From the entrance straight ahead are double doors leading to the large conference hall, and on the left are stairs leading upstairs and leading down to the small basement. On the far right is a small bar against the wall, doors leading to storage and a small kitchen. The bar has four beer taps and the spirit holders on the mirrored wall are empty. The half-wooden and carpeted flooring was recently cleaned. Against the wall under a large old-style window, is a long old wooden bench. Four old brass chandeliers down the middle of the ceiling with harsh lights, some flickering.

"What do you want?" Andy asked.

"Got coke?" Steve asked.

Andy paused and looked at Steve, a grin breaking out on his face.

"Not that kind!" Steve scoffed. "The fizzy drink!"

"I think we have Pepsi," Andy said.

"Same shit," Steve shrugged his shoulders.

Andy went to the bar and poured out a pint of Pepsi, handing it to Steve who exclaimed and laughed,

"So," He took a sip. "What's up?"

"Got a customer that keeps pushing my buttons," Andy said. "Just being a bully."

"That isn't good," Steve shook his head.

"Keeps bringing up my hearing disability," And sighed. "Also had an issue with Marina being a woman."

"Marina?" Steve said. "Is that the one that lives upstairs?"

"Yes," Andy nodded. "The customer also had his car broken into tonight," Andy said. "Had his laptop and phone stolen off the back seat."

"Serves him right for leaving it on the back seat," He snapped. "What did he expect."

"Accused me of stealing them," Andy said. "I wanted to smack him."

"Has it been reported?" Steve asked.

"No," Andy shook his head. "He refused police."

"Wonder what he is hiding," Steve said curiously.

"I had to walk away," Andy said. "He was using my hearing disability and attacking me."

"Sounds like harassment," Steve said. "Do you want me to show my face?"

"Better not," Andy said. "Mark doesn't want any more fuss."

Steve downed the rest of his drink, breathing out.

"That was good," He smiled. "How about this," Steve said. "I will randomly drive up to the car park, notice the car and investigate it and then pop in?"

"That would work," Andy said. "I am pretty sure he is hiding something."

"If he is, then I will find out." Steve placed the pint glass on the bar and Andy moved it to the bottom shelf. "I do regular checks as Mark knows, so it won't give you any grief."

"No problems," Andy said, following Steve to the door. "Thanks."

"What is his name?" Steve said. "The customers?"

"Nick Jones I think," Andy said. "I might be wrong, but his surname is Jones."

"Cheers," Steve said. "See you later."

Andy let himself into reception, nodding at Mark and then sitting down. Marina stood at the counter holding a mug of coffee.

"What's with you?" Mark asked.

"Who is it?" Marina asked.

"Nothing," Andy shook his head. "Why?"

"Looking like you are up to something," Mark said.

"No," Andy said.

"Barn house okay?" Mark asked. "Clean?"

"It has already been done," Andy said. "I checked the bar, and conference hall and then did a backway security check," Andy said. "Found a customer in the staff area."

"I know whom you mean," Mark said. "He likes the quiet there and isn't doing any harm."

"Andy?" Marina said.

Andy got up and walked around to the counter.

"Yeah?" Andy said.

"Any issues with you know who?" She asked.

"No," Andy said. "Where is he?"

"Still in the bar," She looked carefully. "Drinking."

The reception entrance door opened and Steve walked in, waving, and nodding.

"Good evening," He said. "How are things?"

"All good," Mark said. "Can I get you a coffee?"

"No thank you," Steve said smiling.

"Is there a problem?" Marina asked.

"Not at all," Steve said. "We have an agreement to drive through randomly due to the break-in issues."

"I am Marina," She said. "A site manager."

"We have met before," Steve said. "Would you know the owner of the metallic grey Audi parked at the end of the front drive?"

"Yes," She said. "Why?"

"I have noticed the rear passenger window has been broken," Steve said.

Mark looked at Andy who looked up.

"What?" He said silently.

Mark smiled and shook his head.

"We are aware," Marina said. "The owner doesn't want to involve the police."

"Unfortunately," Steve said pulling out a notepad. "I need to speak to them."

"I will go and grab him," Marina said. "He is in the bar."

"Thanks," Steve said as Marina left, making her way to the bar.

"Did anyone speak to you?" Mark asked.

"Not about the car," Steve shook his head. "No."

"He has been a problem," Mark said. "I am close to putting him outside."

"I heard," Steve said.

Jones came storming into reception, looking Steve up and down.

"Yes?" He asked.

"Is the metallic grey Audi yours?" Steve asked.

"It's silver and yes it is," Jones said. "Why?"

"I have noticed the rear passenger window is broken," Steve said. "Are you aware?"

"Yes," Jones said. "And I didn't want it reported to the police."

"No one has reported it," Steve said. "I noticed it when I did a drive by."

"Why do you do a drive by?" Jones demanded to know.

"There have been break-ins," Steve explained. "So we have agreed with the hotel to do a couple of runs a night. Is that a problem?"

"No," Jones said. "I specifically said that I didn't want to take it further, I was going to deal with the hotel manager directly. I believe a disabled person that works here is responsible."

"Why?" Steve asked.

"Because I do," Jones said. "Are you able to search him?"

"Without probable cause or proof," Steve shook his head. "No."

"So why are you bothering me?" Jones said.

"Are you the registered keeper?" Steve asked.

"Why do you need to know?" Jones scoffed.

"Please answer my question," Steve said.

"Yes," Jones said. "The car is mine, purchased outright with cash."

"Thank you," Steve wrote down notes. "The car has no insurance or MOT, and the tax has expired."

"How do you know that?" Jones exclaimed.

"We have the means to check it," Steve said.

"I will deal with it tomorrow," Jones said. "Nothing needs to happen now, I am not harming anyone."

"There is already a warning against the car," Steve said looking through the notes. "You were pulled over last week and warned by London police," Steve said looking up. "You had twenty-four hours to correct this."

"Then give me another twenty-four hours?" Jones said and laughed. "I have the means and the money so I will deal with it tomorrow."

"You have already had a warning," Steve said. "I have a tow truck on the way."

"You cannot do that!" Jones snapped. "I will be speaking to my lawyer!"

"That is fine," Steve said. "Your lawyer will also update you that driving around without insurance, tax and a valid MOT is illegal."

"How do you expect me to get home?" Jones said. "I am an important person."

"To be honest," Steve said. "I don't care."

"Did you put him up to this?" Jones glared at Mark.

"No," Mark said calmly.

"Maybe you," He pointed to Marina. "Because I didn't want a woman dealing with my affairs?" Jones scoffed. "Or was it that disabled runt?"

"Your attitude is harassment," Steve said. "I would think clearly before you say any more."

"If I hear any more insults towards any members of the team," Mark said. "I will close your account

189

and have you removed from the hotel."

"And I will have your job," Jones pointed at Mark who smiled and laughed softly.

"Is this on camera?" Steve asked, pointing to the domed camera above reception.

"Yes," Mark said.

"Again, I warn you, Mr Jones," Steve said. "Any further attitude towards staff, I will take things further, and I promise you, your hotel room is much more comfortable than our cells."

Jones bit his lip, looking down at the floor and then up at Steve.

"Would you like to have a chat with me in the lounge?" Steve asked. "Would that be okay?" Steve asked Mark.

"Sure," Mark nodded.

"Could I get either of you drinks?" Marina asked.

"Whiskey," Jones said. "Going to need it."

"I would recommend coffee," Steve said.

"Fine," Jones said. "Coffee," he looked at Marina. "Please."

"No problems," Marina said. "How about you Steve?"

"Could I have a weak tea?" Steve said.

"I will bring them in shortly," Marina said and left towards the kitchen."

Mark watched as Jones followed Steve into the lounge and closed the door behind him.

"What did you do?" Mark asked quietly.

"Steve asked why I was annoyed," Andy said. "So I told him about the tosser."

"What did you tell him?" Mark asked.

"Just that he was an arse towards me and Marina," Andy said. "Deserves everything he gets."

"I agree," Mark sighed. "But this will probably backfire on us."

"It will be fine," Andy said. "You want a coffee?"

"Yes," Mark nodded. "You still off at two?"

Andy nodded.

"Tell you what," Mark looked at his watch. "If you could do some food for a room service, then you can head off after."

"You sure?" Andy asked.

"Yeah," Mark said. "I think you have had enough stress for the evening."

Marina came up to the counter.

"Dean is sorting them," Marina said. "When I told him what happened, he nearly passed out from laughing."

"Little shit," Mark scoffed. "Andy is going after he has done a room service for me."

Marina looked at her watch.

"Hey, Andy?" Marina said.

Andy moved round to the counter.

"I'll give you a hand then drop you in town if you want?" She said. "I am popping to the store."

"You sure?" Andy asked.

"Course," Marina smiled. "Save you walking."

"Thanks," Andy said. "Meet you in the kitchen."

Andy left the reception, looking down towards the lounge with a grin on his face.

NINE

Andy sat in the reception with his feet up on the worktop, reading a book and occasionally glancing at the security monitor set to the reception desk.

The door opened and Andy dropped his feet from the worktop.

"Stop putting your feet on the worktop!" Mark warned Andy. "Or I will make you polish the brasserie floor!"

"After you did it?" Andy said. "Sure about that?"

"Fine," Mark said. "No coffee tonight for you!"

"You cannot scare me," Andy said, raising his feet closer to the worktop.

"Will send you out with Gary and Keith," Mark said bluntly.

Andy suddenly dropped his feet, and his eyes widened.

"Okay!" Andy scoffed. "No need to be so nasty!"

"How's the group?" Mark said, looking in the mirror as he stood behind the counter.

"Fine," Andy said. "Lindsay is looking after them. Bit rowdy but otherwise fine."

"Wonder if they will go to bed early?" Mark said. "I could do with a chill night."

"No such luck," Andy said.

"Anything left on the list?" Mark asked.

"Barn house is all done," Andy said. "Also tidied up and refreshed for the conference tomorrow."

"Damn," Mark said. "Were you bored?"

"Yes," Andy said. "Set up is only for twenty tomorrow, so I cleared out the extra chairs. Also hoovered it as the carpet was a mess."

"Thought the day porters had done it?" Mark said, picking up a clipboard and reading the notes. "Yeah," he nodded. "Says here they did it."

"They were lying," Andy said.

"Arseholes," Mark shook his head. "I will let Marina know. I heard there were over forty people there today," Mark said. "Some newsgroup thing."

"The cakes are nice," Andy said.

"Cakes?" Mark said. "What cakes?"

"There were some leftover cakes," Andy smiled. "A note saying help yourself."

"Why didn't you tell me?" Mark scoffed.

"You are on a diet," Andy said.

"I swear we will fall out one of these days," Mark said pointing a finger at Andy and trying not to laugh.

"Your other half said to make sure you stick to it," Andy said. "And I am not arguing with her."

"I knew inviting you over for dinner was a bad move," Mark rolled his eyes. "She thinks you are funny, clearly bad taste."

"Must be," Andy said. "She is marrying you."

"Walked into that one!" Mark laughed.

"Did Marina find you?" Andy said. "She was looking for you earlier, wanted your help."

"Yes she did," Mark nodded. "She had trouble with some maths."

"So she asked the geek for help," Andy laughed.

"Well she couldn't ask you could she?" Mark shook his head. "Your maths if bloody terrible!"

A man came up to the counter wearing a white shirt tucked into light blue jeans, tall and overweight with a stomach fighting against his shirt buttons. He has long thinning blonde hair and thick stubble, his glasses resting on the top of his head.

"Evening," The man said. "My name is Paul, I am from the conference group."

"Evening sir," Mark replied with a smile. "How can I help you?"

"We ordered drinks a couple of minutes ago, but the girl behind the counter is taking her time," He said. "Can someone help her?"

"Sure," Mark looked at Andy. "Do you mind?"

"No," Andy said and got up, leaving the bar.

Andy opened the double doors to the bar, smiling at Lindsay when he walked in.

"What's up?" She asked.

"Marked asked me to help out," Andy said. "Need me to do anything?"

"No," Lindsay said. "Already done it," She looked at the group of nine adults, three men and six women, all sitting around three small tables pushed together. "Was it the fat twat in the jeans that moaned?"

Andy nodded.

"Nine drinks in a couple of minutes isn't bad," She said. "H has been getting on my tits all night!"

"Sorry to hear that," Andy said. "We will make his stay rubbish!"

"He cannot talk to me without looking directly at these," She said cupping her breasts. "I had to remind him a couple of times."

"Great," Andy shook his head. "A pervert."

Paul came to the bar, tapping on the counter loudly.

"So how long are these drinks going to be?" Paul asked.

"Coming now," Lindsay said. "Take a seat and I will be with you."

"Who are you?" Paul said looking at Andy.

"One of the night porters," Andy said.

"Oh right," Paul nodded. "Let's get those drinks before they go off!" He smiled at Lindsay, looking down at her chest before walking away.

"See what I mean?" She said. "Fucking freak."

"Sure you don't want any help?" Andy asked.

"Can you make me a coffee?" She asked, pointing to the coffee machine on the worktop. "Please."

"Sure," Andy said nodding.

Lindsay left the bar, walking round to the counters and picked up the tray of drinks, walking over to the group and placing the drinks in front of each person. All dressed smartly, with Paul being the odd one out.

Andy made two mugs of black coffee, adding sugar to one of them and placing it on the bar counter. The doors opened and she walked in, sighing as she placed the tray on the counter.

"Here you go," Andy said pushing the mug towards her. "One sugar."

"Oh you remembered," She said picking it up.

"Should have two," Andy said. "Make you sweeter."

"Cheeky shit," Lindsay laughed. "That guy is going to be a problem," She said. "He has this whole entitled attitude going on with him."

"He will find a nice cosy place at the bottom of the lake if he tries it with me," Andy said.

"You on all night?" She asked.

"Finish as six," Andy said.

"Heard from Charlotte?"

"No," Andy shook his head. "Should I have?"

"Just curious," She smiled. "You won't be mean to her will you?"

"No," Andy said. "Of course I won't."

"Cool," She nodded. "She is an amazing person."

"I know," Andy said. "Put me in the friendzone because her dad doesn't want any disabled people in family."

"I know," She shook her head. "It's not a nice thing is it?"

"No," Andy said. "Anyhow I am going back to reception, give me a shout if you need anything."

"Thanks," She said.

Andy walked towards the storeroom.

"Where you going?" She asked curiously."

"Going the long way," Andy smiled. "To avoid the tosser in the bar!"

Andy opened the door gently and then closed it, nodding at Mark.

"All good?" Mark asked.

"She had the drinks ready," Andy said. "Just that Paul guy being a tosser."

"I think he is going to be a nightmare," Mark said.

"Lindsay said he keeps looking at her tits," Andy said. "God help him when she gets pissed off."

Mark yawned, covering his mouth and looking out the window suddenly.

"What was that?" Mark said in surprise.

"What was what?" Andy said, putting the book down and looking up.

"Saw something outside," Mark said looking.

"Well how the hell will I see it from here?" Andy scoffed, he got up and turned the security monitor channel to show the front of the hotel.   "Cannot see anything," Andy said shrugging his shoulders. "Must be your age getting to you."

"Ha bloody ha," Mark said sarcastically. "Sod!"

Andy laughed.

"Must have been a plastic bag or something," Mark said.

The entrance door opened and a woman walked in, short and slim wearing black trousers and a white blouse. He light brown hair tied into a ponytail.

"There is a swan outside," She said.

"Okay," Mark said. "There is a lake near the Barn house so we do get the occasional duck or swan that pops up to the hotel curiously."

"That isn't what I mean," She sighed.

"Something not right about it," She said. "Nearly took my head off coming back from the carpark."

"Are you okay?" Mark asked.

Andy stood up.

"I am fine," She said. "Maybe get someone in to shoot the bloody thing," She moaned as she walked into the bar.

"Do you want to go and check it out," Mark said.

"Where is the gun then?" Andy asked. "Shall I shoot it?" He said sarcastically.

The door opened and Marina popped her head in, looking around at Andy and then Mark.

"Not letting you have the gun," Mark said.

"Gun?" Marina smiled. "Who are you shooting?"

"No one yet," Andy said. "But it's still early. How are you?"

"Fine," She said. "There is a swan acting weird outside."

"I am going outside now," Andy said.

"I will join you," She said. "I need some air.

Andy left the office, making his way to the entrance, joined by Marina who raced him to the door, laughing as she opened it and tried to stop him getting there.

195

"Cheat," Andy said. "You know I have little legs!"

Marina stood on the steps, looking up at the dark skies.

"Nice and warm," She said. "Makes a change doesn't it."

"Yes," Andy nodded. "When did you see the swan?"

"From the office," She replied. "Something shot past the window and when I went to have a look, it scared the shit out of me."

"Protein shakes will do that to you," Andy exclaimed.

"Tell me about it," She said.

"You hit one twenty yet?" Andy asked.

"I haven't even hit seventy!" She moaned.

"Lazy," Andy said sarcastically and walked down the steps.

The swan swooped down, missing the ground and causing Andy to jump back in fright.

"Jesus!" He yelped. "I can taste the bloody feathers!"

"What is wrong with it?" She said. "Maybe its mate is in trouble?"

"Doesn't have a mate," Andy said. "We only have one left now."

"Really?" She joined Andy at the bottom of the steps. "I thought there were two?"

"Was until a few weeks ago," Andy said. "Someone ran the female over."

"Oh no that is really sad," She moaned. "What happened to the two before? Allain said we had four at one point."

"One was attacked and killed by a fox," Andy said. "Before my time that was, and the other went missing."

"Went missing?" She scoffed. "Did it pack it's bags and run away?" She burst out in laughter.

"No idea," Andy said. "The one that got run over was a sad one, the person that did it came in and said they hit something but not sure what, so Dean went for a walk and found a severed wing, then further down the road a mangled swan."

"That is terrible," She gasped. "Was the person an idiot?"

"Yes," Andy said. "Dean was quite upset."

The swan swopped down again, flying back up towards the Barn house.

"Something isn't right with him," She said, looking at Andy. "It is a boy right?"

"Yes," Andy said. "Can't you see his balls and willy hanging when he flew past?"

"Shut up you moron," She punched him in the arm.

"Let's go back inside," She said. "I'll give the garden team a call and see if they can advise."

Andy nodded and followed her up the steps.

The swan slammed into the road, a bone crunching splatter and thud. Blood splattered up Andy's back and he yelped in shock, falling forward.

"Fuck!" Marina shouted. "What the hell?!"

Andy got to his feet and turned around, looking at the mess of feathers, blood and what was once a swan.

"Shit," Andy said under his breath.

The swan let out a high-pitched groan, one of its wings twitching before it became still, blood pooling around it.

The door opened and Mark ran out, looking at the swan, Marina and then Andy.

"Are you hurt?" Mark asked, noticing the blood splatter on Andy's upper shirt, the back of his neck also had splatters trickling.

"It's not my blood," Andy said.

Marina looked at Andy, gagging.

"You okay?" Andy asked.

"I don't do blood," She said, her hand on her stomach as she heaved.

"Go inside," Mark said. "Go on."

Marina ran inside and Mark watched as she broke into a run for the toilets.

"What happened?" Mark said walking down the steps and looking at the swan.

"It nose-dived," Andy said. "It nearly took our heads off a couple of times and then just, nose-dived into the road."

"Shit," Mark said. "I knew it was depressed," He pointed. "Bit not that depressed."

The door opened and the woman from earlier walked out, a cigarette between her lips.

"I was joking when I said to shoot it," She said bluntly. "Why did you have to shoot the poor thing?!"

"We didn't shoot it," Mark said. "It," Mark paused. "Killed itself."

The door opened and Allain stepped out, gasping in shock. Wearing grey trousers and a white shirt, the arms rolled up.

"What have you done?!" Allain snapped.

"Nothing," Mark said. "The swan killed itself."

"Swans do not kill themselves!" Allain exclaimed.

"Well this one did," Andy said. "Look at my back."

"You have blood on you!" Allain said. "How did that happen, did you kill it?"

"The blood wouldn't be on my back would it?" Andy said. "No I was next to the road when it crashed."

"Poor thing," Allain groaned. "Is it dead?"

Andy walked over to the swan, bending down and gently touching it.

"Well it isn't sleeping," Andy said. "It's neck is practically hanging off!"

"Stop it," Allain said. "You will make me sick!"

"I will get Keith to sort it out," Mark said. "Before the foxes get wind of it."

"I am going to take my cigarette elsewhere," The woman said walking towards the bar.

"Andy," Allain said. "Could I have a catch up?"

"Problem?" Mark asked.

"No," Allain said. "I want to talk about the computers," He said to Mark.

"Oh yes," Mark said. "No problems."

"The lounge in five minutes?" Allain said. "Will let you clean up a little."

Andy nodded.

Allain shuddered and cringed, going back into the hotel.

"What was that about?" Andy asked.

"Looks like your help with the computers last week has been noticed," Mark said. "Marina and Jack spoke to Allain about you sorting the problems out where the company couldn't."

"The company are ripping the hotel off," Andy said. "I am surprised they keep paying thousands for issues the company are causing," Andy scoffed. "It was funny watching the pretend programmer put random codes into the computer to look like he was doing something."

"Go clean up and see what he has to say," Mark said. "I think you will like it."

"Will do," Andy said. "Going to get the blood off my neck first, how bad is the shirt."

"Not too bad," Mark said. "About six spots of blood."

"I will just tell people I had an accident with a nail gun," Andy laughed.

"Knowing you, you bloody would!" Mark shook his head. "I am going to chat to Keith, see if he minds sorting this out."

"He will probably have it in a hotpot within the hour and dish it up to the customers," Andy laughed.

"Not a bad idea," Mark said. "Want some?"

"I don't eat meat you arse," Andy said.

Andy sat on the armchair in the lounge, looking around as Allain looked through his notes.

"Thank you for writing this down," Allain said. "It looks like you know your way around computers."

"It's a hobby," Andy said. "And computers are constantly growing."

"So how long have you worked with computers?" Allain asked, looking at Andy.

"A few years," Andy said. "I recently took up programming but have supported computers for some time."

"Did you go to university and study computers?" Allain asked.

"No," Andy said.

"College?" Allain looked up.

"I went to college yes," Andy said. "But studied performing arts."

"The arts?" Allain said curiously.

"Acting, dancing and singing," Andy said.

"Oh," Allain nodded. "Tracy told me you managed to solve a problem we had," Allain said. "Last Monday?"

"Saturday," Andy said thinking. "They said they couldn't send anyone in until Monday and the system was down."

"How did you fix it?" Allain asked.

"I shut down all connected computers and rebooted the server," Andy explained. "It wasn't a big deal."

"It was for the teams on site," Allain said. "Without computers on Sunday, it would have been much work."

"The system is old," Andy said. "And the company are ripping the hotel off."

"That was mentioned to me yes," Allain nodded. "What would you do differently?"

"Well for one," Andy said. "Get rid of the sever, it is a money guzzler."

"Guzzler?" Allain asked curiously. "What does that mean?"

"It means a waste of money," Andy said. "It is over-kill."

"Really?" Alain said.

"All you need is one main computer, or a mini server," Andy explained. "There are only six computers connected to it, and only three use the hotel software, spend about six thousand and save hundreds of thousands."

"You could do this?" Allain asked.

"Yes," Andy said. "I have a mini network at home of three computers," Andy said.

"Very good," Allain said. "I do not understand computers."

"I will give you an example," Andy said. "You know the front desk computer was playing up last week?"

"Yes," Allain said. The mouse would not work so the company said a new computer is needed.

"Absolute rubbish," Andy said. "Just needed a new mouse."

"You fixed it?" Allain said. "We thought it had been replaced," He gasped. "They sent us a large bill for it, what did you do?"

"Took the mouse ball out and cleaned all the fluff and gunge of the rollers," Andy explained.

"Gunge?" Allain said, shaking his head.

"Dirt," Andy sighed.

"My English is not good," Allain said. "French is easy for me, have you considered learning French?"

"I can barely understand people speaking English!" Andy laughed.

"Myself and the admin manager have spoken and wish to create this role for you," Allain said. "I have spoken to the owners, and they are very happy for me to make this decision, however," Allain said. "It will only be part time to start."

"Not a problem," Andy said. "It's a start and I can still do this role as well, that way it won't impact anyone."

"You have a day job," Allain said. "In a store?"

"I will leave that," Andy said. "I only need to give a weeks' notice."

"When can you start implementing a plan?" Allain said. "To update everything and how long will it take?"

"Once I know what we need, we can get it ordered and I can have them installed in a day," Andy said. "If it is only six machines."

"We may update to eight," Allain nodded. "I would like to offer you this job, when can you start?"

"I can start the research as soon as possible, physically I can be here a week Monday," Andy said. "I am on vacation next week."

"Oh very nice," Allain said. "Where?"

"Les Arcs," Andy said. "Five days of skiing."

"Oh very nice," Allain nodded. "I have been there a couple of times."

"Looking forward to it," Andy said.

"Please don't break your legs," Allain shook his head.

"Not planning on it," Andy laughed.

"You better get back to work and look after the news conference," Allain said. "I will have a letter put together regarding the job, but it is yours, so anything you can do as soon as possible would be good."

"Will do that," Andy said. "I have a friend in the business that can help and will be able to get discounts and so on."

"Good," Allain nodded. "Good."

Allain got up and held out his hand, Andy shook it.

"First time for everything," Andy said and laughed, watching as Allain walked away, wiping his hand on his trousers.

Andy opened the door to reception, looking at Marina who sat down with a bottle of water, looking pale. Mark stood at reception, operating the computer. Paul stood at the counter, a pint of lager in front of him.

"We have several rooms available," Mark said. "How many did you want?"

"Just the two," Paul said.

"Standard?" Mark asked.

"Yes please," Paul nodded. "Two of our delegates have had one too many."

Paul rang the small bell on the counter, giggling.

"I always thought these things were fake," He said, ringing it again.

Mark looked at him, unimpressed.

"Not very loud is it?" He rang it again.

Mark took hold of the bell and placed it under the counter, smiling.

"How would you like to pay?" Mark asked.

"Charge it to the account," Paul said.

"Unfortunately I cannot charge rooms to the conference account," Mark said. "This only covers food and drink I am afraid."

"No that isn't right," Paul shook his head and looked into the bar. "Cathy, come here," Paul said.

Mark looked at Andy, rolling his eyes.

"You okay?" Andy whispered to Marina.

"Yes," Marina said. "Just not great with blood."

"Mad," Any shook his head.

"Last year I was in the gym," She said. "Some guy dropped a weight on his head, cut his scalp open," She laughed softly. "I was squatting eighty kilos at the time, wasn't a good turnout."

"What happened?" Andy asked curiously.

"I fainted," She said. "Face down into the rubber flooring with the weight on my back contributing to sending me down harder."

"Shit!" Andy said.

"Can't you see the scar?" She asked him.

Andy looked closer, noticing the small scar on her bottom lip in the middle.

"No," Andy said. "It's not so noticeable."

"I woke up with blood all over my face, split lip, broken nose," Marina said. "I stood up, looked in the mirror and passed out again, cracking the back of my head. They wouldn't let me stand up after that!"

"Not surprised!" Andy scoffed.

Cathy, a short and slim woman in her mid-sixties, with straight grey hair down to her shoulders, black rimmed glasses and wearing a dark grey suit came up to the counter.

"What is it Paul?" She asked.

"They won't let me charge two rooms to the account," Paul said.

"I have explained that we cannot accept room charges to a food and drink account," Mark said.

"That is correct," Cathy said. "Why are you not running this by me first?"

"You said anything could be charged to the account," Paul questioned.

"Food and drink," She sighed in frustration. "This was made clear."

"Oh," Paul said looking at Mark. "Do we have a card for rooms?"

"Who needs rooms?" She said. "This was discussed earlier, no one wanted a room."

"Matt and Sandy do," Paul said.

Cathy looked into the bar.

"Did you need rooms?" She called out. "Hey, Sandy and Matthew?"

Andy sat in the chair next to Marina.

"I got offered a new job," He said. "Looking after the computers."

"I know," Marina smiled. "I put a good word in for you."

"Aw thanks," Andy said. "Want a hug?"

"Hell no," Marina shook her head. "I want a pizza!"

"Fine," Andy said. "I'll sort you a pizza."

"Andy," Mark said. "Keep an eye while I pop to the toilet."

Mark left the reception and Andy stood in front of the counter, watching Cathy and Paul.

"They don't want rooms," Cathy said and turned to the counter, her mouth opened in shock. "That was an impressive trick," She said.

"What was?" Andy said.

"How you and that other guy swapped," She laughed. "I heard about the swan, how is it?"

"Didn't make it," Andy said.

"I heard there was blood everywhere," Paul said.

Marina gagged and then coughed.

"Is she okay?" Cathy asked in concern.

"Not good with blood," Andy smiled.

"Stop talking about it Paul," Cathy said. "Could we get some more drinks please?"

"Sure," Andy said. "Lindsay is still at the bar."

"I will order these," Cathy said. "Don't want you upsetting anyone else tonight Paul."

Cathy walked away and Paul looked at the counter, shaking his head before walking away.

"Freak," Andy said under his breath and then looked round the corner at Marina, her head resting on the table. "Why don't you go and get some air," He said. "You have lost all your colour again," He laughed. "I'll sort you some food in a bit."

"No it's okay," Marina said breathing in deeply.

"Too bad," Andy said. "Go and sit in the staff room and rest," Andy said. "I will bring you some food, so bugger off and do as you are told for once."

"You wait," She said standing up and pointing a finger. "When you join me at the gym, I am kicking your arse."

"Promise?" Andy asked.

"Yes," She said, grinning as she left the reception, letting the door close gently behind her. Paul appeared at the counter, tapping it.

"Where is the bell?" He said.

"Yes?" Andy walked round.

"Where is the bell?" Paul asked.

"No idea," Andy said.

"It's under the counter," Paul said smiling.

Andy reached for the bell, placing it in the middle of the counter.

"There it is!" Paul said and tapped the bell several times, the loud ring annoying Andy who put his hand over it, moving it back under the counter.

"Not a toy," Andy said. "I know why it was under the counter."

"Spoilsport," Paul moaned. "Can you help the bar girl out?" Paul said.

"I need to keep an eye on reception until my colleague is back," Andy said.

"We would like our drinks quickly," Paul laughed. "She is slow."

"She is working as fast as she can," Andy said. "It's a large group she is looking after."

"I am only being nice because she has a great rack," Paul scoffed. "Anyone else I would have told them straight."

"A nice what?" Andy asked.

"Rack," Paul said nodding.

Marina walked around reception, looking at Andy.

"Never heard that saying before," Andy said. "What does it mean?"

"You know," Paul nodded and smiled.

"Hey Marina," Andy said. "What's a rack?"

"Something you store things on," Marina said walking up to the counter. "I have a laundry rack."

"Oh," Andy said, looking at Paul who became nervous. "Paul here said that Lindsay has a great rack."

203

"Does she now?" Marina looked at Paul.

"Never mind," Paul said nervously and walked away.

"Nice one," Marina said. "Guy is a fucking pervert. I am going to help out Lindsay for a bit," She said. "I need something ice cold."

"See you soon," Andy said and smiled as she walked through the bar, trying not to laugh.

Andy opened the door to the bar, balancing the large pizza on a plate in one hand and a bowl of chips in the other.

"Is that for us?" Paul called out in the small group of seven.

"Afraid not," Andy said. "This is for staff."

"Bit unfair," Paul said.

"Sorry," Andy grinned as he walked past them, walking backwards through the two double doors at the bar.

"Oh Andy!" Marina gasped.

"Told you I would sort out some food," Andy said. "This is to share!" Andy warned her.

"What is it?" Lindsay asked.

"Pizza," Andy said bluntly.

"What kind?" Lindsay stuck her tongue out.

"Just cheese and tomato," Andy said. "Is that satisfactory?"

"It will do," Marina said. "Chips too!"

"Cheese dusted Nachos!" Andy said. "I was hungry!"

Paul came to the bar, grinning awkwardly.

"Can I help?" Marina asked him.

"Can we order pizza?" He asked.

"We don't serve pizza," Lindsay said.

"Then what is that?" He pointed to the pizza, holding up his arms.

"I collected it in town," Andy said.

"Can you go and get us some?" Paul asked.

"Sorry no," Andy said. "I went in my lunch break."

"Do they deliver?" Paul asked.

"They stopped at Ten," Andy said. "Collections until Eleven."

"How much for that?" He said.

"Not for sale," Andy said. "It's our lunch."

Paul groaned and walked away.

"Fucking child," Marina said under her breath, picking up a slice of pizza. "Wow it's still hot!" She exclaimed.

"I heated it up," Andy said.

"Want some money?" Marina asked.

"No," Andy said. "Call it a thank you for the amazing show."

"What amazing show?" Marina asked curiously.

Andy grinned, picking up the nachos.

"Oh that," She scoffed. "Dirty sod."

"What show?" Lindsay asked. "Tell me."

"You know," Marina said. "When he was being a peeping tom."

"Oh that show!" Lindsay laughed.

Paul came up to the counter again.

"Can we get some food?" He asked.

"You can," Lindsay said. "What would you like?"

"What do you have?" Paul asked.

Lindsay picked up a Menu, handing it to Paul.

"Sandwiches and various crisps," She said looking at the clock. "The kitchen closes in twenty minutes and there will be limited service by the porters after then."

"What's your name?" he looked at Andy.

"Sorry?" Andy said.

"Weird name," Paul said.

"No," Marina said. "He didn't hear you."

"Why not?" Paul asked.

"He is deaf," Marina said.

"Oh," Paul paused, looking at Andy. "So what do I do?" He said looking at Marina.

"Ask him again," Marina said.

"Can you tell me?" He asked. "Not a fan of repeating myself."

"I am not speaking for him," Marina said. "Just need to be a little patient and ask him again."

"What did you ask me?" Andy said.

"What your name was," Paul. "But it doesn't matter now."

"It's Bob," Andy said.

"Short for Robert?" Paul said. "My brother is Robert."

"No," Andy shook his head. "Just Bob."

Lindsay started to laugh, turning and picking up a glass of water, glancing at Marina who continued to eat her slice of pizza.

"Here," Andy said handing Paul a notepad. "Write down what you want and I will get onto the kitchen and have the food done as soon as possible."

"Can I get a drink?" Paul asked.

"Sure," Andy said, holding up his hand to stop Lindsay. "What do you want?"

"Vodka and tonic," Paul said. "No ice or lemon."

"Sure," Andy said. "Go take a seat and I will bring that out."

Paul walked away with the menu and the notepad, looking through it.

Andy picked up a glass, pouring a double shot of vodka.

"That is a double," Lindsay said.

"I know," Andy smiled. "Hopefully he will get drunk and piss his boss off."

"Who is the boss?" Lindsay asked.

"Woman with grey hair in the suit," Marina said.

"She is really nice," Lindsay said. "She hasn't looked at my tits yet."

Marina burst out laughing, choking and coughing on the pizza.

"Don't waste it!" Andy warned her and topped off the glass with tonic. "Right let's deal with this fudging moron!"

Andy stood by reception, leaning against the counter. Mark is standing, reading a book perched on the edge of the computer.

Paul stood up from the group of seven, waving to get Andy's attention.

"Oi!" He shouted. "Can we get some service?"

Mark looked up, shaking his head.

"Ignore them," Mark said. "Let's wait until they have a bit more respect."

"It's okay," Andy said. "I will deal with them."

Mark handed a notebook to Andy.

"Any problems let me know," Mark said. "Had enough of his shit."

"You could always throw the bell at his head," Andy laughed softly. "Let the bells ring out for idiots!" He covered his mouth. "Probably hollow up there," He tapped his head.

"He won't be coming back at this rate I tell you!"

"His boss has gone to bed," Andy said. "Probably feeling a bit brave."

"Hello?" Paul called out.

"One moment," Andy said, looking directly at Paul.

"He is drinking a fair bit," Mark said.

"I know," Andy grinned. "I know."

Andy walked out to the group, smiling as he approached Paul.

"About time!" The man said loudly. "Are you deaf or what?" He laughed.

"Yes, I am," Andy replied calmly. "Profoundly in both ears." He smiled.

"Oh," Paul said. "Didn't know that."

"You did," Andy said. "My colleague explained it to you earlier."

"Sorry about that," A woman next to him said. "He always puts his mouth into gear before his brain!" She laughed. Wearing Navy blue trousers, a white shirt with the arms rolled up, her long black hair tightly pulled back and tied.

"Because of the noise, I am going to need someone to write the drinks down," Any said. "Makes all our lives easier."

"Sure, I can do that," The woman said taking the notebook from Andy.

Paul scoffed and shook his head.

"Problem?" Andy asked.

"Just wondering why you cannot do it?" Paul said. "What is the big deal?"

"No big deal," Andy said. "Just harder to follow everyone."

"If you want us to do your job," Paul said defiantly. "Do we get them for free?"

"Unfortunately, no," Andy said.

"Is there someone here that isn't deaf?" Paul smirked. "Someone that can do the job properly?"

"Yes," Andy said. "He will be available in about half an hour or so," Andy started to walk away. "I'll ask him to deal with your order then." As Andy turned his back the woman stood up, putting her hand on his shoulder.

"I will do it," She said. "Ignore him, he is drunk," She whispered.

Andy walked into the bar, noticed one of the delegates eating sandwiches from behind the counter. He is wearing black trousers, polished boots and a white shirt with wine spilt down the front of it. He is tall, slim and balding.

"Really?" Andy scoffed.

"What?" He said looking up at Andy.

"Enjoying my lunch?" Andy asked.

He looked down at the sandwiches and then back at Andy.

"Shit!" He said. "Sorry I had no idea!"

"Don't worry about it," Andy said sighing and shaking his. "The cheese is probably off."

He looked at Andy in concern and pushed returned a half-eaten sandwich back to the plate, wiping his face with a serviette.

"Thought they were for customers," He said.

"That is why we leave them behind the bar," Andy laughed. "So they have to reach over to get them."

"I'll pay for them," He said.

"It's fine," Andy said. "No worries."

"Paul giving you grief?" He said looking at the group.

"Nothing I cannot handle," Andy said.

"Could I get a Guinness?" He said.

Paul walked up to the bar, flipping the pad onto the counter.

"Quick as you can," He said.

"No need to be rude mate," The man said to him. "A bit of respect won't hurt you will it?"

"I am a customer," Paul said. "Oh sandwiches!" He noticed the plate.

Andy picked up the plate, putting it on the counter.

"Help yourself," Andy said with a smile.

Paul took the plate and walked away.

"Hope he chokes on them," Andy said under his breath.

Andy pulled a Guinness, letting it half stand as he prepared the several drinks on the list.

"Been here long?" The man asked.

"Too long," Andy said. "Got a change of job coming up so all good."

"Do you not enjoy it?" He said.

"I don't mind," Andy said looking at the group. "It's complete tossers like him that ruin it."

"Have you hurt your back?" He said pointing at the reflection in the mirror.

"No," Andy said. "We had a suicide earlier."

"Holy shit!" The man gasped.

"A swan," Andy said. "Nose-dived into the drive."

The man looked at Andy opened mouth in shock.

"Was a mess," Andy said.

Paul walked up to the bar just as Andy placed the las drink on the tray, looking at him.

"Yes?" Andy said.

"Drinks?!" Paul said snapping his fingers. "We ordered them ages ago!"

"Well," Andy looked up at the clock. "It has been three minutes, but if you want me to rush them, I can do that?"

"Whatever!" Paul said. "I am dying of thirst!" He stormed off.

"One can hope," Andy said under his breath, picking up the tray, leaving the bar.

Andy called out the drinks, placing them in front of the delegates.

"Vodka and tonic," Andy said placing it in front of Paul who picked up the glass, sipping it and looking at it curiously.

"Just checking," He said. "You might make a mistake with your deafness."

"Doesn't affect my reading," Andy said. "But if it makes you feel better go for it."

Andy placed the last drink in front of the woman that had written down the list.

"Thank you," The woman said. "Is it possible to get a platter of sandwiches?" She asked.

"Don't bother," The man said. "They will be off by the time we get them!" he laughed out loudly, becoming embarrassed when no one responded.

"Well Paul enjoyed mine," Andy said looking down at the empty plate.

"Oh," Paul said. "I didn't know that."

"Sure," Andy said to the woman. "How many platters would you like?" I asked.

"Two mixed please," The woman said. "Can we charge it to the group?"

Andy nodded.

"Oh, porter!" Paul said as Andy walked away. "I have a question." He said clearly, almost patronising.

"Yes?" Andy said.

"Wake up calls?" Paul said.

"Yes?" Andy replied, waiting for the question.

"How do they work?" He asked.

"Well," Andy said. "We program the times into the telephone system and you will receive three calls separate calls until you pick up."

Paul laughed.

"He doesn't understand!" Paul scoffed. "No!" He raised his voice.

"So, what do you mean?" The woman said to him.

"How. Do. I. Arrange. It!" Paul said loudly and bluntly, pausing between every word.

"No need to be rude!" The woman said. "How embarrassing!"

"It's okay," Andy said. "We are used to customers like this."

She shook her head apologetically.

"Either go to reception and leave the details or you can call down from your room," Andy said. "Is. That. Okay?" I said, imitating him.

The group laughed, apart from Paul who looked at Andy, red in the face.

"You making fun of me?" Paul said. "I was being helpful."

"You really wasn't." Andy said.

"I am going to complain!" Paul snapped. "I will have your job!"

"You can have it," Andy said calmly. "You might be able to buy a decent shirt if you save for about three months."

Andy walked back to the bar, placing the tray on the counter and looking up to see the customer at the bar had left, leaving a large cash tip behind the bar.

"That is good of him," Andy said, picking up the cash and putting it into his pocket.

Picking up the telephone, he dialled the reception, looking at the mirror when he saw Mark answer.

"Hi Mark," Andy said. "The group want two platters of sandwiches," Andy coughed, covering his mouth. "They are already made, in the main fridge, can you grab them for the group."

Mark held up his thumb in the mirror to Andy.

"Thanks," Andy said. "Careful, Paul bites."

Andy tidied up the bar and made himself a coffee, looking towards the group every so often.

Half hour had passed when Paul walked up to the bar, slightly drunk.

"Yes?" Andy said when he leaned against the bar.

"Sorry," He mumbled. "Having a stressful day, you wouldn't understand being a porter," he said.

"Okay," Andy ignored the insult. "Can I help you?"

"Could we get another round?" He said forcing a smile. "Same drinks."

Andy looked towards the group and there are only two men and the woman that had taken down the drinks for Andy.

"Which three?" Andy asked.

"What do you mean?" Paul asked.

"There are only three of you," Andy said. "So which three drinks?"

"A lager," Paul said looking. "White wine and a vodka and tonic."

"I'll bring them over in a moment," Andy said.

"Thank you," He said. "I have requested a wake-up call at five in the morning," He looked at his watch. "Need to be ready for an important meeting at eight in London." He nodded and walked away.

"Good for you," Andy said. "I will be over shortly."

Andy had finished cleaning and re-arranging the bar lounge, putting the furniture back where it had come from. He walked into reception when he heard the telephone ring, joined by Marina.

"How's your long evening been?" Andy asked.

"I tell you this," Marina sighed. "That pizza really hit the spot, I loved it."

"Glad to hear it," Andy said. Lindsay gone?"

"I just dropped her home," Marina said. "Going to head off myself in a minute."

"Still in the apartment?" Andy asked.

"Why do you want to come and watch me or something," She laughed, shoving him.

"Someone will come and check shortly," Mark said on the telephone. "I can only apologise, this is not something we allow," He nodded. "Of course, thank you for letting me know."

"What was that about?" Marina asked.

"A complaint," Mark said. "A resident heard someone talking and when they looked through their peephole, they saw a naked man."

Marina burst into hysterics.

"Where?" She asked.

"Top level," Mark said. "You want to deal with it?"

"Oh yes!" She snapped. "Taking Andy with me for protection."

"Of course you are," Mark rolled his eyes. "Let me know if you need me to call the police."

"Can you pass me the dressing gown behind the counter," Marina said. "I'll sign it out later."

"You cold?" Andy sniggered.

"No," She shook her head. "But I bet you he will be! Come on."

Andy followed her to the lift, leaning against the wall as she pressed the call button.

"Sleepwalker?" Andy said curiously.

"Don't know," Marina said.

"I sleepwalk," Andy said. "You should ask Mark about my first week here when I nodded off in the bar, walked into the fireplace!"

"Oh my god!" Marina groaned.

The lift door opened and Marina walked in, Andy following in.

"I had a friend stay over once with his girlfriend," Andy said, pressing the button for the top floor. "They were really off with me the next day, turns out I was sleep walking around the flat, picked up a knife from the kitchen and walked around the flat growling!"

"That is some scary shit," Marina shook her head.

"I walked home from here a couple of months ago, about four in the morning," Andy said. "Fell asleep on the couch and when I woke up, I was barefoot in the local park on a bench."

"You are kidding!?" Marina scoffed.

"No," Andy said. "Luckily my aunt lived nearby and I had some shoes there."

"Surprised you wasn't hurt!" Marina said.

The lift rattled and groaned.

"I hate lifts," She said. "I heard you got stuck in here?"

"Yeah," Andy said. "Came close to wetting myself!"

Marina sniggered, turning her head as she laughed.

The doors opened and they both looked down the corridor, watching as the tall, slim balding naked man walked towards them, his genitals swinging and slapping side to side with each step, the slaps echoing down the corridor.

"Okay stop right there," Marina said holding up her hand and looking away, trying not to laugh.

The man stopped.

"He is a resident," Andy said.

"How do you know?" She asked.

"Unlike you," Andy said. "I looked at his face!"

"Cannot help it," Marina scoffed. "It's like a rabid elephants trunk!"

Andy took the dressing gown.

"Can you cover your tackle for me," Andy said. "I need to lipread and this is going to be awkward."

The man covered his genitals, smiling as Andy got closer.

"Locked myself out my room," He said. "Bit embarrassing."

"How did you manage that?" Andy said handing him the dressing gown.

"I sleepwalk," He replied, putting on the dressing gown and covering himself.

Andy turned and looked at Marina who is looking away.

"You can look now," Andy said.

"Are you okay sir?" Marina asked as she joined Andy.

"I am fine," He nodded.

"You seem quite relaxed," She said. "In public."

"I know," The man smiled.

"Do you suffer with bruising?" Andy asked.

"Bruising?" The man asked curiously.

"All that swinging and slapping," Andy said trying not to laugh.

"Shut up," Marina punched him.   "Which room are you in?" She said. "I have master keys."

"Hyacinth Three," The man pointed to the door.

"Come on," Marina said. "Let's get you back to your room."

"How did you know I was here?" He said. "I was about to call."

"Someone saw you and your penis through their peephole," Andy said calmly.

Marina burst into hysterics.

"She needed that," Andy said. "Been a long night."

Marina let the man into his room, waiting until he locked the door and then ran to the lift when Andy held open the door, shoving him out of the way.

"Interesting night," She said. "Swans and drunk perverts."

"Not forgetting pizza and penis," Andy said.

Marina yelped with laughter as the lift door closed, juddering and groaning.

Andy sat cross legged, reading a book and sipping from a mug of coffee.

"Good book?" Mark asked.

"Yeah," Andy said.

"How many is that?" Mark asked curiously. "Third? Forth?"

"Forth this week," Andy smiled. "Once I start, I just don't want to put them down."

The telephone panel beeped and Mark looked at it, pressing a button.

"Wake up calls done?" Andy asked.

"Yes," He said. "But a six o'clock isn't picking up, three reminders and nothing."

"Who?" Andy asked.

"The irritating twit from last night," Mark laughed. "Can you go and give him a knock?"

"Do I have to?" Andy moaned. "He is probably sleeping off a hangover."

"Let me call him," Mark said and picked up the telephone, dialling the room.

The phone rang out several times and Mark shook his head, putting it down.

"Not picking up," Mark said. "It's been half hour."

"Maybe he stayed with someone else," Andy said trying not to laugh.

Mark laughed, and then suddenly stopped with a straight face.

The door opened and Tracy walked in, looking at both Mark and Andy curiously.

"What are you two up to?" She said.

"Nothing," Mark said looking at his watch. "What are you doing in so early?"

"Couldn't sleep," She said. "Thought I would come in and sort some things out before the day starts," She looked at the sun coming through the windows, yawning. "What's the stain on the road out front?"

"Ah," Mark said. "Our last swan died."

"Oh no!" She exclaimed. "Was it run over?"

"No, " Mark said. "It killed itself."

"Look," Andy said and stood up, showing Tracy his blood splattered back. "Less than a couple of meters away!"

"Shit that is so bad!" She said. "Poor thing!"

"I will pop up to the room," Andy said. "Give this tosser a wakeup call!"

"What have I missed?" Mark said.

"Remember the podgy guy in jeans that kept looking at your chest when he spoke to you?" Mark said. "He pissed off nearly everyone last night."

"How Lindsay never punched his head in," Andy said. "I will never know."

Andy checked the number of the door against his notes and then knocked, waiting.

After a minute, there is no response.

"Good morning," Andy said knocking. "Just following on from your wake-up call."

The door opens suddenly and Paul stood there in small white boxes. Andy stepped back, looking behind around him.

"What?" He snapped.

"Wake up call," Andy said. "We had no response so thought to give you a knock in case."

"Yes I heard it," He said. "No need to go on and on."

"I apologise, but unless the call is answered," Andy explained. "We assume it isn't heard."

"Look," Paul said. "I am an adult and can manage my time," He huffed. "Haven't you got a toilet to clean or something?!" He slammed the door in Andy's face.

Getting a mug of coffee for Tracy from the kitchen, Andy returned to reception, handing it to her.

"You are a star!" She said. "Mark has gone home."

"Cool," Andy said.

"We had Paul call down," Tracy shook her head and smiled. "Complaining about the random porter knocking on his door."

"I think he is still drunk," Andy said. "He was knocking them back."

Cathy came to the counter.

"He isn't responding to me either," She said. "I wonder if he has left already?"

"No," Andy said. "He gave me an earful of attitude when I went up to check he received a call."

"Oh dear I am sorry," She said. "What did he say."

"Asked me if I had a toilet to clean," Andy scoffed and laughed.

"Well I am leaving," She said. "Could you pass this message on to him when he finally comes down?" She handed a note to Tracy who nodded.

"Thank you for looking after us," She said to Andy, handing him a rolled-up twenty-pound note.

"Thank you," Andy said. "It was my pleasure."

"Not all of us surely," She smiled and walked away.

"What was that about?" Tracy asked.

"Paul got a pit patronising and personal over my hearing disability," Andy said. "How he never got my fist in his face, I will never know."

"We are discussing it with Allain today," Tracy said. "Nearly every female that dealt with him had issues."

"He didn't like my pecs," Andy said. "How rude."

Tracy laughed.

"I am going to do a round and then have a break," Andy said. "Beep me if you need anything."

Tracy nodded as Andy left the reception.

Andy stood outside the entrance of the hotel with a mug of coffee, looking up at the cloudless sky, the sun on his face.

Paul burst out from the entrance, struggling with a case and bag as he made his way down the steps towards the waiting taxi.

"Good morning sir," Andy said.

"It's a nightmare!" Paul snapped. "I blame you!"

"What did I do?" Andy asked.

"You know damned well what you did!" Paul said opening the door and throwing his case and bag onto the back seat. "I will be taking things further!"

He got into the front of the taxi and it slowly took off towards the carpark, turning around and leaving the grounds.

Andy laughed, sipping at his coffee and yawning.

"Morning Andy," Spencer said. "What was his problem?"

Andy turned around to see Spencer walking towards him, wearing black trousers, white shirt and a black tie.

"What do you mean?" Andy asked.

"He was ranting!" Spencer said. "At reception about a missed wake up call."

"Oh, he had all three calls," Andy said. "I went up and even knocked on his door, he got the hump and slammed it in my face."

"He blamed you for not doing it right," Spencer laughed.

"Wasn't me," Andy said.

"Yeah," He said. "He was told," He sniggered. "He apparently was up most of the night being sick, put it down to the sandwiches, claims the cheese was off."

"Oh, it wasn't the cheese," Any scoffed.

"Why are you so sure?" He asked, taking a long drag on a cigarette, looking around.

Andy looked at him and smiled.

"Oh dear," He said understanding. "What did you do?"

"Well," Andy said. "He got personal last night and rude, so instead of having single Vodka and tonics," I sniggered. "He had triples."

Spencer started to laugh.

"Silly sod missed an important meeting because he liked a drink," Andy said. "Serves him right."

"Tracy gave him his message and he went quiet, trying to call someone on his telephone," Spencer said. "Was he that bad?"

215

"Ask anyone," Andy said. "He kept looking at Lindsays breasts."

"No shit," Spencer exclaimed. "Damn, I would look but not make it so obvious," He shook his head in amazement. "What was the note?"

"His boss said she was unhappy with his attitude and was thinking about his role within the team," Andy said. "To be honest, I don't think he realised that she heard him slagging her off to reception last night."

"That is cold," Spencer said. "You finished?" He looked at his watch.

"Yeah," Andy said. "Going to shoot off once I have finished my coffee."

"How was the night otherwise?" Spencer asked.

"Dead swan, drunk moron, pizza and penis," Andy said nodding.

"Penis?" Spencer looked at him in confusion.

"You know," Andy said. "Cock, man rod, meat stick?"

"Yes I know what a penis is," Spencer shook his head. "Do I even want to know."

"When you see Marina later," Andy said. "Ask her about the penis on the top floor and watch her giggle like a maniac."

"Sure," Spencer said. "When you in next?" Spencer asked.

"A week Monday," Andy said. "Off on a skiing trip."

"Don't break anything!" Spencer yelped.

The door opened and Tracy popped her head out.

"Before you go Andy can you sort this printer out?" She said. "It's pissing me off!"

"Sure," Andy said and followed her in. "What are you going to do once I fix everything?"

TEN

Andy jumped when the door to the staff room opened and Spencer walked in, holding out his fist in order to fist bump Andy.

"Andy!" He said loudly. "How was the trip?"

"It was great thanks," Andy said. "You okay?"

"I am great," He nodded. "What are you doing here?"

"Making a drink," Andy said pointing to the mug.

"No," Spencer laughed. "I mean what are you doing here, thought you were off until Monday."

"Mark asked me to come in tonight," Andy said. "Something about Dean being off."

"Dean crashed his car!" Spencer said. "He was out with his woman and someone went through a red light," He said. "Crash!" He said loudly.

"Shit," Andy said. "Was he hurt?"

"Hurt his neck," Spencer said. "Both okay otherwise, but the car, rest in peace!"

"He loved that car," Andy said. "Thanks for telling me."

"You want a drink?" Andy pointed.

"No man," Spencer said. "Did you hear?"

"Hear what?" Andy laughed. "I cannot hear for shit."

Spencer burst out laughing, echoing around the room so loud that Andy squinted.

"Charlotte is leaving," He said quietly.

"What?" Andy said in disappointment. "Why?"

"She is going to Manchester," He said. "Uni."

"That is miles away," Andy said. "And a dump."

"You should go with her!" Spencer exclaimed.

"I think not," Andy said.

"Why not?!" He asked.

"No," Andy shook his head.

Spencer groaned, grabbing hold of Andy's shoulders, and rocking him heavily back and forth, pausing.

"You been working out?" He asked.

"Yes," Andy said. "Don't get too excited will you."

"I thought you liked her?" Spencer said sitting on the table.

"I did," Andy said. "But while she listens to her father, nothing is going to happen."

"Her father is a fool," Spencer said. "And so is she."

"Besides," Andy said. "There is someone else on the radar."

Spencer laughed in amazement.

"Oh yeah," Spencer chuckled. "Who?"

"No one here," Andy said. "Someone I work with in the store."

"Wow," Spencer nodded. "You going to ask her out?"

Andy nodded.

"Keep me informed, yeah?" Spence said, holding out his hand.

"I will," Andy said shaking his hand. "Now bugger off and let me enjoy a coffee before the fun starts!"

"Fun?" Spencer said curiously. "Oh, sarcasm!" He said realising.

Andy stood looking into the crowded bar, shaking his head.

"Why did I have to come in today?" He said softly to himself. "Why did I promise Mark I would get in a couple of hours early because the day porters suck."

Marina came from the bar to the reception, sighing heavily.

"My god," She said. "It's a busy night!"

"I can see," Andy said, stifling a yawn.

"How come you are in today?" She said. "Thought you weren't back until Monday?"

"Mark asked me," Andy said. "My own fault for telling him I was home."

"When did you get back?" She asked.

"This morning," Andy said.

"Are you not tired?" She said.

"No," Andy smiled. "Not yet anyhow, I managed to get four hours when I got home."

"How was the trip?" She asked. "Skiing wasn't it."

"Yeah," Andy said. "Met an amazing girl, drank lots of tequila and put my back out."

"Lucky girl!" She scoffed.

"Oh no," Andy said. "Nothing like that, I had an accident skiing!"

"Are you okay?" She asked in concern.

"I am okay thanks," Andy replied. "Tired but okay."

"I need a favour," She said. "Could you look after the stag do in the lounge?"

"Sure," Andy nodded. "How many are there?"

"Five," She replied. "One cancelled luckily. They have had their meal and are using the lounge until late, they know they have to be out at twelve. They have an open account, but after twelve you will need to charge to a room."

"Okay," Andy said.

"They have an order with the bar," She yawned. "Could you grab it and give it to them?"

"Sure," Andy said. "You covering reception?"

She nodded, making her way round to the reception entrance as Andy opened the door for her, making his way to the bar.

218

Andy walked through the bar double doors, smiling, and nodding to Charlotte as she served customers at the bar.

"Nice trip?" She asked him.

"It was fun," Andy said. "Even though I did nearly kill myself on the last day!"

"Oh no!" She said. "When did you get back?" She looked at the calendar next to the till. "I thought you were not due back until next week?"

"Mark asked me to come in," Andy said. "Said the day porters were off."

"Yeah," She said. "None of them turned up today, so Marina has been covering."

"All day?" Andy exclaimed. "Poor girl!"

"How are you?" Charlotte asked.

"I am fine," Andy said. "You?"

Charlotte smiled and nodded.

"I hear you are leaving," Andy said.

"How do you know that?" She said.

"A little bird told me," Andy said.

"Spencer isn't a little bird," She scoffed. "I wanted to tell you myself."

"It's okay," Andy said. "Happy for you."

"Thanks," She said. "Will be staying with my aunt," She smiled. "Took your advice and signed up to art."

"Brilliant," Andy said. "Keep in touch yeah?"

"I will," She said. "Are you okay to take some drinks round to the lounge?" She said. "I could do without the grief."

"Sure," Andy said. "Marina asked me to sort it."

"Thanks," She said. "They are arseholes."

"Are they?" Andy rolled his eyes. "Well they better not give me any shit, too tired to put up with it."

"At least they are going at Midnight," Charlotte said.

"Well," Andy sighed. "I am going they don't find out we have rooms available."

Andy knocked on the door to the lounge and then opened it, walking carefully with five bottles balanced on the small tray.

"Beers for you," Andy said.

The five young men sat around the coffee table, most of the furniture re-arranged. One of the vases under had been moved from the fireplace into the far corner of the room, the other laying on the side. All are wearing identical clothes, black boots, trousers, white shirt, and a dark red waistcoat.

The room smells heavily of cigarette smoke and a hint of urine.

"I take it you are having a good time?" Andy said sniffing. "I hope no one has lost control of their bladder," He looked around. "I am not cleaning it up."

"Coming from outside mate," One of the group said. "Foxes I think," He pointed to an open window.

"Fair enough," Andy said putting the beers on the table in front of each person.

"Where is the hot bird?" One of them said. "We want her, not you."

"She is busy," Andy replied. "So you have me until twelve."

"Is she back at twelve?" One of them said, sticking his tongue out suggestively.

"No," Andy said.

"What happens at twelve?" He said.

Another member of the group threw a beer mat at him.

"We go at twelve," he said shaking his head.

"Are there any waitresses?" Another asked.

"No," Andy said. "You have me, or nothing."

"Suppose you will have to do," One guy said with a badge stating he was the groom to be. "Could we have another round I ten minutes?"

"Sure," Andy replied. "Same drinks?"

"Yeah," He said. "Thanks."

"Let me take these bottles," Andy said clearing up ten empty bottles, carefully placing them on the tray. As we went to walk away, one of the group closest to the door, put his foot out, tripping Andy, causing him to try and steady himself, only for the bottles to go crashing to the floor, bouncing off the door.

"That was clever," Andy said turning round and looking at the person responsible.

"Should watch where you are walking," He said and laughed, a couple of the group joined in.

"Come on man," The groom said. "Not funny."

"Sorry mate," The best man said. "We will ban him from having any more drinks."

Andy picked up the bottles, placing them on the try, staring at the man who tripped him as he walked out the door.

"What happened?" Marina asked.

"One of the morons tripped me," Andy scoffed.

"Are you okay?" Marina asked.

"I am fine," Andy said. "Just not in the mood for their shit."

Allain came out from the side by the restaurant, nodding at Andy when he saw them.

"You are back early," Allain said. "Thought you were on leave until Monday?"

"Mark asked me to help out," Andy said.

"Could I ask for your help?" Allain asked.

"Sure," Andy said. "Let me get rid of this."

"Meet me out the front," Allain said. "It won't take long."

Andy returned the tray and empty bottles to the bar, placing them on the counter.

"Do you mind sorting those," Andy said to Charlotte. "Allain wants something."

"Probably the mess out front," Charlotte cringed.

"What mess out front?" Andy asked.

"No idea," She said. "Looks like something died."

"Oh," Andy said. "Right."

Andy made his way to the terrace from the back of the brasserie, checking the tables and looking for Allain who was standing by the entrance.

"What is it?" Andy said.

"What is that?" Allain pointed to the floor in disgust.

There is a large red puddle, mixed with meat and other unidentified objects. It was trickling down the wall and terrace slabs, making its way to the wall where it dropped into a flowerbed.

"Well that is disgusting!" Andy said.

"What do you think it is?" Allain asked, keeping his distance.

"If I had to guess," Andy said. "It was probably some kind of animal, doubt it's a bird," Andy looked closer. "No feathers."

"Would you be able to clean it up?" Allain gagged, covering his mouth. "Or ask maybe Gary or Keith?"

"Sure," Andy said. "Let me deal with the group first and I will sort it."

"Thank you," Allain said, turning to walk away.

"Any chance we could catch up later?" Andy asked. "Before you finish?"

"Is suppose so," Allain said. "If I get time," He nodded and headed for the brasserie.

"Odd," Andy said and looked at the mess in disgust.

Andy returned to reception, poking his tongue out at Marina.

"What is going on out there?" She asked.

"No idea," Andy said. "Looks like something exploded!" Andy laughed.

"No!" She said cautiously.

"Just don't go outside," Andy warned her. "Trust me!"

"Coffee here for you," Marina said.

Andy let himself into reception, noticing the coffee on the worktop.

"What are you after?" Andy asked curiously. "What have you done to it?"

"What?" She scoffed. "I make you coffee all the time!"

"No you don't," Andy said smiling. "You usually make me tea and I leave it to go cold because I hate tea."

"Do you?" Marina said.

The groom from the group came out of the lounge, walking straight up to reception.

"Yo!" He said loudly. "How you doing gorgeous?"

"My name is Marina," She said. "That is all I respond to."

"You gay?" He looked her up and down.

"No," She said. "Is your fiancé?"

"What?" He said. "What do you mean?"

"Never mind," Marina said. "How can I help?"

"Looking for that guy that bought us our drinks," He said.

Andy walked round to the counter, smiling.

"How can I help," Andy asked.

"Where are the drinks?" he demanded.

"You did say ten minutes," Andy replied. "I was just about to make a start on them."

"I didn't say ten minutes," he laughed. "I said a couple."

"If that is the case," Andy said. "I will get them shortly, no charge for this round."

"Too right!" He snapped and stormed off to the lounge.

"Prick!" Marina said under her breath. "What is his problem?"

"No idea," Andy said. "But I am tempted to bash him over the head with a bottle or two."

"Can I help?" Marina grinned.

"Thought you hated blood?" Andy said.

"Put a bin bag over his head," She said.

"I like how you think," Andy said. "Right, five beers for five tossers."

Andy opened the door to the lounge, looking at the man that had tripped him earlier.

"No trips please," Andy said. "Tips are welcome though."

"About time!" The groom snapped. "That was a long couple of minutes!"

Andy ignored him, placing the beers on the table, the previous ones still half full. One of the men had passed

out, laying back in the couch with his mouth wide open, snoring.

"Is he okay?" Andy asked.

"Yeah," The best man said. "He cannot handle his drink."

"Fair enough," Andy laughed. "Anything else?" He asked.

One of the guys, who had not spoken so far looked up.

"Do you do pizza?" He asked.

"I am afraid not," Andy said. "The best we can do are sandwich platters.

"That will do," The groom said. "I just need to eat something."

"Could we get some sandwiches?" He asked. "Two rounds should do it? He said looking to his friends who

nodded in agreement.

"Yes I can do that," Andy said, feeling a draft from the open window. "Do you want that closed?"

"No it's hot in here," The best man said. "Okay to keep it open?"

"Do you have nachos?" The groom said looking at the menu.

"Could you repeat that?" Andy asked.

"No," He said looking away.

"I didn't hear you," Andy said.

"He is deaf," The best man said. "He probably has to lipread," He said looking at Andy who smiled and nodded.

"That explains why he is so slow!" The groom said loudly and burst into laughter, his two friends following.

"Could you not bring my hearing issue into this please," Andy said and paused. "If you could repeat what you said."

"Nachos!" He said loudly and emphasised. "Could. We. Get. A. Couple. Of. Bowls. Of. Nachos?"

"Yes. You. Can." Andy imitated him.

"You are rude," The groom said. "I may complain."

"That is fine," Andy said. "Does that make you rude too?"

"No it makes me a paying customer," He scoffed. "Go do your job you idiot."

Andy ignored him, leaving the lounge and returning to the office.

"Getting the insults now," Andy said to Marina.

"Want me to throw them out?" She asked.

"No," Andy said. "Let's have some fun."

Allain came up to reception.

"How are they?" he asked. "The stag event?"

"Tossers," Andy replied. "Already having the groom take the micky out of my hearing."

"Sorry Andy," He said. "But you need to just take it, they are paying customers."

"If they continue, they can find another hotel," Andy said. "I am not taking crap from anyone."

"Just let them have what they want," He said. "Try and ignore what they say."

Allain walked away.

"Easy for him to say," Marina said. "I bet if someone called him a frog, he would run crying to his mother!"

"Anyone working in the kitchen?" Andy asked.

"Yes," Marina said. "Gary, believe it or not."

"Could you ring through an order, two lots of sandwiches and nachos."

"Ah," Marina smiled. "I know what you are thinking!"

"Let Gary deal with them," Andy said. "It's going to be a bloodbath!"

"No," Marina shook her head. "Better not."

"Not while Allain is here," Andy said.

The door opened and Mark walked in, smiling at both Andy and Marina, pausing.

"What are you two plotting?" Mark asked.

"Nothing," Marina said. "Well I aren't," She looked at Andy and pointed to him. "Not sure about him!"

"How's things?" Mark said walking up to the counter. "Thanks for coming in earlier Andy."

"You owe me one," Andy said. "The stag group are tossers."

"Well if they continue being tossers," Mark said. "Let me know and I will chuck them out."

"What are you so happy about?" Marina asked him.

"Nothing," Mark smiled.

Gary came to the counter, holding a large platter of sandwiches and a large bowl of nachos. Wearing a white apron over the top of white trousers and a black t-shirt, he is tidier than usual. He has a graze on his chin and black eyes, his nose cut at the bridge.

"Here you go," He said placing them on the counter.

"That was fast," Marina said.

"The chefs made them earlier," Gary said. "We predicted the stag do would want them after complaining about the food."

"Thanks Gary," Marina said. "What's with the uniform?"

"Helped out with the chefs earlier," He said. "Vegetable prep mainly," He said.

"What happened?" Andy asked. "Did you get drunk and fall again?"

"Actually," Gary said grinning. "No!"

"Gary here stepped in when a guy got heavy with his girlfriend," Mark said.

"You have a girlfriend?" Marina said.

"No," Gary groaned. "It was his girlfriend. He got rough with her, so I decided to teach the twat some manners."

"What happened?" Andy said. "Did you kick his arse?"

"He wacked me and everything is a blur after that!" Gary started laughing.

"Thank god for Keith huh?" Mark said.

"Keith saw everything," Gary said. "Headbutted the guy and then dragged him out like a ragdoll."

"Good old Keith," Mark said. "I wouldn't want to get on his bad side."

"What happened to Keith?" Marina asked.

"What do you mean?" Gary asked.

"We I know he has some learning difficulties," Marina said. "Just curious to why?"

"Does he?" Gary looked at Mark. "I didn't notice."

"I am sorry," Marina said uncomfortably. "Didn't mean to be rude."

"I am winding you up," Gary laughed. "Keith was a forceps birth," Gary said. "My old mum struggled to deliver him due to his size and she had some complications, so they had to use forceps."

"Oh no," Marina said.

"The doctor got a little too heavy handed," He said. "Crushed his skull."

Marina gasped.

"But he survived," Gary said. "Always been my little brother, even though the sod is built like a fucking tank!"

"Language," Mark said quietly.

"Sorry," Gary covered his mouth. "He cannot read or write, but he is a cool guy."

"Thanks for telling me that," Marina said.

"Let me get these to the group before they kick off," Andy said and walked round to reception, picking up the platter and bowl before walking to the lounge and opening the door.

When Andy turned and faced the room, the groom is standing in the corner, urinating into the large vase.

"Excuse me," Andy said. "What the hell do you think you are doing?"

"Having a pass" he said. "What does it look like you retard?"

"We have toilets," Andy replied. "Less than thirty seconds away, so if you could not do that and try and be civilised."

"Put it on the bill," The groom said. "What is the problem?"

"No problem," Andy replied. "Evolution hasn't caught up with some people," he muttered.

Andy placed the platter and bowl on the table, moving some of the bottles and collecting the empty ones. The groom leaned over, tapping his hearing aid.

"What is that?" He said.

"It's a hearing aid," Andy replied, stepping away from him. "Don't do that again," He warned him.

"Oh!" He scoffed. "Did I upset you?"

"No," Andy replied. "I just don't like people touching my hearing aids."

"Weird," The groom said. "Is it like one of those retards that doesn't like people touching his head?"

A couple of the men laughed, the best man shook his head in embarrassment.

"How would you like it if you were wearing contact lenses, and someone tapped you on the eye and said, What is that?" Andy said in a sarcastic tone.

"I'd smack them in the face," He said aggressively.

"Fair enough," Andy replied.

"Go on Special needs boy," He said laughing. "Go back to your bar."

"Special needs?" Andy laughed. "At least this special needs boy knows how to use a toilet."

Andy walked away, ignoring the grooms calls for him to come back. He closed the door behind him, holding up a middle finger on each hand to the door.

"What is going on?" Mark said.

Gary stood next to him, looking frustrated.

"Just caught one of them urinating in a vase," Andy told him.

He laughed, thinking I was joking.

"You are kidding?" Mark said. "Really?"

"They were not bothered," Andy replied. "Told me to put it on the bill."

"Jesus!" Marina said. "They are really troublesome."

"One more, and they are gone," Andy said. "Had enough."

"Go grab a break," Mark said. "Meet me in reception in fifteen."

Andy sat in reception, looking up at Marina and Mark talking quietly.

"Did you know?" Marina said. "Mark is getting hitched."

"Poor sod," Andy said.

Mark laughed.

"I am going to tell her," Mark said. "She will beat the shit out of you."

"Don't care," Andy smiled.

A woman walked through the entrance, making a beeline to the counter looking annoyed and disgusted. "She is tall and slim, wearing a blue floral dress and has short blonde hair.

"Hello there," Mark said. "Everything okay?"

"No," She said. "I am disgusted!"

"Why?" Marina asked.

"I was sitting on the terrace," She said. "Enjoying the breeze and some man stuck his head out of the window and vomited!" She groaned. "It's disgusting!"

Andy joined them at the front, smiling at the woman.

"Was this from the lounge?" He asked.

"Yes," She nodded.

"That explains what I saw earlier," Andy said. "I think it's time to abandon this party."

Andy and Mark left the reception, making their way to the lounge.

"What is happening?" Allain said walking from the bar.

"We are shutting them down," Mark said. "They have gone too far."

"It's a harmless stag night," Allain said. "We need to keep them happy."

"Okay Allain," Mark said. "Would you be happy to deal with the vomiting outside of the window and the vase being used as a toilet."

Allain looked at Mark in disgust.

"That is what I thought," Mark said. "I am shutting it down.

"Okay," Allain said and walked away.

"Useless," Mark hissed. "Absolutely useless."

Mark opened the door to the lounge, looking at the groom leaning out the window and heaving, another in the corner vomiting into a vase.

"Where is the other vase?" Mark asked.

"Behind the couch," Andy said pointing. "Looks broken."

"Right guys!" Mark said. "Party is over."

"What is your problem?" the groom snapped and stormed up to Mark who towered him.

"Urinating in vases, damaging property, throwing up inside and outside the window," Any sighed, noticing the vomit down the wall behind the radiator.

"I also had a complaint that one of you were abusive towards one of our waiters," Mark said. "Because of his colour."

"Not abusive," The groom said. "Just my opinion."

"I have had enough," Mark said. "No more alcohol will be served."

"You cannot do that," He growled at Mark. "We are paying lots!"

"I can call the police instead," Mark said to him.

"For what?" He demanded.

"Criminal damage, harassment and so on," Mark said. "So I suggest you leave please."

"Only a manager can decide that," The groom said.

"I am a manager," Mark said. "And I am throwing you out."

"Come on guys," Andy said. "More than happy to provide water and coffee, but you need to leave."

"I ain't having no special needs bar boy telling me what to do on my stag night," He walked up to Andy, puffing his chest up and getting in his face.

Marina walked in, looking at the mess.

"What the hell are you doing?" She snapped.

"Yeah you tell them!" The groom laughed.

"I am talking to you," She said. "You have five minutes to leave, or you can deal with the consequences."

"I ain't scared of no bitch!" The groom shouted in her face, poking her in the chest and grinning.

Marina sighed and brought her knee up between his legs, a thump followed by a yelping groan and the groom fell forward. The best man and the other two men didn't react, the fourth still fast asleep.

"Anyone else?" Marina asked.

"I am going to sue you!" The groom moaned. "I am going to fucking destroy you!"

"For what?" Mark said. "She acted in self-defence, and both myself and Andy will tell the police that."

"All because of the special needs kid there," The groom pointed to Andy.

"Special needs?" Andy looked at Mark.

"Probably thinks you are stupid," Mark said. "Because of the hearing thing."

"I don't think you are stupid," The groom groaned. "I know you are, deafy duck!"

"Wow not heard that one before," Andy scoffed. "Have a few more, if it makes you feel better."

"I am going to complain," he said. "Not having a disabled person do this."

"Complain if you wish," Andy said. "I will be making a statement for the police."

"Do you report all the people you don't like to the police," The groom said.

"No," Andy shook his head. "Only the chavs."

"If you wasn't disabled," He growled. "I'd kick your head in."

"I know the feeling," Andy said. "Your disability is the reason I haven't kicked your head in!"

"What?!" The groom scoffed. "What's my disability?" He demanded.

"Angry chav syndrome," Andy said. "No known cure."

"Go help Charlotte in the bar," Mark said stifling laughter. "Marina and myself will deal with this until the police turn up."

"No need for the police," The best man said. "Can you call us a cab, and we will go."

"I ain't going anywhere," The groom snapped.

"You will," The best man warned him. "This isn't the man I thought my sister was marrying."

The sleeping man woke up suddenly, groaning and mumbling before letting out a prolonged burp, looking around curiously.

"What is going on?" He said. "Did I miss the strippers?"

"It's like release day in here," Marina scoffed.

Andy left the lounge, walking out onto the terrace and leaning against the wall with his eyes closed, feeling the warm breeze against his face. He opened his eyes when he heard a car, looking to see the police car pull up next to him.

"Hey Andy," Steve said. "You good?"

"Usual," He replied. "Up and down."

"Any problems?" he asked.

"Nothing I cannot handle," Andy smiled.

"He is lying!" The groom leaned out from the window of the lounge.

"Who?" Steve said, turning off the engine and getting out. "What are you shouting about?"

"Special needs bar boy," He pointed at me.

Steve looked at Andy curiously.

"Special needs bar boy?" He whispered, trying not to laugh. "New nickname?"

"Yeah," Andy said. "From the tosser that also happens to be the groom."

"What are they up to?" Steve asked.

"Stag do," Andy replied.

"Oh I get you," Steve said and laughed.

"Would you like me to tell the officer what happened?" Andy asked the groom. "Or do you?"

The best man came up behind the groom, trying to encourage him back in.

"Just because we had a bit of fun," The groom said. "He is refusing to serve us."

"Define fun?" The officer said.

"Card games," The groom grinned.

"Urinating into vases, criminal damage, vomiting over the window and harassment of myself and a female colleague," Andy said. "And I found out they were also racially abusive to a waiter in the restaurant."

"Well I didn't like him," The groom said. "Bloody foreigners."

228

"It's time you left," Andy said.

Mark appeared at the window, waving, and giving Steve a thumbs up.

"I suggest that you all calm down," Steve said. "Get your stuff together and go home."

"We are waiting on a cab," The best man said. "Sorry."

"What if we don't want to go?" The groom shouted.

"You can come to the station and discuss things?" Steve said. "And I can give you a special room for the night?"

The groom returned back inside, and Mark closed the window.

"Coffee?" Andy asked.

"I would love one," Steve said. "Maybe my presence will help?"

"Got a gun?" Andy asked.

"No," Steve shook his head.

"Taser?" Andy looked.

"No," Steve laughed. "Just pepper spray and a baton."

"Bloody useless," Andy rolled his eyes. "They will do though!"

"How many of them are there?" Steve said following Andy towards the terrace.

"Five," Andy said. "Although, one of them has been asleep most of the evening."

Steve laughed.

The best man appeared on the terrace, looking nervous.

"They didn't have to call you guys," The best man said. "We are leaving."

"No one called me," Steve said. "The idiot got my attention by hanging out the window and yelling."

"He is drunk," he said. "No excuse but he isn't usually like this."

"Like what?" Steve said. "Rude and abusive?"

The best man laughed, looking at Andy and shaking his head.

"Looks like you have left a disgusting mess," Steve said. "Tell you what."

"What?" The best man said curiously.

"I want the room cleaned up," Steve said. "Whoever decided to urinate into a vase, can deal with that because that is just plain nasty."

"Could make the groom drink it?" Andy said.

"What?" The best man looked at Andy. "Why?"

"It's only urine isn't it?" Steve said.

"And vomit," Andy added.

"Oh no," Steve cringed. "You are telling me that five grown men couldn't use a toilet and decided to use a vase?"

Andy nodded.

Marina opened came outside, breathing heavily and shivering.

"What's up?" Andy asked.

"Sleeping beauty just threw up all over the table," She gagged.

"I am really sorry," The best man said. "If you give me some cleaning stuff, myself and Jack will sort it out the best we can."

"I do hope you have a credit card handy," Steve said.

"I do," The best man said.

"Good," He said. "Back inside and keep your mate in line, otherwise I will have to let him wear my shiny new handcuffs."

Steve followed the best man, Marina, and Andy into the reception. The groom came storming straight up to Steve who put his hands up in defence.

"Woah!" He said. "What's with the attitude?"

"This hotel has ruined my night!" He moaned.

"Come on man!" The best man said. "Stop it!"

"No," The groom scoffed. "We are the customers."

"Look if you don't stop," he said. "I am going to call my sister, is that what you want?"

"Look," Steve said. "Do yourself a favour and calm down," He looked at Mark behind the counter. "Are you happy for them to leave?"

"If they clean up and pay for the rest of the cleaning," Mark nodded. "Yes."

"There you go," Steve said. "I am going to hang around for a while, but if I hear so much as a peep out of him," He pointed to the groom. "I am calling for backup."

Mark indicated for Andy to come over to the counter.

"What?" Andy said.

"Go and wait in the bar," He said.

"Why?" Andy said. "I want to watch him scoop up vomit."

Mark laughed, covering his mouth.

"Just go and wait in the bar," He nodded.

"Fine," Andy said. "Have fun!" He smiled and walked away.

"I will have a coffee Andy," Steve said. "Will join you in the bar shortly."

Andy stood on the terrace, hosing down the wall and the floor, watching the reddish contents wash away. His face is screwed up in disgust, the smell getting to him.

"What happened?" Lindsay asked. "Did something die?"

"That is the contents of someone's stomach from the stag do," Andy said.

"That is disgusting," She shivered. "How were they otherwise?"

"Urinating in vases, harassing the waitresses, using vases as bowling balls, throwing food and drink, vomiting out the window and they have damage the glass cabinet," Andy said. "The groom got quite abusive, but we had the police on site so he de-chaved after a while."

"De-chaved!" Lindsay laughed. "That is a new one!"

"The groom was a scumbag," Andy said. "Kept pushing me because I am sure he wanted me to whack him so he could get a free night."

"Would have been worth it," Lindsay nodded. "Looks like the stones are stained."

"I'll bleach them at dawn," Andy said. "Didn't know you were in today."

"Kitchen," She said. "Helped out with the washing up."

"Oh," Andy said.

"It was actually okay," She smiled. "Got to chill and think."

"What did you think about?" Andy asked.

"I wrote a song," She said. "Going to work on that at tomorrow."

"Oh wow," Andy said. "Would love to hear it some time."

"Considering you are deaf," She said. "You will probably appreciate it!" She laughed, punching him softly.

"Off home?" Andy asked.

"Yes," She said yawning. "I am knackered."

"How you getting home?" Andy asked. "Bit dark to walk."

"Did you see the new motorbike in the staff area?" She smiled.

"Oh you passed your test?" Andy said.

Lindsay nodded.

"Congratulations," Andy said.

"Thank you," she smiled and walked away. "Have fun with the chavs and vomit!"

Andy walked into reception, sighing heavily, and looking at his watch.

"Food and coffee," Andy said to himself. "Then some kip if everyone goes home!"

Allain stepped out from reception, walking towards the stairs.

"Hello," Andy said smiling. "Do you have a moment?"

"I am very busy," Allain said.

"I will be quick," Andy said.

"Of course," He said. "In the Lounge?"

"Better not," Andy said. "Smells of urine and vomit."

"Let's go out onto the terrace then?" Allain said.

Andy followed Allain out to the terrace.

"Who cleaned the patio?" He asked.

"I did," Andy said. "The smell was irritating me."

"Could Keith not do it?" Allain asked.

"It's fine," Andy said. "I had some free time."

Allain nodded.

"Any updates?" Andy asked.

"Updates on what?" Allain said in confusion. "What do you mean?"

"The job?" Andy said.

"What job?" Allain said.

"The computer job," Andy smiled, thinking that Allain was winding him up. "I was expecting a letter by now."

"That will not be happening," Allain said.

"What do you mean it will not be happening?" Andy asked.

"Oh you have not been told?" He laughed. "We have given it to someone more suitable."

Andy froze, the smile disappearing off his face and his heart pounding in his chest.

"What?" Andy said. "What do you mean?"

"We still used your plan," Allain said. "It was extremely helpful, so you should be happy that you contributed, you can put that on your resume."

"The job was offered to me," Andy said. "You said so yourself."

"I know, I made a mistake," He said. "When I spoke to the office manager, she said that the restaurant manager had a nephew looking for a job, and he was much more suitable."

"How so?" Andy asked.

"What do you mean?" Allain asked.

"Why am I not suitable?" Andy demanded.

"He isn't disabled and can hear on the phone," Allain explained. "We need someone that can speak on the phone otherwise it will not work."

"There are ways around it," Andy said. "Faxing, email and so on."

"I know," He laughed. "But he is more suitable and his uncle is a respected manager," He nodded. "The job is his."

"But you promised me the job," Andy said. "You cannot just change your mind due to my hearing loss."

"I can," He said. "I am a manager."

"You do realise this is discrimination," Andy said.

"Call it what you will," He walked to the door. "You still have a job, I can change that."

"Jesus Christ," Andy said and groaned. "All I wanted was a chance," Andy said. "Someone to see past the hearing disability."

"That is one of your weaknesses," Allain shrugged his shoulders. "You need to work on that."

"How can I work on something I have no control over?" And said getting annoyed.

"Oh and please shave," He said pointing to his face. "This hotel has an image."

Andy sat down on the terrace, clenching his shaking fists as a tear ran down his face. He looked out into the lake, his eyes following the outline of the moon light.

"You okay Andy?" Mark said leaning out the doorway.

"Fine," Andy said. "Just want some fresh air," He said. "Won't be a minute."

"No problems," Mark nodded and went back into the hotel.

Andy got up and walked down to the lake, screaming inside, his eyes clenched shut as he kept walking, stopping within inches of the water.

"That arsehole," Andy said. "I knew this was too good to be true! Andy punched himself in the head several times with his palm, grunting and groaning.

A duck stood nearby, quacking at him in agitation.

"You can shut the fuck up as well," Andy snapped.

Andy walked through reception, looking down when he saw Mark standing at the counter, smiling when he saw Andy.

"You okay Andy?" Mark said as Andy walked into reception, picking up his jacket.

"No," He said. "I am done with this toxic place."

"Why?" Mark said. "You are starting the new job soon."

"What new job," Andy asked. "They don't want a deaf person doing it."

"You are kidding," Mark said. "They cannot do that."

"They did," Andy said angrily. "They can find another mug to work nights."

"Come on," Mark said. "You cannot do this to me mate."

"I am sorry," Andy said. "But I cannot do this."

Andy left the office, walking round to the counter.

"I will text you later," Andy said.

"You coming back?" Mark asked.

"Not sure," Andy said. "I need to think."

Andy left the reception and walked through the double entrance doors, breathing in deeply as the cool breeze hit him.

"Hey!" Marina called out from the Barn House. "Where are you going?"

Andy walked down the steps, meeting her halfway.

"He lied," Andy said.

"Who?" Marina asked.

"Allain," Andy shook his head. "The job was given to someone else, and the reason is because I am deaf."

"You are joking!" Marina scoffed. "They cannot do that!"

"He did," Andy said. "And I am going because I am so angry and feel like I am going to cry!"

Andy choked up, turning to hide himself.

"Oh Andy!" Marina said, pulling him towards her and putting her arms around him, hugging him tightly. "If I were you," She said. "Don't drop it, take them to a tribunal."

"No point," Andy said. "I won't get anywhere."

"Just do it," She said. "Go to citizens advice tomorrow and get the ball rolling."

Andy shook his head.

"I am sorry," She said. "But I knew about it and didn't want to say."

"I get it," Andy said stepping back. "It's hard enough being deaf and fighting to gain a career, everyone seems to have an excuse."

"I am sorry," Marina shook her head.

"Oh you cannot join the army, you are deaf," Andy scoffed. "If world war three broke out, they wouldn't care if my ears worked or not."

"What have you tried?" Marina said.

"Army, navy, marines, air force, police, fire service and paramedics," Andy said. "Seems they only way to succeed in anything these days is to not have a disability."

Allain walked out from the brasserie, leaning against the wall.

"Andy!" He called out. "I need you to clean up some mess."

"Do it yourself," Andy said.

"Excuse me?!" Allain said. "You cannot talk to me like that."

"Just did Allen!" Andy said loudly.

"It is Allain!" He corrected him.

"No it is Moron," Andy scoffed. "With a capital M!"

"Careful," Allain said. "I can fire you."

"Too late," Andy said. "I quit!"

"Why?" Allain demanded. "Why are you quitting!?"

"You will find out soon," Andy said and looked at Marina. "Thanks," He smiled. "Catch up with you soon."

"Andy!" Allain called out. "Andy you cannot quit!"

"Yes I can!" Andy waved, not looking back as he walked down the dark lane leading towards the drive through the small woodlands.

"Good night Andy," Marina called out, waving at him as he disappeared into the darkness of the trees.

Walking in the middle of the road, using only the moonlight to watch where he was stepping, Andy mumbled to himself.

His phone buzzed in his pocket and he pulled it out, noticing the messages were from Mark.

"Sorry Mark," Andy said. "Don't take it personally," He said to himself.

Andy moved into the side of the headlights of a car coming from behind him caught his attention, he turned around and shielded his eyes, as the car came to a stop a few feet from him, the lights dimmed.

"Andy?" Charlotte called out. "Come here."

"What?" Andy said loudly. "Cannot understand you."

"Come here Andy!" Charlotte said, waving him over.

Andy squinted, recognising the car.

"Charlotte?" He said curiously. "Thought you left ages ago?"

And walked up to the drivers side, kneeling down when the window is rolled down.

"Why are you walking around in the dark?" Charlotte asked. "Bit dodgy."

"I just quit," Andy said.

"You what?" Charlotte scoffed. "Why?"

"They lied," Andy said. "About the job."

"What do you mean?" Charlotte said. "Get in."

"It's okay," Andy said. "I want to walk."

"Get in the bloody car!" She snapped.

Andy walked round to the passenger side and got in, Charlotte then drove further down and pulled into a layby, turning on the light and facing him.

"So what happened?" She asked.

"There is no job," Andy said. "They gave it to someone else that can hear."

"Oh Andy!" Charlotte groaned. "I am sorry to hear that."

"Yeah," Andy nodded. "A little upset."

Charlotte sighed.

"What are you doing now?" She asked.

"Sitting in the car with you," Andy said and grinned.

"Funny!" She snapped. "No, I mean where are you going?"

"Home," Andy said. "I've a few beers."

"Is that a good idea?" She said.

"No," Andy said. "My good idea was to steal some of the gold letters off the hotel sign at the entrance."

"Wouldn't be the first time that has happened," Charlotte laughed. "Keith tried last year, fell back and broke his wrist!"

"Better give it a miss then," Andy laughed softly.

"There is a twenty-four-hour café near Lakeside," Charlotte said. "How about coffee, cake and a chat?"

Andy looked at her, trying to speak.

"What?" She said. "Are you lost for words Andy?"

"No it's not that," Andy said.

"You don't have to," Charlotte said. "I can drop you home instead."

"No," Andy said. "I would love to," He smiled.

"What are you doing for a job?" Charlotte asked. "I am sure you have bills to pay."

"I have a day job," Andy said.

"You kept that quiet," Charlotte said. "What is it?"

"Home Goods Stores," Andy said.

"No way!" Charlotte exclaimed. "My mum and I absolutely love that store, they do really nice candles and frames!"

"Random," Andy laughed. "Let me know, I can get you thirty percent off."

"I am going to pop in when you are next working," Charlotte said. "Give you some grief."

"What do you do there?" She asked.

"Nothing fancy," Andy said. "Warehouse and shop floor, applied for the supervisor role but got turned down."

"Sorry to hear that," Charlotte said, putting the car into gear and turning the light off. "At least you won't have to deal with Allain anymore!"

"That is true," Andy said. "Still have to deal with bloody customers though!"

Charlotte laughed and pulled away, Andy rolled down the window and put his hand out, holding up his middle finger.

Printed in Great Britain
by Amazon